She felt his ⟨...⟩ tiously over her ⟨...⟩ tall man with b⟨...⟩ the uneven light his hair looked darker than the night and his face was in shadow. She wished she could see his expression and know what he was thinking. Despite his seemingly relaxed posture she could see his tenseness in the angle of his head and the tightly fisted hand held stiffly at his side.

Suddenly he spoke.

"I've had enough air, haven't you?"

"What—" She spun around to face him, startled.

"I said, I—"

"I know what you said, but . . ."

"Yes?"

"Aren't you going to tell me what *you* found out?"

"I'm sure it's of no more interest than your own discoveries."

Sarah knew that wasn't true just from the way he said it.

"Please don't trifle with me."

"Trifle, is it?" he said with harsh amusement. Then his tone changed. "Come here," he said softly.

For a moment Sarah didn't move, didn't even breathe.

"Sarah."

Her name was a whisper on the evening breeze. With slow steps she started toward him. She wasn't sure what propelled her, whether it was her desire to learn what he knew about her brother or something more primitive.

She stopped only when she stood in front of him.

"You never learn, do you?" he said as his fingers brushed against her cheek.

"Learn what?" She whispered, a slight tremor in her voice.

"That there are some places you shouldn't go."

She looked at him questioningly.

"To my house, to the waterfront. And here." With his last words he pulled her into his arms . . .

MAKE THE ROMANCE CONNECTION

Z-TALK
Online

Come talk to your favorite authors and get the inside scoop on everything that's going on in the world of romance publishing, from the only online service that's designed exclusively for the publishing industry.

With Z-Talk Online Information Service, the most innovative and exciting computer bulletin board around, you can:

- ♥ CHAT "LIVE" WITH AUTHORS, FELLOW ROMANCE READERS, AND OTHER MEMBERS OF THE ROMANCE PUBLISHING COMMUNITY.
- ♥ FIND OUT ABOUT UPCOMING TITLES BEFORE THEY'RE RELEASED.
- ♥ DOWNLOAD THOUSANDS OF FILES AND GAMES.
- ♥ READ REVIEWS OF ROMANCE TITLES.
- ♥ HAVE UNLIMITED USE OF E-MAIL.
- ♥ POST MESSAGES ON OUR DOZENS OF TOPIC BOARDS.

All it takes is a computer and a modem to get online with Z-Talk. Set your modem to 8/N/1, and dial 212-545-1120. If you need help, call the System Operator, at 212-889-2299, ext. 260. There's a two week free trial period. After that, annual membership is only $60.00.

See you online!

KENSINGTON PUBLISHING CORP.

PHYLLIS HERRMANN

GOLDEN PROMISE

ZEBRA BOOKS
KENSINGTON PUBLISHING CORP.

ZEBRA BOOKS are published by

Kensington Publishing Corp.
475 Park Avenue South
New York, NY 10016

Copyright © 1994 by Nina Herrman and Phyllis DiFrancesco

All rights reserved. No part of this book may be reproduced in any form or by any means without the prior written consent of the Publisher, excepting brief quotes used in reviews.

If you purchased this book without a cover you should be aware that this book is stolen property. It was reported as "unsold and destroyed" to the Publisher and neither the Author nor the Publisher has received any payment for this "stripped book."

Zebra, the Z logo Reg. U.S. Pat & TM Off. Heartfire Romance and the Heartfire Romance logo are trademarks of Kensington Publishing Corp.

First Printing: March, 1994

Printed in the United States of America

To NJRW on its 10th Anniversary
We owe you our partnership.
Thanks to all the members, especially the first eleven.

Dot Brown
Jennifer Coultas
Mildred Fedorka
Pam Ferguson
Roberta Galli
Judy Reynolds
Christine Tayntor
Vicki Thompson
Suzanne Vandewiele
Cherry Weiner
and
Phyllis

Prologue

The man stumbled along the back streets of the Vieux Carré, catching himself here and there against a wall. He was heading for his special hiding place, a tiny nook nestled in the alley between two storehouses. The night air was thick with the smells of river and bog, and a damp fog glowed around the almost full moon. A heavy silence blanketed him. No one else was about.

He stopped and took a warming swallow from his ever-present bottle. He closed his eyes as his soul absorbed the calming heat. So much pain ... so much guilt. Yes, the guilt was the worst of it, haunting him every moment ever since that day long ago. But soon he would be rid of it. He would tell it all, confess, and then, maybe then he could go home again.

He smiled at the memories of happier times—before The War. Family and friends passed before his eyes, a parade of smiling faces. Suddenly more faces followed, the smiles turning to grimaces and then horror. He groaned out loud, putting up his hand defensively to ward off the phantoms, but to no avail; he could hear their approaching footsteps. With a shrill scream, he started to run, his heart beating wildly in his chest. Too late, too late, it seemed to say, but he ran faster, nonetheless.

At the entrance to the alley, he paused to catch his breath, hurriedly throwing a glance over his shoulder. Nothing. He was alone. Safe. He took another gulp from his bottle, a large one. His hands shook making the bottle jangle against his teeth. A chill ran down his spine and set him to shivering. He scurried into the alley, head down, wanting only to find a dry corner where he could lose himself in his bottle as he had on so many similar nights.

A large shadow suddenly loomed before him, blocking his way. At first he thought it an apparition like all the others that had visited him that night.

"Go away," he muttered. "I've no stomach for you tonight." He lifted the half-empty bottle toward his lips, then froze in place.

"Is that any way to speak to an old friend?" the shadow asked.

A lump of cold dread settled low in his gut. He backed up a step, but the shadow was quicker, once again blocking his way, cutting off any chance of escape.

The fog chose that moment to lift, unveiling the silver-white orb of the moon just above the alleyway. He sagged against the brick wall, his mouth gaping open, his mind too numb to form words. His worst nightmare had come to life.

"I have something for you," the once-familiar voice said. "Something to end the pain. Trust me."

Mesmerized and at the same time terrified by the sound of the voice, he stayed in place while the shadow came to life. His hand was pried open, and his only source of solace was removed—his bottle. Before his drugged mind could produce a protest a new bottle was thrust in his hand.

"Here, let me help you," his nemesis murmured as he lifted the bottle to his mouth.

A faint whiff of almond reached his nostrils in the instant before the corn whiskey burned down his throat. His already fast heartbeat tripled, and he had to gasp for air. Nausea churned in his belly while a sudden dizziness sent him groping for the ground.

He wanted to push the bottle away but had no strength. The full moon dimmed, then faded, a bright aureole round the devil's own face. The devil smiled.

"See how easy that was?" he heard as the world turned black and the pain raced through his body.

And then there was nothing.

Chapter One

Sarah Gentry looked at the dilapidated building and shivered. The sky was a lovely robin's egg blue and the sun shone brightly, yet even with the weight of her dark woolen cape, she felt chilled. She pulled the collar of the cloak closer round her neck. Once she found Morgan Cain everything would be fine; she'd get the information she needed and be on her way.

At least, that was her plan. Cain had a reputation for doing things his own way, and most of the time it had nothing to do with what anyone else wanted. Still, she couldn't turn back now.

Straightening her shoulders, she mounted the steps of the decrepit porch and with a twist of her wrist, rang the bell. Before she could reconsider her actions, the door swung open, and an old woman stared out at her.

"Yeah?"

"I'm here to see Mr. Cain—Morgan Cain."

The woman eyed Sarah from top to bottom. "Cain, is it? Well, follow me. Far be it from me to say what should or shouldn't be done in broad daylight." She turned and hobbled into the gloom. "And shut the door behind you," she called out.

Sarah slowly pushed the door closed, and the darkness inside deepened until she couldn't see a thing. For a moment she panicked, then her eyes began to adjust to the lack of light.

"If you think just because you look like a lady, it'll make a difference, it won't." The old woman's voice came to her from down a dark hall.

"I beg your pardon?" Sarah asked as she scurried after the crone.

"He won't make more of you than of anyone else, I can tell you that, dearie."

"I've only come after information," Sarah explained, her face heating as she caught the woman's implication.

"Sure, and I'm the Queen of England. But mind what I say: do your business and be on your way. This isn't your part of town."

Sarah certainly agreed with that. As soon as she got what she'd come for, she'd be more than happy to leave and never return. A chill ran down her spine when she heard a scratching sound behind the peeling wallpaper. Mice in the wall, she realized, the smell of rotting wood reaching her nostrils. Maybe even rats. She hurried her steps, then nearly bumped into the old woman who had stopped in front of a scarred and battered door.

"Here you are," she said. "You'll find him in there. You don't look like one of his usual, so remember what I said."

Sarah hesitated at the door, watching the woman walk away, her resolve faltering now that she was so close to her goal. What if he wouldn't tell her what he knew? She didn't even want to think about that. She wished he were staying at a more genteel place, but from all she'd heard, this place was typical of the man. In any case, there was nothing to be done about it now. She stared at the door another minute before drawing up the courage to knock. The sound rang hollowly down the long corridor.

"What do you want?" a voice yelled from inside.

Sarah took that as a "come in" and pushed the door open.

"Mr. Cain?" she called out as she stepped into the room. It was empty.

"Well, well. What have we here?"

The voice startled her for she had seen no one enter the room. Yet there he stood, almost directly in front of her—and huge, much larger than she'd ever imagined. He was a newspaper reporter, she'd been told, and the image that had come to her then was of someone small and mouselike, weasling out information bit by bit from here and there to put in his stories. But this was no mouse.

Too late, she remembered the stories of his toughness, of how even his editor at the paper had no control over him. She looked at him and then looked again. He stood well over six feet tall, and there was nothing the least bit mouselike about him. This was a man who lived up to his reputation in every detail.

"Oh my," she said staring at the open shirt unbuttoned almost to his waist. The dark hair on his chest drew her eyes though she knew it wasn't polite to stare, and certainly not at a half-dressed man. But the swirl of hair that disappeared into the waistband of his trousers mesmerized her. She could feel a deep flush rising from her chest up to her cheeks.

"You shouldn't go barging into a man's abode unannounced if you aren't prepared to see him in his natural state." His voice was deep and faintly mocking.

"I—I'd assumed this was your office," Sarah replied with a slight stutter, pulling her gaze from his chest and raising it to his eyes. She immediately wished she hadn't. The dark awareness there made her want to rush back out to the street, but she held her ground. "Please excuse me for interrupting you," she said in a stronger voice. "And for any lack of manners on my part. If you'll finish dressing, we can get down to business."

"Business, is it? What kind of business?" he asked with a glint in his eyes.

She noticed with some discomfort that he didn't bother to rebutton his shirt. "I've come for information I'm told you possess."

"And who may I ask wants this information?"

His question startled her. Though she knew his name, they hadn't been properly introduced, a situation her dead parents would certainly have frowned upon, but Sarah had really had no other choice. It was of the utmost importance that she talk with this man, and she knew of no one who could perform a proper introduction, or would for that matter. He was a most unsuitable man, and all of her acquaintances would have been shocked to the core to think she would deign to spend even the shortest time in his presence.

"My name is Sarah Gentry," she supplied, watching him carefully. He gave no indication that he recognized her name.

"Well, Miss Gentry, to what do I owe the honor?" He walked to a side table and poured a golden-colored liquid into a glass.

He held the glass up in offering, but Sarah shook her

head. Imagine offering a lady liquor, and in the morning no less! She'd been warned against him, told he had no manners or breeding when she'd made her discreet inquiries. She knew he was trying to shock her, but she wasn't easily shocked, not anymore. And given time she might even be a bit amused at the game he was playing.

"As I said, I've come for information I've been told you have."

"And which of my dear friends has been making you such promises?" He took a sip from his glass.

"Oh, so you have friends, I wasn't sure."

"Ah, the little cat has claws, does she? You're right. In my profession we have acquaintances, not friends, informants not confidants. Did you hope to befriend me to get the information you wanted? I can always use a friend, a certain kind of friend anyway."

She chose to ignore his rather pointedly off-color remarks and get to the business she'd come to discuss.

"I understood you might know the whereabouts of a man for whom I'm searching."

His expression hardened. "A man is it? What makes you think I have information on your ... man?" He walked over to the single chair in the room and lowered himself into it without bothering to offer her a seat.

She tapped her foot impatiently, then stopped. It wouldn't do to let her anxiety show. Things like this always took time as she well knew. After all, she'd been through something similar many times before, and after each episode she'd promised herself she wouldn't let herself hope—but hope always blossomed anyway.

This time her lead showed real promise. If Morgan Cain knew half as much as her informant had said, she could be closer than she'd ever been. Why, her quarry might only be a few miles away at this very moment!

"A Mr. Neubald Huggins told me. He said you'd been looking into something that might have led you to Adam."

"Adam?" the infuriating man asked as he brought the glass to his lips as if to take another sip.

"Yes, Lieutenant Adam Gentry, my brother."

The glass was lowered without him taking a swallow. For a moment he didn't speak. Slowly, he placed the glass on the table beside his chair and sat forward.

"Your brother, is it? Not quite as interesting, but you never can tell. What makes you so sure I know anything about him?"

"I've been looking for my brother for quite some time, Mr. Cain. I've heard that you are investigating a piece for your paper which might involve Adam. I'd appreciate it if you'd leave Adam's name out of it and give me any information you might have."

"And why should I do all this?"

"Because it's the gentleman's code."

A low laugh emanated from his throat. "Not a very good reason, I'm afraid. And, as I'm sure you've been told, I'm no gentleman."

"Then how about as a courtesy from one Southerner to another?"

"Evoking the passionate plea of Southern camaraderie will get you nothing, either, but I have another idea."

"Yes?"

"Maybe there's something of yours that I might want—in exchange for giving what information I have."

Sarah's heart raced. It wouldn't be long now. Soon

she'd be with Adam and everything would be all right again, just like it used to be. She stepped closer to Cain's chair in anticipation. "Of course. Anything."

"Anything?" he asked, coming to his feet.

Suddenly he was very close, and very large. Sitting in the chair, he'd lost some of that primal masculine aura, but now she felt it all again: the fear she'd experienced when she'd first set eyes on him, and also the attraction.

"I—I . . ."

"You'd be wise not to make that kind of promise to just any man," he said as he stepped around her, putting some distance between them. "Why don't you tell me what you know about your brother?"

"What?" Sarah whispered, confused by his abrupt changes in subject and her inexplicable awareness of him.

"Tell me about the last time you saw your brother. What did he say?"

"I think you've misunderstood what this meeting is about, Mr. Cain," she said, pulling herself together. *"You are supposed to tell me what you know,* not the other way around. Mr. Huggins might not have shown the best judgment in allowing me to come here on my own, but he's always provided me with accurate facts. He told me you have some new information about Adam—information that you would only give to a member of his immediate family. Well, I'm his immediate family, and I would like that information."

"I think your Mr. Huggins was misinformed."

"You mean you don't know anything about Adam?" Sarah's heart dropped to her feet. She'd had such hope. Surely it all wouldn't end in this dirty little room.

"I didn't say that."

"Then exactly what *are* you saying, Mr. Cain?"

His games were no longer amusing. She'd come so far, and she wanted some answers. She had to find Adam before ... She didn't complete the gruesome thought.

"I'm saying that we each have information that might be helpful to the other. Why don't you tell me what you know, and then we'll see where we are."

Something in his tone had changed, softened, and Sarah felt less defensive. "I don't know too many details about Adam's life in the last few years. As I'm sure you know, he's been wandering about for quite some time."

He nodded encouragingly, and she continued. "The last place he was seen was here in New Orleans, and that was more than six months ago."

"Have you been in touch with any of his friends?"

"Most of his friends haven't seen him any more often than I have. I did meet with several of them in Shreveport, but no one has heard from him in over two years. It just seems so odd. Adam was so close with his friends. He kept up a correspondence with most of them throughout the war."

"Does he have some way of getting money?"

Sarah shook her head. "Not that I know of. I know Mother and Father gave him some when he came home after the war, but that was almost seven years ago. They died shortly after, and he's never asked me for anything. I know he has some sort of pension, but ..."

"Is there any way he could have access to your money?"

"Not without my finding out. Of course, half of all I have is his, but unless I find him soon, I'm afraid there will be less than nothing left." As soon as the words left her mouth she wanted them back. Why had she told him that? She'd told no one about her dwindling fortune, not even her closest friends.

If he'd heard what she said, he didn't react and appeared lost in thought. Then he asked, "How about friends from his company? Did any of them come looking for him?"

Sarah thought back and shook her head. She couldn't remember any of his chums coming to inquire about him. Why hadn't she ever realized how odd that was until now? She'd heard Margaret Rose talk about her son Ebner's friends countless times, how they'd come to visit and help work the plantation, and talk about her lost son, filling the empty space that once was Ebner. But no one had come in search of Adam, no one but herself. And now, if her information was correct, this formidable stranger.

"Your Mr. Huggins must have contacted some of your brother's friends," the stranger now said.

"If he did, he didn't mention them to me. Have you been in contact with any of them or anyone from his company?"

Cain didn't answer. He pulled a watch from his breast pocket and flipped open the case.

"I'm afraid I have somewhere else I need to be. Allow me to escort you back to your hotel."

"I'm not staying at a hotel. Besides, we haven't discussed Adam. What do *you* know about him?"

"Then let me take you to wherever you're staying," he continued as if he hadn't heard her question—or was just ignoring it.

"I haven't made any arrangements as yet."

For a moment he stared at her, his expression clearly

indicating he couldn't believe her words. "You're much too impetuous by half, Miss Gentry. Coming to New Orleans on your own, visiting me unchaperoned. Not booking a room in advance. It's obvious you need to learn a lesson."

Before she could move, he had his arms around her and his mouth pressed to hers. His breath smelled slightly smoky from the drink he'd had and very male. His lips felt firm and warm against hers. Shocked by his actions, she stood still in his embrace, absorbing the strength of the hard masculine body surrounding her and his impossibly clean scent. He was nothing like what she'd anticipated—and exactly as she'd been warned.

Her mind suddenly comprehended where she stood, what he was doing, and she stiffened, her arms coming up to his shoulders to push him away. Before she could launch her protest, he released her and stepped back.

"That and more is what happens when young women venture into unsavory situations," he said, his voice husky and low. "Keep that in mind for the next time. Come along, I'll take you to a hotel I know. They have a very good reputation and only serve the finest New Orleans has to offer."

"I'm afraid I can't do that," Sarah managed to utter, still bemused by what had happened.

Morgan Cain raised a dark eyebrow in question.

"I haven't the money to spare."

"Good God, woman, what in heaven's name did you plan to do?" The stunned expression on his face should have been comical, but coming on top of all her other frustrations, it only irritated her.

"Don't take that tone with me. I can take care of myself."

"Well so far you don't seem to be doing a very good job of it. Don't you have any family to oversee your activities?"

"I'm twenty-five years of age, Mr. Cain, and have been on my own for over six years. I don't need you or anyone else looking over my shoulder."

She gave a brief thought to Philip—he would not be pleased to hear his efforts on her behalf dismissed so summarily, but of late, even his concern over her activities had become overbearing.

Morgan Cain crossed his arms over his chest, clearly battling a temper that wanted to explode. His self-control won out as he asked, in a voice all the more menacing because of its icy calm, "Then just what do you propose we do now? Surely you aren't expecting to stay here?"

Her eyes widened as she realized just how foolhardy she'd been, taking off from Baton Rouge without a plan other than to beard this lion in his den. Well, now that she was trapped here, there truly wasn't anyone else to blame. She thought furiously, turning over the various possibilities in her mind, unwilling to give him the satisfaction of showing her up.

"You don't need to concern yourself over my well-being," she said at last. "I'm sure Geneviève will be more than happy to have me visit."

"Geneviève?"

"Geneveève Michaud, a friend from school. She lives here in New Orleans."

"And does she live nearby?"

"Not far, I think. On the corner of St. Louis and Dauphine."

"Come on, I'll take you there."

"But you haven't told me about Adam," she protested.

"I have some business to attend to right now. After you're settled and have a roof over your head, we'll talk again. There's plenty of time." He held out his hand.

Sarah hesitated a moment, biting her lip, then put her hand in his. It was warm and large, swallowing hers. Ordinarily she didn't like being overwhelmed by a man, but Morgan Cain was different. His size no longer intimidated her. If anything, she felt secure in his grasp, protected. For reasons she couldn't begin to explain, she trusted him. If he said they would talk later, she would take him at his word.

Deep inside she knew there was another reason she didn't press him for an answer. She didn't want her hopes shattered, not quite yet. She wanted to believe she would see Adam—and soon—and this man held the key to that hope. For now, she would let him lead the way.

It didn't take long for them to reach Geneviève's house, and soon Morgan was knocking on the front door of her friend's home. In full daylight he didn't look quite so menacing, though the night's growth of stubble on his cheeks gave him an unsavory air. Her cheeks still tingled from its feel, and his taste still lingered in her mouth. She'd been kissed before, after all she was well past the ideal marriageable age, but never had she experienced the range of emotions Cain elicited in her: fear and exhilaration, recklessness and caution. The mixture was both heady and confusing, as was his attitude toward her.

On the walk over, he'd said nary a word, and neither had she. What was there to say, other than to speak of Adam? And now was not the time for that, or so he had decreed.

The door swung open, and there stood Geneviève, her expression swiftly changing from questioning wariness to pleased surprise.

"Sarah Gentry, how wonderful to see you!" she exclaimed, hugging Sarah with unabashed affection and kissing her on both cheeks with typical French élan. "I thought you were spending the summer in Baton Rouge."

"My plans changed," Sarah said, not wanting to go into more detail while standing on the doorstep. She was disappointed at not finding out more from Morgan Cain and didn't want Geneviève to question her too closely for fear that she might cry. The last thing she needed was for Morgan Cain to think she was weak. So instead she asked with forced bravado, "Are you happy enough that you'll allow me to stay for a visit? I'm afraid I've come to town and not made any arrangements."

"But, of course, *ma chère*, anything for you," Geneviève said, smiling at the younger woman. "Now, you must introduce me to this handsome gentleman who has brought you to me."

Geneviève's eyes conveyed her interest, and after the introductions were made and pleasantries exchanged, she smiled enticingly at him. "Please, Monsieur Cain, come inside and have some refreshment. I must repay you for bringing my good friend to my door."

"You are very kind, Mademoiselle Michaud, but I'm afraid I must decline. Pressing business, I'm sure you understand. But it's been my pleasure to deliver Miss Gentry." Though he was talking with Geneviève, Sarah felt as if she were the entire center of his attention. A rather unsettling sensation. "We'll meet again?"

It was only with his last words that Sarah felt his attention switch to Geneviève.

"For some reason, I am sure of it, Monsieur," Geneviève replied with a speculative glance in Sarah's direction.

"I'll be hearing from you soon, Mr. Cain, won't I?" Sarah asked. She didn't want him to forget his promise—or think that she had. Adam was too important to her.

"To be sure," he said, taking her extended hand in his and raising it to his lips. Sarah felt the color run up her cheeks as his mouth lightly touched the back of her hand. "And you have my address."

Sarah felt her blush deepen at the hidden implication in his voice. Before she could think of a suitable retort, he was heading back in the direction from which they had just come along the banquette.

"An interesting man," Geneviève said.

"I suppose so," Sarah replied noncommittally.

"I think it's more than suppose, but we can talk about that later. Let's get you inside and settled. I'll have Virdie go to the station and get your bags. How long can you stay?"

"How long can you have me? I've some business to take care of here in town, and then I thought I'd stay on for a visit. We haven't seen each other in such a long time."

"It's been well over a year. I've missed you."

"And I've missed you," Sarah replied.

"In that case, you must stay until we run out of things to talk about. And as we both know, that will take quite some time." Geneviève's laugh was filled with happy excitement as they entered the front parlor. "Now you sit here and rest a few minutes while I make arrangements with Virdie and get us both something cool to drink. This weather is beginning to get hot, and you've been out in the sun."

Sarah was grateful for the time alone. She needed to pull her thoughts together and figure out what to do next. She wished she were more like Geneviève—though her friend was only a couple of years older, she always knew exactly what to do. Like sending Virdie for Sarah's bags. And getting something to drink. Sarah always overreacted, rushing forward without a well-defined plan of action and then having to make the best of whatever situation she found herself in.

And what a situation it was this time! For the first time, she felt truly close to Adam. If only Mr. Huggins was right! There had been so many *if only's* in the years since the war, but this time the leads were all so good, she couldn't help but hope the end of her search was in sight.

Geneviève came back in the room carrying a lacquered tray with two tall glasses.

"I brought some lemonade. You're looking better, *chérie*, not so flushed from the sun."

Sarah looked down at her hands neatly folded on her lap—just as she'd been taught at Sennet's Academy for Young Ladies. Though her cheeks had been red, it had been as much because of Morgan Cain as from the sun. And now they were turning red again, much to her embarrassment.

"Did you come down alone?" Geneviève asked.

"Yes. Philip was busy," she said, answering the underlying question. Philip had accompanied Sarah on her last trip to New Orleans, but she hadn't asked him this time, hadn't wanted to. Their relationship was not as easy as it used to be, and some instinct led her to be more careful, not to put herself in a position where she would be even more indebted to him.

"Have you and *Philippe* had a falling out?"

Geneviève's tone told Sarah that her opinion of Philip hadn't changed—even the way she said his name spoke volumes. Her two closest friends had taken an instant dislike to each other the minute they'd met, though Sarah had never been able to figure out why.

Philip D'Arbereaux was one of Baton Rouge's most successful businessmen and had distinguished himself during the War. That he was a very suitable match was beyond question—and handsome, too, in a way few women could resist, except for Geneviève, of course.

Philip had no more liking for the woman who had befriended Sarah during her finishing school days so far from home. Geneviève's house had been her second home during those years, and looking around now, Sarah realized how much she'd missed it, and her friend.

"Philip would have liked to accompany me," Sarah said, stretching the truth a little, "but he had pressing business at home. Because of the urgency of my mission, I decided to come alone."

"Urgency of your mission?" Geneviève repeated in a concerned voice, sitting forward in her seat.

"I think I've found Adam."

"Adam . . . How wonderful, *ma chère*. Where is he?"

"I'm not exactly sure, but definitely here in the city, and that's where Mr. Cain comes in."

"He knows what has happened to Adam?"

"So my investigator tells me, though Mr. Cain wasn't that encouraging when we spoke." As Sarah thought back over her conversation with the man, her doubts surfaced again. "Oh, Geneviève, what am I going to do if I can't find him? I've been looking for Adam for so long that sometimes I have to take out his photograph to remember what he looks like."

Tears welled and threatened to fall onto Sarah's cheeks. She bit the inside of her lower lip, knowing she mustn't let herself cry. She'd promised herself when she left Baton Rouge that she'd be strong no matter what she found out. But sometimes it was so hard, especially when it seemed she was destined to hit dead end.

"Oh, *ma chère*, I'm sure this time you will find him." Geneviève grasped her hand and gave it a squeeze.

"I hope so. If not, I don't know what to do. I'm so afraid I'll never see him again." A tear rolled down her cheek despite her resolution, and she quickly wiped it away with the tip of her finger.

"You mustn't talk in such a way. These things are very difficult, but that doesn't mean you should believe the worst."

"I know, but in my heart I feel such emptiness, such dread when I think of Adam now. And I never used to feel that way. But lately . . ."

"Come," her friend encouraged, "we'll have some tea instead." She pushed the barely touched glasses of lemonade to the side. "Everything will look brighter when you are warm on the inside, yes? I'm sure this Mr. Cain of yours will find Adam in no time." Geneviève reached over and rang the bell for her maid.

"He's not my Mr. Cain," Sarah protested. "We have a business arrangement, nothing more."

"If you want to think so, how can I change your

mind?" Geneviève said with a shrug, but gave her a playful wink.

"For heaven's sake, I've only just met the man."

"Sometimes that is all it takes. One look into each other's eyes, and *voilà* ..." Geneviève closed her eyes and fell back onto her chair, the back of one hand to her forehead as if she had swooned.

Sarah laughed just as she was supposed to. "Geneviève, sometimes you are so very French."

"It is what I am, is it not, even if I have spent most of my life here? I think always in the most romantic way, as you do also, if you would only admit it," she commented in an exaggerated French accent.

"Maybe you're right. Romance must be in the air. Philip has asked me to marry him." As soon as the words left her mouth, Sarah wished them back. She hadn't planned on telling Geneviève about the proposal. After all, she hadn't taken it seriously herself so there was no reason to tell anyone about it, but all of Geneviève's teasing and their laughter had lowered her guard.

Geneviève stopped laughing, and all signs of humor left her face as Sarah's statement sank in.

"Tell me this is not true. And tell me right away."

Before Sarah could answer the maid entered the room carrying a tray laden with afternoon tea.

It was obvious the last thing Geneviève wanted was to fuss with tea, but she knew she had no choice.

"*Merci*, Nettie. Just put it on the table here, and we'll serve ourselves. Then take this other tray to the kitchen, please."

Sarah could see Geneviève's impatience as the maid readied the tea as was her usual custom. She was glad of the respite, for now that she had blurted out her secret, she did not know what to say.

All too soon, Nettie was on her way back to the kitchen, and Sarah had to face Geneviève and her questions. As Sarah had anticipated, Geneviève did not waste a second. "You have not promised to marry him, have you?"

If the subject wasn't such a serious one, Sarah would have laughed at Geneviève's appalled expression.

"No, I haven't. I told him no."

"I should hope so. He is not for you." There was relief in her voice as she picked up her cup of tea.

"But I owe him a great deal," Sarah went on. "You know since my parents' deaths he has been my champion, managing the family's affairs, watching over me. He's stood by me the whole time I've been looking for Adam, long after everyone else told me to give up."

"Thankfulness is not a reason to marry, *ma chère*. I beg of you, don't ruin your life by mistaking gratitude for love. That will never work."

"I did tell him no, Geneviève," she reminded her friend in a gently admonishing tone. She reached for her own cup of tea and took a soothing sip.

"But you have a kind heart. Maybe you will change your mind." Geneviève stared into her cup, preoccupied by her thoughts. Then a small smile curved her generous lips. "But, then, maybe Monsieur Cain will keep you from changing it, yes?"

Sarah choked on her tea. "You're incorrigible. How many times do I have to tell you he's only helping me find Adam?"

"And what does he do that he has this information? Is he also an investigator like your Mr. Huggins?"

"No, he's a reporter for a newspaper. The *Picayune*, in fact."

"*Zut*, now I remember why his name seems so familiar. There's been a lot of talk about him from my friends. Lots of whispering and feminine interest. He has a reputation."

"Oh?" Sarah asked, telling herself her interest was purely for business reasons.

"So you are not interested, eh?"

"I only want to be sure he can be trusted," Sarah insisted.

"With information, yes," Geneviève said, with a Gallic shrug.

"What does that mean?"

"As I said, he has a reputation. They call him *Le Sabre*. They say he can cut you to pieces with the words he writes. But whether he earned his nickname from that or the way he pursues his victims, leaving no quarter, I am not sure."

"That still doesn't explain your cryptic answer."

"They also say he has cut everyone from his life. He is a loner except when he needs companionship. Then he uses women only for his pleasure and for no other reason."

"None of that has anything to do with me. I only need information from him—information about Adam. Nothing else."

"I would not like to see you hurt. I hope what you are saying is true."

"It *is* true," Sarah insisted and tried not to worry about the strangely hollow feeling inside her as Geneviève graciously changed the subject.

Chapter Two

Morgan followed Dauphine Street to Canal, the great commercial dividing line between the old Creole society of the Vieux Carré and the newer American section of the city. The *Picayune*'s offices were located a few short blocks on the American side of Canal Street in a four-story granite building. In minutes, Morgan was at the newspaper office, climbing the stairs to where his desk sat, one thought uppermost on his mind—who was Adam Gentry? And why was his name so familiar?

Morgan glanced over his shoulder to make sure no one was watching, then surreptitiously released a small clasp under his desk. A secret drawer sprang open, and Morgan pulled out a sheaf of papers. Hastily, he stuffed them into his pocket, closed the drawer, and turned away from his desk.

"Morgan, at last," an all too familiar voice boomed out from halfway across the room. "Got my messages, I see. Glad I saw you and saved you a trip upstairs."

Morgan groaned silently. Nathaniel Bayard was his editor, and while the man gave his reporters a lot of leeway, Morgan knew he had been abusing that trust lately. But he didn't want to talk in public, and this floor of the building was full of trained eyes and ears, each longing for the one story that could make his reputation.

"You're right, Nat, we do need to talk." Morgan rubbed his temple with one hand, trying to force himself to relax. "If you don't mind, how about joining me at Ellie's?"

Ellie Hampton was a black woman who ran a restaurant nearby. She took boarders by the week or month and also served meals to whomever stopped by. She specialized in fancy desserts served with the richest, darkest coffee in New Orleans.

Nat's eyes lit up at Morgan's suggestion. "I could use something sweet right about now," he said and absently patted his ample girth.

Morgan led the way down the stairs and across the street. The restaurant was nearly empty at this time of day. He looked around the richly appointed room with its ornate ceilings and mahogany walls, but saw no one he knew.

Ellie herself met them at the door. "It's been a long time, Mr. Cain," she said in a mellifluous voice.

"Too long, Miss Ellie," Morgan replied.

"I've got your favorite table ready. That okay with you, Mr. Bayard?"

Nat nodded, his gaze fixed on the tray of pastries lined up just inside the door to remind patrons not to eat too much at their meal lest they become too full to indulge afterward.

Usually Nat preferred a brightly lit spot in the center of the room where he could see everyone—and, equally important, be seen. Morgan was relieved his editor agreed to the table in the dark corner where he normally sat. It wouldn't do to have too many people take an interest in their discussion.

The two men settled in on opposite sides of the table and decided what they would eat. Nat ordered a rich dessert filled with custard and covered with a sweet red sauce made from the strawberries that were now in season. Morgan ordered a thick bisque soup made from the local crayfish and some of Ellie's hard-crust rolls to go with it. He hadn't eaten a real meal in several days, making do with the meager and unpalatable fare available at his boarding house. The coffee that Ellie placed before them whetted his appetite.

Nat pushed the vase of flowers across the damask tablecloth and off to one side to make room for the treat to come before leaning back in his chair. "So, as Ellie said, it has been a long time since we've seen you, Morgan. I'm not criticizing or anything, after all you are *Le Sabre*, but if Mr. Holbrook asks . . ." His voice trailed off.

Mr. Holbrook, the owner of the *Picayune*, was unlikely to be pleased at the thought of one of his reporters going off on a personal crusade. Though Morgan knew his reputation allowed him a good deal of latitude, he wanted to convince Nat that there was a story here.

"I need your help on this, Nat, but I want it kept confidential."

"Confidential?"

Morgan watched Nat's ears almost perk up at the word. There was nothing Nat liked better than a good story.

"The fewer people who know about this, the better."

"What have you got?"

"This could be big—very big. I don't want to tip my hand too soon. Not to anyone."

Morgan knew he was exaggerating. So far he had very little information to go on and not a clue as to who was behind the murders—if they even were murders. All he had was his sister Annie's suspicions, suspicions borne of her painful widowhood, but he could hardly tell Nat that.

"If this is another of those carpetbagger stories, don't even bother. Since those bastards came down here there's been nothing but greed and corruption at every level. Do you see anyone raising an outcry? Believe me, there is no story so big that anyone cares about it," Nat groused.

Morgan hid his smile. He knew how Nat felt about the carpetbaggers as well as the scalawags. The carpetbaggers had come from the North to take advantage of Louisiana's vulnerable position since the end of the war. The scalawags were worse: Southerners who had thrown their lot in with the outsiders, looting their fellow countrymen without a shred of conscience.

Just to tease him, Morgan said, "If you really think that then why do you keep printing stories about the carpetbaggers and scalawags?'"

"You know the patronage system has run amuck, and somebody has to do something about it. But if that's what you're working on, I can guarantee you no one cares. We already have half our reporters ferreting out information about those damned Republicans—and the other half after the Democrats, though I hate having to admit that since it shows our side's barely better."

"I'm not going after corruption. Leastways, not that kind. I don't even know what side my quarry's on."

Morgan suspected that the man he was after was a Southerner though it was not outside the realm of possibility that a former Yankee soldier was seeking revenge.

At that moment Ellie brought their food, and for a few minutes there was silence as each attacked his plate.

"Mmm-mm, that sure was good," Nat exclaimed as he licked his spoon clean. "You should try it sometime. Might sweeten you up a tad." He grinned, thoroughly enjoying his joke.

Morgan pointedly ignored the comment. Instead, he tore one of the rolls in two and used the smaller half to sop up the last bit of soup from his bowl.

"When's the last time you had a real meal?" Nat asked, genuine concern in his tone.

"Can't remember," Morgan said. "I have more important things to do than worry about what I eat."

Nat laid his spoon alongside his serving plate and folded his napkin as neatly as it had been before he'd used it. "You going to tell me what this story is or not?"

Morgan hesitated. Nat was as close to a friend as anyone he knew, and the most trustworthy. Still, if Morgan himself had had trouble believing the tale his sister told, how would a complete stranger react? Especially someone who did not know Annie as Morgan did.

"I can't cover for you if I have no idea what's going on," Nat added, doing his best to keep his voice level. But Morgan heard the underlying hurt. Nat didn't like it one bit that Morgan didn't trust him with all the particulars.

"All right, I'll tell you. But if you find this hard to believe, don't say I didn't warn you."

Nat nodded and leaned forward as did Morgan, until their heads were only inches apart and Morgan could speak softly enough that no one could overhear a word.

"You might remember my brother-in-law died some time ago," Morgan began.

"Yes. You stayed with your sister for a while after."

"That's right. She was torn apart about it. Seems things had been going bad for her and her husband for quite a while. Since the war ended, to be exact."

"Lots of people had a hard time adjusting when the war was over," Nat agreed. "Wives and husbands were apart too long and saw too much suffering. It all takes its toll."

"Well, James never adjusted. Annie said he had nightmares that haunted him, even during the day. When it got to be too much, he'd just sit out on the front porch and do nothing for weeks on end."

Morgan kneaded the back of his neck, feeling the tension in every muscle as he remembered his sister's anguished face when she'd told him her story. Nat stayed silent. After a couple of moments, Morgan continued.

"Then about three months before he died he started going off, sometimes for just a few days, sometimes for longer. When he came back, he would be quiet, hardly speaking to anyone. He'd smell like he hadn't washed the whole time he was gone and reeked of liquor. He never told Annie where he'd been, and she could only guess what he'd been doing. A few days before he died, James told Annie he had some business to take care of, but he'd be back before she could miss him. He promised her everything would be better when he returned."

"What did he want to do?"

"He went off without telling her any more and never came back. Coroner said it was suicide, but Annie doesn't believe that."

"Why not? Doesn't seem like the man was sound, the

way he carried on, no offense. Maybe it all became too much for him. He wouldn't be the first."

"True enough. But Annie says he would never take his own life and especially not then. After all, he was promising things would be better when he returned, and he'd survived up to that point with no mention of ending it all."

"No one can ever know another's mind. Not well enough to know that, at any rate."

"I agree," Morgan said. "I told her everything you've just said and more. But Annie is stubborn. Said if I wouldn't check things out for her, she'd do it on her own."

"Check what?"

"How James really died. Where he was and who he was with."

"Can't have that," Nat said, a frown furrowing his brow. "Why, the woman could get herself into all sorts of serious trouble."

"So I told her, but she wouldn't give up till I gave her my word I'd look into it."

"Well, how long can that take?" Nat said, then paused. "You don't mean to tell me that's what's been keeping you busy these last few weeks?"

Morgan looked into the distance. "It's not as simple as I thought," he admitted with reluctance. "I can find no one who'll talk about James. No one saw him. No one spoke to him. It's as if he never existed, except of course, that they found his body."

"What are you driving at?"

"I'm not sure ... maybe James didn't want to be found. Maybe he was being secretive on purpose."

"You sound like you don't quite believe that."

"I don't. Annie is right. James was the kind of man who always faced his troubles. Even at the end it sounds like he was planning to do just that. So that leaves only the conclusion that whomever he was meeting doesn't want us to know about it."

"So what do you plan to do? You may never find out who James was meeting, or even *if* he was meeting anyone."

"I know that. But Annie is convinced something happened during the war, something unusual and in her words . . . frightful."

"Lots of frightful things happened," Nat dismissed in a bored tone. "That's hardly a reason to go haring after ghosts that may or may not be there."

"True enough. But so far, every time I've gotten close to anyone who knew James, they've died mysteriously."

"What?"

"I've put together a list of people who served with James in the war. I thought if I could track some of them down, one or the other might know what happened with him. But no one I've tried to find is still alive. And those that are, well . . ."

"Well what?" Nat didn't sound bored anymore. His curiosity was as piqued as Morgan's had become.

"From what I've learned, most of them never rejoined their families. They wander, never settling, haunted by their past. Only thing is, no one seems to know what it is that haunts them—and it looks as if someone wants to make sure no one ever finds out. There are too many suicides and unexplained deaths."

"So what do you think you can do? If the others are all dead, you may never learn what you want."

"They're not all dead. One's in New Orleans. I just have to find him."

"Wait a minute. How do you know he's in New Orleans if you don't know where he is?"

Morgan didn't mention Sarah Gentry. He didn't want her involved in any of this now that she'd given him her meager information. He had his own sources, and he would tap into them now that he had a few more details. Adam Gentry was the key to solving this mystery, Morgan had a bone-deep instinct about it. Without even looking at his list, he was sure Gentry's name would be there. He fit the pattern all too well.

"I've spoken to someone who knows the man," was all he would say.

Nat rubbed a hand over his face. "I don't know, Morgan. This seems a long shot at best. There may be no story at the end—just a bunch of men who were cowards or who are suffering from nostalgia. There are enough of them around, misfits who can't seem to shake the war from their shoulders."

"Yes, I've heard of that, but never like this. A whole company? It's too much of a coincidence. Something happened to this group, and I want to know what."

"This sounds like a wild-goose chase to me."

"Maybe, maybe not. But my instincts are telling me there's something here, something important. If the paper can't give me time to pursue this, I'll go after it on my own."

"You mean quit?" Nat sounded aghast.

Morgan nodded, realizing he meant it. It wasn't an idle threat.

"I see." Nat took a deep breath and visibly held it, then blew it out. "You and I both know you could find a job on any paper in this town or any other. I'll be honest, we don't want to lose you. How about I give you four weeks, no questions asked. Then we'll see what you've got. Fair enough?"

Morgan knew the offer was Nat's way of saving face and accepted it as such "More than fair. I owe you one, Nat."

"What you owe me is a story to blast the competition out of the water. See that you get one." The last sentence was uttered with a smile and an underlying earnestness.

Nat stood and threw several coins onto the table. "I'm paying. You want anything else?"

Morgan shook his head. "Thanks for the meal."

"You look as though you could use it. Don't be too much of a stranger, you hear? I expect to hear from you on this."

"I'll be in touch as soon as I know anything."

With a nod, Nat left and made his way back toward the *Picayune*. Morgan watched him until he disappeared, then he pulled the sheaf of papers from his pocket and flipped through them. Suddenly the name jumped out at him. Lieutenant Adam Gentry. Just as he'd thought.

Morgan smiled grimly as he tucked the papers into his pocket again. Leaving Ellie's, he headed back to the French Quarter, working his way toward the docks and his shabby boardinghouse. As he walked his thoughts turned over the problem of Adam Gentry. Somehow he had to locate the man—and quickly. He would have to try to contact Ossy Burnes. Ossy knew every lost soul that graced the streets and back alleys of the city.

As he made his way along the waterfront, Morgan left word at a number of places, mostly seedy taverns where the down-and-out could buy cheap, watered-down drinks with the few cents they'd begged or stolen, the coins warm and sticky from their unwashed hands. No one admitted to having seen Ossy Burnes, but then few of them were known for their honesty or moral scruples. One way or another, word would get to Ossy, Morgan was pretty sure of that. The only question was how quickly.

When he reached the boardinghouse, Mrs. Ogden mumbled her usual greeting, muttering under her breath about boarders who came and left at all hours, making her come to the door no matter how inconvenient it might be. Morgan ignored her comments. She was being paid well to keep an eye on his things and her mouth shut about his comings and goings.

"Any messages?" he asked, cutting through her muttering.

"Nary a one. You expecting something? Or maybe ... someone?"

The sly, lascivious gleam in her eye told him she was thinking about his earlier visitor—and there was no question about the nature of her thoughts. Morgan clenched his teeth. Sarah Gentry deserved better, but then she'd brought this on herself by her impetuous behavior.

"Just checking," he replied curtly, in a tone designed to cut off further speculation. "I may be going out again soon."

"Whatever you say, dearie." The old lady shuffled off to the back parlor without another word.

Morgan walked down the hall, his thoughts wandering where they would. Without his permission, they veered back to Sarah Gentry. He'd been stunned when she walked into his room this morning. It was as if an angel had wandered into the bowels of hell—and he'd felt like the devil himself beside her pristine, fair beauty. When her bright green eyes had swept over him, lingering on his bare chest, he had felt the touch of fire, burning him on the inside, pooling his blood in his loins. She would have been shocked had she realized the extent of his physical response.

It had taken all his self-control to turn away from her when all he had wanted to do was run his fingers through her auburn hair and see if it felt as soft and welcoming as it looked. Her skin had been unblemished, the color of cream, and her body was slim and feminine with gently rounded curves. A less scrupulous man might have taken advantage of all that innocence, especially in a place where nobody listened too closely or cared what happened next door.

With a sigh, Morgan let himself into his room and quickly checked that no one had been there since he'd left. He'd become clever about such things, leaving a carefully placed hair gently fastened between the door and its frame or a small piece of string tucked into the top of his closet door. Any attempt to open either door would dislodge his markers, revealing the intruder. But tonight, his room was untouched.

Morgan thought over everything Sarah had told him about her brother, hoping to unearth some small shred of information that might help track the man down. His story was like so many others, a reluctant soldier in a war gone bad. A peaceful soul forced to defend his own at a terrible cost. Now he wandered the streets in search of forgetfulness, that much Morgan knew for sure. But what was it Adam Gentry wanted to forget?

Morgan flopped onto the bed and leaned against the wall, throwing an arm over his eyes. The men he'd been seeking were broken, guilt-ridden, and fearful all at the same time. Most of them still relived the war as though it had occurred yesterday instead of ending seven years ago. The intensity of their feelings after so much time separated them from other soldiers, even those who had had some problems readjusting after the war.

Something different had happened to these men, something so shocking, so wounding, that its impact had not lessened after all these years. What could it have been?

Morgan cast his mind back to those awful years, to the pain and disillusionment. He had seen his share of battles and injuries, had tasted fear and smelled death. He had put the horrors behind him after a while, into a place he never looked, shutting himself off so he could go on living.

The images blurred before his eyes, and he fell into a restless doze, the elusive memories dancing just out of reach.

A noise at the window brought him out of a troubled sleep to full alertness. The sound repeated—a handful of gravel against the shutter. In a single lithe movement, Morgan stood and pressed himself against the wall by the window. Carefully, he peered outside, surprised to see how late it was. The moon was high in the sky, the sun long since gone. He must have slept longer than he realized.

A shadow moved under the magnolia tree, and another shower of tiny stones hit the outside surface of the wall he leaned on. Morgan recognized the hunched shape and the hacking cough that emanated from the ghostly apparition.

"Ossy?" he called out in a hushed voice.

"Yeah, boss. You wanted to see me?"

Morgan nodded, then realized the other man couldn't see him. "I'll be right down."

"I'll wait here, boss," the other man replied, and the shadow disappeared beneath the tree.

Morgan grabbed his dark jacket as much because it made him harder to spot as for any additional warmth. The nights stayed warm this time of year. He slipped out the back door without bothering his landlady, carefully closing the door so it didn't latch shut and he could return the same way, unnoticed.

The old soldier was leaning against the tree trunk, his breath rasping. He coughed twice when he tried to say hello, then reached into his pocket and took a swig from a battered flask.

"You shouldn't drink that stuff," Morgan said, nodding in the direction of the flask. "It's not good for you."

The old man gave him a gap-toothed grin. "Nope, but I sure like it. Makes life go down a wee bit better." He smacked his lips as if to get the last bit of taste from them. "What can I do for you, boss?" He coughed again.

Morgan waited until the spasm had passed. "I've been wondering about someone I just learned was in town."

Ossy didn't say anything until Morgan drew a few bills from his pocket, enough to keep the old man pleasantly soused for the next week, providing he cooperated.

"So, who you want to find?"

"A soldier, like the others I told you about. This one's named Adam Gentry. Used to be a lieutenant."

"Gentry, huh? Don't know no one by that name, but Adam, now. There was talk of someone like him." Ossy looked decidedly worried.

"What kind of talk?"

"I don't think you're gonna like it," the soldier whined.

Morgan bit down on his impatience, knowing that the old man was rattled enough as it was.

"Why not?"

"They found him just a little while ago. Dead."

"Dead!" Morgan let loose with a string of epithets and pounded the tree trunk with his fist, oblivious to the pain. "Damn it! How the hell did it happen?"

"No one knows for sure. Maybe he just wanted to die."

"He's wanted to die for a long time—probably seven years. So why tonight?"

Ossy shrugged.

"Do you know where it happened?" Morgan demanded.

Ossy's eyes opened so wide Morgan could see the whites all around the man's irises.

"I ain't going anywhere near there. And neither will you, if you know what's good for you." The old man shuddered and crossed himself.

"Just tell me where it happened. I'll go by myself."

Morgan pulled another couple of bills from his pocket and added them to Ossy's pile.

The former soldier swallowed noisily. "I don't like this. I don't like this at all."

"All I want to know is where it happened and what they found."

"I already told you what they found: they found him dead. That's all there was to it."

He reached out for the money, and Morgan pulled it back, just out of his grasp.

"Was he shot or stabbed? Was there any injury? Could he have been poisoned?"

"I don't know. I don't know." The old man began to whimper, and Morgan cursed under his breath. The liquor had been quick in taking over the old man's mind. A few more minutes and Morgan would get nothing more from him, nothing of any use, at least.

"Ossy, listen to me. This is important. Where was Adam found? Can you tell me that?"

He put the money in Ossy's hand but closed his own around it, making sure the man knew the money would be his if he could but answer this last question.

"Down by the docks, in this small alleyway. You know, where he always went."

"Show me?"

"But—"

"Just close enough that I can find it myself. All right?"

The old man trembled, and Morgan was sure he would refuse, but suddenly he straightened his back, looking once again like the soldier he'd been so long ago. "All right. I can do that. Adam, he was one of us, you know—he fought in that damned war just like I did."

"Thanks," Morgan said and followed the other man's lurching gait through the back roads and alleyways of the worst part of town, until they reached their destination.

The alleyway was deserted. Situated between two storehouses near the docks, it would have gone unnoticed unless you were looking for a place to hide. Morgan cursed his lack of foresight in not bringing a candle so he could see in the narrow causeway. The moon was still high in the sky but not shining at the right angle to illuminate the hidey-hole.

Ossy had run off as quickly as he could, leaving Morgan to the gruesome task of pawing through the dead man's meager store of belongings. The alleyway smelled unpleasantly of human habitation and something else. The elusive smell barely floated on the breeze, and Morgan wasn't sure if he actually smelled it or it was simply his imagination. Almonds. Cyanide.

But was it murder or suicide? How could he ever tell? Still, who would choose cyanide as a way to die? Morgan shook his head. None of it made sense.

And then he thought of Sarah. Who would have thought that a man like Adam Gentry would have a sister like her? She was everything her brother wasn't: innocent and pure, genteel and soft, sheltered from the harsh realities of life.

But not any longer. There was no harsher reality than a death in such a place. He wished he could spare her but knew he couldn't. She would keep searching if no one told her the truth, wearing herself out emotionally and financially for a lost cause. Morgan only marveled that she hadn't given up long ago. She had spirit to go along with her impetuousness. He hoped his news wouldn't break her.

Clenching his jaw, he turned his steps back to the boardinghouse. He'd see her first thing in the morning when he was bathed and clean-shaven.

Chapter Three

Sarah paced from one end of the small front parlor to the other. Ever since Morgan Cain sent word that he was coming to see her this morning, she hadn't been able to think of anything else. He must have some information about Adam. Why else would he be coming over ... and so soon?

She'd been certain he'd known more than he was letting on, and now he had something to report. Maybe he was even bringing Adam with him! Sarah could barely contain her excitement. She wished Geneviève were here, but her friend had been called out to her mother's house early this morning. Sarah had offered to go along, but Geneviève had refused, claiming her mother's emergencies were rarely anything to worry about. Still, Geneviève had not wanted to ignore the summons as her mother was quite elderly.

"Can I bring you morning tea, Miss Sarah?" Geneviève's mulatto maid asked as she entered the room, dust cloth in hand.

Sarah turned and smiled at the young woman.

"I don't think I could keep anything down, but thank you anyway, Nettie."

"You do seem a bit excited this morning, if I may say so," the other woman said as she straightened the cushions and the lace doilies on the backs of the chairs. Nettie's statement might seem forward to anyone overhearing them, but Nettie had been with the Michaud family since childhood. After the war, she'd accepted employment with Geneviève, happy to stay with the family who'd raised her and have a job that didn't entail outside work or worse.

The war that had liberated the slaves all too often "liberated" them to a life with no future, to starvation and deprivation the likes of which she'd never seen before. She was one of the lucky ones, having formed a friendship with her employer that broke the bounds of what others might consider proper. But Geneviève had never let others' opinions sway her, and Nettie had blossomed with her new freedom.

"I'm expecting some very good news—as well as a visitor," Sarah told her.

"That visitor wouldn't be that handsome gentleman that escorted you here yesterday, would it?"

"How did you guess? Did you see him? Do you really think he's handsome?" Sarah didn't know what possessed her to ask such a question, but now that she'd said the words, she wanted to hear Nettie's answer.

"Doesn't matter what I think. It's what you think that matters, and you must think him handsome to have asked in the first place."

Heat filled Sarah's face, and she turned away, suddenly shy about the direction the conversation had taken. She did find Morgan attractive in a very dark way. He touched some wild chord inside her and made her body vibrate with awareness—of him and of herself—but she could never admit that to anyone.

"What matters to me most is that he knows Adam's whereabouts."

"Oh, Miss Sarah, do you mean it? He knows where Mr. Adam is?" Nettie came to Sarah's side, her eyes bright with hope. "I'm so happy for you. I know how hard it's been these last few years. I remember when you were children, and you'd come to the big house so we could all play together. It seems so long ago now. So many things have changed."

"And best that they have, I think. I know—"

Sarah's reply was interrupted by the ringing of the front bell. When the maid would have answered the summons, Sarah stopped her. "Don't bother, Nettie. I'll go. I don't think I can wait another minute to find out about Adam."

"I understand. You go on, then." With a fond smile, Nettie changed direction and headed back to the kitchen.

Sarah tugged the bottom of her light green shirtwaist into place and smoothed the material of her darker green skirt. She glanced in the hall mirror to make sure her hair was still neat and tucked one wayward auburn strand back into the knot at the top of her head. Taking a deep breath, she opened the door.

Morgan Cain completely filled the doorway. His dark eyes stared down at her. With excited eyes she looked behind him but saw no one. Her heart dropped though she realized how foolish her hope had been. It was unlikely that he would have found Adam so quickly. But maybe he'd gleaned some new information. Yes, that must be it.

"Won't you come in," she said, putting a smile on her face.

She showed him into the parlor, refraining from hurtling questions at him only by exercising all her self-control.

"Shall I ring for tea?" she asked with her best company manners.

He appeared uncomfortable as he looked around the feminine room, but all he said was, "Tea will be fine. Is Miss Michaud here? Perhaps she would care to join us."

"Geneviève had to go see her mother," she said as she rang the bell for Nettie, a bit disappointed that he wanted to see Geneviève. "Some family emergency. But I'm sure she'll be back soon." The polite conversation was more than she could bear. Without intending to she blurted out what had been uppermost in her mind, "Have you news of Adam?"

Before he could answer Nettie entered the room carrying a tray set for tea.

"I think you were ringing for this, yes?" she said, placing the tray on the table in front of Sarah.

"Thank you, Nettie."

"If you need anything else, just let me know," she said with a wink for Sarah, then nodded her head in the visitor's direction before leaving the room.

"I find tea very relaxing in the morning," Sarah said as she poured out two cups. She found it hard to believe that her voice sounded so natural when all she wanted, all she could think of, was Adam, seeing him and holding him close.

"Sugar? Cream?" she asked, waiting out her guest. This was his story to tell.

"Nothing," he returned and reached out to take the

cup she held toward him. He placed it on the occasional table beside his chair. "I do have news of your brother."

His tone sent a chill through Sarah's body, but she ignored it. "You've found him. How wonderful! When can I see him? Why didn't you bring him with you?" She rose from her chair and stood before him, ignoring the prickly feeling at the back of her neck and the heavy feeling in her chest.

He stood, too, and took a step toward her. "I'm afraid the news I have isn't good. There's no easy ... Your brother's dead."

The words hit her like a sharp blow, pushing the air from her lungs and leaving her light-headed and gasping for breath. She reached for the back of a nearby chair to steady herself, and Morgan put out his hand, as if to catch her.

She shuddered and stepped away from him. "No, you're wrong," she said, her knuckles turning white as she gripped the chair. "You've made a mistake."

"There's been no mistake."

His voice was gentle, but firm, brooking no disagreement, leaving no hope of misunderstanding. Still, she couldn't accept it. She must have heard wrong. Her brother, her dear Adam, he couldn't be—

"You can't know that. You can't be so sure. Why, Gentry's a common name. There must be over fifty families just in New Orleans. You've mistaken Adam for one of them."

"I haven't," he said softly, his voice coming from just behind her. It was the softest she'd ever heard him speak. "My contact got in touch with me late last night. The body was taken—"

"No, I don't want to hear this. Get out! Do you hear me? Just get out—now!"

"That won't change anything."

The implacability of his tone infuriated her. Didn't he realize he'd just destroyed her world? Didn't he understand she couldn't just abandon Adam to such a fate?

The rage inside her took over, and she flew at Morgan, demanding that he leave as her fists pounded ineffectually at his chest. The pain inside her was so great, she thought she might explode. She fought against his arms when they closed around her, channeling her anger toward him so she wouldn't have to face the hurtful truth.

But it wouldn't go away. As Morgan tried to soothe her, she knew he hadn't lied, and the rage suddenly abandoned her, leaving her lost and empty. A wave of hurt crested in its place, then broke, spilling over in tears. Her sobs shook her to the very core, obliterating every thought save one: Adam was no more.

Never again would he call her name, or smile at her in that sad, wistful way he had. Never again would she hold his hand or feel his joy or know his love. All she had left of him was her memories—and the precious gold locket he'd given her on her sixteenth birthday, before the war had destroyed his soul.

She didn't know how long the storm of crying lasted. All she knew was that she'd found a safe harbor from which to face her pain and loss. No matter how strongly her grief tore at her, his arms were stronger still, holding her together when she thought she would break apart.

As her sobs slowly eased, she became aware of the world again, of the heat from his body and the scent of his skin, of the gentle way he held her, so unlike what she had imagined when she'd seen him at the boardinghouse. She felt fragile and feminine—and knew that wouldn't do at all.

She was alone now, with no parents and no brother. She had to be strong; she had to face what needed to be done. She tugged herself free of his hold.

"Are you all right?" he asked.

"Yes, I think so." She took a deep breath and covered her face with her hands, needing a moment of privacy to pull herself together. "I'm sorry." She lifted her head to look at him and motioned with her hand to indicate all that had just passed, especially her loss of control.

"It's to be expected, under the circumstances."

"You were saying something about having taken the . . ." Her voice broke, and she couldn't bring her self to say "body."

"I'm not sure you're ready to cope with this just yet."

"Whether I'm ready isn't the issue, is it? I want to do this for Adam. I need to."

He stared at her intently, and she thought she caught a glint of admiration in his eyes but it was hidden as quickly as any other emotion he might be feeling.

"All right. They took his body to the Girod Street Cemetery."

"Girod Street? But isn't that where—"

"Yes. They thought him an indigent. If you like, I can make other arrangements."

The Girod Street Cemetery was the oldest of the American cemeteries, lying across Canal Street from the Vieux Carré. Once it had been one of the grandest in the city, but that was before the war and the great epidemics of '53 and '66. Now it was largely abandoned, used as a resting place for the very poor.

Sarah's first impulse was that she didn't want him

there, not with the lost and forgotten and those nobody wanted. But what would Adam have wanted? That thought came rushing hard on the heels of the first. Adam had spent the past few years among the lost and forgotten. Had he wanted to lose himself? And what was it he wanted to forget?

"Will he be all right there?" she asked, as if anything would ever be all right for Adam again. A hysterical bubble of laughter threatened to erupt from her throat as she heard her words, and she had to bite down hard on her lip to keep the laughter from escaping.

"I'll send word that you'll cover expenses, and they'll keep him from a pauper's grave," Morgan said. "Some of the better families still use the Girod, you know, the ones who have family tombs there from the old days."

The better families. What a strange idea that was in the wake of the terrible conflict that had torn the land apart, turning its deepest traditions upside down even as it sought to give freedom to the downtrodden.

"I just want him to find peace. Lord knows, he never found it when he lived." She turned to the window and saw the bright sunny day. A bird hopped from one branch of the tree in the inner courtyard to another, singing a merry tune. How incongruous that life should go on so happily outside her window on one of the saddest days of her life. She sighed, and the breath caught in her throat for an instant, but she regained control without succumbing to tears. "Could you tell me how Adam died?"

"The police think he drank himself to death."

"Is that possible?"

"It's not impossible."

There was something in his tone that made her turn

and look him in the face. "Does that mean you don't believe them?"

He shrugged, but his expression remained neutral. Still, she sensed he wasn't convinced. And neither was she.

"Well, I don't believe it. Why now, after all this time? It doesn't make sense."

"His life was not easy—or particularly safe, you know."

"You don't have to coddle me and weigh every word just because you think I might be offended," she told him, irritated by his reticence. Why did men think women needed to be so sheltered? It only made things more difficult. Why, for all she knew, she might have found Adam months ago if only someone would have told her the truth about his life instead of her having to find it out for herself—and too late, at that. "I know how he lived, and where, more or less. What I don't know is why, but I intend to find out."

She'd caught him by surprise, she could see that. His brow furrowed, and he looked every bit as menacing as he had the day before in his room, all harsh angles and planes.

"This is a dangerous business, not something you should be throwing yourself into on a lark."

"This isn't a lark," she answered, her own brow furrowing so he would know the seriousness of her intent. "I want to know what happened to Adam and how he ended up like this. And I won't let anything stop me." She looked straight at him as she finished speaking, letting him know her last sentence had been directed at him.

She could see his jaw clench, the muscles on the side

of his cheek standing out in high relief. Even his dark eyes appeared to glow with an inner fire made up of anger and something else she could not fully make out. Then he blinked, and it was gone.

"Listen," he said, his voice once again calm and detached. "Your brother was found in an alley, down by the river where only the rats run around with impunity. There are more murders and robberies down there in a day than there are in this part of town in a year. People die for all sorts of reasons—and for no reason at all. No one knows what happened to Adam, and in all likelihood, no one will ever know. Is that blunt enough for you?"

If he was trying to scare her off, he was doing a good job.

"And what about Adam?" she whispered, once again near tears. "He didn't deserve to die like that."

Morgan ran a hand through his hair and made a frustrated noise, halfway between a sigh and a growl. His eyes looked anywhere but at her, finally resting on a distant view out her window, as if he wished he were out there too rather than cooped in here with her. Some small feminine part of her felt hurt at the rejection, but her more sensible self was relieved.

"No one deserves to die like that, and too many have," he murmured more to himself than to her. Then he snapped his gaze back into the room and looked directly at her. "I'll check around, ask some questions."

"Thank—"

"Don't thank me yet. I want you keeping out of it, you hear? No impulsive trips to the docks, no sneaking around alleyways, no asking questions you shouldn't."

Her spine straightened of its own accord. Who was he to order her around?

"You could get killed, don't you understand?" he demanded without letting her interrupt. "Or worse ... Give me your word that you'll leave this to me or I won't tell you a thing. I'm far better equipped to get the information you want."

It was blackmail, plain and simple. And effective. She already knew how difficult it was to get information from anybody. After all, she'd been trying for years and had had to resort to Mr. Huggins for help before she got very far in her search.

"You'll tell me everything you find out?"

He nodded.

"All right. You win. But promise me you'll find the person who murdered Adam."

He looked instantly wary and alert. "What makes you think he was murdered?"

"It stands to reason. If he didn't drink himself to death, someone must have killed him—the one fact I do know is that he's dead. And you must think so, too, or you wouldn't be warning me off and investigating it yourself."

"I would be warning you off no matter what. I told you already how dangerous that area is, and I'm telling you again. You don't want to be coddled and treated like a lady, then I'll give you the same treatment I'd give to a man. You gave me your word, and I'm holding you to it. Now I'd better go and start checking things out. I'll be in touch."

Within seconds he was gone, and Sarah stood alone in Geneviève's parlor. She felt lost and abandoned, though in truth, Adam had left her long ago—at least the Adam she remembered from her childhood. She fingered the locket at her neck, the locket he had given her. It was all she had left of him. The hope that she would someday get him back had kept her going. Now that hope was irrevocably shattered.

Only later, after she'd cried herself dry, did she realize that Morgan had never denied thinking that Adam was murdered. In fact, he'd made his escape as quickly as he could before she could question him further. He was too clever by far, but next time she would be prepared. She would find out exactly how Morgan Cain fit into the picture, for she knew without a doubt that he was part of this mystery too.

Morgan cursed under his breath as he left Geneviève Michaud's house. What was he going to do now? He knew he didn't have much time before Sarah would yield to her impulsiveness, promise or no promise. If only her friend had been there, she would have understood his need to keep Sarah far from his investigation. A woman of her sophistication would have accepted whatever story he chose to tell without his having to go into detail, unlike Sarah.

Though he had left her behind, he still carried her image with him. Her grief had torn at him despite his detachment, a detachment cultivated by every reporter in order to do his job. Morgan had cultivated it deeper than most, perhaps because he had more to forget, more to put aside than others. He never let himself get involved with the people of his stories or the people he met in his life. At least he tried not to.

Sarah was proving to be the exception. Since when

had he promised to share information with anyone other than his editor? And why now? Bright green eyes came to mind, and skin as smooth and creamy as new-fallen snow. She had grit and determination—and was just foolhardy enough to plunge into the thick of things if someone didn't take her in hand.

That thought brought him up short. To take someone in hand meant taking on a responsibility, something he had successfully avoided since the war. And yet the thought of leaving Sarah to her fate never crossed his mind. Without his knowing quite how, he had made a commitment to her—to see this thing through, to try and set things right. Why, if he wasn't careful, she'd be thinking of him as a damned hero, before long. And Lord knows, he was anything but hero material.

Nor was she a classic damsel in distress, waiting to be saved. She was convinced that accepting responsibility for her own fate as well as her brother's, lay in her soft, delicate hands. He shook his head, knowing how dangerous her feisty spirit was, how likely to lead her into trouble, for she'd come too close to guessing his thoughts. If she sensed there was more to his story than just her brother's death, there would be no stopping her. He had to solve this problem, and quickly. For Sarah was right—he did think it was murder, just as he had become convinced his brother-in-law's death was no accident.

Morgan turned his steps toward *Smoky Row*. Though it was just a few streets from where Sarah, in her innocence and purity, was staying, it was a world apart. No one ventured down that dangerous block unarmed. The poor women who made their living in its squalid shadows would just as soon drag a man off the streets and rob him as provide the services for which some were all too eager to pay.

Morgan scouted out the block from across the street. The banquettes on either side were crowded and smoky, filled with shouts and screams, curses and vulgar laughter. Women from seven to seventy sat in various stages of undress along the road, some on chairs, others along the curb of the sidewalk itself, hawking their wares as they smoked and drank and fought over the few misguided men who wandered in through the day. The men who visited were equally desperate, at least those who didn't make their living off the women as pimps and procurers.

"Wanna good time, Mistuh? Come on ova heah!" a woman called from the opposite corner. She wore a filthy dress that hung on her too thin body, baring one brown shoulder and nearly half her chest.

Morgan guessed her age to be around seventeen going on fifty—her eyes a generation or two older than her face. He crossed the street.

"I want information," he said as he neared her.

"Information?" She spat on the ground. "Information don't pay my bills." She turned to go.

"I'll pay for your time."

"You will? Then come right along. Bettine can give you all the time you need."

She put her hand on his arm and tugged, as if to pull him down the street. He knew better than to follow. Rumor had it more men were murdered or robbed on this block than in the whole rest of the city.

"We can talk just as well here," he said, refusing to budge.

"Talk?" She looked him over from top to toe, her expression as bold and brazen as any he'd seen. "I don't know what's come over you white boys. Always wantin' to talk, talk, talk."

She leaned against him, her hand going unerringly to his crotch. "You sure you don't wanna do anything more interesting, sugah?"

Morgan grabbed her by the wrist and jerked her hand away. She was both pathetic and disgusting, her body no cleaner than her clothes, her choices narrowed to this seething dark world of shame. She was missing half her teeth, and up close he could see her body was covered with half-healed scabs and running sores.

"You want my money, you'll do as I say, you hear?"

She nodded sullenly. "Whatever you say, Mastuh."

He let her go, and she pulled up the top of her dress, but when she let it go, it once again flopped down her arm, baring most of one breast. She leaned against the wall of the shack behind her and thrust her hips out in what she must have thought was a provocative pose. Morgan was unmoved. The squalor and venality of the street overwhelmed whatever baser urges she might be trying to waken in him.

"I want to know about a soldier," he said.

"You and everyone else," she said in a bored tone. "What you wanna know?"

Morgan began to describe Adam Gentry, relying on what Ossy Burnes had told him.

"How come ever'one's looking for the same one?" the whore asked.

"What do you mean?"

She shrugged and looked meaningfully at his pocket. Morgan reached in and pulled out some money, letting her catch a glimpse of silver to loosen her tongue.

61

She licked her lips, and Morgan could almost hear the thoughts racing through her mind as she weighed her information against the money she would gain. She was deciding how much to let out now, and what to hold in reserve for bargaining.

He dropped a few coins in her hand. "Tell me what you know. If it's of interest, I'll give you the rest."

She looked greedily at the money still in his hand. He moved it out of her reach and carefully checked around to be sure no one was sneaking up on him from behind. It was not unheard of for the whores to work together to lure a man off the streets, then club him over the head and steal everything he owned.

"First tell me who else is looking for soldiers."

"Lots of folks," she replied, dashing his hopes. "But only two or three want your soldier."

"*My* soldier?" The fine hairs on his neck stood up at her words. Could someone else have been searching for Adam, perhaps the killer? "Who are they? Can you describe them?"

"Could be, less'n I forget, o'course." She eyed his hand again.

He gave her a couple more coins, well aware that he was paying her more than she could earn on a good day on this street. But time was his enemy. He did as he must.

"Well, one of 'em was a soldier, just like your man. Still wore his grays 'ceptin' they ain't any color no more."

"Did he say why he was looking?"

"Just that they was friends once."

"And that's all?"

She gave him a blank, waiting look. He reached into his pocket again for the last of his coins.

"If you want this, you better tell me all you know."

"I done told you all. He said the other soldier was his friend, and he wanted to talk to him about somethin' important. That's it!"

She faced him with her hands on her hips and her face thrust belligerently up toward his. "You done finished talkin'? Cause I is. I got better thing to do with *my* time."

"Just one more thing, then you can go about your business."

"What's that?"

"You said there was someone else looking, too. What can you tell me about him?"

"Don't know much. Fancy gentleman, I hear tell, but with a hunger for sweet young'uns. Can't get that here, you know. Got to go up to Basin Street, to one of them fancy houses where they buy the girls fresh from their mammas."

"What do you know of such things?" he asked, grabbing her by the arm.

"Let me go. You asked to know. Don't blame me if you don't like what you hear," she replied, trying to pull out of his grasp. Her eyes widened with fear though she was no stranger to men's brutality. He knew he held her more tightly than he'd intended and let her go at once.

"What else do you know about him?"

"Nothin'. Like I said, I hear tell 'bout him. That's all."

"That's it, then?"

She nodded and held out her hand. Morgan dropped the last of his money into it, and she scurried away, looking over her shoulder once to check that he wasn't following her.

His jaw clenched, Morgan set out with grim purpose for Basin Street, just outside the boundaries of the French Quarter, the Vieux Carré. As he walked, he tried to sort out what he had just heard. That another soldier would be looking for Adam was not a surprise. From what his sister, Annie, had said, her husband had been looking for his mess mates at the time of his death. What if he wasn't the only one searching?

But the gentleman—that was a new twist, and one to which he had no answer. If the man was after virgins, there was no telling what kind of man he was. The question was how to track him down. Basin Street was much more sophisticated than *Smoky Row*. To a passerby, it looked just like any other well-tended residential street with trees lining the sidewalks and an air of gentility. But that was misleading. Anyone watching for any length of time would be sure to notice the number of men stopping at the houses, sometimes for just a while, sometimes for much longer.

The madams who ruled here made plenty of money and were protective of their clients, knowing that return business was key to their profits. They wouldn't take kindly to anyone who was too curious or who might bring the law down on their heads.

He stood beneath a tree and scanned the houses, trying to decide where to start. This business was getting more complicated by the minute.

By the time Geneviève returned home, Sarah was in control of her emotions. Geneviève paled when she heard the news but was quick to turn her attention to Sarah and her needs.

"What will you do now?" she asked.

"I don't know. Morgan ... that is, Mr. Cain said he will make arrangements for the funeral. They've taken Adam to the Girod Street Cemetery, and Mr. Cain will see to it that he gets a proper grave."

"Can you afford that, Sarah? I'll be glad to help."

Sarah stiffened. So far she'd managed to keep her financial situation private, except for her lapse with Morgan. Had he talked to Geneviève?

"I have money put aside for Adam," she said crisply, though it had not been set aside for this—never this. She had wanted to build a new life with Adam, to give him a fresh start. Now all she could do was bid him farewell.

"I didn't mean to pry, Sarah. I know how hard it has been, and with your search for Adam ... I guess I assumed things might be difficult now. The war left many in tightened straits."

"I'm sorry," Sarah said, knowing from Geneviève's tone that the other woman had been hurt by her abrupt response. "You're right, things are more difficult now, but I'm not in the poorhouse yet."

That was true as far as it went, though she had little idea how she would live once her money ran out. She gave a wan smile, which was the best she could come up with under the circumstances.

"If I can help in any way, you will let me know, yes?"

"Yes, of course. I didn't mean to snap. It's just ..." Tears gathered in her eyes as the overwhelming events of the day caught up with her again. "Oh, Geneviève, what am I going to do without him?"

Geneviève put her arms around Sarah's shoulders,

tears filling her own eyes. "I don't know, *chérie*, but we will find a way. We have no choice."

The two of them sat together for a long time without speaking, each lost in her own thoughts. A tentative knock on the door made them look up. Nettie stood there, an uncertain expression on her face.

"The police are here. To see Miss Sarah," she explained. "Should I tell them to come back another time?"

Sarah rubbed her palms across her cheeks to wipe away the traces of her tears. "No, no. I want to see them. Please show them in, if that's all right with you, Geneviève?"

"Yes, if you are certain now is a good time. We can always—"

"No, please. I need to know what they've learned about Adam."

Geneviève turned to Nettie. "Put them in the front parlor. We'll be right there."

The two policemen looked uncomfortable amidst Geneviève's collection of porcelains displayed on ornately carved tables spread about the room. They sat on the edge of her satin settee as if they were afraid their combined weight would overwhelm its delicate structure. When the two women entered the room, the policemen stood, the younger one blushing as he looked to his older companion to take the lead.

"Good afternoon, gentlemen," Geneviève said, sensing their discomfort. "Please be seated and tell us how we may be of assistance."

The older policeman took the lead. "I'm Sergeant Belmont and this is Officer Parker," he said, still standing and turning his cap around in circles in his hand. "We understand you've, uh, been told about your brother?"

This last was directed at Sarah. She nodded.

"Yes, well." He cleared his throat. "It seems to us . . . well, there don't seem to be no delicate way to put this . . . We think he, uh, did hisself in. Wouldn't be the first time for the likes of him, if you get my meaning."

He stared down at his shoes, and his companion flushed an even brighter red as he, too, looked anywhere but at the two women.

"I'm sorry gentlemen, but I don't believe that, and if you'd known him, you wouldn't either."

The men looked up apologetically, the younger one saying, "Did you see him to talk to lately, miss? He may have changed, you know."

"Not that much, not so much that he'd take his own life. You just don't want to take the time to investigate his death, do you?"

"Now, miss, it's not like that at all," the sergeant said. "There just isn't much to go on, him having been found in an alley and all. I wouldn't want to raise any false hopes."

"I think he was murdered, and I want his death investigated. If you can't do it, I'll have to find someone who will."

The men looked a bit alarmed and turned to Geneviève, hoping she would see reason.

"We're doing the best we can, ma'am. There's a lot of crime out there, and we try to keep up. But frankly, there doesn't seem to be much anyone can do here. Besides, no one saw what happened. You do understand?"

Geneviève nodded. "We can only ask that you do your best," she said.

The sergeant nodded. "Again our sympathies, ma'am," he said as he and his colleague took their leave.

Sarah wasn't as pacified as Geneviève. "What does that mean? Will they investigate or not?" she demanded the minute the policemen were out the door.

Geneviève closed the door behind them, then leaned against it.

"I don't know, *ma chère*. I don't think they'll search hard no matter what. Their minds are made up."

"They're wrong, you know. Surely you believe that?"

"I want to as much as you do, but"—she shrugged her shoulders—"they are right about one thing, you know. Who of us can know what was in Adam's mind these past few years? Who can know what demons haunted him?"

"That's just it, Geneviève. If we could find out what happened to change him, we would know. That's why this investigation is so important."

"We may never know," Geneviève replied and reached out to stroke Sarah's hair as if she were but a child.

But Sarah stepped back. "No. I refuse to believe that. I *will* know what happened even if I have to do the investigation myself!"

Geneviève frowned. "But, Sarah, you can't possibly hope to learn what has happened. Where will you go? Who will you talk to? Leave this in the hands of the police, I implore you. I couldn't stand to lose you, too."

This time, when Geneviève reached for her, Sarah stepped into her embrace, recognizing her friend's need for comfort and reassurance was as desperate as her own.

"Don't worry," she whispered. "I won't let anything happen to me." *But I won't stop my search, either*, she thought to herself. *Somehow I will discover what I need to know!*

Chapter Four

She stood before him in wanton innocence, luring him as the Sirens of old had lured the sailors to their deaths. And how eagerly they had gone, as eagerly as he now reached for her. Her skin was even softer than he'd imagined, her lips like ripe strawberries, sweet and flavorful and ready for the plucking. Her hair blew about her like a copper nimbus, the wind lifting it in the air, the sun turning it into golden fire. The flames licked at him as the long strands wrapped around his body, drawing him into her web, closer and closer still. The heat of her body burned him wherever they touched.

Morgan groaned with the exquisite pain of it. He turned over and groaned again. This time the pain was anything but exquisite. The dream faded, and reality intruded—the hard ground beneath him, the stone poking into his sore ribs, the pounding headache at the back of his skull. He raised a hand and gingerly felt around the lump forming at the back of his head. Not too bad, considering.

He opened one eye and sat up. A wave of dizziness assaulted him making his stomach roll. He took a deep breath, and the world settled back into place. He felt his pockets from the outside. Empty. He'd been robbed as well as beaten. Fortunately he'd had nothing irreplaceable on him—nothing except a little money, hardly enough to keep even a drunk happy for long.

He thought back on his afternoon. He must have hit a nerve at Miss Jassie's or maybe simply asking questions was enough to unsettle the denizens of New Orleans' netherworld. The newspapers had been having a field day with what was going on in this part of town, and maybe the locals had gotten tired of it. Morgan had been making progress in his investigation when someone had recognized him as a reporter for the *Picayune*. Though he was not generally known by his physical appearance, someone visiting Jassie's house could have recognized him—maybe even have been a colleague, for all Morgan knew.

In any case, the damage had been done. Before he knew what happened, Jassie's bouncer had hit him over the head with a blackjack and dumped him in the back alley. From the way his ribs felt, the bouncer must have gotten in a kick or two for good measure. Morgan shook his head at his carelessness, then immediately regretted the action. Another wave of dizziness caused him to grab his head. When it passed, he slowly eased himself to his feet, using the wall for support.

The light from a nearby street lamp glowed in the damp fog that had risen with the moon, its golden color reminding him of his sensuous dream. He closed his eyes and once again saw Sarah as his mind imagined her, silky skin and rosy lips, hair the color of fire and eyes as green as a newborn leaf. His body hardened, and he blinked, shattering the image even as he chastised himself for his errant thoughts. Since when had he dreamed of someone like this? He must be getting soft, something he couldn't afford.

Grimly putting his fantasy aside, he clenched his jaw and pushed his body off the wall, staggering a couple of paces toward the street before getting his footing. A hackney cab passed, the horse ambling slowly by, in no hurry to get anywhere. Morgan wished he had the price of a ride home in his pocket, but he'd been picked clean. Sighing, he stepped onto the banquette and headed for his boardinghouse, wishing with every painful step that it lay closer.

Sarah felt listless and without purpose or direction once Adam was buried. For so long finding him had been at the heart of every step she'd taken, every committee she joined, every new person she'd met. All her energies had been devoted to her quest. And now, suddenly, it was over. Day after day she wandered aimlessly around Geneviève's house or followed her about on a variety of small errands throughout the French Quarter. But everything seemed to be happening at a distance, almost as if to someone else, and none of it seemed to matter one way or another.

Though Geneviève shared some small measure of her grief, the other woman made an effort to find solace in the business of living, in shopping and visiting friends, in seeing her mother and walking in the gardens of Jackson Square. For the first few days she allowed Sarah to wallow in her sorrow, bringing her breakfast in bed and lending her shoulder for Sarah's tears when the memories overwhelmed her. But today was different. After a week of indulging her and letting her glide through life in a numb haze, Geneviève's attitude changed.

"I thought we might go out today and buy you a dress for the charity ball this evening," she said over breakfast.

"A dress? For a ball? But Geneviève—"

"The ball is for a good cause. We are raising money for the soldiers, men like Adam who were hurt by the war. We need everyone to come. Besides, it will be good for you, too."

Geneviève continued to describe the ball and the various people, including herself, who were responsible for planning it. Sarah listened halfheartedly, not wanting to disappoint her friend. When Geneviève once again insisted she come, Sarah tried to gracefully decline, but Geneviève wouldn't hear of it.

"You must attend. This is a charity ball that has meaning for you, no?"

"Really, Geneviève, I'm not sure I'm up to it. Adam is still very much in my thoughts—"

"And so he should be. But do you think this is what he would have wanted for you if he was his old self? Be honest, *ma chère*, Adam's been dead to you for much longer than a week. You have not heard from him for a long time. No letters, no contact. You have mourned him the past five years and more, is that not so?"

Sarah nodded reluctantly. Everything Geneviève said was true, still something inside her was not yet ready to go on.

"But I always had hope."

"I know, but now you must move on with your life. And this ball is for a very good cause. Many soldiers will be helped by the money raised tonight. Adam would have wanted that, I know." For a moment Geneviève stopped speaking as if her throat had become constricted. "He and I were very close at one time. Did you know this?"

"You and Adam?" Sarah said with amazement. "But—"

"When your family came to visit you at school in your last year, do you remember Adam was on leave and came along?"

Sarah's hand went to the locket around her neck. "He was happy then," she recalled. "Happier than I'd ever seen him."

"Was he? I hope so." The words sounded wistful and full of longing. Sarah shook off her self-absorption and looked sharply at Geneviève. The other woman stared at her hands which were clasped tightly together in her lap. "Your brother and I found we had many things in common that week," Geneviève went on, not looking up.

Her voice trembled and Sarah realized her friend was worried about Sarah's reaction to this news.

"Were you—" Sarah hesitated, unsure she should voice the question that immediately popped into her mind.

"We were . . . very fond of each other. If we'd had more time together, who can say what might have happened?" She looked into Sarah's face, as if to check what effect her words were having.

"It must have been hard on you both," Sarah said, understanding for the first time that Geneviève's sorrow was no different than her own.

"Yes, it was, especially when he again left for the war. Then he came home at the war's end, and nothing was the same. The change was so deep I felt the man I knew had died. Didn't you feel it also?"

"I was a child when he left for the war, but I remember how he laughed and joked. He loved being with people—and they loved being with him."

"But not when he returned."

"No. Then he became so . . . distant. He never laughed and hardly talked and if the war was mentioned . . ."

"I know." Geneviève sighed. "I kept thinking he needed more time to put it all behind him. But it only got worse. Sometimes I felt like he was somewhere else even when he was in the same room with me."

"Me, too," Sarah said, her voice rough from unshed tears.

Geneviève leaned over and squeezed her hand. "I know it is hard to think about him in such times."

"What I can't understand is why he changed so much."

"War changes a man," Geneviève said in a matter of fact tone.

"But Adam was changed more than most, don't you think?"

"Perhaps . . . But that is all in the past. It makes no sense to dwell on it now."

"I can't let it go, not when I don't understand what happened. *Something* must have changed him—and I want to know what."

"We may never know, Sarah. Then what will you do?"

"I'll worry about that when it happens. Right now I feel I have to try. Adam was too good a man to be forgotten or put aside as if he never mattered."

"But what can you do?"

"I don't know," she said, but her thoughts flew to Morgan Cain. He could help her, if only he would—but even if he wouldn't that would not deter her. She was going to find out what happened to Adam no matter what. "I'll think of something."

Geneviève gave her a worried look. "I wish you would leave this to the police, *chérie*. It is far too dangerous for a woman."

"Maybe so, but the police aren't interested, and I can't just sit by and do nothing."

In fact, unbeknownst to Geneviève, she had already begun her investigations. A streak of guilt raced through her at the thought for she had broken her promise to Morgan Cain. Just two days ago she'd gone out on her own, trying to track down information about Adam. She'd felt she had no choice. She had waited patiently at Geneviève's expecting some word, but she'd seen neither hide nor hair of Morgan since the funeral.

He'd made it clear enough that Adam's life had been lived on the fringes of civilized society. Perhaps he shared the police's attitude and was content to turn his attention to other matters. While she longed for his assistance, knowing how wide his network of contacts must be, she still couldn't sit and just wait. After all, why should he care about her or her brother?

"What about your Morgan Cain? Can he help?" Geneviève asked, as if she read Sarah's thoughts.

"I don't know." She got up to pace impatiently. "I've heard nothing from him in days."

"Then that gives you yet another reason to come to the ball. For all we know, Mr. Cain will be there. I understand he has some interest in this charity, though he doesn't like it known."

Geneviève's last argument was the most convincing. If Morgan Cain would be there...

"I'll go," Sarah conceded, not wanting to disappoint her friend either.

"Good. Now, what shall we do about a dress, *hein*? I know. Let's go upstairs and see if I don't have something you can use. I have a particular dress in mind. Come along."

They went upstairs to Geneviève's dressing room. She opened a large armoire and a riot of silk and satin spilled out.

"I am one of the lucky ones, you know. I still have many fine things."

She stuck her head and arms into the closet, and Sarah heard the rustle of fabric as her friend hunted for a dress. She still had doubts about going tonight, but there might be someone there who'd known Adam since many veterans of the war would be attending. For all she knew there might even be someone from his company. And this could be her chance to get some information out of Morgan Cain.

"Ah, here it is—the perfect gown," Geneviève said, pulling her head out of the armoire just as someone knocked at the door.

"There's a caller for Miss Sarah," Nettie said as she entered the room and went to Geneviève's side to help with the dress.

Sarah's heart began to beat in double time. Morgan Cain. The thought of seeing him sent ripples of heat through her. What was it about the man? She'd never reacted to anyone this way before—especially someone she wasn't even sure she liked. Maybe it was his dark, brooding manner or his untamed masculinity—whatever it was she couldn't get him or his kiss out of her mind. She'd been kissed before, more gently and with greater tenderness, but those kisses had barely caused a ripple in her awareness. But the memory of Morgan's touch and his tender caring when he'd told about Adam's death stayed with her, catching her unaware whenever she let her guard down.

Knowing he was standing in the foyer filled her with a sudden urgency. Without waiting for either Geneviève or Nettie, she rushed out the door, only slowing her pace when she reached the stairs. She peered over the top railing to the foyer below, but no matter how she craned her neck, she could see no more than a pair of legs encased in brown trousers.

Pressing her hand to her stomach to stop its fluttering, she started down. She'd gone no more than four steps when she realized her visitor wasn't Morgan Cain. The body wasn't large enough, hard enough. This man, whose back was toward her, was of much smaller stature and noticeably different clothing. A pang of disappointment cut through her making her gasp softly.

The man turned around and she recognized him. Forcing a smile onto her face, she completed her descent.

"Why, Philip, what a surprise."

"Sarah, my dear," he said and took her hand, raising it to his lips, then pressing a kiss to its back.

She suppressed the urge to tear her hand from his grasp. All she could think of was how much more she had enjoyed Morgan's lips against her hand. She mentally shook her head. She mustn't feel this way. Philip was her friend and mentor. He'd come here out of concern for her and deserved better.

"I was devastated to hear of your loss," he continued. "Is there someplace we can sit and talk?"

"Of course, how rude of me. Come into the parlor," she said and led him into the front room.

She showed him to the couch, then perched on the opposite end.

"This is quite the surprise," she reiterated, unsure whether she was pleased or irritated.

"I could hardly stay away once I'd heard of your devastating loss. I am only sorry I couldn't get here sooner, to be here for Adam's funeral, but I had some pressing business. I would have done anything to spare you such sorrow."

He slid closer to her. "Are you all right?" he asked in a lower tone.

"Yes, I think I am," Sarah replied, realizing as she said the words just how true they were. When her parents had died, she'd been wracked by feelings of loss and abandonment, whereas now she felt more a gentle sadness. Unknowingly she had been mourning Adam for the last five years, and his death had brought the period to a close.

Now her predominant feeling was of anger, anger at the waste of such a young life, anger at the war and all the damage it had caused, anger at the man who had murdered her brother, taking his life from him before he'd had a chance to recapture it for himself. Where once she had sought her brother with single-minded intensity, now she wanted his killer. Geneviève was right. She would go to the ball and ferret out every bit of information she could.

"I am glad to see you are managing so well on this sad occasion, but I'm sure you must want to go home.

I took the liberty of coming down to escort you back, Sarah. The sooner your life is returned to normal, the sooner you will feel like your old self."

At Philip's words, she gave a start.

"That's very kind of you, Philip, but I'll be staying on in New Orleans a while longer."

"But you can't." The words burst from him, and Sarah gave him a startled look. "I mean, you have obligations in Baton Rouge, friends who will want to see you, to express their condolences. Now that this business with Adam is finished you can get on with your life."

"I'll have time for that later. For the moment, I've decided to stay on and visit with Geneviève. There really isn't anything in Baton Rouge that needs my urgent attention."

Before Philip could reply, there was a knock at the door.

"I just wanted to make sure you didn't need anything," Geneviève said as she stepped into the room.

Philip was already on his feet. When Geneviève saw him with Sarah, the look on her face said everything.

"I didn't realize you were in town, *Philippe*."

"I've only just arrived. I thought I'd come to take Sarah back home. So many people have missed her since she's been gone."

"But she's only just arrived, and we've hardly had any time together. I absolutely refuse to let her go."

The two adversaries faced each other, seemingly oblivious to Sarah's presence.

"As I was just saying," Sarah intervened before their battle grew. "I've told Philip I'll be staying on for a visit."

"And for your investigation, too."

At Geneviève's words, Philip sent a questioning glance in Sarah's direction.

"What does she mean? Is there something you haven't told me?" he demanded.

Sarah recoiled from his overly familiar tone. He had no right to address her as if she owed him any explanations. While she appreciated all he had done for her, she had her own life to lead, a fact he seemed unwilling to accept.

"I saw no need to trouble you," she said. "However, it is hardly a secret that I've decided to look into Adam's death."

"Look into his death? Whatever can you mean?"

"I don't believe the police report on their conclusions. I don't think Adam died from too much drink."

"Now, Sarah, be rational. Adam was on the streets for a very long time—and he was drinking even longer. Don't you remember the last time he was home? It would certainly seem that—"

"I don't care what it *seems* like. I know it isn't true," she said with conviction.

"Then how do you think he died?"

"*I* think he was murdered."

"Why that's the most preposterous thing I've ever heard. Why would anyone want to murder him? He had no money, nothing of worth, did he?"

"No, but—"

"Did he double-cross someone?"

"No, I'm sure he didn't, but still—"

"I think you're trying to whitewash his death, Sarah. Make it more respectable, if you will. It's never pleasant to think of one's relatives as having taken their own lives."

Sarah heard nothing after the word respectable. "Respectable? How do you make a violent death respectable?"

"By making it happen by someone else's hand. I think you can't accept that Adam took his own life."

"I know Adam wouldn't do that."

"You haven't seen Adam in over five years. You don't know anything about it. You're just fooling yourself and wasting time."

"I'm sorry that you think so, but it is my time to waste, as you put it. Don't you agree, Geneviève?"

It stung that Philip could be so dismissing of something that was so important to her. She had always thought of him as her friend, as someone to turn to in times of trouble, but ever since his ill-timed marriage proposal, things had changed. She was seeing sides of Philip she never knew existed. All she wanted was for him to understand her need to see this to completion.

Geneviève sent her a reassuring smile. "I think Sarah has a right to find out exactly how Adam died. She's worried and searched for all these years. He was her only brother, you know."

"I'm afraid *Geneviève* does not understand all the issues, my dear," Philip countered addressing only Sarah. "This is not a woman's concern nor should it be. It is far too unseemly and will lead nowhere. Surely *you* can appreciate that."

"We're talking about my brother, Philip," Sarah replied, her voice filled with a new resolve. It no longer mattered what Philip thought. She was going to find out how Adam died, with or without his approval. "I can't give up."

"Well, I don't see that you'll get very far without

help." His smug self-assurance undermined her confidence. Geneviève must have seen her waver for when she hesitated her friend jumped in with, "Sarah has help."

"You have help already?" he asked in some surprise.

"Not really. There's a newspaper reporter who has shown some interest, but I'm not sure he'll want to pursue the matter." As Sarah finished speaking, she sent a telling glance to her friend. For some reason she didn't want Geneviève to say anything more about Morgan Cain.

"A reporter?" His expression hardened. "Why, such a man can hardly be trusted. He would never have your interests at heart. Really, Sarah, if you need help, you should turn to your friends, not to strangers. I have considerable experience in public service and know about these things. I can see that it'll be best if I help you after all. Now tell me, where were you planning to start?"

For someone who, only moments before, had been so opposed to her quest, Philip had certainly done an about-face. But what he said was true: he did have considerable experience in public service and knew countless officials at all levels, some of whom could prove extremely useful. His political career was about to take off.

As a Southerner, he'd found many avenues blocked because of his glorious war record, but he'd worked relentlessly at building support and was now considered a major force, especially among the Republicans. The party of the Union had broadened its base, though many Southerners thought of it with contempt, calling its members carpetbaggers and worse. But Philip claimed there was no use fighting the inevitable. If the

South were to prosper, men like him had to be accepted by the party in control, had to gain power for themselves so they could help their homeland recover.

Now he had his eye on bigger and better things. He'd set his cap on a congressional seat and was working assiduously to insure his election. And he had contacts that would undoubtedly be useful.

"I would be most appreciative of your help," Sarah said. "And to tell you the truth, I haven't a plan of action as yet."

"Perhaps not, but at least you know where to start," Geneviève put in. "We're going to the Decoration Ball tonight."

This last was said with a certain hauteur, and Sarah knew her friend was simply trying to even the odds in this strange game they were caught up in. She only wished Geneviève had chosen a different area to take a stand. She sent Geneviève a quelling look and got a confused look back. Then Philip spoke, "A wonderful idea. I'd be more than happy to escort you, my dear," he said, smiling at Sarah, and Geneviève realized her mistake.

"Really, there's no need," she said. "Sarah and I will accompany each other. She is my guest, after all."

"Geneviève is right. We can manage just fine and wouldn't want to put you out," Sarah added. "I know there are many people you have to see while you're here in the city. We certainly don't want to interfere with your plans."

"Nonsense, you're my first priority, and I'm sure there will be people of interest at the ball. I'll be able to kill two birds with one stone, so to speak." He smiled, but for the first time Sarah wasn't charmed either by his looks or the apparent warmth in his gaze. Instead, she felt backed into a corner, unable to escape.

"That would be fine," she said politely and forced a return smile.

"However, we women need some time to get ready," Geneviève said. "So if you will excuse us for a while . . ." She let her voice trail off suggestively, but Philip did not take the hint.

"I just have a question or two, if you don't mind. I need a bit more information if I'm to be of help to you, Sarah."

"Oh? What sort of information?"

"I know this might be painful, but . . . have the police given you any of Adam's belongings?"

Sarah shook her head. "They said they'd bring me what little he had when they finished their investigation, but I haven't seen anything yet. I'm sure there won't be much."

"There might be some clues, nonetheless. I think you should let me know immediately when anything arrives."

"You're right. Perhaps I should have contacted them and made sure I received Adam's things sooner. But with everything happening, I—"

"Don't fret, my dear. I'm here now and I'll be more than pleased to handle these unpleasant matters. It would spare you the pain, don't you think?"

Before Sarah could answer, Geneviève said, "It's kind of you to offer, I'm sure, but it really is getting late, and Sarah and I must prepare for tonight. Let me show you to the door."

She stood and Philip had no choice but to follow suit though the look he gave Geneviève promised retribu-

84

tion. Sarah sensed she would have a long and tedious evening, one way or the other, with the two of them sniping at each other like this, however well-intentioned they each thought they were.

"Geneviève is right, Philip," she said and laid her hand gently on his forearm. "We really do have to get ready for tonight. But I can't tell you how happy I am that you've changed your mind about my decision. It means a lot to me to have your approval and friendship."

"It is not friendship I want from you, *mignonne*," he whispered for her ears alone.

"Right now that's all I can promise," she replied equally softly and knew she lied. Friendship was all she could *ever* offer him, but he wasn't ready to accept that, and she didn't have the energy to convince him otherwise today.

"Then that will have to do for now," he said and made his departure with a brisk nod in Geneviève's direction.

"I don't like that man," Geneviève said.

"So you've said numerous times before." Sarah gave her friend a wry smile.

"What do you see in him?"

"I told you before. He helped me through some of the darkest days of my life. Even now he is willing to help though he doesn't agree with what I am doing."

"Well, I hate to be so negative, but I have to wonder why. Take care you don't put yourself in a position where you have to pay a price you do not want, *ma chère*. A man like that does nothing without reasons of his own."

* * *

Sarah looked around the large ballroom. A sea of people filled the huge expanse, milling about, talking, and laughing as they waited for the orchestra to start the next selection. The festive mood clashed with her own more subdued feelings. Adam's death still hung over her even if she had accepted that he'd been lost to her long ago.

Her dress matched her mood. Unlike the more flamboyant clothes of the other women, her lavender silk dress with its cream lace trim featured a demure neckline and a matching overskirt with only two flounces. The pleated underskirt was of the same cream as the lace. Geneviève and Nettie had made the few alterations needed to make the bodice a perfect fit, assuring her that no one would fault her presence at the ball.

Philip stood beside her also looking about the room as if he were trying to locate someone.

"Do you have friends attending?" she asked.

"No, I'm just interested. You can never let an opportunity pass, you know. Look, there's John Palmer. Remember I mentioned him to you? He could be a big help in my run for the congressional seat. I think I'll just go over and have a word with him." He started to leave, then turned back, "With your permission, of course."

"You mustn't worry yourself about me. I'll be fine. Geneviève is just over there. I'll join her group."

Philip frowned as he looked in the same direction, but apparently found no other solution as he nodded and then took off without a backward glance. Though she didn't like to admit it, she was glad to see him go. For some reason she didn't want Morgan to see them together, providing he was even here. She hadn't seen him on her last perusal of the room though he would be easy to spot even in a crowd because of his height, to say nothing of his unmistakable presence.

"Have you seen him?" a voice whispered from behind her.

Sarah turned with a start. "Geneviève, you scared me."

"Only because you were so intent on finding a certain face in the crowd, yes?"

"I was just enjoying the music," she returned, making a point of tapping her foot.

"As I was saying, have you seen him yet?"

"No." As soon as the word left her mouth, she knew she'd betrayed herself.

"I thought so. Now I am here and can help you look," she said glancing about the room. "I see you have managed to get rid of *Philippe*."

"I did not get rid of him. He saw someone he knew and decided to reintroduce himself."

"No doubt someone who could help him politically," Geneviève said almost to herself.

How was it that Geneviève could see Philip so much more clearly than she could herself? When she'd left Baton Rouge she'd had some doubts about her decision, but seeing him again, she knew the answer she'd given him was the right one. She didn't want to marry him. It wouldn't be right, especially now that she'd had a taste of passion. Whatever else lay between her and Philip, passion had played no part. She'd been too young and naive to realize that, too inexperienced to know. But the brief kisses from Morgan Cain had opened her eyes. Any chance Philip might have had to convince her theirs was a special relationship had vanished beneath the onslaught of emotions Morgan Cain awakened without even trying.

"Oh, look. There he is!" Geneviève said in an excited voice.

"Where?" Sarah asked, her heart giving a strange jump.

"Over by the side door, under the balcony," Geneviève said, pointing discreetly in that direction.

At that same moment Sarah spotted him. He was dressed in black as were most of the men present except on him it looked far more dark and mysterious. The white of his shirt contrasted starkly with the darkness of his hair and skin. She found she was unable to tear her gaze from him. For several long minutes she stood transfixed.

"Well, are you going over to see him?" Geneviève asked impatiently.

"I couldn't."

"Of course you could. You two are almost colleagues, working together, combining skills to unravel what happened to Adam."

"I'm not sure he thinks of us as working together. I know there's information out there that I need. And I'm sure he has the capability of finding it. Whether we'll find it together or not is another story."

"Ma chère, I see the way he looks at you. He will help."

At Geneviève's words, Sarah felt the heat rush to her face. Certainly in her innermost secret self she hoped what Geneviève said might be true, but was it a realistic dream? She wasn't sure. Was it without danger? Almost assuredly not. But something kept her hoping, kept her seeking out his assistance. And it was more than his being the only one with the information.

"He has seen you," Geneviève said as she flicked open her fan and spoke from behind it. "See, he is heading this way."

Sarah looked up and straight into his eyes. They seemed to burn into her. She swallowed dryly, unsure what to do or say. In the end, it didn't matter. He held out his hand, and she placed hers in it. Without a word, he swept her out onto the dance floor.

Chapter Five

Neither of them spoke as they danced around the room, but an unusual tension stretched between them. Sarah felt raw and vulnerable. There were so many questions she wanted to ask but didn't dare: something in Morgan's face kept her silent. He looked so serious and remote. Nary a smile cracked his features, and now that she thought about it, she couldn't remember ever having seen one on him. But his grimness tonight seemed deeper, as if he were fighting an inner battle he wasn't too sure he would win.

Still, she couldn't help but be aware of the strength of his arms around her and the accomplished way he moved across the dance floor, making her feel light and graceful as her skirt swirled about them.

Despite the perfume-laden air surrounding them, she thought she could detect his special scent, as dark and masculine as the man himself. A thrill ran down her spine, leaving little bumps on her skin in its wake.

The silence between them stretched, magnified by the flirtatious snippets of conversation and high-pitched laughter that reached her as other couples danced past.

"Have you found out anything about Adam?" she finally found the courage to ask.

"Why don't we just dance and enjoy the music."

His voice held a warning she chose to ignore. "I didn't realize you were enjoying it."

"Ah, so the little cat strikes again," he growled.

When she would have pulled away, he tightened his grip and drew her closer to his chest, closer than was proper in polite society.

"If you'd just answered my question—" she started to explain.

"Don't qualify it. Just dance."

She allowed him to continue guiding her around the floor, but now instead of relishing being in his arms, questions about Adam invaded her mind. Had he found something out—something that cast a bad light on her brother? Was that the cause of his suppressed anger?

He must have sensed her change of mood, for within moments he suggested they get some fresh air.

She could feel his impatience as he walked behind her, edging their way to the same side door he'd entered earlier. When they reached the door, he stepped in front of her and pulled it open, then nodded for her to precede him. The small courtyard outside was attractively lit with Chinese lanterns mounted on poles. At the moment it was deserted.

She'd taken no more than a few steps when his voice stopped her.

"So, did you have an interesting time at the riverfront?"

The words seemed to explode from him. For a moment Sarah couldn't speak. Of all the things she'd expected him to say this wasn't on the list.

"Cat got your tongue?" he asked nastily.

"I can explain." Though why she felt the need to she didn't know.

"I'm sure you can," he said, his voice dark and gravelly.

"Maybe I haven't gotten across to you just how important my brother is—was to me. I'm willing to do anything to clear his name—anything. And if that means going to an area that some people think of as unacceptable, then that's too bad. I'll do whatever I have to when it comes to Adam's memory."

"Even lie?"

"I've never—"

"You promised me you wouldn't go—"

"You browbeat me into that promise with wild tales of the waterfront and rats."

"And how farfetched were they?"

Sarah shivered. They weren't farfetched at all; to the contrary, all that he'd said was true. But none of that mattered.

"You were right. There were many things I would have rather not seen." He gave a snort of satisfaction, but before he could say anything, she added, "But I'd go through far worse to clear Adam's name."

He snorted again, then asked, "Did you find anything of interest?"

"As I'm sure you already know, not a lot."

She turned away from him and walked to the edge of the courtyard. The building where the ball was held overlooked a curve of the Mississippi, and she stared unseeingly at the levee that blocked her view of the river.

A welter of emotions raged through her. She took a deep breath, hoping to regain her sense of control.

Nothing was working out the way she'd hoped, and the man behind her was only adding to her confusion. She no longer knew what she wanted of him, couldn't begin to guess what he expected of her. In the heavy silence she faintly heard the orchestra start another set.

She felt his eyes burning into her back and glanced surreptitiously over her shoulder. He was leaning against a lamppost, a tall man with broad shoulders and a sleekly muscled strength. In the uneven light his hair looked darker than the night and his face was in shadow. She wished she could see his expression and know what he was thinking. Despite his seemingly relaxed posture she could see his tenseness in the angle of his head and the tightly fisted hand held stiffly at his side.

Suddenly he spoke.

"I've had enough air, haven't you?"

"What?" She spun around to face him, startled.

"I said, I—"

"I know what you said, but . . ."

"Yes?"

"Aren't you going to tell me what *you* found out?"

"I'm sure it's of no more interest than your own discoveries."

Sarah knew that wasn't true just from the way he said it.

"Please don't trifle with me."

"Trifle, is it?" he said with harsh amusement. Then his tone changed. "Come here," he said softly.

For a moment Sarah didn't move, didn't even breathe.

"Sarah."

Her name was a whisper on the evening breeze. With slow steps she started toward him. She wasn't sure what propelled her, whether it was her desire to learn what he knew about Adam or something more primitive.

She stopped only when she stood in front of him.

"You never learn, do you?" he said as his fingers brushed against her cheek.

"Learn what?" she whispered, a slight tremor in her voice.

"That there are some places you shouldn't go."

She looked at him questioningly.

"To my house, to the waterfront . . . And here." With his last words he pulled her into his arms and his lips covered hers.

Her heart jumped, and a liquid warmth filled her body, pooling low inside her. She knew this was the passion the poets wrote of, and for the first time she understood why. Magic and wonder flowed through her. Her knees trembled, and she clung to him, reveling in his strength.

His mouth shifted over hers, and a small sigh escaped her. He took advantage of her parted lips to slip his tongue inside. Desire surged when his tongue swept her mouth, touching places that had never been touched before, arousing emotions that until now had been hidden.

His hands moved from her back to her shoulders, his fingers tracing the hollow of her neck where her gown dipped slightly. She wished now that she had worn a different dress, one cut low enough that she could feel him against her breasts where her skin tingled and ached with unfamiliar yearning.

Morgan leaned against the lamp pole behind him, his hands sliding from her shoulders back to her waist as he pulled her even closer. Now they were pressed together along their entire lengths, and she could feel the muscles of his chest, hard and solid under her palms. And hot, even through the smooth fabric of his shirt. As hot and burning as she herself felt.

His hands pressed her hips closer, and she could feel the rigid length of his arousal against her. She moaned as a surge of longing sprang to life in her most feminine core.

His lips glided along her jaw, his breath leaving a warm, moist trail that cooled in the evening air and sent flickers of delight racing along her skin. She felt alive as never before. Beneath her hands his heart beat as wildly as hers, and she knew she was not alone in her feelings.

When his tongue flicked her ear she thought she would melt. Her arms crept around his neck so her fingers could burrow into his hair. Its sleek resilience felt rich and silky. She turned her head to kiss him in return, and once again his lips met hers.

This time her lips opened of their own volition, and her tongue rubbed against his, sending frissons of wanting to every nerve ending in her body. She no longer recognized herself in this wanton being that had sprung to life in his arms. She'd never felt such an intense response, such a loss of herself in another. And then she couldn't think at all as she yielded to the sensations besieging her, his taste and his scent, the feel of the delicate skin at the back of his neck, the distant sound of music filling her ears, and in the center of it all, Morgan.

He eased his mouth from hers long before she was ready, the parting slow and tender. He rested for a moment, his cheek lying against the top of her head while he just held her. After a while her heart rate slowed and her lungs remembered how to work. Her arms felt heavy and languorous, and she lowered them to his waist. Beneath her ear she heard his heartbeat slow as well until their rhythms matched.

Morgan lifted his head and looked down into her eyes.

"I think it might be time to head back inside. Your friend might be wondering where you are."

"Philip won't worry. He has other things on his mind tonight," she said in a dreamy voice. For a moment longer she kept her head against his chest, breathing in the smell of him and marveling at what had just happened, at the feelings still swirling inside her.

Then she noticed his sudden stillness and knew something was wrong. Slowly he straightened and held her away from him. She looked into his eyes and tried to understand the sudden change.

"I thought you came with Geneviève," he said carefully.

"I did—I mean we came together . . . with Philip."

"In that case, allow me to show you back inside." His voice was cold and distant, as if nothing burning had passed between them.

Her heart skipped a beat as she realized how Morgan was interpreting her words.

"No! You don't understand," she said, digging in her heels. "I'm not going inside until we've talked."

"I don't think there's anything else to say."

"There's a great deal left to be said." She wouldn't let the evening end like this, not with some stupid misunderstanding. She watched him, afraid he'd walk off and leave her, but to her relief he only turned and walked a few paces away.

"Do you think I would . . . kiss you like that if I were here with another man?"

"Wouldn't you?"

"Of course not."

"Then exactly who is Philip?"

"He's a friend of the family." And he was. It was only in his mind that he was more.

"A good friend?"

"A very good friend. He stood by me after my parents died and supported my quest to find Adam from the very beginning."

"I see."

"What do you see? To me he is only a friend."

"And how does he see himself, I wonder? Doesn't he think of himself as something more?" His question was purely rhetorical.

"I've told Philip exactly where things stand."

"Have you now?" he said almost to himself.

"Philip has been a very good friend, and he believed in my search for Adam long after everyone else gave up."

"I think I understand," he said softly.

"No, you don't. Come meet him, *then* you'll understand."

"Maybe I'll do just that," he answered.

For a moment Sarah was relieved; the crisis had passed. It wasn't until they were back inside that she noticed the challenging glint in his black eyes.

Silently she prayed that Philip was busy in some back room with his political cronies, out of sight and unobtainable. She caught Geneviève's eye and sent her a silent plea for assistance. Within a minute, Geneviève came to greet them.

"How are you enjoying the ball?" she asked, her eyes aglow with mischief. "Better than *Philippe*, I hope. I don't think he has danced even once. Come, I will show you."

Sarah closed her eyes wishing the ground would open

up and swallow her. How could Geneviève so misunderstand her signal?

As Geneviève led the way to a small anteroom off the main ballroom, Sarah tried to imagine what else could go wrong.

The fates must have been listening to her thoughts and decided to play a nasty trick, for the minute she walked into the side room, Philip spotted her with Morgan. He stood and without a word to his friends, came over to her side and slipped his arm possessively around her waist.

"Sarah, where have you been? I looked all over for you."

"You couldn't have looked all that thoroughly," Geneviève contradicted. "After all, you've been in here for all of the past hour—even before Sarah left the ballroom."

"You left the ballroom?" Philip asked, ignoring Geneviève. "But why? I thought you wanted to dance, and you must have known I was in here."

Sarah took a deep breath. "I guessed as much. You always gravitate to one of the back rooms, but—"

"What do you mean?" Philip interrupted, his voice suspicious. "Why didn't you come join me if you were done dancing?"

The way you usually do, hung in the air, and Sarah realized with a guilty start that in the past she did usually join Philip at some point in the evening though she'd never even thought of doing so tonight. Perhaps Philip recognized it, too, and that explained his slightly petulant tone.

"I was with a friend." She looked at Morgan, not missing the angry light in his eye as he glanced at Philip's arm still nestled around her waist. "Let me introduce him."

She stepped hastily out of Philip's hold just as Morgan

98

said, "I'm Morgan Cain and you are Philip D'Arbereaux, I believe?"

"Yes, I am," Philip replied, pleased at having been recognized. "Perhaps we've met before?"

"I doubt that. I don't move in your circles," Morgan said, his voice hard and dismissing. "I simply recognized you from your description."

He looked pointedly at the one blond lock adorning Philip's otherwise dark head. The lighter hair cut across one temple in a triangular swath and was hard to miss.

"Morgan works for the *Picayune*, Philip," Geneviève said. "You'd best be careful what you say in front of him. You wouldn't want any of your wheeling and dealing to get out in the press."

Sarah gave her friend a sharp glance. Instead of helping her put a damper on the men's obvious antagonism to each other, Geneviève was fanning the flames. The other woman shrugged helplessly, a ploy Sarah saw through right away. Geneviève preferred Morgan over Philip and wanted to make sure Sarah saw the two men in the same light she did.

"Philip is a businessman in Baton Rouge," Sarah said before Geneviève could get in another inflammatory word. "He's thinking of running for political office."

"I know. I've heard about him," Morgan said, his tone even more contemptuous, much to Sarah's surprise.

"All good things, I hope," Philip said with a laugh, apparently misinterpreting Morgan's intent completely. "Sarah has been most supportive of my ambitions."

He took her hand in his and gave her a fond, possessive look as if her support of everything relating to him was a foregone conclusion.

"Interesting things, shall we say," Morgan replied, his

attitude suddenly different. "What exactly are your plans?"

"We haven't completely settled our strategy, but we're building a political base. Do you think you might do a story on my campaign?"

"It's possible. As I recall I heard John Palmer was thinking seriously about supporting you. Is that true?"

"John has been a big help, introducing me around and making sure I meet the right people."

"I understand he's a carpetbagger," Morgan said in a conversational voice.

Philip's face suffused with color. "I think you've been misinformed. While it's true that John is from the North, he has Louisiana's best interests at heart."

Morgan's eyes narrowed. "And I think it's time—"

"Time you gave me that dance you promised," Sarah interrupted as she extricated her hand from Philip's. She wasn't sure whom she was protecting. All she knew was that she didn't want them to take this particular conversation any further.

Sarah glared meaningfully at Geneviève who took the hint with ill grace, making a face at Sarah behind the men's backs though she said, "And this is ours, I believe?"

She took Philip's arm before he could protest, but the glance she shot at Sarah told her she would pay for this favor.

Without another word the two couples returned to the dance floor and mingled with the other dancers as they waltzed around the room. Within seconds Morgan had swept Sarah across the floor and far from Philip and Geneviève.

For several minutes neither Morgan nor Sarah spoke. This time the tension arcing between them had no mysterious source. The two men's antipathy for each other had been immediately clear. Sarah sighed. She'd hoped to diffuse Morgan's hard feelings by having them meet. Instead, the meeting had worked against her, increasing the men's animosity fivefold.

Though Morgan danced as fluidly as ever, Sarah could see the muscles in his cheek working as he clenched his jaw over whatever thoughts he was thinking. His face looked carved from granite, not a single soft line easing his fierce expression. She should have been frightened. Instead, she was intrigued. He was like dynamite with a lit fuse, ready to explode. But the explosion never came. His iron self-control held it in check, and were she not close enough to see the tiny signs of his anger, she might never have known it existed.

Though she thought of herself as anything but adventurous, an exhilarating excitement ran through her. She was holding a tiger by the tail and enjoying the experience. Of course, she knew that the trick in such an exercise was not getting hurt when you let the beast go, but for the moment, Morgan seemed willing to stay in her arms.

"Your friend should choose his associates with more care," he said after a while, his voice low and dark.

"You don't like them?"

He shrugged. "How long have you known him?"

For a moment she debated whether or not to answer, but decided she had nothing to gain by keeping silent. "Philip moved to Baton Rouge right after the war ended. He met my parents and through them we met."

"Since he's such a *good friend* you might tell him—"

"I told you before, Philip and I are friends, nothing more."

"Then someone should tell Philip that."

"He's merely taken over for my parents. He feels protective."

"But what's he protecting you for—himself?"

Morgan's persistence was beginning to irritate her. "I think I'd like to change the subject."

Morgan looked like he was about to argue and then nodded, conceding to her wishes, and they danced in silence. Sarah wasn't sure she liked this any better. He was stiff and unresponsive, and she couldn't wait for the music to end.

When the waltz finished, Sarah suggested they might do with some refreshment.

"Would you like some punch?" Morgan asked.

"Thank you, that would be lovely. I'll wait here."

She gave him a smile, and he went off to fight the crowds surrounding the refreshment table. In the meantime, she craned her neck looking for Geneviève and Philip.

"I've lost him if it's Philip you're looking for," Geneviève said from behind her. "And none too soon, I might add. I thought I'd be bored to death by his unending political aspirations. Don't you ever tell him you get tired of hearing it all?"

"Stop sneaking up on me, and no, I wouldn't tell him such a thing. And I hope you had the sense not to either."

"Just barely, *ma chère*, just barely. If the music hadn't ended, I'm not sure what I would have done."

"Where's Philip now?"

"Gone off with one of his cronies. Good riddance, I say."

Before Sarah could reply, Morgan returned with her drink and graciously handed Geneviève the other cup.

"But you got this for yourself," Geneviève protested, trying to give him back the glass.

"I'm not really thirsty anyway," he returned.

"Then I simply must repay you. You'll come to dinner. Tomorrow evening, yes? Sarah and I would love to have you."

He looked from one to the other. "How can I say no to such a pretty invitation?"

"Wonderful. We'll see you about eight?"

Morgan nodded.

"We'll have to invite another to even the numbers. Who do you suggest?" Geneviève asked as she looked around the room only to come face-to-face with Philip.

"There you are," he said to Sarah as he joined the group. "What have I missed?"

For a moment no one spoke.

"You're just in time to be the recipient of an invitation to dinner tomorrow," Sarah said brightly, filling in the gap. "We were just arranging to get together," she added with a wave of her hand to indicate herself and the other couple. Though she would have preferred not to bring Philip and Morgan together again, Philip had been such a large part of her life for so long, she found she couldn't snub him now.

"I'll be looking forward to Nettie's cooking. She always comes up with the most perfect combinations. Remember the time about three years ago when we came for a visit?"

Sarah bit her lip, realizing she'd given Philip another opportunity to make sure Morgan knew how close they'd been. Nothing was going her way tonight, she thought as Philip's voice droned on and on, and then felt guilty for her thoughts. Finally the music resumed, and when Philip asked her to dance she accepted with just the quickest glance in Morgan's direction, but he already had Geneviève halfway to the dance floor.

The rest of the evening became a blur with glimpses of Morgan dancing with any number of different women, but never again with her. By the time Philip escorted them out the door in the early hours of the morning, Morgan had disappeared without another word.

The carriage pulled to a halt in front of Geneviève's house and Sarah wanted nothing more than to collapse in her bed. Philip escorted them to the door, but sensing Sarah's preoccupation kept the good-nights to a minimum.

"Finally you have learned how to handle Philip," Geneviève said wearily as they hung their wraps on the clothes tree. "Don't talk to him. Next time you must learn to do that when I am not the one who must keep up the conversation."

Sarah smiled. "I was tired, and Philip understood. And thank you for your diligence on my behalf."

"Now we must get to sleep for we have a very full day tomorrow."

"I'd like to join Nettie when she shops for dinner, if you think she won't mind."

"She'll enjoy the company, I'm sure. I'll leave her a note about the plans and mention you."

Sarah kissed her friend on the cheek and headed upstairs to her room as Geneviève walked in the direction of the kitchen. She hadn't been this tired in a long time. The combination of the ball and everything she'd gone through recently was beginning to take its toll. She removed her clothes and readied herself for bed, hanging up Geneviève's gown but allowing everything else to fall as it may. And then she slipped into bed.

The fresh sheets felt and smelled wonderful. She stretched her legs relishing the feel of the material against her body. All she wanted was to sink into a deep sleep and forget everything. But sleep wouldn't come, no matter how she tried.

When she closed her eyes she saw Morgan Cain— talking with Geneviéve, moving across the dance floor with lithe grace, pressing his lips to hers as he held her close. She could still feel his lips touching hers, his hands holding her close, his long length pressed against her. She'd never been that close to a man before, never felt the physical evidence of his desire—until today, in Morgan's arms.

It scared her.

Not only had she felt Morgan's arousal, she had known her own. The rapid beat of her heart, the shallow breaths, the flush on her face, the heat in her center, the yearning, aching need that permeated her very being.

She turned over, lying on her back, and there he was; she could almost smell his scent. She kept her eyes tightly closed, her breathing slow. The spell was too fragile to break, too wondrous to let go. She saw him smile as he stood above her, the smile she'd always longed to see, and she liked it. She felt closer to him then, safer, protected.

His fingers touched her cheek, feathering down to her jaw and then back up. Her skin tingled, coming alive beneath his fingertips. She turned her face toward him, and he cupped her cheek, drawing his thumb back and forth across her mouth. Her tongue came out to moisten her lips, and she encountered his thumb with its tip. She tasted the saltiness of his skin and felt its slightly rough texture. When she would have raised her hand to touch him, she found she had no control over her muscles, that her commands went unanswered and again she saw him smile.

His eyes perused her entire length, lingering at the swell of her breasts, the dip at her waist, the flare of her hips. And everywhere his gaze touched she felt her body burn with wanting, desire flaring to life inside her. She needed him closer, his body near hers as it had been during their kiss.

As if he heard her thoughts, he lowered himself to the edge of the bed. He leaned over her and his hand blazed a path along her neck, then moved to the top of her nightdress. She shivered in anticipation when his fingers played with ruffle of lace that banded the neckline of her nightdress and ran down the buttoned front.

At each button he stopped and traced its shape. Then slowly his fingers opened the top button—then the second and third, moving down until they all were undone. For a moment he did nothing. Then with his gaze still holding hers, his hand moved under the open flap to her bare skin.

At his first touch she wanted to speak, though whether to ask him to stop or to go on, she didn't know. But no sound came forth and his hand moved again, brushing her breast. It hovered, barely touching her. And then with just the lightest of strokes she felt his fingers move, grazing the tip of her breast. He looked deeply into her eyes as if he could read everything she was feeling and then began to rub the swollen tip. A shiver ran down her spine, followed in quick succession by waves of heat. His eyes were like black pools of mystery, drawing her into their depths.

She arched her back, offering herself to him, and he cupped her breast with his palm, enclosing her softness with his fingers. All thoughts were wiped from her mind. She shivered, wanting more. And then with just the lightest of touches she felt his hand move to the other side, rubbing the swollen nipple until she thought she would cry out from the pleasure rushing through her veins to every corner of her body.

His hand slid lower, pushing away the night dress until she lay naked before him. She writhed with need and moaned, seeking an even closer contact, craving an ease to the hunger burning within her.

His hand caressed her from shoulder to hip, leaving small fires burning in its wake, and still she wanted more. His hand moved slowly over the softness of her stomach, outlining the indentation of her belly button and then slipping downward toward her feminine core, to the secret place that ached with a longing she knew only he could satisfy. Closer and closer he inched. Her body quivered with anticipation, waiting for the final touch.

A branch hit the window, blown by the wind, and Sarah jerked upward, startled. The dream evaporated. She moaned a protest, trying desperately to call it back, but to no avail. Morgan's image slowly drew away, disappearing into the shadows from which he had come, his eyes holding the promise of wonders yet unknown.

She sat up in bed and pulled the nightdress close. Her hands trembled and her breathing was labored. What would have happened next, she wondered, if the wind hadn't woken her? She couldn't begin to guess, not with her limited experience. All she knew was that the yearning ache low within her still lingered, leaving her unsettled. Now the night seemed lonelier than usual, her bed no longer a haven.

Getting up, she moved to the overstuffed chair near the window, taking the sheet with her. Wrapping herself against the wind, she sat in the dark, watching the stars move across the heavens, listening to the tree branches beat against the house. How insignificant were men's lives against the magnificence of the sky—and yet how magnificent human life could be, its loss so irrevocable.

Adam's death made her want to celebrate life, to fight the emptiness that had swallowed him. A silent tear made its way down her cheek, unnoticed. Life was much more complicated and confusing than she'd ever dreamed. And more wondrous, she had to admit.

She wished she'd had another opportunity to talk to Morgan at the ball, but he'd left without a word. Would he come to dinner as invited? She desperately hoped so. There was so much she wanted to tell him, so much she needed to know—about herself as well as Adam. And Morgan Cain held the keys.

A bird called in the distance, and she smiled through her tears. Dawn must be around the corner though it was still dark. And with dawn would come another day, another chance to fix the mistakes of today. She wiped her cheeks and leaned her head back as a feeling of peace finally stole over her.

Sarah and Nettie walked along the banquette in search of the perfect ingredients for the perfect meal. Morgan was coming to dinner, and Sarah wanted everything to go flawlessly—from the meal to the conversation. Unfortunately, while she could control the meal, the guests were another matter altogether. Having Philip and Morgan at the same table would be a trial, but there really wasn't anything she could do about it.

For some reason they had taken an instant dislike to each other. At one point, when Geneviève had mentioned that Morgan worked for a newspaper, she could have sworn that Philip paled. But when she looked again, he seemed his usual self hoping for some free press.

Morgan's negative attitude toward Philip went beyond mere animosity. The way the two men had gone after each other made her shudder—and wish only one of them were coming to dinner.

But with Geneviève at her most impish, Sarah had felt compelled to compensate. The result was the fix she was now in, and she saw no way out. She had to hope the two men would put themselves out for her sake and show some restraint.

"What do you want to serve, Miss Sarah?" Nettie asked as they came to the market.

"Something special," Sarah said and sniffed the air appreciatively. The smell of the freshly baked bread, the rows of produce, and the meat stalls made her pleasantly dizzy. "Do you have any suggestions?"

"Your guests might enjoy a truly Creole meal."

"What a wonderful idea! What do we need to get?"

"We can pick up a number of things here, but I think I might need to go down to Tante Zabelle's for some of the fixin's. I'm not sure you should be coming along, though. It's not in a section of town where ladies go."

"Please let me come," Sarah cajoled. "I won't be any bother, I promise."

She knew that Tante Zabelle's wasn't far from where Adam's body had been found. Going with Nettie would provide a certain safety. Though she didn't dare voice the hope, she wanted the opportunity to ask a local resident a few questions. Maybe Tante Zabelle or one of her customers would have greater insight into what might have happened than the police.

For a moment Nettie looked like she might refuse and then, hesitantly, she nodded her head. "But you must be careful. That can be a dangerous area."

After her last foray to the waterfront, she knew exactly how dangerous the area could be. "I know. I'll be careful."

"All right, then. Let's see what we can find here first."

Nettie picked over the produce and haggled with the vendors over price and quality, and before long they had more than they could carry. After hiring a cab to take the supplies back to Geneviève's home, they headed over to Tante Zabelle's.

Nettie took her to a Spanish style house with a walled inner courtyard. She knocked on a dark wooden door. Sarah cast furtive glances about but saw nothing threatening. Suddenly a peephole in the door was whisked open and then shut again, and the door opened.

"Come in, my child," a broad-faced woman of color said to Nettie and gestured for them to enter.

The outer wall hid a lush, fragrant garden featuring a fountain in the corner that was surrounded by flowers of every color. Water sprayed in diamond droplets into a bright blue pool. The courtyard was vividly alive, teeming with so much light and color it almost overwhelmed the senses.

Nettie and Sarah stepped through the door and into this magic world. The air felt cooler in the shade of the spreading magnolia tree whose leathery leaves covered half the courtyard. Beneath the tree, in large clay pots grew ferns and ivies in rich profusion, together with other plants Sarah had never seen before. The palette of scents rising from this garden revealed the plants to be herbs of mysterious origin.

"What can I get for you on this bright morning?" the dark-skinned woman asked.

"The best. That's why we've come," Nettie joked and the older woman laughed.

She led them through another door and into the building. Sarah found herself in a large room containing all types of produce, spices, and meats. On one side of the room was a large trough filled with damp Spanish moss under which was nestled both large and small crabs and wooden slat boxes filled with crawfish, on the other a long table piled high with vegetables and greens from someone's late spring garden. Hanging from the walls were strings of dried red peppers and garlands of garlic. And the same wonderful aroma that permeated the market also filled this room: the smell of freshly baked bread.

"Of course you come here for the best. It is all I have. But first, you must introduce us," she said, looking toward Sarah.

"Tante, I'd like you to meet Miss Sarah, a friend of Miss Geneviève's."

"Pleased to meet you, child," she said with a smile.

"And how is that devilish Miss Geneviève? Up to her same tricks?"

"I'm afraid so," Sarah said, amazed that Tante seemed to know her friend so well.

"That child was always a handful."

Sarah sent Tante Zabelle and Nettie a questioning look. It was Nettie who answered.

"Tante worked at the Michaud House when Geneviève and I were small. Then before the war came to New Orleans, she left and started her business."

Then Sarah understood. Tante had been a *free woman of color*, even before the war. A woman who owned herself and was accountable to no one, who could go where she pleased.

Tante shook her head and tsked. "She'll never settle down, that one. Not until some man takes a hold of her. Now what can I get for you two?"

"We need the fixin's for a special dinner. A special Creole dinner," Nettie told her.

"Who is it you're trying to impress, *mes belles?*"

"Miss Sarah's friend, Morgan Cain."

Sarah saw a brief flicker of something in Tante's eyes, but it was gone so quickly she decided it had been a trick of the light.

"He is your beau, then?" the other woman asked.

"No," Sarah hurriedly corrected her, "just a friend."

"But a special one?"

"Yes, a special one," she conceded. Even to herself she had been afraid to think of him as more.

"Then we must find you something equally special."

While the two women looked over the fish and produce, Sarah wandered about the room deciding how best to broach the subject of her brother's death.

"Miss Sarah," Nettie called, bring her attention back to the task at hand. "I've picked up what I need. Is there anything else you can think of?"

Despite her nervous trepidation she decided to plunge ahead. "Tante Zabelle, I was wondering if I might ask you a question?"

The older woman and Nettie exchanged glances, and Nettie lifted her shoulder very slightly, to indicate she did not know what Sarah would say.

"To be sure. I will try to answer if I can," Tante Zabelle said.

"My brother was found dead near here last week. Perhaps you heard of it?"

"There are many who are murdered here in these parts, others who simply die of one thing or another. But your brother, he would be the soldier?"

"Yes. His name was Adam. Adam Gentry."

"I am sorry for your loss. I have brothers of my own. What do you need to know of me?"

"I believe he was murdered. I want to find out by whom. Have you heard anyone talk of his death?"

"There has been much talk about it, missy. Seems there is a great deal of interest in what happens down here. Specially when a white man gets himself killed."

"Then there are people who think he was killed? Who are they? How can I find them?"

The older woman shrugged. "Most of the talk comes from outside the district. The police have been asking many questions as well as a number of other men."

"The police?" That surprised her as the last she'd heard they had written off this case.

"And others as well," Tante confirmed.

"Who are the others?"

Tante shook her head. "I do not know. They are not from here, and they come at night, asking their questions and buying forgetfulness with their money."

"But why? And why the interest in Adam?"

"That I do not know. But surely as his sister, you might know more than me."

Tante's words hurt. As Adam's sister she had longed to know more of her brother, but he had not wanted her to. When the war was over, he came home restless and strained, jumping at every noise and unable to sleep the night through. But he would not talk to anyone of his experiences, not even her though she was his closest relative.

Now she had no clue as to why men would come in such secrecy to learn about his death. The entire situation was fraught with layer upon layer of complication and intrigue, too much so for an accidental death or suicide. Her conviction that he had been murdered grew stronger.

"I wish I could find someone who knew more," she said wistfully, feeling as if she'd hit another dead end.

"I might know such a one," Tante Zabelle said, although with some reluctance.

Sarah didn't say anything, letting the silence do the work for her. When Tante Zabelle began speaking again, Sarah let out the breath she hadn't realized she'd been holding.

"I will check with my Lafcadio. He knows many of the people questioned, and he likes to keep his finger on what's happening in our community. If he knows anything, I'll get in touch with Nettie."

"I would be grateful to you for *anything*," Sarah said.

"You are a good girl," Tante replied. "I fear for

you—the road you have chosen is not an easy one and betrayal lies in wait. Take care that it does not catch you."

When Sarah would have questioned the woman, Nettie silenced her with a look.

"What did she mean?" Sarah demanded when she and Nettie were on the street again.

Nettie shrugged.

"Then why didn't you let me ask her?"

"It's not done."

"What?"

"Tante Zabelle has the power. She uses it when and how she sees fit. It is not for us to question her. She has told you what you need to know. The rest is for you to discover."

Nettie's remarks made no more sense than Tante Zabelle's but Sarah knew better than to press the issue.

Thoughtfully she walked by the maid's side, thinking back on Tante Zabelle's words. Betrayal. She gave a shudder. Who had been betrayed? And by whom? Was that the reason Adam had been killed?

But she couldn't imagine Adam betraying anybody. Perhaps he was the one betrayed. But then why was he killed? The answers eluded her while Tante Zabelle's warning sent a shiver down her spine.

Chapter Six

Sarah straightened the bodice of her dress as she looked in the cheval mirror. She liked the dress's dark amber color, the way it set off her hair and skin. She wanted to look pretty this evening, to show Morgan how special she thought him. But Philip would be there, too, and she had no wish to hurt him. In his way, he'd given her his devotion, and her loyalty to him prevented her from wanting to flaunt the new feelings burgeoning inside her. The dress suited her purposes perfectly, showing off her figure without being flamboyant.

The front bell rang, and Sarah caught her breath. Who would arrive first? She couldn't wait to see Morgan, to have his deep voice whisper in her ear, to feel his hard masculine strength beneath her fingers. Heat filled her cheeks as she thought back to the dream she'd had the night before and the part Morgan had played in it. She hoped when she saw him she'd react normally.

What was taking Geneviève so long? Sarah couldn't wait to make her appearance downstairs, but good manners dictated she wait for her hostess. At last she heard her friend's footsteps in the hall and threw open her door.

"You look lovely," Geneviève commented as she swept into the room, her deep blue dress swirling around her. The color matched her eyes, giving them an extra sparkle.

"As do you," Sarah commented, but her heart skipped a beat at the hint of mischief in the other woman's voice. She had hoped this troublesome mood would not surface tonight.

"This evening should prove to be very interesting," Geneviève said with a relish that confirmed Sarah's worst fears.

"Geneviève, promise me you'll be good."

"Of course I'll be good."

Sarah tried to stare her down as their gazes met in the mirror, but without success.

Geneviève put on her innocent face and pouted prettily at her reflection.

"How could you even think anything else?" she asked in a tone that belied her question.

"Because I remember some of your antics at school."

"But that was such a long time ago. I was much younger then."

Sarah just shook her head. "For such a sensible person, sometimes you amaze me."

"A little amazement is a good thing, yes?"

"A *little* amazement, maybe, but not tonight. Just having Philip and Morgan in the same room together will be amazing enough without you stirring things up even more."

Geneviève opened her eyes widely. "Me? Stir things

up in my own house? Why, I would hardly need to do such a thing, now would I?"

Sarah shook her head resignedly. After last evening's mischief, Geneviève would not have to do anything at all. The men would be primed for battle, and it would be left to Sarah to keep them from drawing blood.

"We'd better get downstairs," she said. "It won't do to be late to our own soirée." She took a last look in the mirror. "Does my hair look all right?"

"As always. You have such a wonderful hair color, no one can resist admiring it. I've seen the men watch as you go by. If you weren't so innocent, you would see it, too."

"Really, Geneviève." Sarah laughed at her friend's exaggeration, but was secretly pleased. She remembered how Morgan had looked at her, how he had run his fingers through her hair. A warm glow filled her. She hoped it pleased him for she had taken extra care today, heating up the irons so each curl would lie perfectly in place, brushing its long length until every lock shone brightly.

"Now don't you worry," Geneviève said with a last look in the mirror. "Everything will go as planned. Shall we make our appearance?"

The two women headed downstairs to their guests, but when they entered the front parlor only Philip was present.

"My, how lovely you both look this evening. I feel honored to be in the presence of two such beautiful ladies."

Geneviève just stood there staring blankly at Philip as if he didn't exist compelling Sarah to jump into the silence. "Why thank you, Philip. You look quite dashing yourself."

"And has your other guest—Mr. Cain, wasn't it—arrived?"

"Not yet. But I'm sure it will only be a matter of time before he gets here," Geneviève finally said. "Something must have detained him."

"I'm sure you're right, but on the other hand, you know little about him other than the fact he is a journalist. Perhaps some story detains him. Do you know what he is working on?"

"Other than helping me because of Adam, I really don't know much about his work," Sarah said. "He did say he would be here, though."

"In that case, why don't we sit and talk for a while. I very much want to tell you about my meetings with William Bennett and Cal Strand. They were very encouraging. I think my political career has started most fortuitously."

"Let me just check with Nettie on dinner," Geneviève said, excusing herself.

Philip did not seem in the least disturbed by her departure as he escorted Sarah to the settee and spoke to her of his plans. His goal was a seat in Congress, and he was doing his best to rally support among the influential businessmen and politicians. Sarah noticed that most of the people he mentioned were Northerners.

"Don't be foolish, Sarah," Philip remarked when she mentioned it. "The South lost this war. We won't survive if we don't join the winning side."

"Is winning all that matters?"

"If you don't win, you don't have the power you need. With power, you can accomplish anything you want. Men will follow you into battle and do what you say. It's the only way to change things, believe me."

Why did men always think about the world in terms of win and lose, she wondered, though she didn't say anything to Philip, knowing he would not understand. Women sent their sons to battle, heartsick at the thought of losing them, while men plotted new and ingenious ways to vanquish each other. Even Philip, whom she thought of as having the height of civilized manners, seemed to have this bloodthirsty streak inside, a need to win at all costs.

"I can see we've talked enough of politics," he said to her then. "You see now why men do not feel women have a place in our political life. The subject merely bores you. Let's talk instead of all the friends who miss you in Baton Rouge."

Sarah wanted to protest. Politics did not bore her. It was Philip's self-centered descriptions that didn't hold her interest. But the talk of old friends distracted her, and she was surprised to see how much time had passed when Geneviève returned.

"I don't think Nettie can hold dinner any longer. Why don't we go in and when Mr. Cain arrives he can join us," Geneviève suggested.

Sarah and Philip concurred and before long dinner was served. The Creole food was wonderful, but Sarah couldn't enjoy it. Every mouthful tasted like ashes, for the one person she'd wanted to share dinner with had never arrived.

The evening stretched interminably. All Sarah wanted was time to herself, time to think about what happened with Morgan, where he might be, why he had not come. She paid desultory attention to Philip's attempts to converse, losing herself in her thoughts whenever silence prevailed, making only the most limited responses.

When the meal was over, Geneviève joined them in the front parlor, but her comments were few and far apart. And her yawns grew bigger and bigger and much more pointed. Sarah gave her a censuring glare, but she merely smiled and then yawned again. She soon made her excuses and retired for the evening, clearly having had her fill of Philip.

Sarah wished she could do the same, but Philip showed no propensity to leave. If anything, Geneviève's departure pleased him, for it meant time alone with Sarah.

"As I've said before, New Orleans seems to be the city of action. It's beautiful and right on the river," he was saying. "Besides, if I want to make my move for Congress, this is the city and the powerful people I'll have to win over."

"I'm sure you're right, but Baton Rouge has a lot to offer, too. It has been your home for any number of years. I'm not sure I could live here all the time," Sarah replied merely as a conversational gambit.

"You can't be serious? But I—" Abruptly, Philip stopped speaking, then continued. "Sarah, I think there are things that we should straighten out between us. Things have already been left unsaid too long."

Sarah could think of nothing to say that would divert Philip from the conversation to follow. Frantically, she searched her mind for a less personal distraction, but she could think of nothing.

"Really, Philip, I'm sure—"

"You know how I feel about you," he said, grasping her hand and pulling her to her feet in front of him.

"We've discussed this already," she reminded him. "Besides, I'm in the middle of investigating Adam's—"

"Sarah, face facts. Adam is dead, and there's nothing you can do about it. He wouldn't want you running all over and putting yourself in danger for his sake. He'd want you to have the life you deserve, married to a good man with children playing at your feet."

Before she could answer, he pulled her into his arms. She quickly turned her face when she realized his intent to kiss her, but that didn't stop him from placing frantic little kisses on her cheek, her eyebrow, her jaw.

"No, Philip, please don't."

"You know I've been waiting for you, Sarah, and now it's time we made some decisions." He held her against him with one arm around her waist while the other hand held her jaw so he could slant his lips over hers. His mouth felt wet and hot against hers. Too hot. She felt his desperation and strength of will—if she wouldn't come to him of her own accord, he'd impose himself.

Her blood ran cold. Twisting with all her strength, she turned her head and freed her lips. "Let me go. Now," she implored.

At the sound of her voice, Philip suddenly released her. She stepped back. Instinctively her hand went to her mouth to wipe away the violation. Her stomach heaved once, and she swallowed dryly, regaining a precarious control over her panic. She wanted to run and hide, to get away from Philip and never see him again. He wasn't the man she'd thought she knew.

"Please forgive me, Sarah. I didn't . . . I couldn't . . . I know you're slipping away from me and I couldn't let you go. For so long I've thought of you as . . ." He stopped, looking contrite and appalled at his own behavior.

Gazing at him, she remembered all he'd done for her, all his help. Maybe she'd been at fault, too, accepting his assistance without thinking what payment he might want in return. Had she led him on without even realizing it? She thought not. He'd always had lady friends, women he escorted to various social functions related to his work and social position. He'd only taken Sarah when one of them canceled at the last minute, or so it had seemed at the time.

Thinking back, she realized his lady friends had canceled with increasing regularity in the past year or so, leaving Sarah to act as his hostess more and more often. Funny but she hadn't noticed that, preoccupied as she was with her increasingly desperate search for Adam. For her, Philip had always been a "friend of the family," someone she associated more with her parents than herself. Her careless thoughtlessness was partly to blame for this, she decided. Philip deserved to be let down gently.

"Philip, you must understand. I think Adam *would* want me to do what I felt was right, and trying to track down who murdered him is something I have to do."

Visibly reining in his emotions, Philip said, "You haven't the knowledge or the information to handle this, my dear. Be reasonable."

"By myself I might not, but I'll get help. I have help."

"From whom? Morgan Cain?" The disdain in his voice was evident. "I can see he's a very reliable person. He can't even show up for a simple dinner invitation, and you expect him to help you locate Adam's murderer—if there even is such a thing?"

Sarah had had about all she could handle. "You're

free to hold your own opinion, as I'm free to have mine. I think it might be best if you left now, Philip. It's getting late."

"Sarah, please see reason. You—"

"There's nothing more to say. I'm very tired, and I feel a dreadful headache coming on. I'd like to rest. You can see yourself out, can't you?" She didn't wait for his answer but flew out of the parlor and up the stairs to her room before he could utter another word.

Shutting the door behind her, Sarah rushed to the washstand. Grabbing the pitcher, she splashed water into its matching bowl and frantically washed her face. She wanted the feel and taste of him gone. She wished he had accepted her word in Baton Rouge when she'd told him she wasn't ready to marry. Her mistake had been that she wasn't firm enough to convince him.

What a mess everything had become! And where was Morgan Cain? Why had he sent no word? Had their kiss meant nothing to him? Suddenly, she felt very much alone, and the tears she'd kept at bay downstairs began to flow. She buried her head in the cloth she was using to dry her face as the sobs shook her so no one would hear her cry.

When all the tears were spent, she walked to her bed and collapsed into its softness. She'd had such hopes for the evening, spinning fantasies born of longing and need—and the brief taste of passion she'd felt in Morgan's arms. What a fool she had been, bumbling about like a horse with blinders, seeing only what she wanted to see and nothing more.

Everything had changed, everything was different, and she wanted it to be the same, the way it had been before the war with her mother and father alive and her brother contented and happy. She fell into a troubled sleep, a confusion of images flashing before her closed eyes—Philip with his startling lock of blond hair against the jet black, Morgan looking past her as if she didn't exist, Adam beckoning to her to save him. Her feet were rooted to the ground and she couldn't move. Her breath came faster, and she woke with a start, her heart beating wildly.

Her pillow was hot and damp beneath her head. She turned it over, relishing the coolness of its other side. The moon had risen and now shone through her window, a mere crescent, marking the days she'd been in New Orleans. Soon it would fade to nothing and begin anew, just as she had to. Did the moon remember its past as she did? Did it long for times gone by or tire of the endless cycle of change and renewal?

It shone with silver splendor against a midnight black sky just as it had when she was a child. She could remember sitting outside in the spring, listening to the crickets chirp and her parents talk. Adam would be playing in the yard with his friends, and she would lie there on the grass with her favorite doll and watch the moon and stars. How protected she'd felt then.

And as she drifted off to sleep again, it was as if her memories became true. She was back in her home, back with the people who loved her . . .

A knocking at her door pulled her from the most wonderful place, a place she didn't want to leave. She tried to block out the sound, but it grew louder, more persistent. Then her parents and brother disappeared, and she was again alone in the darkness of her room. The moon was no longer shining through her window, but the sky was still dark.

"Sarah, are you awake?" she heard Geneviève call as she knocked yet again.

She sat up and noticed she had forgotten to change out of her clothes. The turbulent events of evening came back to her, and she remembered locking her door.

"I'm coming," she said and quickly wiped the traces of tears from her face. She flew to the door and quickly unlocked it. "What is it? What's happened?"

"Philip is downstairs demanding to see you," Geneviève said, then seeing how Sarah was dressed, asked with concern, "Are you all right?"

Sarah nodded though a shiver ran down her back. Philip. What was he doing here? "What time is it?"

"Three o'clock. He wouldn't take no for an answer, *chérie*, but you do not have to see him if you do not want." She gave Sarah a concerned look. "I should not have left you alone, *hein?* It was cowardly of me, but I have never liked the man. I am sorry—it did not go well, yes?"

"It wasn't your fault. There was a . . . misunderstanding." She shrugged off the unpleasantness as if it had been minor. "No matter."

"I can send him on his way, if you like."

"No, I'd better see what he wants. It must be important if he came in the middle of the night. Give me a minute to freshen up, and I'll be down."

Geneviève nodded, not looking at all happy. "Do you want me to join you?"

In a way Sarah did but knew that would be cowardly. "I can handle him on my own. There's no point in both of us losing sleep. If you could just tell him I'll be another minute, that would be fine."

"Are you sure?"

"Yes. I'll be fine."

Geneviève headed down the stairs, and Sarah slipped back into her room to repair her face and hair. She wouldn't give Philip the satisfaction of knowing how much he had upset her.

From the quiet in the front hall, Sarah knew Geneviève was already gone. As soon as Philip saw her, he crossed the room and grabbed her arm.

"Sarah, you must go home right away. I'll make all the arrangements. How quickly can you pack? You don't need to take everything; Geneviève can send the rest. Just throw together what you really need—"

"Philip, what are you talking about?" She pulled her arm from his grasp and stepped back from him.

"I'm talking about your safety, even your life."

"Have you been drinking?" she asked. Nothing she could think of would have Philip acting like this—except maybe liquor. "This doesn't make any sense."

"Sarah, you must listen to me. I know I behaved badly earlier this evening, but have I ever steered you wrong? You know I only want what's best for you."

"Philip, please. Just tell me what's going on." She'd had about all she could take from Philip in one day, and she didn't bother to hide her irritation.

"All right. I will," he said, and Sarah caught a malicious gleam in his eye. "Your friend is wanted by the police, and I don't want you sullied by your connection. The best thing you can do is let me take you home immediately. You know I've always taken my responsibility to your parents seriously."

"What friend? And why are the police involved?"

"Morgan Cain, of course. Weren't you a bit suspi-

127

cious when he didn't show up tonight? I knew the man was up to no good."

Though he didn't smile, Sarah could hear the deep-seated satisfaction in Philip's voice. Her heart raced as trepidation gripped her.

"Where is Morgan? Please, tell me what's going on."

"Murder, that's what. And Mr. Cain is in the thick of it."

For a moment, Sarah was too stunned to speak. *Morgan a murderer?* While he no doubt had a dangerous side and could defend himself if need be, she didn't believe for a moment that he was a murderer.

"Where did you get your information?" she challenged Philip.

"From a very good source: John Palmer. Remember? I pointed him out to you at the ball? Well, after seeing all of us together last night, he thought I might be interested in what the chief of police told him."

"And that was?" Sarah resented having to pull each tidbit of information from Philip as if it were a bad tooth in need of extraction.

"That your friend was down on Smoky Row and had a tangle with some prosti—, uh, woman. Now she's dead, and he's the one who killed her."

"I don't believe it," Sarah said, stunned by Philip's explanation.

"Well, this Bettine woman is dead, there's no question of that. And you can't deny he wasn't where he should have been, can you? I hear he's on the run and no telling how dangerous."

When Sarah didn't speak, he continued. "Now will you get your things together so we can leave before something happens to you?"

"Philip, first of all, I'm not leaving in the middle of the night no matter what's happened. I'll think about what you said and let you know in the morning what my plans are. Until then, I think you should go back to your hotel and get some sleep. I'll be perfectly safe."

When he would have argued, she merely opened the door and waited for him to leave.

"I'll be over first thing in the morning. Have your trunk packed," he ordered as he walked out the door.

She bolted the door behind him, and slowly climbed the steps. She didn't believe Philip's tale, especially knowing his ill feelings toward Morgan. He'd been fed some misinformation and was only too happy to act on it. Whatever mix-up had occurred, she was sure it would all be straightened out by morning. Though her words sounded convincing in her own ears, she couldn't help but wonder where Morgan had been tonight and what had been so important that he hadn't even sent word that he couldn't come.

Her room was dark, just as she'd left it. She crossed to the lamp on her bedside table intending to light it. There was no way she would sleep again tonight. A noise startled her just as she got out a match, and she half turned. A dark shadow crept up behind her. When she would have screamed a hand covered her mouth. For a moment she thought she would faint, then she recognized the touch.

"It's me. Don't scream," Morgan's voice mouthed in her ear.

She nodded, and his hand left her mouth, but he didn't move away.

"What are you doing here?" she whispered as softly as he had. "Wait, let me light the lamp."

She started to strike the match, but he stopped her. "Not until you've drawn the curtains."

Her heart resumed its rapid pace. Why the secrecy? Unless Philip had been telling the truth. Did the police want Morgan?

A sense of danger closed in on her. Using all her self-control she walked to the side window and closed the shutters. Then she drew the heavy curtains over the panes. She went to the window overlooking the back alley and noticed the bottom casement stood open. He must have climbed up the back porch, onto the roof, and entered her bedroom through it. Again she closed the shutters and drew the heavy curtains so no light would escape.

"May I light the lamp now?" she asked, working to hide the tremor in her voice.

She saw a movement from his direction and took that as his assent. She struck a match and lit the lamp. Only then did she turn to face him. A soft glow encompassed the area by the bed, but the light didn't touch him for he had moved to a dark corner. She could barely make out his features.

"To what do I owe the honor of this *late hour* visit?" she asked with false bravado.

"Always the little cat, aren't you? I wasn't the only one visiting you at such an inappropriate time, now was I?"

So he'd seen Philip's visit.

"At least he chose a more conventional method of entry. He used the front door."

"And so would I if you hadn't already . . . had . . . a guest." His last words faltered, and she heard him take a swift breath. "Why was he here?" he asked.

"Not that I owe you an answer, but under the circumstances you do have an interest in what he said."

"Oh?"

"Yes. It seems there was a murder tonight."

She watched him shift his weight from one foot to the other and thought he made a small sound, but she wasn't sure.

"There are always murders in a city this size. I could cover one for the paper every day. And sometimes I do."

"But are you ever the accused?" She tensed as she waited for his reaction.

"What?" he asked incredulously, his body jerking forward. Then he grunted as if in pain and clutched his left arm. "That's the—What else did he say?" he managed to get out through gritted teeth.

Sarah picked up the lamp and walked toward him. The light revealed a dark red patch high on his shoulder.

"My God, you're hurt. Come and sit on the bed."

"I want to know what else he said."

"As soon as you sit down I'll tell you everything. All right?" she coaxed as if he were a small child, the bribe an incentive to get him to do her bidding.

On his face she saw the strain of his ordeal and the realization that he probably couldn't go much farther. Slowly, he eased himself down on the edge of the bed. It was as if he'd used the last of his strength to talk and now he was drained, but he didn't want her to know it.

"What happened?" she asked as she placed the lamp on the table and reached out to inspect his shoulder.

"You were going to tell me what D'Arbereaux had to say," he said and stopped her hand.

"I can do two things at once, you know." She kept her voice steady despite her alarm. All that blood didn't bode well. "I can look and talk at the same time. Where do you want me to start?" As she spoke she unbuttoned his shirt.

"With what he was saying about a murder." His words were clipped as he watched her release the buttons one after another.

"Let's ease this off," she said, pulling the material from his good shoulder, then lifting it away from his injury. "Is this a knife wound?" She'd seen a number of bayonet wounds at the hospital were she'd volunteered during the last months of the war and this looked very akin to one.

"Or something similar." He winced with pain as she lifted off the shirt and threw it on the floor. She turned back to face him.

She knew she had to wash out his wound, but for a second she could do nothing but stare. She'd seen any number of naked men having worked at the hospital, but none had looked like him. Except for his injury, his skin was sleek and smooth, dusted with dark hair that flared in a triangle on his chest then came together in a tight band that disappeared in the waistband of his pants.

His muscles were firm and his body toned. A couple of scars stood out against his olive skin, mementos of the war that still held so much sway over their lives. She wanted to run her fingers along them, to see if his skin felt as vibrant as it looked, and the thought shocked her. Suddenly she was short of breath and her hands were shaking. To hide her confusion, she reached for the pitcher and bowl.

"Who am I accused of murdering?" he rasped as she bathed his wound.

"A woman in a place called Smoky Row. She had an unusual name. Something like Betty, but not quite."

"Bettine?"

"You knew her?"

Sarah looked down at the bowl in front of her and watched the red water swirl as she rinsed out the cloth she was using to clean his wound. She was afraid to look at him, afraid of the truth she might see in his eyes, so she walked over to the bureau and began searching for bandages.

"I've met her. She gave me some information on a story I'm working on."

Sarah bit her lip, but she had to ask. "And she was alive the last time you saw her?"

"Very much alive, if you can call that kind of life living."

Sarah allowed the breath that she'd been holding to escape. She believed him. She had absolutely no reason to, but she did. She took a sheet from the bureau and began to tear it into strips.

"The story you were working on didn't have anything to do with Adam, did it?"

He hesitated, and then, as if he'd made a decision, he nodded. "Bettine lived in the area Adam and others like him frequented. Ossy Burns gave me her name."

"Who's Ossy Burns?"

"Another soldier. Knew Adam."

Sarah stood very still. "Does he know how Adam died?"

"If he does, which I doubt, he's not telling."

"I need to talk to him."

"Maybe so, but he won't talk to you. Ladies don't figure much in his life. You would only embarrass him and make him tongue-tied."

Sarah considered his words. Was he telling her the truth or simply trying to keep her out of trouble?

As if he read her mind, Morgan said, "Listen, if you're so intent on meeting him, I'll try to arrange something. But I'm warning you now, I'd probably get a lot more out of him without you there."

"Yes, but how will you arrange anything with this mess going on? You never told me why you're here."

He sighed. "I had nowhere else to go where they wouldn't find me," he admitted with obvious reluctance. "I need to plan what to do next, especially with the police after me. I'm sorry I had to involve you."

She heard the weariness and discouragement in his tone and also the determination. If there were a way out, he would find it. She knew that in the deepest part of her.

"I'm glad you came," she said and knew it to be the truth. A warm glow of happiness filled her born of the knowledge that when he'd really needed someone, he'd turned to her.

"The main thing is for me to get away before you're drawn in any deeper."

"First we have to get you bandaged. If you bleed to death, you'll be of no use to anyone. Now don't move. I just have to get something."

She gathered up the bandages and went to her trunk, rummaging through it until she came up with a brown bottle.

"This will hurt," she told Morgan pulling the cork

from the bottle of alcohol and pouring some of it into the wound.

His indrawn breath and the barest of grunts was his only reaction.

"I'll wrap it up, but you need to lie down and not move around for a couple of hours if you want the bleeding to stop. When was the last time you saw her?"

Her last sentence was a non sequitur, but he seemed to follow her train of thought and understood she spoke of Bettine.

"A week ago."

He looked into her eyes and she saw no guile lurking in his. A flash of relief coursed through her.

"Let me help you ease back against the pillows. Did she have any information?"

He didn't answer right away. She could tell from the way he clenched his jaw that he was in pain.

"She didn't have much to say," he said after a minute. "Only that there were two other men looking for Adam right before he died. She didn't know either of their names, but she was able to give me a description." He paused again to catch his breath. "Of course her descriptions could match half the men in New Orleans—one in army gray, the other dressed as a gentleman."

Sarah pulled the cover up over his chest. "Well at least that proves something is going on, doesn't it?"

"Her death could be telling us a lot more."

"You think she was murdered because of what she knew?"

"You can get killed in that part of town for any number of reasons. Maybe she made off with more of her client's money than she should have or maybe she was moving in on someone else's territory or—"

"Or maybe they thought she knew something they didn't want repeated."

Morgan nodded his head. "Exactly."

"Do you have an alibi for the time she was killed?"

"Not likely."

"What happened?"

"To me? It's a long story. I got a message to go to Smoky Row. I'd talked to Bettine before and asked her to send for me if she remembered anything more."

"So you thought she sent for you."

Morgan couldn't hide his surprise. "Yes. You believe me?"

"Shouldn't I?"

He shook his head. "You're too trusting."

"What happened then?"

"I was jumped and locked in a cellar, tied hand and foot. They left a guard outside the door. It took me a while to work myself free. The guard stabbed me when we scuffled as I made my escape."

"What happened to him?" She almost didn't want to hear, but if she was to be of any help to Morgan, she had to know the worst.

"I knocked him out. By now he could be anywhere. Probably letting his contacts know what happened."

"I take it you're not turning yourself in?"

"Again, not likely."

Sarah looked around the room. What were they going to do? She couldn't hide Morgan in her room forever. She figured they were safe for the night, but not for much longer.

"Do you have an alternate plan?"

"I have friends out in the bayou. One of them has a cabin I can use."

"Good," she said glad that the problem had been so easily solved. "We'll head out after you've had some rest. Just before dawn will be best."

"*We* are not going anywhere," he countered, but his voice didn't hold the same command as earlier. She could tell the loss of blood had weakened him.

"Argue all you like, it will only weaken you more. When you get up in several hours' time you'll see exactly what I'm talking about. Besides, it was my brother's death that got you into this, and it looks like you're being framed because of it. I'm not letting you go off without me," Sarah said, starting to gather together the things she would need for the trip.

She'd expected an argument from Morgan, but when she turned back toward the bed she found him fast asleep. All the better. She needed her rest, too, if they were leaving in a few hours.

Chapter Seven

Sarah glanced over at Morgan. He was still asleep, and she hated to disturb him. He needed all the rest he could get, but all too soon the sun would be up, and by then she hoped they'd be out of the city.

She'd packed everything she could in her old carpetbag, not knowing how long they'd be gone but thinking it might be a while. Now she sat down to write Geneviève a note telling her not to worry and asking that she keep Sarah's departure a secret. Geneviève knew she was still investigating Adam's death and would understand her sudden disappearance. To convince her friend that she was safe, Sarah added that she would contact Geneviève at her summer home as soon as possible.

Philip was a bigger worry, especially after his visit last night. He'd been altogether too pleased to tell her of Morgan's troubles. At least he had no knowledge that Morgan had come to see her so he wouldn't tie the two of them together. She needed a plausible reason to keep him from coming after her.

Furrowing her brow, she bent over her page again

and told Geneviève the message to relay: that after their *altercation* the day before, she'd needed to get away by herself for a few days and think things over. Philip knew he'd overstepped the bounds of propriety, had admitted it himself in the middle of the night. Surely he would understand her desire to be alone for a few days. Besides, he had his own pressing political concerns, and Sarah had to hope they would occupy him and keep him from giving chase.

Satisfied that she'd left no loose ends to entangle her later, Sarah folded the note in two and placed it on the bureau where Geneviève would be sure to find it.

Snapping open the watch pinned to her blouse, Sarah knew there was no more time to lose. She walked to the bed and looked down at Morgan, noting how rakishly handsome he looked even in sleep, his rough-hewn features covered with a day's growth of beard, his impossibly thick lashes lying in dark crescents above his cheeks.

She felt his forehead gently, checking for fever, and was relieved that he felt only the slightest bit warm. She moved her hand to his cheek, dragging her fingers lightly over his skin, enjoying the different textures of his face, smooth where his skin was bare, scratchy where the stubble protruded. Though she knew better, she couldn't keep herself from absorbing everything she could about him as he slept, imprinting him on her memory for all time while safe from anyone's gaze.

"That feels nice," he suddenly murmured.

With a start she jerked her hand back and saw that his eyes were open and watching at her.

"I—it's almost daybreak," she stammered. "We need to get going if we want to make it out of the city before dawn."

She took a step back, but even from this distance she was aware of him as a man, of his subtle, masculine scent, of the even, deep breaths he was taking, of his clear, dark gaze locked on her.

"How do you feel?" she asked to distract him.

"I've felt better," he said, tentatively moving his shoulder and grimacing with pain. "And I've felt worse. What time is it?"

"Almost five."

Pushing himself up, he swung his feet over the side of the bed. Sarah heard him groan, and rushed around the bed to help, but he motioned her away.

"How long will it take you to get ready?" she asked as she turned her back and quickly washed her face in the fresh water she had retrieved from the kitchen after he'd fallen asleep.

"I'm ready now."

"Good. Then we can leave by the back stairs."

Picking up her bag, she started to the door only to be pulled back when his hand reached out and grasped her upper arm.

"I told you before, *we're* not going anywhere."

"We had this discussion last night, and it's settled. I'm going with or without your permission."

"We didn't settle anything," he said obstinately. "As I recall, I fell asleep."

"Yes, and you look all the better for it. After what you've been through you should still be in bed."

He scowled ferociously at her, but she merely stuck her chin out at a defiant angle, daring him to do his worst. As if her words were a challenge, he grabbed the bedpost and came to his feet. Before she could say a word, he swayed and little drops of sweat broke out across his forehead. His hand tightened on the bedpost, the knuckles white against the dark wood as he struggled to keep his balance.

"Are you dizzy?"

"A little," he was forced to admit as his knees buckled under him. Luckily he slumped onto the bed rather than the floor, since Sarah wasn't sure she would have the strength to lift him if he fell that far.

"Sit for a minute before you try to get up. You've lost quite a bit of blood. It shouldn't surprise you that you're unsteady on your feet."

She crossed the room to the small mahogany table in front of the window and picked up the tray she'd placed there earlier.

"I brought this up in case you wanted something," she said, and placed the tray on the table near the bed. "Maybe you should try to eat a little. You'll feel better if you do."

"Thank you."

He picked up a currant roll and took a bite. Sarah brought him a cup of water to drink. "I'm sorry I don't have coffee. I didn't want to stir up the stove."

"This is more than fine."

He finished eating in silence. When he was done, he stood again. This time he didn't wobble. Sarah kept a close eye on him when he let go of the bedpost and took a couple of steps.

"Don't worry, I won't make you catch me," he said with amusement, looking down on her from his superior height.

"Maybe not. But if I had to I could always prop you against a wall. Do you think you can make it down the stairs?"

"If we take it slow."

Sarah picked up her carpetbag and prepared herself for another confrontation. It didn't come. Morgan quietly opened the door and motioned for her to precede him. She wasn't ready for his sudden capitulation and had to swallow the biting remark she'd readied for the battle she was sure would ensue. Once again he'd done the exact opposite of what she'd expected. As in times past his reversal of temperament probably meant he had something else up his sleeve. She just wondered what it was this time.

Stepping out of the bedroom, she looked up and down the hall. It was empty. She nodded, and they tiptoed along the corridor and down the stairs like two ghosts, making nary a sound. They'd made it to the kitchen, and Sarah had just put her hand on the back door knob when Nettie's voice stopped her in her tracks.

"You can't go with him, Miss Sarah," Nettie called out in a frantic whisper.

Sarah turned toward the girl, wanting to relieve her fears. "Nettie, you mustn't worry. Everything will be fine."

"But you mustn't go with *him*. Tante told me to tell you."

"Nettie, you're talking nonsense. We're going to find out who killed Adam. You know what that means to me."

"But Tante says he's not to be trusted. He'll betray you just like he did Etienne." Nettie looked at Morgan. "Did you think you could keep it a secret? I can't let you take her."

"Nettie, please. This is no time for histrionics," Sarah protested with some exasperation. She looked over at

142

Morgan. He stared back at her, then headed toward the door.

"I'll let you and Geneviève know where we are when it's safe." She started after him, afraid he would use the maid's fears as yet another excuse to leave her behind.

"Please don't go, Miss Sarah," Nettie called out after them. "Tante is never wrong."

"Goodbye, Nettie," Sarah called out as she and Morgan slipped out the door. "Don't worry. I'll take care."

The heat was oppressive, hovering over the water of the bayou in shimmering waves. The pirogue in which they were traveling sliced through it like a knife.

Morgan looked over at Sarah. She was sitting ahead of him in the front of the dugout while Etienne sat in the rear handling the difficult craft with the consummate ease that came from years of practice. The other man had met them soon after daybreak with a wagon and supplies just outside of the city. The message Morgan sent before reaching Sarah had been relayed, and Etienne had been happy to help.

Though she hadn't complained, Morgan could see Sarah was feeling the intensity of the early morning heat. Her red hair was curling in the humid air and slipping out of her carefully arranged topknot. He watched in fascination as she pulled out the few remaining pins and, with a couple of well-placed swipes, straightened out the tangles, then tied it back with a green ribbon so it fell down her back in a riot of color all the way to her slim waist.

His fingers tingled with the urge to stroke the fiery tresses, and he wondered if the heat was getting to him, too. He should never have allowed Sarah to accompany him to this godforsaken area, but he hadn't had the strength to force her to stay behind. She was as obstinate as she was beautiful, and if he were honest, he'd admit that he needed her. The stab wound had taken more out of him than he'd wanted to acknowledge.

He dragged his eyes away from her as he felt himself hardening with desire and shifted on the hard boat bottom to ease the constriction of his clothes.

After Nettie's parting remarks, he was surprised Sarah had gone out the door with him much less insisted upon it. Nettie's implications would have turned many others away, especially under the circumstances. Here he was, wounded and wanted for murder with Nettie shouting about betrayals of the worst sort. Why hadn't Sarah dug in her heels and stayed put? Her faith in him only made the real secret he kept all the more damning.

He twisted around to see how Etienne was faring and to take his mind off Sarah. It wasn't like him to allow an infatuation such control over his life. Since he'd met her she'd been in his thoughts more and more.

"How much farther?" Morgan asked his friend. He'd visited this area several times before, but until he got acclimated everything tended to look alike—one inlet similar to the next, each cypress covered with Spanish moss hanging like old men's gray beards, alligators sunning themselves on half-submerged branches or slithering into the water to speed away from the boat.

"Not far, my friend. Ten minutes at the most. There, see that inlet? That is where we harvest the old cypress. Remember?"

Morgan turned with care and looked in the direction

Etienne was pointing. Now that he mentioned it, the place did look familiar.

"Some things are beginning to look less foreign, as if I've seen them before," he agreed. He braced himself against the side of the pirogue so he could face Etienne more easily. "You haven't asked what this is about, why I sent for you in the middle of the night. Aren't you the least bit curious?"

"I figured in time you would tell."

"You are very trusting. What would you say if you knew you were piloting one of the most wanted men in New Orleans?"

"Is it so?"

Morgan nodded. "As of last night, or so I'm told."

"How did you acquire that honor?" Etienne asked casually as he concentrated on navigating around a tree stump protruding from the water.

Morgan looked toward the bow of the boat aware that Sarah was listening to every word of his conversation and decided if she was going to be a part of this he wouldn't spare her either.

"It seems I killed a whore on Smoky Row."

He friend stopped paddling, a look of shock on his face. *"Sacrebleu,* how could such a lie have started?"

Though he had half anticipated such a reaction, Morgan was still moved by Etienne's unequivocal response. In a world turned so suddenly upside-down, his friend's unswerving loyalty was a balm to his troubled soul.

"Thank you for your faith, my friend," Morgan said, deeply touched. He looked into the distance, squinting against the brightness of the sun glinting off the ripples in the water stirred up by the hot breeze sweeping up the bayou. Collecting his thoughts, he said slowly, "I think it may have been started by someone who thinks he'll be better off with me out of the way."

"Out of the way? Is this some story you're working on?"

Morgan saw a movement from the front of the boat and realized Sarah had turned her head just the smallest bit to better catch their conversation.

"Either I'm sticking my nose into something that someone doesn't like or I'm getting closer to something someone wants kept secret."

"Do you have any idea who or what it could be?"

"Several," Morgan said shortly, not ready yet to voice his suspicions. "And as soon as I'm feeling better, I'll do some investigating. Until then, I wait."

"*We* wait," Sarah interjected without turning around.

"For the moment," he agreed, having no other choice. For now they would be traveling this part of the adventure together, but after they left the bayou it would be another story.

Etienne sent him a questioning look. Morgan merely shrugged. How could he explain Sarah to Etienne? His friend was used to a woman who knew her place, who stayed at home cleaning and cooking and bearing him children, with never any thought of talking back. Sarah didn't fit that mold at all, and Morgan found to his surprise that he liked it. She brought things to life inside him that he'd thought long dead. Every time he brushed against her anger and determination, he felt more alive.

"Here we are," Etienne said as he guided the boat through the overhanging branches of a tall cypress and into a hidden inlet. He let the boat bump against a rotting dock. Deftly he jumped from the dugout onto the crumbling wooden boards and held the vessel steady while Morgan and Sarah disembarked. The air here was a little cooler as the inlet was shaded on all sides by the tall cypress trees, but that was the place's only saving grace.

Morgan hadn't been expecting much, but even to his eye the decrepit homestead looked daunting. The house at the end of the long dock was built on stilts that sank deep into the murky waters of the bayou in the front. The back was anchored to solid ground. The boards of the house were covered in green algae, and Spanish moss draped over the edges of the roof from the trees overhead. He glanced over at Sarah in time to see her take a big swallow.

"The inside looks better," Etienne assured them and smiled jovially. "Come, I will show you and then bring in the supplies."

Before Etienne could stop him, Morgan grabbed a sack with his good arm. He felt the painful pull on his injured side, but it wasn't nearly as excruciating as on the night before. Sarah's preparations must have helped. Maybe he'd be back on the investigation sooner than he expected.

Sarah followed his lead, picking up one of the smaller packages along with her carpetbag. He opened his mouth to protest, then caught the look in her eye, and clamped his mouth shut, leaving the words unsaid. Her pointed look encompassed his injured shoulder and the bag he carried before returning to his face, challenging him boldly. He fought down a grin and stepped back to let her go by.

The three of them walked in a single file to the sorry cabin. Etienne pushed on the door, and it swung back on rusted hinges to reveal a single room. An open fireplace graced one end and a large bed the other. There were two makeshift chairs sitting in the center. The place had a musty odor, and dust motes danced in the air where the sun broke through the green cover in shining shafts.

"I've some blankets and linens here as well as some other items to make your stay more comfortable," Etienne said. "Let me just get the last of the things from the pirogue and then we'll talk."

Morgan dropped the sack he'd been carrying with a thunk. His shoulder ached painfully from the strain but he wouldn't give Sarah the satisfaction of hearing him complain. A cloud of dust rose from the floor, making him sneeze twice. That didn't help his shoulder, either.

Sarah stood silently by the door, watching him, her eyes wide and slightly glazed. She lowered her carpetbag and package to the floor more carefully, barely raising any dust. They stood in silence until Etienne returned.

"There, that's everything," Etienne said after he piled the last of the supplies in the corner. "Is there anything else can I get you?"

"This will do fine. I can't tell you how much I appreciate all you've done," Morgan said, walking over to his friend and clapping him on the back. Etienne had offered the best he had. His family was not well to do, yet he had given all he could with no questions asked.

"Yes, this will be quite cozy once we're settled in," Sarah put in. Morgan could hear the lack of certainty in her tone, but made no comment on it. She was trying her best to accommodate herself to the strange situation and he could only admire her tenacity. "It seems cooler here than out on the water," she added with an attempt at a smile.

"Always is. Something about all the trees and moss. Anyway, this is nothing. It's still early yet. Wait a month if you want to feel heat." Etienne grinned, then turned to Morgan. "You'll be all right here?"

"Don't worry. I just need a little time out of the city to try and figure out what's going on."

"If you need anything else, you will call Etienne, *non?*"

"You've done more than enough.'

"Between friends, there is never such a thing as *enough*. You saved my little Lynette for us. We will never be able to repay you." Etienne's voice filled with emotion, and he turned away to clear his throat before saying, "I'd best be getting on. Octavie's near her time, and she likes me close by."

"What do you want? A boy or a girl?" Morgan asked, smiling at the news.

"After five girls I deserve some peace and quiet. I'm hoping for a boy," Etienne said with a sly smile, pretending to be tired of women. He spied on Sarah from beneath his dark brow, watching for her reaction.

Knowing that Sarah would be unable to pass up such a blatant challenge, Morgan jumped in. "Don't let him fool you. Each of those girls has him wrapped around her little finger."

"They are my sweets," he said with a laugh, then sobered. "You take care. I don't think you'll be found here, but you never can tell. Depends on who knows what."

"We will, my friend," Morgan said. "We'll see you again?"

"No doubt. Maybe if you have time you two can stop

in to see us. There's a small boat behind the house. I know Octavie would enjoy the company of a woman. With just the girls, she sometimes misses talking woman talk."

"If I can remember the way, we might just do that," Morgan said walking his friend out the door.

After seeing Etienne off, he looked around the outside of the house. As far as he could see in any direction, there was nothing but nature, no other people, no other houses. As he stood in silence, he heard the hum of insects, the call of birds, the snap of water as the fish and alligators fed. The isolation of the place served as its security. To find them here, someone would have to know where to look and have a way to get here—no mean feat unless one had grown up on the bayou.

Morgan felt some of the tension leave his body. They were safe here for the moment. The local birds would alert them at anyone's approach, setting up a ruckus as they warned each other of a potential danger. Etienne had left them food and a rifle. A couple of fishing poles stood on end in a corner of the porch, leaning against the shack that would be home for the next few days. They wouldn't starve, one way or another.

Alone, he might have enjoyed his few days' enforced stay here. With Sarah . . . a different tension filled him as he thought of her sitting in the boat so proudly, her chin tilted in that stubborn way of hers, ready to take on the world. A fine sheen of sweat had covered her skin, giving it an almost ethereal glow. And that hair—thick and flowing like a waterfall of fire, catching the sun's brightness and magnifying it a thousand times.

Closing his eyes, he could imagine burying his face in its luxuriant softness, wrapping it around them both as he took her, letting its sweet flowery scent transport them to another world as he plunged into her womanly depths and lost his soul. A deep shudder shook him, shattering the dream. A man on the run had no right to be thinking such thoughts. There was work to be done if they were to be comfortable by nightfall.

To his surprise when he walked back into the cabin, Sarah had a fire going and a pot put on to boil.

"I would have done that for you," he protested when he saw all her work.

"With that shoulder, showing off for Etienne was more than enough," she said with a sniff.

Morgan didn't bother to correct her—he'd been showing off for her, not Etienne, behaving like some ten-year-old schoolboy, and she hadn't even been impressed.

"My shoulder's feeling much better," he lied. It still ached from his foolish actions, but at least the bleeding had stopped from what he could tell. The reddish stain seeping through his bandage had not increased in size.

"But not that much better. Besides you don't want to strain or pull anything. Quite frankly, I'm not sure that you shouldn't have had a stitch or two in that wound," she said as if she were trying to scare him.

"If that's needed, you can do it," he returned bluntly, wanting to give her some of her own back.

She paled, but Morgan felt no satisfaction at his win. Her irritation and fussing came from concern for his well-being. He shouldn't blame her for not seeing him in a more heroic light when he came to her injured through his own stupidity.

He sighed and ran his hand through his hair. Since when had a woman's opinion mattered to him so much?

Since Sarah, a small voice whispered in his head, but he squashed it mercilessly.

"What are you cooking?" he asked to change the subject.

"Etienne left some potatoes and clams. I thought I'd make chowder before the milk goes bad."

"Is there anything I can do?"

"Sit."

"But—"

"Sit or I won't be responsible when I have to take a rusty needle to that cut in your shoulder," she threatened pushing a small bag of clams at him. "Here, if you're feeling so much better, take these and shuck them for me. I only need eight or ten."

Morgan sat down. Though he didn't like to admit it, he was feeling a little weak. He hoped he didn't embarrass himself by not being able to open the shells. He picked up the curved knife she'd placed on the table and made the first cut, then pried open the clam, depositing the meaty insides into the bowl Sarah had left for the purpose.

As he worked his way methodically through the sack of clams, he watched Sarah go about her business, peeling potatoes and onions and cutting them up into the boiling water. Her movements were graceful and feminine, and her hair swung in tempo with them, a bright swatch of color in an otherwise drab environment.

He wondered what she was thinking as she worked, if she had regrets at having accompanied him. He couldn't think of many women from her station who would have adapted to the circumstances with such ease, making the best of the primitive conditions.

And primitive was the best one could say of the place.

The room held the barest of essentials—one bed, two chairs, a couple of cupboards. It probably would have been better with the opposite arrangement, but essentials didn't stretch to two beds. Before long they'd have to confront that dilemma. He wasn't sure what would happen, wasn't sure what he wanted. His body and his mind warred, each certain it knew better.

His body wanted Sarah, no question there. Just watching her cook was enough to make him harder than one of those cypresses just outside the window. His mind pulled in the opposite direction, reminding him of all the reasons why wanting Sarah was foolish. The problem was, he kept forgetting them every time he looked in her direction.

Her luscious lips were pursed in concentration, practically begging to be kissed. Her hands moved quickly and with sureness as she worked, making him wonder what they'd feel like stroking him, kneading his muscles the way she was kneading the dough for biscuits. Her backside was rounded and tempting when she bent over to check the pot. His hands itched to cup her, to treasure those feminine curves and hold them close.

He shifted on the chair and she looked up.

"Are you all right?" she asked.

"Fine," he said, amazed at how good he was getting at lying.

"You don't look fine. You look kind of strained."

Morgan rolled his eyes. She didn't know the half of it.

"It's been a long day," he said noncommittally.

"Yes." She glanced around at the room as if she couldn't bring herself to look at him. His gaze followed hers, noting with dismay just how shabby everything looked.

"I hadn't realized when I brought you on this escapade that the conditions would be quite so primitive."

"You didn't bring me. I chose to come, and in case it's escaped your notice, I haven't complained."

"I did notice," he said softly. *That, and so much more.*

She looked at him quickly, then her glance jumped away only to fall on the bed. He saw her flush.

"Just so you know, I plan to sleep on the floor," he said to reassure her. "Etienne brought extra blankets."

"You will do no such thing," she retorted. "You're hurt and need your rest. I'll make do with a pallet."

"That's ridiculous. I already told you I'm feeling better."

"Then why did I see you yawn a moment ago?"

"Is there a law against yawning?" he bridled. She could get his back up without half trying, and he knew the reason why. He wanted her, with every cell in his body. Frustration made him edgy, but that was no reason to take it out on her. "Sorry. Maybe I am a bit tired."

He had no intention of letting her sleep on the floor, but they'd argue that out later. He really was tired. After all this morning's moving about and carrying, his shoulder was beginning to throb.

Her belligerence turned to concern. "You need to rest. Let me just make up the bed." She scooped up the bedding Etienne had left and crossed the room. "It's a feather tick."

He could barely make out her words for she was bending over the bed and beating at the covering.

"And not the least bit dusty, thank goodness. I was a bit worried given the conditions here. Etienne must have seen to its airing. Just a couple more minutes and you can lie down," she said, turning to face him.

She looked so lovely, flushed from her exertions, her long length of hair falling over her shoulder. He nodded his head without realizing it.

"Good. I'll just get the linens and you'll be all set."

He started to get up to help, but she shooed him back to the chair.

"I can handle this. You save your energy for the things I can't do," she insisted.

He smiled to himself. She was very good at this, he thought, making him think he'd be needed later when she knew she'd make sure there was nothing for him to do. It had been a long time since he'd been coddled like this, and he found he was beginning to like it.

Sarah watched as Morgan began to stir. The last rays of the setting sun filled the cabin with a rosy glow. The light flickered across his face, highlighting his cheekbones and the dark growth of beard making him look both mysterious and dangerous, and totally male. She wondered what he'd look like with a full beard. Would the hair be soft or springy? Would it tickle when they kissed?

She flushed and looked away. Maybe a beard wasn't such a good idea, not if the mere thought of it left her so breathless. Then again, it would be a good disguise when they headed back to the city—the city with everything they were hiding from.

Hiding. The word held so many meanings for her now that she let herself think. She'd spent the day putting aside her worries, refusing to let all the conflicting thoughts settle in her mind, not wanting to face the enormity of her actions. Now, with nothing to do but wait, her conflicting thoughts refused to be put aside.

Had Philip been right about Morgan? He'd never steered her wrong before, helping her in her search for Adam, lifting her spirits when she'd given in to despair. But Geneviève had never liked him, claiming his every action had a selfish motive. And after his behavior just the night before—was it really so recently?—she felt she hardly knew him. So much had happened in the past twenty-four hours, it seemed like a lifetime. That there was no love lost between Philip and Morgan had been clear from the start, particularly once Philip realized Morgan would not be an asset to his political career.

On the other hand, Geneviève had warmed to Morgan at once, encouraging Sarah's interest in the man. Surely Geneviève was a good judge of character—she'd always been so before. But what about Nettie's words? She'd looked at Morgan with such contempt, accusing him of betrayal, of turning on a friend. Etienne, she'd said. Could it be the same Etienne they'd met? But if so, why was he being so helpful? Was Morgan blackmailing him?

No, she wouldn't believe that. Etienne had been too sincere, too eager to help with even the smallest things to insure their comfort.

It was all so confusing. Now, here they were, alone in the back of beyond. Sarah couldn't get home if her life depended on it—and for all she knew, it might. How could she have been so impulsive? So sure of herself one minute, so unsure the next? How had Morgan managed to turn her entire life inside out so quickly? She bit her lip, afraid she knew why but unwilling to confess the truth, even to herself.

Morgan turned again, but did not wake. He must have been even more tired than she'd thought. The trip out had been a strain even on her, and she wasn't injured. But he'd fought his tiredness, trying to prove something. Whether it was to her or himself, she wasn't sure. She thought she'd handled him well. At least, she'd gotten him to sit still while she put the bed together.

Though he'd tried to fight it, the tiredness had won out. As soon as his head had hit the pillow, he'd been asleep. Now the sun was beginning to set, and he was only just starting to stir.

Sarah got up from her chair and swung the pot of chowder back over the fire so it would heat. She'd spent the hours while Morgan slept trying to clean the cabin and put away their provisions. Now she went to one of the cupboards sitting beside the fireplace and took out a few of the biscuits she'd made to eat with the soup.

"What time is it?" Morgan asked in a scratchy voice.

Sarah opened her watch. "Nearly seven."

"Why'd you let me sleep so long?"

"You needed your rest. You can't get better if you overexert."

"But there were things I had to do."

"Such as?" she questioned. She could think of nothing he had to do that couldn't wait until tomorrow. They were going to be here some time.

"Things," he replied grumpily.

She smiled to herself at his mood. She usually woke up cheerful, but not everyone was the same. She could see that their enforced proximity was going to be a learning experience.

"Are you hungry?" she asked in a mild tone.

He didn't answer immediately, as if the question involved great thought. "Is the chowder you were making earlier still hot?"

She took that to be a yes and made up a bowl for him. Setting it on a plate with a spoon and some biscuits on the side, she brought it over to him.

When he would have gotten out of bed, she forestalled him. "There isn't a table, so you might as well stay put. Prop yourself up with some of those pillows. That's right," she said watching him do her bidding. When he was settled she handed him the soup and went over and ladled a bowl for herself. She pulled a chair over toward the bed and started to eat.

Neither of them spoke. The only sounds were the clinking of their spoons against their bowls and the occasional snap of burning wood in the fireplace. After a while, Sarah wasn't sure how to break the silence, so she kept her eyes trained on her bowl and concentrated on not accidentally slurping.

"The chowder was very good."

She was so surprised to hear his voice, she almost dropped her soup bowl on the floor.

"I'm glad you liked it," she said gathering up the dirty dishes since they were both finished and taking them over to a bucket by the hearth. When she turned back to ask him if he wanted anything else, she saw him swinging his legs over the side of the bed.

"I thought we decided you should stay in bed."

"*We* didn't decide anything," he said pushing himself to a standing position. When he started to wobble she ran to his side.

"See, I told you you're too weak to be gallivanting about."

"I'm not gallivanting. And I'm fine now. I just lost my balance for a second," he said, though he didn't push her away.

With her arm around his waist, she could feel the hard strength of his muscles under her palm, the taut firmness of his thigh next to hers. Her hand gripped his side and of its own volition began to massage the flesh above his waist.

"I have to make a trip outside," he told her.

"I'm not sure that's such a good idea. You probably shouldn't even have been out there this afternoon."

"Well, now I have to go."

"Whatever you need I can do for you."

"I think it might—"

"Just tell me and I'll—"

"This is something only *I* can do. Do you understand?"

And then she did. She let go of him as if he were made of fire. She felt her face begin to flush from embarrassment. He had been asleep most of the afternoon so it made sense that he'd need to . . . use the privy.

"But if you'd like to come along and help . . ." He let the sentence trail off. It was obvious he'd seen her embarrassment, and unlike a gentleman, had chosen not to ignore it. Not only to not ignore it, but to draw attention to it.

"I'm sure you can manage on your own," she replied in the most prim voice she could muster.

"I'm not so sure. You know, you were right before. I am a bit weak. Maybe you should—"

"I'll clean up the dishes now if you've finished having your fun."

"For the time being, I guess," he said and chuckled under his breath as he made his way out the door.

When it closed behind him, she gave a sigh of relief. This time alone together was going to be more challenging than she'd anticipated. She'd given little thought to what coming with him would mean beyond her need to discover Adam's murderer. Now she was faced with a reality far more powerful than any she could have imagined.

Her arm still felt the warmth from his body; her fingers still tingled from the touch of his skin. His male scent, musky and potent, clung to her, reminding her with every breath of just how close they'd been.

She looked over to the corner where the bed stood. It loomed large in the room. What would happen tonight when they were alone and it was dark and there was only the bed, waiting? Suddenly Sarah felt light-headed as if there were no air in the room. She knew Morgan wouldn't do anything she didn't want, knew it with the deepest, most feminine part of her. Her faith in him was unshaken.

But what of her? What did *she* want?

Chapter Eight

Though she wanted to put it out of her mind, thoughts of what the night would bring stayed with Sarah as she washed the tin bowls and cutlery from dinner. By the time she was finished there was barely any daylight filling the cabin. When she'd cleaned up earlier she'd found two kerosene lamps, both full. Etienne, it seemed, had thought of everything. She set the larger one in the middle of the floor and struck a match to its wick. A warm glow filled the space. She left the smaller one unlit, unsure of their fuel supply. There was no point in being wasteful when she had no idea how long they would have to stay here.

Now that the lamp was lit, she realized that Morgan had been gone for quite some time, more time than was needed she felt sure. What if he'd gotten dizzy and fallen? Her heart started to race. She quickly opened the door and walked out on what could be called a porch though on this particular building she wasn't sure. The boards seemed to move with each step she took.

She stood still and cocked her head, listening. The only sounds she heard were the croaking of frogs and chirping of insects. Even the birds had settled down for the night. She headed around to the back since there was nothing out front except water. Walking to the end of the porch, she peered into the darkness. She'd been out here earlier in the afternoon and knew there was solid ground all around, but without a light to show the way, she was hesitant about venturing farther. She decided to wait five more minutes. Then if he didn't appear she'd get the lamp from inside and see if she could find him.

As she waited for the minutes to tick off, she imagined him in all kinds of dire predicaments. Suppose he had fallen down and was unconscious, how would she get him back to the cabin? Or what if he'd tumbled into the water and some alligator was ripping him to pieces? She'd heard they could swallow a baby in one gulp, and if you were swimming, they would grab you by the feet and pull you under until you drowned and then save you for dinner.

"Decided on some fresh air?"

At the sound of Morgan's voice, Sarah screamed and jumped two feet, nearly falling off the porch. Then she turned and rushed into his arms.

After imagining him at the bottom of the bayou it felt good to feel the strength of his arms around her, to see him standing there without an alligator bite on his body. And then she remembered his shoulder.

"I'm sorry I shouldn't have—your arm," she said in a wobbly voice and began to pull from his embrace.

"Never mind about my arm," he said tugging her back against him. "Tell me what scared you."

"I'm not scared," she said, but her tone of voice wasn't even convincing to her own ears.

"You've never struck me as a woman who'd run from shadows. Though sometimes I wish you were," he whispered in a tone so low she was sure she wasn't supposed to hear. "Now tell me what it is."

"It's foolishness. Sometimes women get this way." She didn't want to admit to what she'd been thinking. "I'm fine." Though on her final words, she shivered.

"It's getting chilly out here. Maybe we'd better go inside," he suggested, but he didn't move. They stood together, his arms wrapped around her, his warmth permeating her body, filling even the tiniest, most hidden corners.

Was this what she'd hoped would happen when they came here? Had she wanted time alone with Morgan, to get to know him and understand him?

She didn't know the answers to her questions, but she suspected there was an element of truth there if she dared to look. Now was not the time for introspection, however, not when she was nestled in the shelter of his arms and liking every minute of it. His hand moved rhythmically up and down her back in a soothing motion, and she relaxed against him. Every once in a while he'd run his hand through her hair. Everything was slow and leisurely, as if they had all the time in the world.

A cool breeze blew off the water, ruffling her skirt. The night noises resumed around them, the lapping of the water, the rustling of the trees, the calls of one animal to another as they went about their nightly chores. Beneath her ear she heard Morgan's heartbeat, steady and strong, blending with the other sounds. She felt a strange peace settle over her, all sense of time and place evaporating into a single unity.

Then she felt him loosen his hold. She wanted to protest, to recapture that sense of oneness, but before she could utter a word his hand gently tilted her chin up until she was looking into his eyes. Only she couldn't see anything in their dark, fathomless depths, couldn't tell what he was thinking . . . or feeling. And then it didn't matter for his mouth was covering hers.

It was just as before, that same magic when his lips touched hers. Her whole body quivered and it wasn't from the chill in the air or her thoughts as before, but because of the emotions he ignited inside her. Wherever they touched, she felt consumed. She didn't know which way to turn or what to do, only that she wanted this to go on forever.

Her mouth clung to his, and this time she initiated the dueling between male and female. Her tongue touched his, and the fire within her spread. She moaned her acquiescence when he took over, leading her down paths she'd never before traveled.

Earlier his hands had soothed; now they enflamed, touching, tantalizing, making her want to beg for more. She'd never felt this way before. She even forgot to breathe until he gently took his lips from hers. She stood enthralled, her eyes searching his face, aware that he too was out of breath, his lungs expanding and contracting beneath her palms.

He touched her face, feathering his fingertips across her forehead and down to her jaw, then retracing the path until he could cup her cheek. She closed her eyes, giving herself over to her other senses. His thumb danced back and forth across her lips, just as it had in her dream, and as in her dream her tongue came out to lick her lips and encountered his thumb with its tip. She tasted the saltiness of his skin and felt its slightly rough texture, dream and reality combining. Her eyes darted open, and she saw his tender smile. This was no dream but a far more potent reality.

Closing her eyes again, she gave herself up to the rapture, half knowing what would happen because she'd dreamed it, but never like this, never with such intensity, never with such yearning. She wanted all of him, and from the way he touched her, she knew he wanted her in return. As if he'd shared her dream, his hand traced a path along her neck and then moved to the top of her dress. She shivered when his fingers played with the green piping that banded its neckline, then ran down the buttoned front of her bodice.

At each button he stopped and traced its shape. She held her breath, anticipation making her giddy. Slowly his fingers moved back to the top button. With infinite care he slipped the white mother-of-pearl circlet through the buttonhole. The two sides of her bodice separated, pulled apart by her swelling breasts. He leaned over and kissed the delicate skin now exposed to him, and a shiver of delight ran down her spine. His tongue darted out, warm and wet, tasting her as she had tasted him.

Her moist skin gave off a flowery scent that combined with his in an intoxicating blend. Sarah breathed deeply, barely noticing that he'd undone three more buttons until she felt the evening air brush coolly against her. Morgan lifted his head and stared, an expression of wonder on his face.

"You're so beautiful," he whispered. His fingers slowly reached out to stroke her, his touch so light she wasn't sure she even felt it. Then they skirted along the edge of her corset to rest on the swell of her breast. Instinctively she arched her back, wanting to get closer, to increase the pressure of his touch. In response, his hand began to move ever so slowly over her bare skin tracing a tantalizing pattern of small circles between her collarbone and the lace decoration at the top of her corset.

With each sweep, her breathing became more labored until she thought if he didn't touch the part of her that ached most, she would faint from wanting. And then, when she couldn't stand another second of waiting, his finger moved downward under the lace and lightly brushed her aching nipple.

She couldn't believe the storm of feeling he unleashed inside her, the weakness in her knees, the throbbing in her womb, the aching need in her other breast where the nipple puckered just as tightly as if it had been stroked as well. Her fingers closed around the wooden rail at her back and she moaned, wanting more, filled with longings she didn't recognize but which were all the more intense for her inexperience.

Morgan shushed her, drawing her into his embrace and wrapping his arms around her.

"Hush, little one," he whispered near her ear. "It'll be all right. Just give it a minute."

She wanted him to touch her again, to ease the flaming need inside her, but he merely hugged her to him, until the wanting burned itself out, leaving only the tiniest embers still glowing deep inside her.

He held her away from him and gently pulled the halves of her bodice together, sliding each button back through its hole, until she was fully dressed again.

"It's been quite a day," he said then, "and I think we need some time to put everything in its proper place."

"You're right, of course," she replied a bit stiffly. And

he *was* right. So why didn't she feel more grateful for his restraint?

He put his hand around her waist and turned her toward the cabin. "You're a wonderful woman, Sarah. Special in so many ways."

The light from the lantern shone through the window of the shack highlighting the planes and angles of his face. She looked up at him, searching his face and the depths of his eyes. She saw the same confusion she felt reflected there, the mix of desire and hesitation, the knowledge that now was the time to stop and the regret. He was open to her as never before, letting her see into his soul. And there was more—a promise for the future lurked behind the turmoil and confusion, a hope of better things. For the moment it was enough.

"We'd better get inside before the bugs eat us alive," he whispered at last.

"Yes, we should," she said strangely comforted.

They walked into the cabin together. The lamp seemed overly bright after the dimness of the night, and Sarah blinked owlishly. When her eyes adjusted, the first thing she saw was the bed. For all that had passed between them, it still loomed as a formidable adversary, a threat to the peace she'd felt just moments ago.

"Do you think you could make a pot of coffee over that fire?"

Morgan's voice came to her as if from a great distance. At first she didn't understand the words, and then she grabbed onto them like a lifeline.

"I can't promise how good it will taste, but I'll give it a try."

"While you're doing that I'll get some more wood.

We'll want to keep the fire going most of the night. It can get mighty damp here this time of year."

She wanted to stop him, to tell him that carrying the wood would strain his shoulder and maybe do more damage, but she kept quiet. She needed time alone to sort out what had happened between them, and maybe he did, too.

Walking to the cupboard, she pulled out the battered pot and set about making the coffee. All too soon she had the filled pot hanging over the fire. Now there was nothing left to distract her from her thoughts.

She spread an old quilt on the floor by the fireplace and sat watching the flames, looking for the answers to all the uncertainties plaguing her. Tonight might well be a turning point in her life, she thought, depending on what happened. Was that what she wanted?

She thought of how little time had passed since she met Morgan and yet how well she knew him despite their short acquaintance. She'd seen aspects of him she was sure no one else ever saw, known his kind and gentle side as well his more aloof persona. She'd known Philip much longer but never felt a hundredth of what Morgan could make her feel with a simple touch.

The pot began to boil, filling the air with the rich smell of coffee. Sarah pushed it off to the side of the fireplace so it could simmer, and sat back on the quilt.

Her thoughts returned to Morgan, remembering how he'd helped her come to terms with Adam's death, the way he'd tried to protect her and shield her from life's uglier side. He was a man of honor, no matter what anyone said. He'd even put his life at risk trying to get the information she wanted. And when he kissed her, she was transported to another world.

She smiled drowsily, wondering what other new worlds he could open for her. She laughed at herself. Here she was worrying about something that more than likely wouldn't happen and certainly not tonight. She didn't even know what Morgan was thinking, if he was feeling the same things she was. He had been as involved as she in that kiss, but she'd heard how men were different than women, how men could— She yawned and lost her train of thought. Today had been such a long day. She'd just close her eyes for a few minutes and then try to sort everything out.

When Morgan walked back into the cabin with a small load of wood the last thing he expected was to find Sarah slumped across the floor in front of the fire. He rushed to her side, his heart beating wildly. It settled when he realized she wasn't hurt, only asleep. Slowly and quietly he placed the wood in a neat stack beside the fireplace, doing his best not to disturb her.

He straightened and looked around the cabin. It looked neat and much cleaner than before. The rich smell of hot coffee filled the air, giving the place a homey atmosphere. With the dishes drying in one corner and the fire dying down, the place felt cozy and welcoming, something he wouldn't have thought possible when they'd first arrived. And it was all due to Sarah's efforts.

He looked down at her curled up on the quilt, her face flushed from the warmth of the fire and her exertions. She must have been exhausted, he thought with a pang. She'd been up most of the night tending to his arm. Thinking back, he wasn't sure if she'd slept at all last night, between packing her bags and preparing his breakfast.

Despite their fatiguing trip, she'd worked the whole afternoon as well, fixing the soup and cleaning the cabin, all without a word of complaint. He knew few people, even hardened soldiers, who would cope so well.

He owed her a lot. She'd kept his spirits up despite his injury and the mess he was in now, forced him to stay on his toes both literally and figuratively just to keep up with her. She deserved her rest, and she didn't deserve to have it on the hard wood floor of the cabin. The only question was how he could get her onto the bed. Would he be able to lift her with his good arm and a little help from the other?

He took in her uncomfortable position and knew he'd have to try. With extreme care he hunkered down beside her and rolled her upper body gently onto his weak arm. Then as quickly as he could, he used his other arm to swing her up as he stood.

With long purposeful strides, he walked to the bed and laid her carefully on the feather tick. As he stood his arm felt the strain, and he rubbed it absentmindedly, his attention all on Sarah. She stirred briefly, then turned to her side without awakening. He smiled. All her arguments about the bed were for naught, he thought. Tonight they would share it. It was the only way they would both get the rest they needed, though Morgan had some doubts about how well he would rest with Sarah so close beside him.

Sarah turned in her sleep and bumped up against a wall. Turning back she bumped into another wall, although this one was somewhat softer, she thought drowsily. She opened her eyes but the room was dark. Then the softer wall moved and turned toward her.

"Are you awake?" Morgan asked.

She didn't know what to say. Her mind whirled trying to recall exactly what had happened the evening before, but the last thing she remembered was gazing into the fire.

"Sarah?" he whispered again.

"Yes," she replied in a very small voice.

"Go back to sleep. It's still the middle of the night," he said and then turned onto his back, no longer looming over her.

The fire had burned down but still glowed red, reflecting onto the ceiling over the bed. In the muted light she could make out the outline of Morgan's face. His profile was distinctly male, from his strong jutting nose to his equally determined chin now covered by a thick growth of beard. She was close enough to see the rise and fall of his chest when he breathed and the flat plane of his stomach, loosely covered by the sheet.

Her gaze drifted downward, and she caught herself up sharply, feeling a blush come to her face. He was wearing no shirt, and if she hadn't turned her eyes away quickly, she might have discovered how little else he was wearing. Every inch of her skin prickled with an awareness of how near he was, how easy it would be to snuggle close and touch him, to run her fingers along his skin and learn his different textures. She nearly groaned aloud. How on earth did he expect her to go back to sleep?

She shifted again, trying to determine what she herself was wearing. She didn't remember undressing, but then, she didn't remember getting into the bed, either. She did recollect being so tired her eyes would no longer stay open. Had she fallen asleep on the quilt? It seemed the only answer. And then Morgan must have put her to bed, undressing her in the bargain.

She groaned as she realized both her top and skirt had been removed, leaving her shoulders bare and her legs unencumbered by the weight of her petticoats.

"You all right?" Morgan whispered.

"Yes, yes. I'm fine," she whispered back, knowing she wasn't. But since Morgan himself was the cause of her discomfiture, or more exactly, her reaction to him, what could she say?

She curled up, hugging the edge of the bed. She was never going to get back to sleep. Not with him so close. Not after realizing how undressed she actually was. Not after—

"Sarah, stop twitching."

"I'm not twitching," she denied vehemently, turning to face him. "I'm positioning myself for sleep."

"Do you think you'll be through *positioning* yourself soon? All your squirming is . . . disturbing me."

"As I recall, I said I'd sleep on the floor."

"And what kind of gentleman would I be to allow that?"

"What kind of gentleman gives a lady his bed and then climbs in afterward?"

Morgan let out a loud laugh. "You have an answer for everything, don't you?" he said rolling over and facing her.

"No, not for everything," she managed to get out. Now that they were eye to eye she wasn't quite as brave.

"Good, because once in a while I like having the last word."

"And—"

"God, woman, you never quit."

Before she could frame a reply, his lips were on hers, coaxing and teasing, playing with her. Slowly the kiss changed from merely a way to silence her to a kiss of blossoming passion. Sarah opened her mouth, and Morgan's tongue plunged inside, warm and wet and hungry, probing every hidden recess, then withdrawing provocatively, challenging her to follow. And follow she did, reveling in his taste, at once familiar and mysteriously male. His teeth felt sharp as they gently nipped her, his tongue soothing as it stroked across the tiny pain.

Her hunger for him grew even as he tried to satisfy it. With every taste she wanted more, wanted him more deeply until she lost herself in him. Her arms went around his neck, her fingers burying themselves in his nape, holding her to him.

After a while, he pulled his lips from hers. "Sarah, you do realize where this will lead, don't you?"

She didn't want him to leave.

"Yes," she replied breathlessly.

"If you want me to stop, you have to say so now because in a few more minutes, I won't be able to hear a word you say. Do you understand?"

"I understand and I want you to kiss me again."

Morgan groaned with desire and gathered her into his arms.

"God, I've wanted you since that first morning you walked so confidently into my room."

"You have?" she asked in wonder. She thought he'd wanted nothing but to be rid of her, at least at first.

"How can you doubt it? And now I want to love you very, very slowly until you beg me . . ."

Sarah's heart started to race. "Beg you to what?"

"Never stop," he said, and then there was no time for words. His mouth was on hers again, and all she could think of was his heat and her desire. His lips sucked on hers then moved lower, leaving a wet trail as he nibbled his way down to her corset. Deftly he opened the clasps and eased her from the confining garment. Beneath it she wore a short camisole and pantalets of the thinnest fabric. As Morgan leaned over her again, his lips met hers.

Before she realized quite what was happening they were both naked and she was cradled in Morgan's arms. With infinite care, he began her journey into the world of lovemaking. And he did so with the utmost attention.

His lips touched hers ever so lightly and then went on to kiss her eyelids, cheeks, and throat while his hands moved over her back from hip to shoulder.

She mimicked his actions, running her hands down his back, following the contour of his hips and buttocks. His muscles tensed at her touch and she marveled at his strength, at the supple feel of flesh against her skin. Her hands slid up his back, following the valley of his spine, then spread to his shoulders until her fingers brushed against fabric and through a fog of wanting she remembered his injury.

"Your shoulder—"

"My shoulder's fine," he whispered in her ear. "You let me worry about that." When he finished talking, his tongue came out and teased the tip of her ear, sending ribbons of desire through her.

Gently he turned her onto her back. His hand

reached out and lightly touched her breast. Her breath quickened at the contact. This was so much better than her dream, she thought. She felt a hot, bubbling need begin to build within her.

His fingers massaged her nipple until it was a hard throbbing center of longing. Then he moved to the other, and soon it was in the same state. His fingers felt rough against her skin, yet it wasn't pain she experienced when his hand moved to the softness of her stomach and drew small circles around her navel. When the tip of one finger dipped inside, a cascade of shivers raced down her spine and a deep languor filled her very center.

She moaned her compliance, though she wasn't sure to what she'd agreed; she only knew she wanted more.

He bent his head, and his lips surrounded one aching nipple. At first they were a soothing balm, then his tongue wrapped around the tip, flicking relentlessly, and she began to writhe, arching her back for closer contact. When he backed off, she placed her hands behind his head and drew him closer, silently begging him not to pull away.

He lifted his head just far enough to look into her eyes and smile. His face was flushed, his eyes heavy-lidded with passion, his mouth as full and swollen as hers felt. She'd never seen a man aroused and felt a surge of purely feminine power that she could bring him to such a state. Then her own feelings of arousal took over, and she gave a sharp tug, wanting to draw him closer. He yielded to her plea, tonguing first one breast and then the other, pausing only to kiss the valley between.

When she thought the ecstasy inside her could peak

no higher, his hand slid down toward her most feminine self, teasing her as he approached the place she most wanted his touch. He touched her lightly, barely making contact as he ran his fingers down the outside of one thigh and up the other. A liquid warmth filled her, making her feel boneless and pliant. With slow, deliberate movements, he separated her legs until he had access to the inside of her thighs and then his fingers repeated their earlier journey on the more tender skin. Each time he reached the heart of her he'd linger a little longer and then move on, until at the top on the last circuit, he stopped.

She gasped for breath as his fingers slowly reached for her most private part. She pulled away, but losing his touch was unbearable. She stretched forward again. Immediately his fingers set to work, touching her in ways that had her head thrashing against the pillow in wanton desire. Suddenly she was shooting into the sky, higher and higher until she came to the edge and began to float back to earth.

Her breathing was erratic, coming in small bursts, and perspiration rolled from her face. She felt both exhilarated and spent, craving more yet needing time to recover. She'd been shattered into a thousand tiny pieces and made whole all at the same time, but something was missing.

Gently Morgan smoothed back her hair and wiped her brow with the edge of the sheet. He lay beside her, his hand idly stroking her until she calmed. In his face she could still see need etched with passion. Though her own desire had been slaked, she knew his still burned fiercely though he made no demands. For a while, she was content to lie by his side, passively absorbing his soothing touch. His hand felt warm against her cooling skin and she snuggled against his side.

All too soon, his gentle stroking was no longer enough, and she turned on her side so she could more easily reach him. Her hands burrowed into the hair on his chest, and when she accidentally brushed her little finger against one of his flat male nipples, she felt him shudder. She tried to withdraw her hand, but he placed his own on top, holding her to him.

"Don't be afraid to touch me," he murmured hoarsely.

"I didn't want to hurt you."

"This kind of pain I could bear forever," he said, and she knew then that she was giving him the same agonizing pleasure he'd given her. Gathering her courage, she dipped her head and ran her tongue around his nipple, just as he'd done to her. His deep groan gave her a feeling of feminine power, emboldening her to repeat her action.

Suddenly he flipped her onto her back, his mouth on hers as he moved over her. She felt the rigid length of his manhood brush against her leg and a frisson of fear ran through her. Before her mind could form words of protest, he slowly and carefully positioned himself between her legs. His lips captured hers again in a kiss so drugging, so encompassing that everything else faded into the distance.

And when she thought she could feel no more, his body pushed forward into hers. She felt him press at the very core of her womanhood, felt her own flesh ease apart so he could enter. He filled her slowly, exquisitely, rocking against her so that with each thrust he captured more ground, until he was buried so deep inside her she felt him a part of her soul. Nor did he stop then. Waiting only for her body to accommodate his size, he stroked her again, nearly leaving her entirely so that she felt bereft with wanting, then filling her again and again until the tension that built inside her threatened to snap like a wire.

Again she climbed the heights, waves of pleasure carrying her higher and higher until she soared. Through her own cries she heard him call her name as the spasms shook them both. She held on to him tightly, shaken to her very core, her arms and legs trembling as she fought to catch her breath.

He lifted his weight from her, holding himself on bent elbows as his lips again sought hers. His kiss was sweet, meant to calm. His body was slick with sweat, smooth and slippery as she ran her hands over his back, holding him to her for a few more minutes. Gradually their breathing slowed and their hearts no longer raced.

Morgan lifted his head to look down on her. His face was still flushed, his hair mussed. But a look of peace softened his features.

"Are you all right?" he asked in a low whisper and nuzzled her neck.

"Very all right," she said, smiling to herself. She was sure he could hear the smile in her voice even if he couldn't see it. Then she remembered his arm. "How about you? Is your shoulder hurting?"

"Only a little, and this is well worth a little pain. I just hope . . . you didn't hurt too much—"

She was surprised at his hesitancy, especially after all they had shared.

"It only hurt for a moment. Hardly at all."

She felt a blush rise at such intimate conversation.

She wanted to ask him a very private question herself but was unsure how to start. She chewed on her lip.

"It's probably best to just say whatever it is straight out," he told her, his tone indulgent.

She looked into his eyes and found them open and strangely vulnerable as if he had dropped all his barriers just for her. She could do no less in return. "Do you . . . I mean is it always this . . . wonderful when a man and woman . . ." Her voice petered out as she tried to decide how to best phrase her question.

"Make love?" he finished for her.

She nodded.

He stayed silent for so long that she was afraid to hear the answer. Maybe she shouldn't have asked after all. Then he squeezed her to him and kissed her forehead.

"What we shared was very special, Sarah," he said softly. "Rare and precious . . . just like you."

His last words were so faint, she wasn't sure she even heard them correctly. A wave of languorousness took over her body, making her suddenly sleepy. Though she wanted to keep her eyes open, her lids felt weighted with lead.

"I'm glad," she told him in a sleepy voice. "Very glad."

Then she drifted off to sleep in the shelter of his arms.

Chapter Nine

When Sarah woke, she found she couldn't move. Whenever she tried, an arm tightened around her. She opened her eyes to a room filled with the pale blue light of dawn. When she turned her head to the side, she found dark eyes staring at her from mere inches away.

Morgan.

Heat suffused her face as she remembered everything that had happened last night.

"I hope that isn't regret I see," he said cautiously.

"No—I mean of course not. Why would you ever think that? After all, I didn't ... couldn't ..."

"God, you're beautiful. Did you know that?"

He braced his head on one bent arm and gently pushed her hair back from her face with the other hand. She shook her head, afraid to speak after the mangled mess she'd made of her last attempt.

"Your hair is so soft," he continued as he carefully laid out the strands like a halo about her head. "And when the light hits it, it looks like fire." He ran a lock through his fingers, reverently feeling its texture before putting it in place. "And your eyes"—he brought his face close to hers—"they're the greenest I've ever seen, greener even than the water at the far end of the bayou with the sunlight filtering through. And so full of mystery, I could dive inside them and never learn all your secrets."

His words affected her like a physical caress, setting fire to places he'd made her aware of for the first time mere hours ago.

She licked her lips and he cupped her cheek, stopping her. Before she knew it, his tongue had replaced hers, stroking across her upper lip, lingering at the corner of her mouth, then making the return journey along her bottom lip. She took a shuddering breath as he raised his head and smiled at her, his gaze moving from her eyes to her lips, then down to her toes, pausing along the way at her breast and her waist . . . and the triangle at the juncture of her legs.

She felt a melting heat bubble up from her core, dampening her.

"Your body was made for mine," he said hoarsely, his voice deep and incredibly dark. "Look how it curves so naturally into mine."

He drew her closer as he spoke, tucking her along his side until she lay half on him. His hand found her breast and his fingers began to rub the nipple. It tightened into a bud at his first touch, every nerve ending quivering as he stroked her.

"Are you very sore?" he asked.

Lost in a haze of pleasure, she didn't understand his question at first. Then his hand moved down her stomach and further still. His fingers tangled in the delta of dark red hair, and she ached for him to touch her more intimately.

"I don't know," she answered in a muffled voice. Everything was so new to her. Was she supposed to feel so achy? Did men and women usually talk about such things? Would he think her brazen for wanting his touch so much?

"Let's see," he whispered, and his hand brushed lightly against her very center.

She moaned her pleasure and flexed her hips, pressing against him. He cupped her with his hand, his fingers slowly exploring, and her body remembered—remembered all the joy and pleasure his touch had given.

"No, I'm not sore, not at all," she managed to tell him. Her arms went around him, her fingers kneading the muscles of his good shoulder as she pulled him to her.

He kissed her hotly and she responded with everything inside her.

"What kind of monster have I created?" he asked with a soft chuckle.

"The kind who likes your touch."

He smiled and moved his hand. "Do you like it here?"

She moaned her yes.

Again he parted her and touched her ever so lightly. "And here?"

She twisted her legs around his hand trying to pull him closer.

"Then I think I know exactly what you want."

His body moved over hers and he proceeded to show her just how right he was.

The second time Sarah woke she was alone in the bed, the covers twisted so that she lay half naked in the bright sunlight filling the cabin. For a moment she didn't move, memories of all she and Morgan had shared the night before flooding through her. She smiled. Who would have thought it could be so wonderful, so exciting, so addicting? As she lay there remembering, her body began to ache for release. And all she'd done was think of him!

"Well, lazybones, are you going to stay in bed all morning?"

His voice came from the corner by the fireplace. Sarah hastily pulled the quilt up.

"You needn't be so modest. What do you think I've been doing for the last half hour?"

Once again heat filled her face. "That's not a very gentlemanly thing to say."

"I think we've already established the fact that I'm not a gentleman. And after last night you can be very sure of it. But I will consider your modesty and take a stroll out on the dock while you dress. I've brought in a bucket of water for your use." He pointed to a spot on the floor near the fireplace. "Etienne left us a towel and soap which I've laid by the bucket. Call me when you're done."

"Thank you," she managed to get out before the door closed behind him. She heard his footsteps ring hollowly on the wooden planking.

Pulling the quilt around her, she struggled to a sitting position. First she'd bathe and dress as quickly as she could before Morgan took it into his mind to come strolling back in here. Then she'd set about fixing something for breakfast.

She'd barely finished buttoning her shirtwaist when he opened the door and walked in.

With a startled yelp, she turned to face him. "You could have knocked. I might not have been dressed."

"I thought we'd already established my credentials. Besides, I've been keeping an eye on you through the window."

She was about to give vent to a regular fit when she realized he was teasing her. She could see the mischief in his black eyes.

"You're a devil, all right," she said with a resigned laugh. "What would you like for breakfast?"

"Anything will be fine," he said, crossing the room. "But first I need this . . ."

He took her in his arms and gave her a very satisfactory kiss. She hadn't realized until that moment how much she needed the reassurance of his touch, the knowledge that he didn't regret the night before or think less of her for it.

She flung her arms about him as the kiss deepened, reminding her of passion awakened, desire fulfilled. Then slowly he eased back, gentling the kiss until it spoke of friendship and a quieter joy, a banking of passion to another time.

"Now, where were we?" he asked, standing with his arms wrapped around her waist.

"Breakfast," she reminded him, struggling to remember herself.

"Right. Do you have enough wood for the fire?"

"I don't know. I haven't had a chance to check."

"I'll go look," he said, setting her free.

She noticed that he rubbed his injured shoulder as he walked toward the fireplace.

"Does your arm hurt? You, uh, used it quite a lot yesterday." She couldn't quite bring herself to say last night.

"It's fine."

"I think I'd better take a look at it. Besides, it should be rebandaged. Here sit on this chair." She pointed to the chair by the window where there was a lot of natural light. The look she gave him brooked no argument.

Gathering up a basin of water and a flannel rag, she removed his bandage and inspected the wound. While it didn't look any worse than before, it also didn't look a lot better. "I think you might have reopened it a bit."

"It's nothing major, and well worth it as I told you last night."

He ran his hand along her back and down to her behind, gently stroking her. Desire threatened to bloom again inside her.

She shifted just out of reach. "I think we'd better talk about something else while I do this."

"I like this particular conversation, but if you prefer, pick another topic."

"Why don't you tell me about Etienne?" The words burst from her. Until then she hadn't realized herself that Nettie's words still lingered in her mind.

"What do you want to know?" Morgan asked, folding his hands on his lap. She seemed to have found the perfect topic to squelch his desire.

"I don't know. What would you like to tell me?"

"Are you talking now about the maid's accusation when we left Geneviève's house?"

Her hands stilled as she sensed dangerous ground. But she'd given herself to him fully without knowing the answers to her questions. Surely he couldn't begrudge her the truth. She couldn't believe Nettie was right—but she wanted to hear it from him.

"I guess I am."

Silence filled the air. She waited for him to begin, and at first she didn't think he was going to. Then he started to speak.

"About five years ago Etienne came to me and asked for my help. He'd gotten my name from an associate and came to see what I knew about a problem his family was having.

"He said his niece Lynette had disappeared. She'd gone to live in New Orleans with a woman named Odette Lamonte, but when Etienne's brother, Guy, had tried to find his daughter, Odette said she didn't know what he was talking about. Etienne and his brother didn't know where to turn. You've met Etienne. You know he doesn't have much, but he is a good man, willing to share what he has."

Sarah nodded, not wanting to say anything and break the spell.

"Odette had promised to help establish Lynette in the city, for a fee. Etienne and his brother scraped together the money, but it didn't last long. Then Odette told Lynette she'd become very fond of her and would care for her herself if she cut off contact with her bayou family.

"Lynette was just a child, barely fifteen, but very beautiful. Guy and his wife had great hopes that she would escape the poverty of their lives with Mrs. Lamonte's help. They couldn't believe their daughter would be so completely torn from their lives. When they didn't hear from her, Guy became anxious and came looking for her. No one seemed to know of the girl; not one of the neighbors admitted to having seen her."

"What did he do?" Sarah asked as Morgan paused again. She dipped the flannel into the bowl of water and gently washed around the wound.

"He came with Etienne to the city and tried to find her, but they didn't know where to start." He laughed harshly. "Men such as Etienne and Guy couldn't begin to suspect the depravity others fall to. It never even crossed their minds."

From the anguish in his tone, she knew this story wasn't easy for him to tell.

"But you helped them?" she prompted.

"Oh, yes. I knew just where to look After all, that's how I make my living consorting with the lowest of the low to get my stories."

"What did you find?"

"Things no lady should know."

His bitterness frightened Sarah, and for a moment she wondered whether she really wanted to hear the story. But she knew her curiosity would continue to nag at her if she didn't see things through. Moreover, Morgan needed to tell this story. It was festering inside him, and now that he was talking, she wouldn't have him stop.

"Ignorance never profited anyone. There are a lot of things in this world women could protect themselves from if only they knew about them."

"There are things *no one* should have to know about, but they exist anyway." His expression was weary and defeated, his eyes even darker than usual as though some inner light had been dimmed.

She wanted to put her arms around him and give him comfort, but she knew he would view it as a sign of weakness. His weakness. For all their talk about the frailty of women, Sarah knew men were no different.

They felt pain and discouragement, joy and happiness just as deeply. But at such moments, they seemed to push those emotions away, as if they were unseemly. It made her sad.

"What happened to Lynette?" she asked softly.

"You're sure you want to know?"

She nodded. She had finished washing off his wound and began tearing clean strips from an old sheet to wrap it again.

He shrugged one shoulder. "When you've heard enough just say so."

She could hardly make out his voice when he began speaking again.

"Lynette was young, only fifteen, but that didn't matter to them. In fact, it was to their advantage. You see she was highly impressionable and could be easily taught. And she was a virgin—something highly prized, but not for the right reasons.

"When Etienne came to see me, I sensed an interesting story. I had just started this job, and like many reporters I was eager to make a name for myself. I had heard rumors, of course. Who doesn't in a city like New Orleans? Anything could be had for a price. *Anything*.

"But you know, you don't really believe it, not in your heart of hearts. Still, I was curious and tenacious, and slowly the truth was revealed, layer by layer until it could no longer be denied."

Sarah folded one swatch of material into a square and laid it against his shoulder as he spoke, then started wrapping the bandages around it. He didn't look at her as he continued, his voice flat and hard.

"Odette Lamonte was no fallen aristocrat. She was the daughter of a prostitute and had plied the trade herself when she was young. But she was ambitious and wanted more for herself."

"You can hardly blame her for that," Sarah murmured, her heart going out to the woman. "Imagine what a life she'd led. It can't have been easy."

"Save your pity," Morgan said harshly, "until you hear what she did. She had a small shop in the Vieux Carré, and most of her clients were male. No one thought much about it as she sold articles primarily for men—everything from cravats to snuff boxes to fancy sleeve link buttons. But that was just for show. Oh, she made a good enough living that way, good enough that no one suspected her of anything underhanded. But the men who visited her often made more than one purchase, for you see, Odette specialized in girls—young white girls.

"And can you guess what kind of girls brought the highest price?"

Sarah swallowed dryly, almost afraid to hear what was coming next, for he had already implied as much. Girls like Lynette—young and untouched.

"That's vile," she exclaimed. "Who would do such a thing? Who would trade on another's misery, especially an innocent's?"

"Why do you think I told you to stay out of that part of town?"

He stood up impatiently and pulled away from her, pacing in the narrow confines of the room.

"Wait, just let me finish," she pleaded, and he stood still just long enough for her to tie off the bandage so it wouldn't come undone. The instant she completed the last knot, he strode to the window. She doubted he was seeing the green cypress forest or hearing the birds cheerfully calling back and forth. He was in another time and place.

"I remember her shop," he said almost to himself. "Tidy and compact with two small tables and several chairs so clients could examine the merchandise at their ease. She had two books she kept behind the counter. If you said the right words and flashed enough money or if you had the right connections, you could get to see them.

"I'd heard enough to hint strongly that I was interested in a special product. I made sure she knew I had the money to pay for it. After a couple of visits, she indicated she might be able to help me. All I had to do was come back just before the store closed.

"That night I went back as she suggested. She let me and another man in, then brought us each one of her books. They were filled with pictures, mostly of girls though there were a few boys, some dressed scantily, some not at all. And all young—some of them not even ten years old, and all on the block for the right price."

Sarah sank into the second chair and folded her arms about her waist in a protective gesture. She wanted to stop him but it was too late. Now they both needed to get to the end of the story.

"I looked through the book," Morgan continued. "I couldn't believe what I saw." He swept his hand across his forehead and down the side of his face, and Sarah knew the worst was yet to come. "The other man wasn't satisfied, complaining he'd been promised better and was willing to pay what it took.

"Odette turned to me. 'How about you?' she asked. 'You want to see my special dolls, toys so rare they only have value once and then never again?'

"I agreed, of course. Anything for the story, right?

She went to the back room and came out with a leather portfolio. It contained only a few pictures. The man and I paged through them slowly. Suddenly I recognized Lynette. She looked just like her mother, only much younger. I asked for her. Odette smiled apologetically. 'She has already been promised to another,' she said. 'Perhaps I can interest you in someone else?'

"I refused, insisting on Lynette. She told me if I had a little patience, she would be a lot less expensive in another two days.

"Two days! I was just in time, but I still had to find her. Help came from a most unexpected source. The other man was one of Odette's regulars. When she left the room to get us coffee, he told me what he knew of how she operated, selling the virgins for a premium price the first time, then selling them again and again to those who preferred them young.

"The man knew where she kept the most select of her charges, a house just two blocks away from the shop, where Odette herself lived. The house held several apartments. Etienne and I went there in the dead of night. When we burst into the apartment, Lynette was alone, dressed in a gauzy dress. She stared blankly at the wall not recognizing her uncle. She'd been drugged to keep her docile.

"We were about to leave when Odette arrived with her client, a legislator of some repute. He was incensed to see that we had gotten to Lynette first—he complained loudly that the privilege had been reserved for him, that he'd paid, and paid well."

Morgan turned away from the window and dropped into the nearby chair. He rubbed his face with both hands then stared at the floor, bracing his elbows on his knees. His hands locked together, the knuckles showing white as he leaned his forehead against them.

"Odette was furious, too, thinking I was just infatuated with Lynette because of her picture. It wasn't until she recognized Etienne that she realized she was in trouble. I could hardly keep him from killing her on the spot. Hell, I was ready to beat someone myself, but there was Lynette to consider.

"We got her out of there and reported the situation to the police. Odette disappeared. The legislator denied any complicity and the police let him go."

"Let him go? Just like that?" Sarah couldn't believe it. Her sense of outrage had been stretched to the limit. "How could that happen? How could a man be like that? So depraved?"

At that moment, Sarah felt she left the last remnants of childhood innocence and naïveté behind. The horrors of war had taught her much about the depths to which man could sink, but at least there had been a purpose there. Each side thought it was defending a way of life, whether defending its honor or trying to free the slaves. But this, this was beyond anything she'd ever imagined—the cruel use and abuse of others for fleeting pleasure, with no thought of the consequences to the victims of the abuse.

"The police had been bought off. It's not so unusual," Morgan said. "Especially nowadays."

"What happened to Lynette?"

"Etienne took her home. She recovered from the drug and, fortunately, had little memory of all that had happened to her. We were lucky we got to her before that bastard did.

"But when nothing else happened, Etienne became

angry. Lynette had suffered and no one cared. He came to me and asked that I publish the story. The paper insisted that we use their real names, but that didn't stop Etienne even though his family didn't want to face the humiliation of public exposure. They were afraid Lynette would be ostracized, but he finally convinced them that they needed the story told so that others wouldn't be fooled in the same way. They agreed and I wrote the story."

He shook his head over the memories. "I can remember how important I felt, taking on a legislator. I was filled with moral outrage, and it poured into every word I wrote. But the legislator was well connected. He put the word out that I was an opportunist, making use of the ugliness to make my name and trying to dirty him, too, because of our political differences.

"Some of the mud stuck to him, some to me. Who knows what Nettie or her friend have heard. All I know is that Lynette made a narrow escape.

"The only good part is that several other families thanked Lynette's for speaking out. They said it saved their daughters from the same fate."

"I'm glad you got to her in time," Sarah said, and then shivered. These kinds of things happened all the time, and she wasn't even aware of it. Why had she always been so protected? Why had it taken her brother's death before she could be enlightened? Look what ignorance had done to Lynette's family. "Thank goodness her family had the courage to let the world know what's out there. No wonder Etienne is such a good friend. His whole family must be grateful to you."

Morgan frowned. "They shouldn't be. I only got involved for the story. And it worked. Despite the slurs on my character, my editor knew the truth. He's let me follow my instincts since. That story did exactly what I'd hoped for my career."

His self-deprecating response was not what Sarah had expected. She could see it disturbed him to have gained from another's misfortune.

She got up and crossed to his side, then laid her hand on his good shoulder. "Just because you benefited doesn't mean you didn't do the right thing. From what you say, neither Guy nor Etienne could have found Lynette on their own, certainly not in time. And the police were not interested in helping—I can understand that. Look at how they have treated me and Adam."

He stood abruptly, shaking off her touch. "And here I am again. There's a story here, too, you know," he said gruffly.

"Yes, I've known that from the start." She came up behind him and put her arms around his waist, resting her head against his back. "I came to you, remember? I knew what I was getting into, and so did Etienne. We're both grateful for your help and understand your professional requirements. There's no need to apologize or feel guilty, Morgan."

He stiffened. "I never said I felt guilty."

"Not in so many words. You're an honorable man, Morgan Cain. I'm sure you did everything you could to save Lynette, and you succeeded. I hope you'll be as successful in helping me find Adam's murderer."

"You know this may be a wild-goose chase. I never did get that legislator punished."

"You tried. That's what counts. Is he still in office?"

"Who? Palmer? He's still in politics. Fancies himself a

king-maker. Works behind the scenes to help people get elected."

"Maybe you'll be able to get him on something else."

"You have great faith in me, little one," Morgan said and placed his hands over hers, holding her tight. "I am not the noble knight you're making me out to be."

"Maybe not. But you're the closest I have."

"Then I'll have to do my best to live up to your needs."

"Well, there is one need you could live up to right now, I'm sure," she said and gently nipped his back.

"Ouch! What was that for?" he asked as he spun in her arms until they stood hip to hip, facing each other. He dropped his arms to her waist, holding her as she held him.

"That's better," she said. "Much more promising."

"Promising, huh? How about this?"

He lowered his mouth to hers and kissed her with a soul-deep desperation she felt down to her toes.

She matched his ardor, knowing the morning had taken something out of him and wanting to replace it with something of her own, something to heal his hurts.

And then she stopped thinking as he swept her into his arms, heedless of his injury, and carried her back to the bed where he gently laid her down. Laughing, she reached up and pulled him on top of her.

"Now that's what I call promising," she whispered, as she felt his hard length against her, and then there were no more words.

Chapter Ten

Today would be their last day in the bayou. Sarah tried not to think about it. Looking back, it seemed the past two weeks had sped by in an instant, yet it was as if a lifetime had gone by since she'd left New Orleans. And in a way it had.

So much had changed—the way she looked at herself, the way she looked at Morgan, the way she looked at the world. Some of the changes were joyous and fulfilling, others grim and frightening, but from all of them she'd learned and matured. She felt she truly was a woman now, not just because of her sexual experience, but also because she'd shed the blinders of childhood and learned to see the world through different eyes—Morgan's eyes, she was the first to admit.

He'd taught her more about her body than she'd thought there was to know and awakened emotions more profound than she'd ever dreamed of. They'd made love often, in the morning and at night, even in the middle of day. Sarah would have been scandalized if she hadn't been swept into the sensual spell Morgan created every time he touched her.

More importantly, he'd shared their sensual voyage, letting her know in thousands of tiny ways that he was as moved as she was, that he too was making discoveries about himself. He made her feel feminine and powerful, greedy and satiated, loved and loving. He also kept her aware of the dangerous side of life, of the troubles awaiting them when they returned to New Orleans, as they would tomorrow.

But she still had today. If anyone had told her two weeks ago that she'd feel comfortable riding in a small boat in the middle of a steaming bayou, she would have laughed and called them crazy, but here she was. Once again she sat in the front of a small pirogue, but today only Morgan sat behind her guiding the boat. They were heading for Etienne's house to make the final arrangements for getting home.

Tonight would be their last together here in the bayou, and though she was pleased to be meeting Octavie and Etienne's children, what she really wanted was to spend time alone with Morgan. Once they were back in New Orleans, she had no idea what would happen—at any level. Their investigation had been halted just as they had started making progress, or at least Morgan assumed that. Why else would someone have tried to stop him?

More frightening to Sarah was the thought that what they'd shared was an interlude outside of their normal lives. Would the special closeness she and Morgan experienced survive being transplanted back to the city? And what would happen when they finally found Adam's murderer? Where would that leave them?

Sarah shivered despite the heat and looked over her shoulder. Morgan smiled back, his teeth gleaming whitely against the dark beard that gave a dangerously exciting edge to his already masculine looks. She liked the way it felt against her skin and on every part of her body.

"Watch yourself, the bayou narrows up here and the moss hangs right over into the boat. If you're not careful, it'll hit you in the face," Morgan called out.

He must have noticed she wasn't paying attention to where they were going. No doubt her dreamy expression gave her away. She'd better keep her mind on the business at hand.

"Where did all this moss come from anyway? I don't think I've ever seen so much," she said grabbing some from overhead and then twirling it between her fingers.

"Here in the bayou there's certainly an abundance. In the old days it was known by other names. The Spanish called it *Frenchman's wig*, while the French called it *Spaniard's beard*. But there's an old legend I like better."

Sarah half-turned in her seat. "How does it go?"

Morgan stopped paddling and placed the paddle crossways in front of him, leaning it on the two sides of the boat. The craft rocked gently on the shifting water, tiny waves lapping against its side. Insects hummed around them and an occasional frog croaked.

"Long ago an Indian mother and her two children were caught out in the bayou when a terrible storm suddenly blew up. The storm was followed by a terrible chilling cold. Taking refuge in a large tree the mother begged the moon to shine on them, for without its warmth they might die. In the morning when they awakened, the sky had cleared and all trees were covered in moss which hung down around them, giving warmth to the marooned group. The small son cried out, 'Mother, the moon heard us; she tore up the storm clouds and threw them down upon us. Look, there are none left in the sky!' And that's how we ended up with so much moss."

"That's a lovely story."

"Yes, it's much better than the one about the dead Indian princess whose hair turned gray and became the moss."

Sarah shivered. "Decidedly," she agreed. "I'm glad I got the Indian children legend instead."

They laughed as Morgan resumed his paddling, happy just to be together. Morgan pointed out various sights along the way, an egret fishing for his lunch, a particularly handsome old cypress, a large crayfish crawling over some rocks by the shore.

Before long they turned off the main canal and up a side inlet that formed a small bay. Morgan called out as they approached another long dock much like the one at their cabin.

When there was no response, Morgan shouted again. This time four little girls, ranging in age from about three to nine, came running out of the large house that was set back some distance from the water. The house stood in a large sunny clearing. It was much bigger than the shack Morgan and Sarah shared in the bayou.

Before Sarah had a chance to really look at the place, the four girls reached the dock.

"Come quick, come quick," one of the middle girls called out. "Papa says Maman is having our new baby."

The oldest one nodded, her head bobbing up and down with excitement as she added, "Papa, he is very worried. He can't come to see you. You have to come in."

Morgan grabbed hold of the dock and pulled the boat close to its edge.

"Can you climb out?" he asked Sarah.

Sarah had her doubts what with the full skirt she was wearing, but she was willing to give it a try. Bracing herself on one of the dock's supports, she slowly stood. The boat rocked under her and drifted out from the dock. Morgan pulled it back in and reached out a hand to help her.

Sarah bit her lip. Landing in the bayou loomed as a large possibility if she tried to clamber onto the dock. She realized she would never make it if she simply tried to step out of the boat. For one thing, the dock was too high to easily climb onto. Seeing no other alternative, she turned cautiously so her back was to the dock, then plopped her bottom down on its surface and lifted her feet from the boat which swung crazily out. It wasn't the most graceful way to disembark, but at least she was still dry.

Morgan smiled and then hopped out and helped her to her feet while the oldest girl secured the pirogue with a rope.

"I'll show you where they are," the middle girl said.

"Thank you, Gabrielle," Morgan replied as the little girl grabbed his hand. He reached out for Sarah's with the other and the six of them ran for the house. As they approached, Sarah could see that the house had been added to over the years, each time with a different material. Part was made of stone, another part light-colored wood, another dark and weathered. But for all the differences it had a stately grandeur. There was a garden on the far side and the house was accessible by both water and road.

The interior of the house seemed dark after the blinding brightness of the noonday sun. Sarah found she was having trouble seeing much at all. A sudden scream pierced the air, and she and Morgan looked at each other, then down at the children.

"Why don't you girls stay down here while Sarah and I find your papa," Morgan suggested.

The girls looked frightened and clung to the oldest who bravely said, "That's what Papa wants us to do. He said to wait in the kitchen."

"Good idea. We'll come down and check on you as soon as we know what's happening."

The girls ran down the hall toward the back of the house, and Morgan glanced toward the stairs. "This sounds like the wrong time to be visiting."

"Not if Etienne needs our help," Sarah replied.

"You don't mind?"

Before she could answer, Octavie was screaming again and Etienne's voice had a desperate note to it as he tried to soothe his wife.

"We'd better go up," Sarah said.

They followed the sound up a flight of steps to a room off to the left.

Morgan stood at the open bedroom door and knocked on its frame. "Etienne, what can we do to help?"

"I am not sure," the man confessed. He was sitting on the edge of the bed, his wife's hands clasping his tightly. Though his voice was calm, his expression revealed just how fearful he was. "Octavie says never has the pain been this bad. Not for any of the others."

"There is no one else who can help? A midwife, perhaps?"

"The baby is early. Tante Philomine usually comes when there is a problem, but she has gone to visit her daughter in Baton Rouge for the month. There is no other woman nearby."

He looked past Morgan to Sarah, hope written clearly in his eyes. Morgan also turned to gaze at her. She looked back at him, a blank expression on her face. What did she know about having babies? All her medical experience had centered around the hospital during the war. And soldiers didn't give birth. She wanted to tell them that, but when she looked at their faces she realized they were turning to her for guidance. Since she was the only other woman in the room, they expected her to be able to do something as if it were inbred or something.

She edged into the large room. The bed stood in one corner, a beautiful quilt draped over the footboard. Several bureaus were placed along the walls and a chifforobe graced one corner. Pictures of various saints hung on the walls around the room, and a large crucifix held the place of honor over the bed.

Sarah took a deep breath and crossed to the opposite side of the mattress from Etienne. She looked down at the woman lying in the bed and smiled.

"I am sorry," Octavie murmured. Sweat beaded her forehead and her clothes were twisted around her. Two pillows were stacked beneath her head, their covers soaked.

"There's no need to be sorry," Sarah replied soothingly.

"I wanted your visit . . . to be nice," the woman said with a groan that ended in a small scream as another contraction shook her.

When the contraction ended, Octavie lay still, catching her breath, her eyes closed.

Sarah waited a few seconds, then asked, "Why don't you tell me how you're feeling?" Not that she'd be able to deduce much from what she heard.

"Like something is not right."

Sarah nodded as though the words had meaning for her and picked up the woman's hand. It felt a little clammy, but her pulse seemed steady. Sarah laid Octavie's hand back down on the coverlet. "How is this different from your last birth?"

That sounded like a fairly intelligent question, Sarah thought. Octavie had considerable experience at childbirth while Sarah had none. She'd heard women talk about the births of their babies, usually with one or two tales of horror thrown in for good measure. Other than that she had no practical experience. Her best bet was to get the older woman to tell her everything she could.

"I'm not sure I can explain it."

"Try!" As soon as the word was out of her mouth Sarah realized how desperate it sounded. "It would be a help," she finished in a calmer tone. If Octavie could put what she was feeling in terms that Sarah was able to understand, they might be able to come up with a workable plan.

"With my other babies everything was easy. Some pain, yes, but then they come. But this one is not coming. The pushing is not right."

"How far is the nearest doctor?" Sarah asked Etienne.

"Many miles," he replied.

Sarah already knew the midwife was unavailable, but she would give anything to have another woman around, preferably someone who knew about birthing. "Aren't there any other women nearby?"

"Miss Etta lives about five miles due east."

"How long will it take you to bring her?"

"Maybe two hours."

Two hours. It seemed like an eternity under the circumstances, but if that was the best they could do, then she would have to live with it.

"Can we get her here? Maybe you can go, Morgan, and—"

Etienne shook his head. "He would never find her. The directions are too complicated. I'll have to go."

His reluctance to leave his wife was evident, but Sarah could see no other way around it. And if Miss Etta knew anything at all, she'd be miles ahead of Sarah.

"Why don't you head out as soon as we get situated here. We need to change the bedding and get Octavie into something loose and dry."

Etienne nodded and gave his wife an encouraging smile. "You are in good hands, *non?*"

Octavie managed a weak smile. "You will not be long?"

"*Non*, I will hurry."

He stood to go, then bent to place a kiss on his wife's forehead.

"What about the girls?" Octavie asked him.

"They are downstairs," Sarah answered for him. "We told them to wait in the kitchen. If you like, I can check on them before Etienne leaves."

"Would you, please?"

Sarah nodded and quickly left the room. She heard Octavie groan behind her and knew she was having another contraction. How had she gotten into this, Sarah wondered, a sense of panic building inside her. She reached the kitchen and found the four girls sitting together in a large chair, their arms around each other, their faces pale and frightened.

Sarah smiled to reassure the girls. She was determined not to show exactly how scared she was even though she was quaking inside.

"I'm going to need help from all of you. Can you do that?" she asked.

"I'll help," the oldest girl said and extricated herself from the jumble of her sisters to stand in front of the chair.

The others followed her example, a chorus of "Me, too's" filling the air.

"I knew I could count on you," she said approvingly. "First let's all introduce ourselves, and then I'll assign jobs. How will that be?"

The girls nodded and told her their names. The oldest was Juliette, then came Gabrielle, Josephine, and Lisette. The baby, Imogene, was sleeping in the other room.

"And I'm Sarah. It's nice to finally meet you. Now, why don't we decide what needs to be done."

She wasn't really sure what she'd need, but boiling water would keep them busy for a while as would preparing for the new arrival.

"I'll need hot and cold water and perhaps some clean sheets and blankets," she said. "And a place for the new baby. Then we'll need food for everyone. Can you manage that?"

Juliette stepped forward proudly. "Maman taught me to cook. I can do everything."

"We can help," the three younger girls chorused, crowding around their sister.

"Good, but be very careful. When the water is ready, you come get me or Morgan to help you, you hear?"

They nodded solemnly, and Sarah breathed a sigh of relief. Children could be so unpredictable at times of crisis. So far, it looked as if everything was working out.

"Etienne is ready to go," Morgan said, walking into the kitchen just then. "Is everything set here?"

Sarah nodded and told him what they'd arranged.

"Good. I'll help the girls if you want to go back up to Octavie."

"All right," Sarah said, though her heart raced at the thought of the responsibility she was accepting. What if something went wrong? What if she lost the baby . . . or worse, Octavie? She swallowed and forced herself to hurry up the stairs.

Etienne left quickly once Sarah arrived, pausing only long enough to give his wife one last kiss and squeeze her hand.

Sarah had barely settled herself in the chair by Octavie's side when the woman moaned.

"The pain is starting again," she cried, and Sarah turned to help, letting Octavie grab onto her hands until the pain passed. She'd have to do more than this, but she was at a loss as to what it would be.

"I don't know what is happening," Octavie said tearfully. "Can you check that all is well?"

"O-of course," Sarah replied, her heart in her throat. She wished now that she'd paid more attention when the married women talked about their experiences. Somehow she'd always thought there would be plenty of time for such concerns after she was married. It looked like she'd just run out of time.

She turned the covers back from the foot of the bed, and Octavie pulled the white nightdress she was wearing up over her stomach.

The baby might be early, but Octavie's belly looked enormous as she lay prone on the bed. Sarah tried to remember everything she'd ever been told about giving birth. The few things she'd gleaned she now did; checking Octavie's stomach and then the birth canal. This was not the time for modesty on either of their parts and they both realized it.

"Everything looks as it should," Sarah said, though what it should look like she wasn't exactly sure. "We'll wait for the next pain and then see." She pulled the coverlet back up just as the door opened.

Juliette peered in. In her hands she held a small cradle.

"My father made it," she said with pride. "For me when I was born."

"And each of my other babies were placed in it as soon as they arrived," Octavie said, with a catch in her voice.

"As this one will be," Sarah replied with assurance. "Please, Juliette, bring it in."

The young girl smiled, then glanced worriedly toward the bed as she placed the cradle in a corner.

"Will you be all right, Maman?" she asked, her dark eyes wide.

"Do not worry, *ma petite.*" Octavie pasted a smile on her face to ease her daughter's fears. "I'll be fine, but I need your help. Would you make sure Imogene is still sleeping and if not keep her busy? Would you do that for me?"

"You know I will, but couldn't I stay here with you? I'm sure I could be of help here. Gabrielle and the others can watch the baby."

"Thank you for wanting to stay. I'd love to have you, but I'll feel better knowing you're watching Imogene. You have such a way with her. You know she likes it better when you play with her than anyone else."

Sarah smiled inwardly. Octavie knew just how to handle her daughter, keeping her occupied with a special job so she'd spend less time worrying and fretting over what was happening.

Juliette nodded her head reluctantly, then kissed her mother on the cheek. She had just reached the door when Octavie said, "And one more thing—keep your father busy when he returns. You know what a worrier he is."

She and her daughter shared a secret smile, and then Juliette hurried to do her mother's bidding.

"She is a good girl, that one," Octavie said. Then another contraction began. "My God, will it never end?" she cried out.

Sarah thought the bones in her hands would break the way Octavie gripped them. When Octavie loosened her hold, Sarah wiped the perspiration from her face with a damp rag.

"I understand Etienne would like a boy this time," she said to distract Octavie.

"Etienne wanted a boy every time before the baby was born. Then, when he sees he has another girl, he smiles like he has just received the best present on earth," Octavie said in an indulgent tone.

"I've found that most men don't know what they want until they have it," Sarah said.

"What's this I hear? Are you women defaming us menfolk?" Morgan said as he pushed open the door with his shoulder, his arms filled with clean blankets and sheets.

The women laughed at his outraged expression.

"No, we were just telling the truth," Sarah countered. "Isn't that right, Octavie?" She glanced down at the dark-haired woman and winked.

"Most certainly. You should listen to her, Morgan."

"You say that because you women are plotting a conspiracy. Even when Etienne gets back we'll still be outnumbered." He put the bedclothes down on one of the bureaus and came to stand by the bed. "I think you'd better have a boy this time," he said to Octavie with a teasing smile. "We need to start evening the sides here."

"Octavie will have whatever she wants, isn't that so?" Sarah replied, looking back to Octavie. But Octavie didn't hear her, another pain was coming.

"I'm sorry."

Sarah brushed aside her apology. "Here grip my hands."

Octavie took her at her word, and Sarah felt her fingers crushed once again as Octavie tried to hold on through the pain. Instead of focusing on Octavie's pain this time, Sarah focused her attention on how long it lasted.

"The last two contractions have lasted longer," she said.

"That's good, isn't it?" Morgan asked.

"I think so," Sarah replied, sitting down in the chair beside the bed. She rubbed her hands together, massaging her painful fingers. She didn't want to complain about them, not when Octavie was in such dire straits, but she wasn't sure she could last the entire labor helping Octavie through her pain like this.

Morgan squatted beside her and took her hands in his, running his thumbs gently over the tops. His strength was comforting, letting her know she was not alone. Not many men would willingly help out at a birthing, especially if neither the child nor the woman was theirs.

He raised her hands to his lips, kissing the back of the left and then of the right. His lips felt warm and supple; his beard soft and silky as it brushed against her skin.

"You're doing fine," he whispered for her ears only. Did he sense her fear and uncertainty, she wondered. No matter, she was grateful for his silent support. "Now, let's see what we can do about making Octavie more comfortable."

He stood and collected a couple of clean sheets. Deftly he rolled Octavie to one side and pulled the old sheet off the bed. With Sarah's help, he put the new one in place, then went to the other side of the bed and repeated the process until the clean sheet lay neatly beneath her.

"Let me cover the pillows," he said, helping Octavie to lift her head. "Now, where do you keep your night dresses?"

"Surely you don't intend to change that, too?" Octavie asked with mock horror.

Morgan laughed. "Not if I want Etienne to let me live to see another day. Sarah can help you there."

Octavie smiled at him.

He seemed to have a way with women, Sarah reflected, noticing how easily he had charmed the four girls in the kitchen earlier and now claimed their mother.

Octavie's smile slipped as another contraction came, and she reached blindly for a hand, grabbing Morgan's instead of Sarah's. He helped her ride out the pain, then when she let go, he turned to Sarah.

"You can't do this until the baby is born," he said, rubbing his own hands together.

"I have to," she replied.

"No you don't. Give me a second."

He went to the pile of sheets and selected a small one, most likely from the baby's bed. Like the others it was threadbare but clean. He stretched it out by diagonal corners, then tied two large knots at either end.

"Here, Octavie, pull on this when you feel the pain," he said and placed one knot under each of her hands.

"Thank you, I did not mean—"

"I know. When the pain is great, one does as one must." He smiled encouragingly at her.

"You are a good man, Morgan," she said. "Even if you do not know it yet."

The cryptic remark puzzled Sarah, and she looked at the other woman questioningly. But Octavie was already anticipating the next pain and had turned inward.

"I'd best go help the children," Morgan said. "Call me if you need help."

Sarah nodded, her attention on the struggling Octavie.

"Will the baby be here soon?" the woman asked when she was able.

Sarah set about checking her again. She wasn't sure

if things were different or the same. She was in over her head and she knew it.

"It won't be much longer," she said, knowing that Octavie needed to hear the words to keep her spirits up.

"I hope you are right," Octavie said. "That Morgan, he is a good man, you know."

"Even with a nickname like Le Sabre?"

"That is the world's impression of him, not those who know him. He's a man you could trust with your life, if you were so inclined." Octavie looked at her with a speculative eye.

Sarah looked away, not yet ready to share her innermost hopes and feelings. "He wouldn't be easy to handle."

"No good man ever is, but if you learn the right way, it can be worth every minute."

Sarah already knew that. The question was not so much her own feelings as Morgan's. Despite their wide-ranging conversations, there were subjects they never touched on—they spoke little of the past and less of the future outside of their plans for tracking down Adam's murderer.

"Speaking of handling, you managed Juliette very well," Sarah said, wanting to change the subject.

"After the second or third one you finally learn," Octavie replied with just a trace of pride, easily distracted when the subject of her children came up. Then she grimaced as she shifted in bed. "My back is really starting to hurt."

"Why don't you roll over on your side and I'll rub it? That might help."

"I couldn't ask you to do that," Octavie exclaimed. "Guests shouldn't—"

"But you *would* ask me to deliver your baby?" Sarah interrupted and laughed gently. "Come now, roll over and let's see if rubbing helps."

With reluctance and some difficulty Octavie rolled a quarter turn away from Sarah. When Sarah asked, she pointed out where the pain was centered. The rubbing helped, but only to a point. The contractions still came and went with no discernible pattern, some close together, others far apart, some strong and others weak. Sarah felt sure this was not normal, but she didn't know what to do to help things along other than to try and make Octavie feel better.

She was still rubbing Octavie's back when Morgan came back into the room. He was carrying a bucket of clean, warm water. Sarah asked him to place it by bed and then hand her a few flannel cloths.

Dipping the cloths into the water, she gently wiped her patient's brow. As she repeated this action, Octavie finally fell into a light sleep.

"What do you think?" Morgan asked in a soft voice.

"I wish I knew," she answered, then motioned for him to move away from the bed so that Octavie could get the sleep she so desperately needed. "This isn't something I'm at all familiar with. I wish Geneviève were here. She's the one everyone always turns to in an emergency. She even delivered a baby right after the war ended. She has experience in this type of situation."

"You'll do a wonderful job," he said with unquestioning conviction.

Sarah just wished she believed it herself. "I hope you're right. I'm not even sure what any of the symptoms mean. Any suggestions?"

She looked over at him expectantly.

"How many babies do you think *I've* delivered?"

"But you said you were brought up on a farm. Being a boy and all, weren't you out in the barn when the cows or pigs gave birth?"

"Yeah, but they pretty much took care of themselves . . ." His voice trailed off as if he'd just thought of something. "There was one time, but . . ."

"I'm desperate here," she coaxed softly so Octavie would not hear. "Anything you can tell me will help."

"Once one of our mares was in trouble. The symptoms were a lot like Octavie's. We called our neighbor over. He'd had some training with animals."

"What happened?"

"He said it looked like the foal hadn't turned. And then he—" Morgan stopped speaking.

"He what?"

"This part is sort of—"

She interrupted him, her voice even softer than before. "Nothing you can possibly say can be more personal than what we've shared this past week. Agreed?"

He looked at her and cupped her face.

"You're right. I guess my mother's preaching on what is and isn't proper conversation with a lady keeps popping up." He cleared his throat. "Anyway, he said he had to turn the foal. It was coming back end first, and if we couldn't get it turned, we'd probably lose both the mare and the foal. Then he stuck his arm inside the mare and started manipulating the foal."

Sarah blanched. Even for a horse, it sounded rather brutal. She looked over her shoulder at Octavie. "Do you think that's what might be wrong here?"

"I don't know. It's the only explanation I can come up with, but . . ." He shrugged.

Sarah thought for a moment. "All the stories I've heard said the head always comes out first with babies. I suppose I'm going to have to do what your family friend did if your guess is right." Sarah looked down at the napping woman and unconsciously straightened her back. "I'll wait until the next pain passes and then check."

She turned her gaze back to Morgan. "Promise me if Etienne doesn't get Miss Etta in time you'll stay and help," she said in an urgent whisper.

He nodded, not hesitating an instant. She felt a sense of relief flow through her. With Morgan by her side the problems ahead seemed much less daunting.

"Thank you," she murmured.

At her words, he reached over and clasped her hand in his. She looked down at their entwined fingers, his so dark and strong, hers white and slender. They looked so right together. United they could conquer anything, she thought.

His words mimicked her thoughts. "We can do this. Besides, Octavie's much more relaxed now that you're here. Sometimes just knowing there's someone close by who seems knowledgeable helps the most."

"I hope you're right."

Octavie began to moan and their conversation ended. Reluctantly, Sarah let go of Morgan's hand.

"I'll wait outside until you're done," he murmured.

Sarah nodded and headed back to the bedside.

After the pain had passed, Sarah checked the woman once again. Her heart caught in her throat. Not wanting to scare Octavie, she mumbled a few reassuring words. The instant Octavie closed her eyes, Sarah darted to the door and motioned Morgan back in.

"You were right. The feet are facing down. At least, I think that's what I felt. Oh, God, what should we do?"

The panic she'd been keeping at bay threatened to overwhelm her.

"We'll handle whatever happens," Morgan said. His hands framed her face. "Believe me," he added and leaned over to press his lips to hers. Just when their kiss would have deepened into more, a trio of giggles pulled them back to reality.

The door opened wider, and the three younger girls edged in. "We wanted to see Maman. Is that all right?"

"I'm sure she'd love to see you, but you mustn't tire her," Sarah told them trying to act as if they hadn't caught her kissing. She looked over and saw Octavie was awake and motioned for the girls to go on over.

As the girls trotted over to the bed, Sarah turned back to Morgan, "They'll take her mind off her worries for a few minutes as long as we don't let them tire her."

Sarah listened to the girls excited chatter as they talked about the new baby and the names they had picked out. When Octavie motioned that the pains were starting again, Morgan herded the girls out of the room and Sarah moved back to her side.

She placed her hands on Octavie's stomach, hoping she'd feel some change, some difference, and though she did feel movement she could read nothing from it.

The next half hour passed with Sarah sponging off Octavie's face and arms, and Morgan taking the cooling pan of water back to the kitchen and replacing it with hot. Of Etienne and Miss Etta there was no sign.

Sarah was just about to take a break with a walk out in the front yard, when Octavie screamed out.

"The baby is moving. Here, feel it." Octavie's breaths

came in pants as she took Sarah's hand and placed it on her stomach.

Her belly pitched and rolled, but whether that was a good sign or a not, Sarah had no idea. When the pain ended, Sarah decided to check the birth canal in the hopes that there would be a change.

"Octavie, it's happened. I see the head," Sarah called out in an excited voice. She said a silent prayer hoping everything would now proceed quickly and naturally.

Morgan reentered the room carrying a bucket of clean water. Sarah gave him the good news while he filled the pitcher on the dry sink. He smiled and leaned over to give her a kiss.

"I knew you could handle this," he said as his lips left hers.

"Let's wait until we have a baby before congratulations are handed out," she said, afraid to assume too much too soon.

Sarah had no sooner sat down in her chair again than the next pain started.

"The pains are coming closer now. That means the baby will be here soon," Octavie said, grimacing. "Already I need to push."

Now that things were back on track, Octavie seemed to know exactly what to do which proved a relief to Sarah. Morgan came over and held Octavie's hand while Sarah followed Octavie's directions and made preparations for the birth.

When the next pain started, Octavie told Sarah to move down and be ready when the baby came. Sarah did as she was told and soon the baby's head and shoulders appeared. She took a damp cloth and cleared the baby's nose and face and then as the next pain started

Octavie pushed the baby out into Sarah's waiting arms. She looked up into Morgan's eyes and saw such a depth of emotion that she had to look away or be overcome herself.

With a loud cry Etienne and Octavie's first son made his presence known to the world.

Sarah sat on the front porch of the dilapidated cabin she'd called home these past two weeks and looked out at the bayou. She watched the moon slowly rise, its reflection gliding across the water's surface like a silver ribbon. The night noises had become so familiar she almost didn't hear them anymore. They were just part of the whole atmosphere that made these past two weeks so special.

The day's events still whirled in her mind, as if by reliving her experiences she could gain control over what had happened. She laughed at herself. What had started out as a social call to thank Etienne for his hospitality had turned into a drama she had no wish to repeat. It felt good to just sit and do nothing, though tomorrow would be a different matter.

But she wouldn't worry about that tonight. Tonight was her last night alone with Morgan and she wanted it to be special—one last night stolen from the fabric of her normal life to pretend everything would work out perfectly.

She sighed. She had no more control over her own life than she'd had this afternoon with Octavie's and her son's. Whether she wanted it or not, time marched relentlessly onward sweeping her with it to God only knew what fate. Would they find Adam's murderer? And if they did, what would happen then?

She shook her head hoping to shake off her thoughts as well. Tomorrow was soon enough to start worrying again.

"What are you thinking about?" Morgan asked as he came up behind her, his hands going to her shoulders and rubbing them lightly.

"You're very good at sneaking up on people, aren't you?" she said with a smile and bent her head back, relaxing into his touch. She wanted to purr like a kitten with a bowl of cream—he had magic hands. "I was just thinking what a full day we had."

"A slight understatement, my dear. You were the heroine of the hour."

"It's a good thing they didn't know what a total coward their heroine was," Sarah said with a rueful laugh, letting her head flop forward and turning her neck as he rubbed. She'd felt like such a fraud when they were all thanking her for everything she'd done.

"What are you talking about?" Morgan gave her shoulders a shake, then squatted in front of her. "The only difference between a hero and a coward is that the hero keeps going even though inside everything is screaming at him to stop. And that's exactly what you did. You kept going even though you didn't know what was coming around the next bend."

She looked down into his dark eyes. "With your help. If you hadn't been there, I'm sure I would have been out and running."

"Not you. Never you," he repeated earnestly. "And now Etienne and Octavie have their little boy."

"And they named him Adam." Tears pooled in her

eyes and fell over onto her cheeks before she could wipe them away.

Morgan reached up and gently brushed her cheeks with his thumbs. Then, holding her face still, he pressed his lips to hers in a short, chaste kiss made all the sweeter for his restraint. Sarah took a hiccuping breath and smiled through her tears. Morgan lifted her into his arms and settled into her chair himself, cradling her in his lap.

"A most fitting name, Adam, don't you think? Especially for the first boy after five girls—and in honor of your bravery and courage."

Sarah didn't argue with him over his last words, since she knew she couldn't win. She just enjoyed being held in the warmth of his embrace. He made her feel cherished, and she wanted to share that feeling with him.

She looped her arms around his neck and idly played with the hair growing at his nape. Soft and thick, it was longer now than when they'd arrived and had a slight curl. She twisted a lock around her finger and tugged gently.

Morgan dipped his head back, and when his mouth was level with hers, she ran her tongue over his lips. He let her control the kiss for a few minutes as she teased and taunted him by darting her tongue in and out of his mouth.

Then he took over, opening his mouth over hers and sucking on her tongue, drawing her in. She felt his heat and the sharp edge of his teeth as he gently nipped at her. His hand moved to the back of her head holding her in place while he reversed their positions, ravaging her mouth with total expertise.

He pulled the pins from her hair until it fell around

them, allowing it to wrap around his hand like a silken rope, holding her prisoner to his plundering. His taste and scent surrounded her, and her hands clung to his shoulders, clutching at him with a soul-wrenching need. She wanted more, all of him, as if by making love she could tie him to her forever, forging invisible bonds that would stretch but not break.

He kissed her with equal desperation as if he too were afraid of the consequences of leaving this haven and wanted to burn the memory of her into his mind for all time. With quickly indrawn breaths they reached for each other's clothes and removed them in a frenzy. When Morgan finally touched her breast, Sarah felt ready to come apart in a million pieces.

The moonlight turned his golden skin silver and highlighted the lithe lines of his body, masculine, sleek, and aroused. He stood, and she could see he was ready for her. In one lithe movement he lifted her into his arms and strode inside the cabin and to the bed.

Chapter Eleven

The man standing beneath the street lamp leered as Sarah walked by, his few remaining teeth stained and jagged. Morgan wanted to punch him but refrained.

"Do you think he recognized us?" Sarah asked worriedly once they were out of earshot.

"No. He had other things on his mind." Even to his own ears, his voice sounded clipped and angry.

"What other . . . Oh."

"Yes. Oh."

So she was finally realizing the full ramifications of her insistence on joining him. He ought to be shot for allowing it, but he'd been more afraid she might go off on her own and get in over her head without someone to watch over her.

"I can't see why he would want me dressed like this. It's not as if this dress Etienne gave me is the least bit attractive or revealing."

The dress in question was an old and shapeless brown dress sent for her use by Octavie who no longer needed its bulk now that Adam was born. An even darker scarf covered her head, hiding her hair with its telltale auburn color. The costume's purpose was to keep her from being recognized.

"I doubt your clothes matter for what he has in mind."

Her eyes darkened at the bluntness of his words. Morgan knew he'd frightened her, but he wanted her wary and on her guard.

After their time together at the cabin, it would have been easy to be lulled into a sense of complacency. But this was no parlor game they were involved in. It was a grim and lethal fight to the finish. Whoever was behind the killings of the soldiers was willing to do whatever it took to protect himself and his secrets, even killing completely innocent bystanders, though Bettine was hardly innocent in the traditional sense. Still, all she'd done was talk to him, and Morgan felt responsible for her death.

"I don't want anything happening to you, don't you understand?" he asked, taking Sarah's hand in his.

It felt small and fragile in his grasp, but vital and alive. He wouldn't be able to stand it if she were hurt . . . or worse.

"Nothing will happen," she replied. "I'll be careful. Besides, I have you to protect me."

She dropped a kiss on his hand and a shudder stole through him. Her faith was gratifying and terrifying. No mere human could protect another from all the dangers the world had to offer—he'd learned that lesson all too well. He held her hand tightly as he steered her past a drunken man asleep on the pavement next to a wall.

"I wish you would consider staying with Geneviève until this whole thing is over."

"By now she's left the city. She finds the summers

here too hot and humid. But I'm sure we could use her house, if you like."

"You seem to forget I'm wanted by the police. I don't think they'd take too kindly to my setting up camp at Geneviève's."

Sarah chewed on her lower lip in the way she did when she was worried.

"Do you think they still want you? Even after all this time?"

"Ordinarily the murder of someone like Bettine wouldn't be investigated with any diligence or for any length of time. But you said Philip knew the police were looking specifically for me. That's very different from having to pursue an investigation for some unknown man."

He could feel her tremble. "This is all my fault," she said. "If I hadn't come to you about Adam, you would never have sought out Bettine."

He put his arms around her. "You know that's not true. Adam is only one of several soldiers I've been pursuing. Chances are I would have spoken to Bettine or someone like her even without you. Don't worry. We'll get to the bottom of this soon enough."

She smiled at him though they both knew he had no way to predict how long it would take. Her faith in him, and her trust, were precious gifts, and he knew he would walk through Hell itself to protect her. But how long would her faith and trust last once she knew his past? He should have told her everything before they'd made love, but he'd never spoken of those years with anyone and the habit was too hard to break. Now it was too late. She needed him, and he couldn't desert her even if it meant betraying her innocence.

Her hand snaked around his waist, and she slipped herself under his arm, her head leaning against his chest as they walked. The heat from her body seared through his clothes; the sweet flowery scent from her hair rose to his nostrils, familiar and new all at the same time. His body reacted as it always did when she was near, hardening and heating.

She tilted her head back, her eyes slumberous with desire. By the light from a nearby open window he could see her pupils dilating until her eyes were as black as his. Her lips parted and her tongue darted out to lick them. Without thought, he lowered his mouth to hers, tasting again her feminine sweetness. She opened to him without guile or false modesty, welcoming him in that trusting, impulsive way she had. He wanted to drown in her, to sink so deeply he would never again need to come up for air. But they were in the wrong place and this was the wrong time.

Slowly he lifted his head. Closing his eyes, he whispered, "You make me forget myself."

She ran her hands up and down his back. "Mmm," she murmured into his chest.

"Hey, lady, save some o' that for me," a crude voice said from behind them.

"Yeah, I want some, too," a younger voice put in brashly.

The two men snickered drunkenly.

Morgan turned around, shielding Sarah with his body. How could he lose all sense of place like this?

"Keep moving," he ordered.

The two men scattered.

He turned back to Sarah. "Are you all right?"

She laughed aloud. "We're a pair, aren't we?" She

looked up at him, her face glowing, the scarf sliding back to reveal a lock of hair as bright as flame.

"I guess we are." He couldn't help but smile back despite his worry. How long it had been since he thought of himself as part of anything! He'd been on the outside for so long, he'd forgotten what it was like to belong. Even his job let him observe rather than act, and he'd always liked it that way, never getting too involved, never risking his very soul, not like that one time ...

"Now what?" Sarah asked.

He sighed and came back to the present. "Now we try to find Ossy Burnes."

"How do we do that?"

"Every time you say 'we' trouble follows. You're going to have to let me take the lead on this. The parts of town Ossy frequents are worse than any you've been in so far."

"I'll do whatever you say."

She said it so earnestly, an outside observer would have believed it. Morgan knew better. "I wish."

"What does that mean?"

"It means I wish you were somewhere safe, waiting."

"I'd go crazy with worry. Besides, I've been a help so far."

He couldn't deny that. Still, the bayou was a safe haven compared to what they were going to do next.

"Listen to me, what we're about to do may get dangerous quickly. Do you still have the knife I gave you?"

She nodded and patted the misshapen pocket on her dress.

"Good. Now follow my lead. And for God's sake, keep your face covered. I don't want anyone getting a good look at you. Is that clear?"

She nodded again, her expression sober. "We'll do fine," she said with that sweet naïveté he found both appealing and wholly dangerous.

He took her to the worst of the bars and hotels, pretending to be drunk and newly married, making sure he stayed between her and any kind of danger.

"Hey, anybody seen good ol' Ossy?" he slurred at one establishment after another. "Gotta show him my new missus."

Finally at a particularly seedy tavern, a young black man said, "He ain't been around lately. Probably holed up in that shanty of his."

"Oh, yeah?" It was the first he'd heard that Ossy had a place of his own. The man had always been cagey about his whereabouts, preferring to come to him rather than the other way around.

"Yeah, you know the place, out by the slaughterhouses."

"Thanks. We'll go find him. Old Ossy loves a good celebration."

The other men snickered and sent along their greetings should he be found as Morgan escorted Sarah out of the fetid bar and into the damp night air.

"Now what?" she asked.

Morgan rubbed his hand over the back of his head and down to his neck. His muscles felt hard and tense, accurately reflecting his mood. "Now we try to find Ossy's shack and hope he's there unless you're willing to be reasonable and wait here in town for me."

"I want to be there, Morgan. Please. Ossy may be the last person to have seen Adam alive . . . except for his killer. I *need* to talk to him."

Her words came as no surprise. Her determination and courage were indomitable, especially where Adam was concerned. A man would be lucky to have all that loyalty and perseverance directed at him. Still Morgan's muscles tightened another notch. How could he protect her in the nether world they were about to enter? On his own he knew just what risks to take, what price to pay. His mother had drummed the value of human life into his head from the time he was a child. Thou shalt not kill, the commandment demanded. No excuses, no conditions, no extenuating circumstances. Simply the law, from God's hand.

He'd broken the law once and the deed still haunted him. Did his mother know of his sin? Did she look down on him from the heavens and condemn his act? And for what? He'd lost everything that day, his self-respect as well as the life he'd tried to save. His mother had been right: killing did not pay, no matter the reason, right or wrong.

Alone, he would obey her strict edicts, no matter the cost to himself. But with Sarah . . . the cost would be too much. And yet, he could not bring himself to bare his very soul to her, to explain, and see her respect for him disintegrate.

"All right. Stay by me and be prepared to do whatever I say instantly. There may be no time for discussion, no chance for us to argue. Do you understand?"

"Thank you, Morgan." She reached up her hand and stroked his bearded cheek. "Everything will be fine, you'll see. I'll do exactly what you say."

He took a deep breath, wishing he had a tenth of her assurance. His skin tingled where her hand had touched him, and he longed to have her in a safe place lying naked beneath him. The image came to him strongly—her face flushed with passion, her heartbeat wild to match his own, her skin so soft and feminine, her taste far sweeter than any wine. The urge to sink into her and forget the bloody past filled him to overflowing. He wanted nothing more than to turn his back on the evil he feared they would find, to finally close the door on the hellish war that should have been part of the past but kept infringing on the present.

He looked into her eyes, and her trust pierced his heart like the deadliest of knives, cutting him deeply. He was trapped, caught between the competing demands of the only two women he had ever loved. There was no way out, though, not as long as someone was out there taking life after life. He would have to give chase and win, whatever it took, without counting the cost to himself.

Grimly he turned away from Sarah. Without looking back, he took her hand in his and pulled her to his side.

"Come along," he rasped and strode briskly down the street.

The slaughterhouses were located at the lower end of the city, on the waterfront. The abattoirs, as they were called, were open sheds surrounded by pens where the cattle to be butchered were bought and sold. The area was dirty and smelly, no place to take a lady, particularly at night. The butchers were primarily Gascons who kept to themselves, speaking their own special language.

He could feel Sarah shudder at the sights and sounds near the slaughterhouses. The scent of blood and death mingled with the smell of manure from the closely penned animals. The heavy air pressed down on them.

A few shadows lurked in the recesses of the buildings they passed but none approached them. Morgan didn't say a word as he led her through the streets, his hand tightly gripping hers as he searched the dark corners for even the hint of a threat. Every muscle was taut, and his heart beat loudly in his ears as his body prepared to parry even the slightest danger.

Sarah kept silent, too, and he wondered what she was thinking. This was a side of life to which few ladies were ever exposed—the very bottom of the social scale, people whose lives were so marginal they could barely be said to be living. And every one of them desperate enough to do most anything for a few coins or a swallow of whiskey or even the boots on a man's feet. Morgan tightened his grip on Sarah's hand as if by simply holding on to her he could keep her safe.

They skirted the abattoirs and headed toward the levee. There, along the river, stood an odd assortment of shacks constructed from scrap lumber and the sides of shipping crates fastened together in a haphazard manner. Their walls listed in every direction and were covered with an assortment of tin and thatch to keep out the rain.

"He lives here?" Sarah asked, horrified. "These . . . these places aren't fit for an animal much less a human being."

Morgan didn't answer. What could he say?

A baby cried in one of the shacks, and a man cursed and threw something that hit the wall with a loud thunk. As they neared, a dog barked and the baby continued to wail.

"Probably hungry," Morgan bit out looking in the direction of the noise. The war had been over for years. Why were so many still suffering? Would it never end?

"Oh, God," Sarah said and covered her face with her free hand.

"Do you want me to take you back?" Morgan asked, feeling her shock and dismay as if it were his own.

She shook her head. "I'll . . . just give me a minute."

The baby stopped crying and the small town quieted again.

Sarah took a deep breath. "How will we find Ossy?"

"I'll have to ask. Stay behind me, all right? I don't want anyone taking notice of you."

"All right," she whispered.

She sounded subdued and a bit frightened. Morgan wished he could have spared her this. How long before she realized this squalor had been her brother's as well as Ossy's? Still, it was better that she saw it with him than alone.

As they approached the nearest shack, a man lurched out of the shadows. Morgan heard Sarah gulp down a breath and tightened his grip warningly so she wouldn't scream.

"Could you tell me where Ossy Burnes lives?" he asked the man.

"What's in it for me?" came the slurred reply.

Morgan flipped a coin. The man gnawed at it, making sure it was the real thing before pointing to a sagging structure at the edge of the compound.

Morgan maneuvered Sarah around him so he didn't have to turn his back on the stranger, and they inched their way to Ossy's shack. There were no windows, and the door consisted of an opening between the two packing crates that served as the wall.

"Ossy?" he called in a soft voice from directly outside.

A low groan sounded from within followed by a hacking cough that Morgan recognized. Still, he needed to be certain Ossy was alone before letting Sarah near. At the same time, he couldn't leave Sarah by herself while he checked out the shanty.

Given no choice, he thrust her just inside the door and stepped in front of her, his muscles poised against any attack. None came.

"Stay here," he whispered as his eyes adjusted to the deeper dark of the shack, then made his way cautiously across the floor, swearing once when his foot hit something hard.

"Ossy? How are you doing, my man?"

A grunt came from a dark shape in the far corner. Morgan lit a match, striking it against the bottom of his boot. In the quick flare of brightness he saw that the shack was empty save for a small crate that served as table and a straw pallet in the corner. As the light dimmed, Morgan could just make out the outline of a small man huddled on the pallet, shaking with chills despite the warmth of the evening and the threadbare blanket covering him.

"Who's there?" the man rasped, then set to coughing again.

The wooden match burned down to his fingers, and Morgan dropped it to the floor where it guttered out. In the dark, sounds were magnified, the beating of his own heart, the rasping breaths from the man on the floor, the rustle of fabric as Sarah moved to his side.

"Is it Ossy?" she whispered, her voice filled with an odd combination of compassion and dismay.

"Yes. Give me a minute here, and I'll introduce you." He reached into his pocket and pulled out another match. "I think I saw a small candle over here . . ." He made his way to the up-ended crate and ran his hand over its rough surface. "Here we go," he added when he found the last remaining stub of a candle and lit it.

"Hey, Ossy, it's me, Morgan. How you doing, old man?"

"That really you, boss, comin' to see ol' Ossy?"

"It's really me. I brought a friend to meet you."

The old man smiled and tried to sit up, but a fit of coughing shook his body. Morgan frowned. The man sounded much worse than he had just a couple of weeks ago.

"When did you last eat?" he asked when the coughing stopped.

"Don' remember," Ossy mumbled. "Wanna drink."

Morgan touched his hand to the man's forehead. "He's burning with fever. We need to get him someplace we can take care of him."

"Where?" Sarah asked, her voice cracking.

"We can try my boardinghouse. Chances are no one knows I stayed there."

"What about the landlady? She knew your real name."

"She's easily bought. Besides, she's no friend of the police."

"How will we get him there?"

"I'll have to carry him, at least part of the way. I'll take you there first, then come back for him."

"No. I don't want you to have to come around here twice. Can't we take him with us?"

"I can't protect you if my arms are full."

Just then Ossy coughed again, great hacking coughs that came from the very heart of him. When he finished, his lips were lined with a dark foam. In a brighter light, Morgan knew the foam would be red.

"We can't leave him, Morgan," Sarah said. "He'll be dead by morning."

"You're right. Let's go. We should be able to get a hack now that it's almost light."

He knelt by Ossy's pallet and wrapped the blanket more tightly about the man. "Hang on, buddy. We're going to take you somewhere more comfortable."

"I need a drink," the sick man insisted querulously.

"I'll give you a drink after we get there," Morgan promised, ignoring Sarah's outraged exclamation. "You ready?"

Without waiting for Ossy's response, Morgan blew out the candle, then hefted the man into his arms. He weighed next to nothing, a skeleton of skin and bones.

Clenching his jaw, Morgan made his way to the entrance of the shack and peered out. Nothing stirred.

"Follow me and stick close," he ordered Sarah, "and let me know if you see anything the least bit suspicious. All right?"

"Yes," she murmured. "I'm right behind you."

She laid her hand on his shoulder, letting him know she was near. Taking a deep breath he led the way out of the shack and back around the slaughterhouses until they reached Peters Road. There, he stood Ossy on his feet, his arm around the feeble man to prop him up while he hailed a passing hack. The carriage was old and dilapidated, the horse mangy and with dull eyes, exactly the kind of vehicle Morgan wanted, knowing the driver wouldn't be too fussy about who his passengers were.

"What's with him?" the driver demanded, eyeing Ossy with suspicion.

"Tied one on, I'm afraid," Morgan answered. "We're

taking him home, do you mind?" The look he gave the driver dared him to protest.

"I guess not. Mind he doesn't get sick or nothing inside."

"Not to worry. We'll take care."

The driver nodded, and Morgan gave him the address. He settled Ossy in the corner, propped up by the side of the carriage, then lifted Sarah inside. Her eyes looked bruised, with deep purple coloring beneath them. Her face was pale from strain. The lack of sleep and myriad shocks from their adventure were taking their toll.

"Come on, sweetheart," he murmured. "Just hang on a little bit longer."

She managed a wan smile, and Morgan squeezed her hand, gaining as much comfort from the contact as he gave. She was still sweetness and light, touched by all she saw, yet somehow still clean and pure—like salvation for his soul. He tucked her into the opposite corner from Ossy then plunked himself between them.

"All set, driver," he called out, and the hack slowly pulled away from the curb.

Sarah felt a blessed numbness settle over her as she sat in the carriage. She'd seen more than she could bear this evening and wasn't yet ready to deal with it all. Had Adam lived like that? The thought darted through her mind, and a harsh denial escaped from her lips. Morgan sent her a worried look, and she bit down on her protest.

He'd done so much tonight and she could see the strain was taking its toll on him as well. The lines bracketing his mouth were deeper than before, and his eyes looked haunted. Beside him, Ossy broke into another coughing fit, and Morgan turned to support the man before he fell off the seat. His gentle compassion reached right into Sarah's heart. If she hadn't already been falling in love with him, he would have won her over in this instant.

The carriage drew to a halt in front of the boardinghouse Sarah remembered from her first meeting with Morgan. It looked just as sorry in the early hours before dawn as it had in the bright morning light.

Morgan jumped from the carriage. "Wait here a minute," he said and turned to the driver. "I'll make some arrangements."

He quickly strode to the front door of the boardinghouse and rapped loudly. After waiting for a minute, he knocked again and yet again.

The door opened and Mrs. Ogden, the landlady, stood there in a ratty housecoat, her hair in a disheveled mess.

"Whatcha want?" she demanded loudly. "It's the middle of the night." She had a gun in her hand that she held none too steadily, pointing it right at Morgan.

Sarah caught her breath. She could see Morgan hush the woman and then lean close to talk. Mrs. Ogden seemed to be complaining, though whether it was about the lateness or something else, Sarah did not know. Just as she began to despair of the situation ever working out, Morgan trotted back to the carriage.

"Thanks for waiting," he said to driver. "If you hold on for a second, I'll just go inside and get your payment."

"Hey, what's this?" the driver protested. "You trying to gull me?"

"No. I would be a fool to take money with me where you picked me up, don't you think? Any penny-ante crook could come after me, and I'd be broke."

"We-ell, I guess so," the man allowed.

"I'm just going inside for a minute. I'll be right out. Besides, how far could I get him if I wanted to disappear?"

As if on cue, Ossy let out another round of coughs. Sarah leaned her head out the window. "He's getting sicker by the minute. We've got to get him into bed."

"Sick, is he?" the driver asked, looking worriedly down. "Get him out, then. You promised he wouldn't mess my rig."

"And he won't. Now you stay put a minute."

With those words, Morgan came back to the carriage and reached in for Ossy, lifting him easily. "Come along," he said to Sarah, and she was only too glad to comply.

"Do you really have no money?" she asked, appalled that such a thought had never occurred to her.

"I left most of it with Etienne. For the baby," he added defensively, his face reddening.

Sarah wished she could hug him on the spot. Instead, she hugged the thought of his generosity to her. Then another thought occurred.

"How will you pay the driver? Do you need money? I have—"

"No," he cut her off. "I have money hidden in my room. As you know, I never did have a chance to clear out my things. Mrs. Ogden has saved the room for me kindly enough. We'll put Ossy there and make other arrangements later."

Sarah followed him to the chamber, noting the strange way he examined the doorway before he entered.

"Someone's been in here while I was gone. No surprise, though, probably Mrs. Ogden herself. Pull down the bedcover and I'll settle Ossy."

Sarah ran to do his bidding, stacking the meager pillows on each other to support Ossy's back. Morgan laid the frail older man down and drew the cover over him. Ossy's head lolled back and his eyes closed.

"Is he asleep?" Sarah asked.

"I'm not sure. Let me go pay the driver and see if I can get Mrs. Ogden to warm some broth for him. I'll be back as fast as I can."

He went to the closet and carefully scrutinized the door just as he had with the room.

"What are you doing?" Sarah asked unable to contain her curiosity.

"Checking if anyone's been poking around my room."

"And have they?"

He moved over to the bureau and examined each drawer separately. "Looks like it."

"How do you know?"

"I marked things before I left. See here?"

She crossed the room to his side and looked where he pointed. A short length of red thread lay on the carpet, so unobtrusive she would never have noticed it if he hadn't pointed it out.

"I placed this right on the edge of the middle drawer, like this." He picked up the piece of string and suited his actions to his words. "It fell to the floor when the drawer was opened."

"Clever," she said, though a shiver ran down her spine at the thought that such precautions were necessary. "Are any of your things gone?"

"I don't see anything obvious. Maybe Mrs. Ogden was simply looking for money to pay for the room since I didn't return."

"Did she find any?"

"I don't know, but I doubt it. I'll check."

He went back to the bed and gently pushed it one foot to the side. It resisted his efforts at first, then slowly gave way. The floor beneath the bed was not as smooth as elsewhere and Morgan slipped the knife out of his boot and gently pried up one of the floorboards. Reaching into the opening, he pulled out a bag and peered into it. "Doesn't look like she found this, at least. I'm pretty sure she'd as soon have taken it all as just what was owed her."

He pulled several greenbacks and coins out of the bag and put them in his pocket, then placed the bag back in its hiding place and carefully wedged the floorboard back in place.

"If anything happens to me," he said, "remember where the money is hidden. I want you to have it."

Sarah's stomach quaked. "What do you mean?"

"Don't be afraid. I don't intend to have anything happen. This is just a precaution." He placed a tender kiss on her lips. "I'll be right back. Lock the door behind me and don't open to anyone else."

Morgan left and Sarah went back to the bed. Ossy was breathing regularly but with a rattling sound in his chest. Sarah felt his forehead and found it hot. Looking around the room she spotted a pitcher standing next to a bowl and cup. She crossed the room and filled the cup with water, then returned to the bed.

Ossy was mumbling in his sleep. "No. Stop!" Sarah made out as she leaned over him. She wiped his face with a corner of the blanket and his eyes blinked open. They looked glazed as he looked past her.

"Mr. Burnes, would you like a drink?" she asked.

She snaked her arm under his neck and propped his head up, then held the cup to his lips.

He thrust his hands out in front of him in a defensive posture.

"No, stay back," he screamed. "Don't touch me. I won't help. I won't!"

He started to whimper and tears fell from his eyes. He was lost somewhere in the past and Sarah didn't know what to do. His skin felt so hot he was probably out of his head. She laid him back down on the pillow and went to Morgan's bureau, opening each drawer until she found what she was looking for—a large square handkerchief.

She filled the bowl with the remaining water from the pitcher and brought it over to the bed. Dipping the handkerchief in the water, she washed first his face, then the scrawny arms sticking out of his ragged clothes. Ossy kept muttering and thrashing about on the bed.

A few minutes later Morgan walked into the room holding a tray with three bowls.

"Here, I brought you some soup. You must be starving. How's Ossy?"

"Not well. I'm trying to get his temperature down, but he's very restless."

"Sit over here and eat," he said and placed the tray

on the small table in the corner. "I'll take over for you. I brought some plain broth for Ossy."

"I'm not sure he's up to eating anything. I couldn't even get him to take some water." She indicated the cup on the small end table with a flick of her hand. A feeling of crushing despair filled her. "What if we're too late? Ossy's so sick. What if he can't tell us what happened?"

Morgan put his arm soothingly around her shoulders. "Then we'll find someone who can. That's the best we can do. Now you go eat some of that soup and bread. You'll feel better and more able to face the world."

He leaned down and kissed her, giving her a portion of his strength and calm.

"Go on, now," he said.

Sarah dragged herself out of the chair, looking bruised and fragile. Not for the first time, he wished she would let go of this search before it destroyed her. She was bearing up extremely well under the circumstances, but things would be getting worse before they got better. Ossy was unlikely to survive another day, as far as Morgan could tell. His skin was sallow, and in the two weeks since Morgan had last seen him, he seemed to have been consumed from the inside until nothing was left.

He watched her until she was settled at the table and had eaten the first bite of soup. Satisfied that she was all right for the moment, he turned his attention to Ossy, lifting his head and pouring a few drops of water down his throat. The man swallowed convulsively, then rooted around looking for more. Morgan gave him another couple of sips before putting the cup away.

"Give it a little time, Ossy," he whispered. "I'll give you more in a minute." He didn't want to make the man sick.

Ossy closed his eyes and sank into a stupor again. Morgan squeezed out the wet handkerchief and washed Ossy down. His skin was feeling a bit cooler.

Suddenly Ossy's eyes opened wide and he sat up in the bed.

"Easy, Ossy," Morgan muttered and tried to push the man back down, but Ossy resisted.

"Stop them," he yelled. "Make them stop now. There won't be anyone left. No more! No more!"

He clutched at Morgan's arms with surprising strength, his clawlike hands digging into Morgan's muscles in his urgency.

"Hush now, Ossy. It's all over now. Hush," Morgan crooned, but Ossy was beyond hearing him.

"No, no. Don't you see. It's just women. Women and children. You've got to stop. You're killing them all!"

He began to shriek. "No," over and over again.

Morgan looked toward Sarah. She stood on the other side of the bed, her eyes round with shock, her arms wrapped around her waist as if she were trying to keep from coming apart.

"It's over, Ossy. You're safe here. Can you hear me?" Morgan grabbed the older man by the shoulders and gave him a slight shake.

The madness drained from Ossy's eyes, replaced by a look of recognition.

"That you, boss? How you find old Ossy?"

"A friend told me where you were. How are you feeling?"

"Don't have much time left."

There was nothing Morgan could say to that. "Would you like some water?"

"Don'tcha have anything stronger?" the man asked with some of his old slyness.

"Afraid not," Morgan replied and reached for the cup. "Here, have some of this."

Ossy grimaced but accepted the water. He drank half the contents, then was wracked by another coughing fit. Morgan handed him the dry handkerchief from his pocket. Ossy held it to his mouth until the coughing fit passed. When he brought it away from his face, a bright circle of red covered the middle. Morgan folded it over, hoping Sarah hadn't seen it.

Ossy leaned back. "Not much longer now," he said with a sigh, almost as if he welcomed death. He lay silent for a while, staring at the ceiling. "Never told you about the war, did I?" he said at last, turning toward Morgan.

"Not much, no."

"Shoulda. Mighta helped that Adam boy. Then again, who knows, huh?"

"What would you have told me?" Morgan asked almost in a whisper, wanting the man to continue but afraid he would pull back at the last minute just as he had all those other times.

"About the town. What we did. How we hid it." He sighed and fell quiet again.

Morgan felt his stomach knot tightly. "What did you do?" he asked, though he already had his suspicions.

"We killed them all, you know."

"Yes, I thought so . . . Can you tell me where?"

"Croxton's Mill," he said with a small sigh, almost as if he were relieved to finally get it out in the open.

"Why there?"

Ossy shrugged. "No special reason that I know of. Maybe just because it was there."

"Can you tell me about it?"

"We'd fought that morning. It was terrible. Them Yankees were all over, everywhere you looked there was a blue uniform with a gun pointed at you. People were dying like flies. Friends, you know what I mean?"

Morgan nodded. He'd been on the battlefields himself though not like this. He'd come to save lives rather than take them, for all the good it did.

"We all ran in the end. Just every which way. Things got all mixed up. Men from one mess mixed up with those from another. Even the officers ran. No one told us where to go, what to do. And then it was quiet. Birds singing, the sun shining, just as if the battle never happened.

"It was too much, I guess. Why should everyone else get to live when we had to die? I don't even remember who fired the first shot, but before long we were all shooting. Just bang, bang, bang. Anything that moved." He closed one eye and lifted his hand, sighting over it as if he held a pistol.

From the other side of the bed, Morgan heard a gasp. Sarah stood there, whiter than a ghost, as if hypnotized by the old man's words. He wanted to go to her but knew he couldn't. Ossy didn't have much longer and as long as this lucid period lasted he had to stay with the man.

"Then what?" Morgan asked.

"After a while nothing moved. We kept shooting, hitting the trees, the ground, even the dead, not that they cared anymore. And then the red haze cleared, and there we were, in the middle of a battlefield where we were the victors.

"Some victory, eh? Women and children lying dead on the ground, not more'n three guns among them. And then he made us bury them, deep in the ground where no one would find them, no one could tell.

" 'Dig,' he yelled and threatened to shoot if we didn't do it. 'Dig, faster.' " Ossy's voice mimicked someone else's, and Morgan could sense the nightmare taking over the man's brain again. "All those dead," he whispered, his voice breaking. "So many, so many. Only Hedda left to tell the tale."

"Hedda?" Morgan sat up. Could this be the break he'd been searching for. "Who's Hedda? Who yelled at you, Ossy? Who made you dig?" He grabbed Ossy by the shoulders and looked into his face, willing him to hang on just another minute.

"The commander, of course," Ossy said. "He wanted Hedda for himself. Beautiful Hedda. Such a one has never been seen before or since."

"Who was the commander, Ossy?" Morgan demanded harshly, trying to break through the grip of the nightmare.

"Oh, God. Oh, God, what did we do? We killed them all! We'll burn forever. I don't want to go. No! No!"

He began coughing again and desperately gasping for air. Morgan heard a rattling sound come from his chest and the coughing stopped. Ossy slumped over.

Morgan eased him back onto the pillow. For a moment he looked down and then pulled the blanket over him.

He looked up at Sarah. She looked at him through haunted eyes.

"You knew about this, didn't you?" she asked in an accusing tone.

He came around the bed and reached for her but she stepped away.

"Didn't you?" she insisted.

He passed his hand wearily over his face. Time to pay for his sins.

"I suspected something similar."

"How? Why?"

"Mostly because someone was going to such lengths to keep things quiet. I knew whatever had happened had to have been pretty horrendous. That doesn't leave much scope when you consider how horrendous war is in and of itself."

"Did Ossy know Adam?"

Ah, now they had reached it, the crucial issue. And there was nothing he could do to stop it. She would never forgive him a lie, but could she forgive him the truth?

"They weren't in the same company, but . . ."

"But they were both there, weren't they?"

"Yes."

She stood still as a statue, absorbing the hurt. Would she turn away from him now, the bearer of bad tidings? Would she blame him for tarnishing her memories of her brother? He stood helplessly watching her, waiting for his fate to be decided.

With a sudden cry, she flung herself into his arms. "Oh, Morgan, how could it have happened?" she said through her sobs. "How could anyone do such terrible things?"

Morgan held her while she cried out her anguish. She was losing her brother all over again and in a much more absolute way. Even her good memories would be forever tarnished.

After a while, her sobs calmed.

"Come and sit," Morgan murmured and led her back to her chair. He knelt in front of her and combed her hair back over her forehead where it had loosened from the knot she wore.

She leaned into his touch. "It's so hard to believe," she whispered. "Adam was . . . I don't know. Kind and gentle. Not really cut out to be a soldier. He was a true gentleman. I don't know how this could have happened. I just can't believe it."

"War changes people in all sorts of ways."

"But this? This is beyond comprehension. Could Ossy have been lying—exaggerating, maybe?"

Morgan shrugged. In his gut, he knew Ossy's words had the ring of truth. And the man had known he was on his deathbed.

"There's only one way to find out," he said at last. "Go to Croxton's Mill and see what I can find."

Sarah shuddered. "I can't even think of it. It's just so awful."

"I'm sorry, Sarah. I should never have allowed you to be a part of this."

She stroked his cheek. "This isn't your fault. I would have found out about it one way or another. It's been a help that you were here."

She gave him a weak smile even as her eyes filled again. "It's just so awful," she repeated.

He sat back on his heels and pulled her to his lap,

holding her tightly while her grief poured out of her again.

After a while she stopped crying and they sat, arms entwined, absorbing comfort from the simple human touch.

The sound of hoofbeats clattering on the cobblestones caught Morgan's attention. It sounded as if a troop of riders were outside. He lifted his head to listen more closely.

"What is it?" Sarah asked.

"Shhh," he said quickly and set her back onto her chair. With a warning finger on his lips, he rounded the bed and opened his room door a crack.

He could hear the front door open and Mrs. Ogden's voice saying, "This way. I did like you told me. I let him in and sent for you."

The man's voice was too muffled to understand.

"I would have, except the boy was nowhere around. He came in the middle of the night, he and his friend. 'Tweren't no one around to send. Anyway, he's still in his room, so what's the fuss about?"

Morgan shut the door and locked it. He quickly searched the room for another way out.

"Grab your things. We've got to leave," he said to Sarah.

"What's happening?"

"I think our dear landlady has turned me in. Sounds like a whole troop of policemen are coming down the hall."

"What about Ossy?" she asked as she gathered the bare necessities.

Morgan glanced at the bed. Ossy was beyond pain

and guilt now. "He'll be fine where he is. Nothing more can hurt him. You ready?"

She nodded. The trust in her eyes warmed him, and he knew she had his heart forever. Women like Sarah did not come along very often. He only wished he could live up to what she deserved.

Grabbing her hand, he led her out the little-used back door and along the wall surrounding the back courtyard where he'd talked to Ossy the night Adam died. They slipped out the rear gate and into the alley backing onto the buildings.

"Hurry," Morgan urged as they ran toward the next street. "The police will be out here any minute."

Hearing a noise behind them, Morgan pushed Sarah into a shadowed doorway at the far end of the alley. Craning his neck around the edge, he watched as the policemen surrounded the building they'd just left, sealing off the backyard as well.

"Are they coming after us?" Sarah whispered.

"No. I don't think they know we're gone yet. Let's get moving before they find out."

Morgan checked the alley one more time and saw it was clear. Grabbing Sarah's hand, he ran the last few feet to the street and into the sunshine.

Chapter Twelve

The wagon rumbled to a stop in the middle of a narrow dirt road choked with weeds. A few burned-out hulks of what had once been houses or stores stood scattered along the road. Sarah looked around at what once had been Croxton's Mill. It was obvious that no one traveled here very often.

"This is it?" she asked, not quite believing her own assessment.

"If the directions were accurate, yes."

The place was more barren than she'd expected. She'd thought there would be something more, perhaps a few hardy souls who still eked out a living, maybe a chicken or two and a dog. Not this emptiness. What could they possibly learn from this wilderness?

"I thought there would be ... more," she said, not trying to hide her disappointment. This was the first real lead they'd had, and her anticipation had grown with each mile they'd traveled. Maybe that was why the reality was hitting her so hard. After all, Ossy had painted a pretty grim picture of the events that had taken place here. She realized now that in the deepest part of her, she hadn't fully believed him.

She looked over at Morgan. The muscles in his cheek were working and his jaw looked clenched. He stood up in the wagon and surveyed the land around them. Was he trying to picture the place as it had been before the violence? A shiver ran down Sarah's spine. She could almost see the ghosts, hear the screams of the fallen. She closed her eyes tightly and willed her wild imagination to stop torturing her.

"Stay here," Morgan said curtly and jumped to the ground. He wandered from ruin to ruin, stopping here and there to look at the ground more closely. Her gaze followed him. What was he looking for?

They'd been driving since early this morning and with each mile he'd become more distant, pulling into himself and shutting her out. She wasn't sure why, though she suspected Ossy's death had affected him more than he wanted to admit. He'd never spoken of his war years, skirting the issue every time they got close. Perhaps being here brought back unpleasant memories. She shivered again.

The sun beat down and the sky was blue, but the birds were silent as if even they knew what had happened here.

Suddenly she couldn't stand sitting alone anymore. She jumped down from the wagon and walked across the high grass to join Morgan as he walked the perimeter of a grove of trees. She was still wearing the dress Octavie had given her, and she found the skirt cumbersome. If it wouldn't have drawn unwanted attention, she would have preferred a pair of britches. Sneaking around back alleys and rushing around in the bushes called for more appropriate clothing—male clothing.

"There doesn't seem to be much here," she called out as she reached him.

"From what Ossy said, I didn't expect much," Morgan replied. "When they took off back in '64 everything was pretty much gone."

The bramble had grown up in the center of the grove, and he pushed it aside to step in, his eyes intently searching the ground. She couldn't imagine what he was looking for. When she would have followed, the briars caught at her bare arms and her long skirt, entangling her hopelessly. She stepped back, and he went on without her.

She sighed and chewed on her lip. She had hoped that if she left him to himself long enough he'd begin to talk about what was bothering him. But so far he seemed to want only his own company. If he didn't want her with him, there wasn't anything she could do to change his mind, at least not now. She'd have to wait for her time. But it was hard. What had happened to the man she'd come to know in the bayou?

She walked back to the horse and wagon and led the animal into the shade. Morgan must have been distracted to allow the bay to stand in the hot sun like this. Absently rubbing the horse's muzzle, she thought back over the tumultuous events of the last twenty-four hours. Her whole view of the world had changed, leaving her unsure and vulnerable. Things she'd thought true were just illusions. Where she had seen goodness, there had been evil, and she'd never come close to realizing it. Could she even trust her judgment anymore?

She tied the horse to a tree and wandered off, lost in her thoughts. She could hear the trickle of a small stream and further in the distance Morgan moving through the underbrush. What did he hope to find? She looked around but saw nothing out of the ordinary.

As she wandered into the woods, she saw the remains of what had been a house. Cautiously, she made her way over to the foundation. She knew snakes lived in just such places. Making as much noise as she could to scare off any creatures that might be housed in the rubble, she sat down on a large flat stone.

Soon Morgan would stop looking about and they'd have to move on, but to where? There'd been nothing left in Croxton's Mill to even hint at what had happened eight years ago, only Ossy Burnes's fractured recitation—unless they could locate Hedda. Right now that seemed an unlikely prospect.

She wished she could talk to Morgan. She needed to put her brother's actions into some perspective. To suddenly find out he'd been a murderer . . . It just couldn't be true. Adam wasn't that kind of man. He couldn't have . . . wouldn't have done anything like that. Not the gay, laughing Adam who had taken her on picnics and into town to the traveling shows, not even the more reserved and quiet Adam who had given her the gold locket and told her to follow her dreams and not allow anyone else to change them.

And yet how else could she explain the changes in her brother? What had eaten at his insides until he couldn't stay in one place, couldn't bear to be with those who'd known him and loved him before the war? Something had happened, something too awful to live with. Had it been here?

She looked around at the drying grass, the gently rolling land covered with trees, the road now going to nowhere, and tried to see it as it must have been that day. What had made the men coming through this town behave the way they did? Why had they done things as a group that they never would have done as individuals? Had some madness overtaken them or had someone ordered them to kill—or maybe both?

A chill ran through her, raising little bumps on her arms. She felt around the back of her neck for the chain that held her locket and gently tugged, pulling the gold ornament from inside her dress. It was a large locket and nearly covered the palm of her hand. She rubbed her fingers over its engraved surface. It felt warm and comforting, taking her back to a time that was less confusing. She needed to remember Adam as he was then, she thought shakily, otherwise this nightmare would overwhelm her.

"Sarah! Sarah, where are you?" she heard Morgan shout from beyond the trees in a tone that indicated he'd been calling to her for some time.

"I'm just here," she called back, rising to her feet and starting in the direction of the wagon.

They both rounded the edge of the grove at the same time.

"Don't ever wander off like that again," Morgan snarled, his hands coming out to grasp her upper arms.

She felt the bite of his fingers and for a moment she was afraid he was going to shake her mercilessly. Instead, he crushed her to him, his arms circling her tightly.

"Something could have happened to you. I've lost so much. I won't lose you," he said, his voice muffled by her hair.

Sarah held on to him. She could feel the tremors

shaking him and wondered if he had found something disturbing in his search.

"I wasn't lost," she said. And she hadn't been, not in the way he meant. "I was just looking around. When you went off on your own into the brambles, I couldn't follow. I decided to look in a different direction."

"You should have stayed with the horse. At least then you'd have transportation and water. You would have been safe." He leaned back and looked into her eyes.

"I was safe. There isn't a soul within miles."

"You can never be too careful, don't you know that? Besides, there *was* someone around. A man."

"Out here?" she questioned and then understood the significance of his words. "Did you talk with him? What did he say?"

"I met him back there, on the other side of the grove."

Sarah could see the excitement in his eyes. He'd discovered something that would help them in their search. Suddenly things didn't look as bleak as they had just a few minutes before.

"What did you learn?" she asked, her own excitement building.

"That there were several families that moved to a small town called Barner's Creek right after the war started, before the massacre. It's about five miles up the road, though no one comes this way much anymore. It's possible someone there might know the families that stayed in Croxton's Mill."

"Did the man you met know anything about Hedda?"

"No, he'd never heard of her, but then he's always lived over in Crighton. That's about ten miles the other side of the river. He was only out this way today because he's headed to Dawson to visit some friends. We were lucky to see him."

Grabbing his hand, she began pulling him toward the wagon. "Let's go before it gets too late," she urged, forgetting about Morgan's intense searching.

"I want to stay here a little longer. Will you wait by the wagon for me?"

"What are you looking for?"

"Proof," he said succinctly.

"Proof?"

"That the massacre really happened and wasn't just a tale embellished over the years by the local folk to explain the abandonment of the town."

"What kind of proof?"

He looked away from her. "I'm looking for a mound of earth that's out of place. I just want to check the other side of the road. Will you wait here?"

She nodded, perplexed. Then she understood. Ossy had said they'd had to dig and dig. The grave. Oh, God, he was looking for the grave where the women and children had all been buried. Her knees sagged with weakness and her stomach turned over. She ran just into the trees and was horribly sick. The heaving continued long after her stomach was empty. When it stopped, she made her way back to the wagon and leaned against it feeling cold and shaky. She closed her eyes so she wouldn't have to look at the place again. But it didn't help—the image was burned on her memory for all time.

Hot tears seeped from her eyes, and she brushed them away as fast as they fell. What good were tears now? More was needed, much more. These innocent deaths had to be avenged or at least remembered. The world had to know this dirty secret so it wouldn't happen again. War was ugly enough as it was. But what had happened here was unconscionable and had to be exposed, even if Adam's reputation was destroyed with the others.

She heard Morgan's steps as he returned.

"Did you find what you were looking for?" she asked, keeping her head down.

"I think so."

He sounded as wounded as she felt. She gazed at him then and saw that coming here was as hard for him as it had been for her. She wanted to go to him and wrap her arms around him but sensed that he needed to stand alone right now. Men were like that, hanging tightly on to their emotions and hiding them from the world. Unlike her, he had released none of his pain, keeping it all inside where it was tearing him apart.

Adam had done that, too. And in the end he hadn't really needed the murderer to end his life. It had been over long before.

"What do you think happened?" she asked.

He shrugged. "What Ossy said. A bunch of soldiers had been routed and came here, most from Adam's company, some from others. Somehow the massacre started, and no one could stop it until everyone was dead. Blood lust is like that. I've seen it happen."

His voice sounded bleak, his eyes dark and strangely empty.

"But how did it start?" she whispered.

He shrugged. "It takes only one person to set it off. A leader, someone who makes it all right for the others to throw off their usual restraints. The war helped. The men had already killed. They'd seen their friends die just that morning and knew they could have died, too.

Might still die, in fact. All that fear and anger is a potent force. All they needed was someone to point them in the same direction."

"And who was that someone?" she asked in fascinated horror. She could see it happening as he described it, see the group take on a personality of its own, sucking up each individual's will as it gained strength until they felt above all law, above all sense of right and wrong.

"That's the question, isn't it? I think it was an outsider, someone who happened to be at this place at the same time as the others. Maybe he even held a position of authority in another troop. But this was a time out of time for him."

"What makes you say that?"

"Because I've checked out most of the people in Adam's company and because it makes sense. The leader wouldn't risk getting turned in by the soldiers once their madness had ended. He would have to disappear. But the records show that no one in such a position deserted at that time."

"And who's killing the soldiers now?"

"Someone who knows who was here and who wasn't. Someone who was involved."

"The leader," she said with sudden understanding. "He's making sure no one ever turns him in, isn't he?"

"That's what I think."

"And now he knows you're looking for him." Her heart began to race in fear. The man they were seeking was even more ruthless than she'd imagined in her naïve way.

"And I'll find him."

He said the words with such grim determination that Sarah knew there was nothing she could say to dissuade him, to keep him from putting his own life on the line. And yet, she understood him, too for her quest to avenge Adam had broadened in scope as a result of their stop in this place of ghosts. She wanted nothing more than to find the man who had destroyed so many lives and had no compunction about destroying more. He had to be stopped, and she would do everything in her power to see that he was.

They left Croxton's Mill then, heading for Barner's Creek. Within the hour they'd arrived in the little town: a few houses clustered around a crossroads. Sarah wasn't even sure you could call it a town. Nor did she see a drop of water. No doubt the town was named after a stream that had long since dried up.

The wind blew and the dust lifted off the road, swirling around her head. She coughed and thought back to the bayou and how much better she'd liked being surrounded by water to being consumed by dust. She pulled her scarf closer around her face, hoping to keep her hair and mouth clean. There was no telling the next time she'd be able to bathe. She wasn't even sure where they'd be spending the night. It all depended on the information they got on Hedda.

Morgan stood beside her. He'd been watching the houses, waiting. They'd traveled the whole five miles meeting no one, not even seeing another house. This could well be the closest town to Croxton's Mills—or where Croxton's Mill had been—at least in an easterly direction. If they didn't get some information here, Sarah didn't want to think where that would leave them.

"We'll have to start knocking on doors," Morgan said,

nodding in the direction of the first house, a nondescript building with a porch that was falling off on one side.

"Shall I go to the next?" she asked, looking past the house he indicated.

"This may be the country, but that doesn't mean it's filled with churchgoing folks who'll invite you in for cake and coffee."

"You could have just said no."

Sarah's gaze met his. She allowed him to see the hurt his words had caused her.

"You're right," he said and took her hand in his, rubbing his thumb over its back. "This whole business is getting to me, I guess. It's hard to imagine, a whole town disappearing like that, and all on the whim of some crazed soldiers, including James. Annie will be heartbroken."

She'd forgotten he had a personal stake in this investigation, one that went beyond Adam. She remembered now that his sister had set him on this investigation, convinced her husband had been killed for some reason. Now Annie, too, would have to face the pain of realizing her husband had been a monster, if only for a single afternoon. And Morgan would be the one having to tell her.

"Do you think we'll ever know how it happened?" she asked.

"We're getting close, I can feel it. I'm not saying it will be easy, but I think we'll have it unraveled soon enough."

Sarah suspected it had something to do with his nose as a journalist that gave him a sense of what was to come. She hoped he was right. With each new piece to the puzzle, they also found another mystery that had to be solved: Adam's murder, Bettine's murder, and now the massacre.

"Let's go to the first house," Morgan said. "Promise me you'll let me do the talking."

Sarah nodded and he led the way to the house. Sarah wasn't even sure someone lived there from the way it looked. They climbed onto the rickety porch and Morgan knocked on the door, then stepped back.

The door opened a crack and a voice called out, "What do ya want?"

"We're looking for some information."

"I ain't got any."

Before the door could slam shut, Morgan jammed his foot between the door and the casing.

"I'll make it worth your while," he said, jingling the coins in his pocket.

The eyes peeking out of the crack in the door brightened at Morgan's words, and a hand popped out, palm up. "What do you want to know?"

For the first time Sarah realized how well Morgan knew this world. He'd been here before, among the poor and hungry for whom a few coins made all the difference. He knew how to get what he wanted, how to barter need for information.

"What happened over at Croxton's Mill?" Morgan demanded.

"There is no Croxton's Mill."

"That kind of answer will have these coins heading back to New Orleans with me. Now, what do you know about Croxton's Mill?"

"I knew some people that lived there."

"Now that's more like the answer I want to hear." Morgan dropped a coin in the man's hand, and it disappeared in an instant. Sarah saw that Morgan had not moved his foot from the door, apparently not trusting his informant to hold up his end of the bargain. "Did you live there before the war?"

"Nah, but my uncle did."

"He live around here?"

The hand came out again. Morgan considered it for a moment and then placed another coin on the palm.

Again Sarah watched the hand whip inside. She couldn't imagine what it must be like to live out here, where the coins Morgan had just given made the difference between starvation and survival.

"There'll be more if you know what I need," Morgan promised.

"What's that?"

"Your uncle, does he live around here?"

"Maybe he does and maybe he doesn't," the voice said in a sly undertone.

Morgan looked over at Sarah and then nodded for her to step off the porch. He was just turning to follow when the voice called out, "Where you goin'?" The man sounded panicked that his source of funds could so easily dry up. "I know a lot."

Morgan looked back over his shoulder. "You might, but you don't look like the type who wants to make some easy money."

"I do. I have a family, you know." The door opened wider, and Sarah could see not only the man, but a woman and small child as well.

"That's your problem, not mine. I told you, I have need of information, not charity. You just want to gouge me. I'm sure there are others here who will be more willing to tell me what I want to know."

He turned and walked toward the next house, jingling the coins in his pocket. Sarah followed him, glancing over her shoulder at the family now standing on the porch. She could sense their desperation, but Morgan was unmoved. She didn't like this side of him, the efficient reporter, uninterested in anything or anyone beyond his story. She'd felt him becoming colder and more distant ever since they'd left the bayou and come back to the city. It was as if a shield had come down around him, and he wasn't letting anyone too close—particularly her. For a while, at Croxton's Mill when they'd held each other, she'd thought she'd been imagining it, but now she wasn't so sure.

"Wait, please," the man called out, chasing after them. He got in front of Morgan and started running backward. "I'll tell you whatever you want. Please."

His desperation tore at Sarah. Why didn't Morgan stop?

"What can you tell us?" she asked.

"About my uncle. Whatever you want to know."

Morgan stopped walking. A cold, triumphant smile crossed his face as he caught Sarah's eye.

"His name?"

"Abner Prugh," the man said without hesitation.

"And he lives?"

"In that brown house with the chimney. I can take you there if you like." He pointed across the street.

"That won't be necessary." Morgan reached into his pocket. "A word of advice. Next time negotiate up front. This is a buyer's market, my friend."

Sarah couldn't believe her ears. For an instant she thought Morgan was going to leave without paying the man. She glanced over at the man's family. The woman stood behind the child, her arm draped over the boy's thin shoulders. She looked older than her years, already worn out with the strains of daily life.

She turned back in time to see the man stuff his hand in his pocket. What had Morgan given him? Had he paid him or sent him packing, knowing full well that almost anyone in the town could have given him the information he wanted?

"Thank you, mister," the man said, backing away from them. "I'll remember what you said the next time."

She couldn't bring herself to ask Morgan what he'd given the man, but judging from the man's expression, he'd been satisfied. As Morgan turned toward the uncle's house, she heard him mutter, "Hell, he's got a wife and child." She knew then that he'd been more generous than he should have been.

She followed him across the street. "Do you think Mr. Prugh will be able to help us?"

"Remember the man I met said most of these people moved before the massacre. Let's wait and see what Prugh has to say."

Again Morgan knocked on the door, only this one was in better shape and attached to a house in reasonable condition.

When there was no answer, Morgan knocked again and called out, "Mr. Prugh, your nephew sent me over," which wasn't exactly true, but it had the desired effect—the door opened.

A woman of indeterminate age looked both Sarah and Morgan over from head to toe before asking, "What can I do for you?"

Her tone was quiet and respectful. She must have seen through the veneer of their ragged clothes and realized they were the kind of people you didn't often see in a small out-of-the-way town like Barner's Creek. She put her hand to her hair, quickly smoothing it into order.

"We're looking for some information about Croxton's Mill. Do you know anything?"

"My husband and I lived there until a few years before the war started. He wanted to go to New Orleans and get himself some fancy job. Said he was tired of working the land for someone else and getting nothing back in return except more work."

Sarah felt hope blossom. This woman might be just the key they were looking for. She certainly liked to talk, probably didn't get much company this far out. Now all they had to do was find out about Hedda.

"But we didn't really keep up with anyone from there," she finished.

Sarah glanced up at Morgan knowing disappointment was written on her face, but he didn't look down at her. He was intent on getting answers. "Do you know what happened to the town during the war?"

"I heard tell some Yankee scum came in and blew the place up. Didn't no one escape. Abner was telling me we'd have ended up dead if'n he hadn't hustled us off to the city. I told him dead might be better."

"Who you blabberin' to, woman?"

Instantly she stopped talking and turned toward the voice. She whispered something to him.

"You don't know who they might be, woman. And don't go shushing me," Sarah heard the man mutter just as he stepped out on the porch.

"Abner Prugh, at your service. What would it be that you folks might be wanting?"

265

"Information about Croxton's Mill or more precisely someone who lived there."

"That so? I did know a great many people before we moved."

"Did you know a woman named Hedda?" Sarah asked, not wanting to wait for Morgan's more roundabout way of asking. She felt him stiffen beside her. She'd probably hear about this later, but she couldn't wait any longer.

"Hedda Winslow?" the woman asked.

Sarah nodded, excitement building inside her. There couldn't be that many people with the name Hedda from a town as small as Croxton's Mill. If nothing else, they now knew Hedda's last name.

"I'll do the talking here, woman," Abner said, pushing his wife to the side.

Why was it that the men of this world always wanted to do all the talking, even when they didn't have anything to say, Sarah thought.

"We *used* to know Hedda. She was a distant cousin on my mother's side," he added cautiously. "Exactly why do you want her?"

"We're trying to locate her. Do you know where she ended up?" Morgan asked.

"Went off with some soldier. Wooed by the promise of silks and chocolates." There was disgust in his voice. "Never did understand that woman."

"Now, Abner, Hedda just wanted a better life, just like you when you decided we should go for that better job in New Orleans."

"That isn't the same thing at all, woman. I was going out to work. I wouldn't call what Hedda did work exactly. And after what those soldiers did . . ."

"Have you heard from her since?" Morgan asked to get them back to the original question.

"Too ashamed to show her face around here. That fancy officer dropped her as soon as he found something better, no doubt. Heard tell she went off to New Orleans after that."

Sarah's heart fell. But they'd just come from there, she thought, and it was too dangerous to go back, what with Ossy's death and the police still on the lookout for Morgan. Sooner or later their luck would run out.

The woman whispered something to Abner, but he shook his head.

"That's the most I can tell you," he said flatly. "More than that I don't know. I wish you luck." He backed up, shepherding his wife behind him, and closed the door.

Sarah kept her eyes on the woman. Something wasn't right. Abner hadn't told them everything, she was sure of it.

Morgan turned and stepped off the porch, but Sarah didn't move.

"Sarah? Are you coming?" he asked.

"I have an idea."

"Sarah, I don't th—"

"Morgan, you asked me to trust your instincts. Well, this time I'd like you to trust mine. You've met these people. Do you think they'd kill me?"

"Of course not."

"So there's no reason we shouldn't try a little experiment. Come back up here," she whispered.

"Sarah, I'm warning you—"

"I'm going to knock on the door. When Abner opens I'm going to ask for water and I want you to keep him busy while I go with his wife. Just do it, please, without a big debate."

For a moment he looked as if he were about to argue, then he took the two steps in one bound and was beside her on the porch.

Without a word, he raised his hand and knocked. Mrs. Prugh answered the door once again, and before she could say a word, he starting speaking.

"I'm sorry to bother you again, but might I ask you for a glass of water for my wife. She's had a long trip, and for the last five miles there wasn't a house to be seen."

Sarah nearly swallowed her tongue. His wife? Where had that come from? He was lucky she hadn't gasped out loud and spoiled his game.

"Why, of course. You come on in, honey, and follow me out to the kitchen. If you've come from Croxton's Mill there wouldn't be nary a place to get something cool to drink," she said in a motherly voice. "I'll get you a nice glass full of water. By the way, my name's Aggie."

Sarah smiled her acceptance. "Thank you, Aggie, it's been a long trip. My name's Sarah."

She left Morgan standing on the porch as she followed Aggie back toward the kitchen. She glanced over her shoulder and winked as she continued her conversation with her hostess.

Morgan sat on the porch railing, leaning against the wall of the house. Sarah'd been in there well over a half hour. Abner'd come out and talked for all of two minutes about *them corrupt Yankees* and then headed out to his garden patch out back. Morgan had been cooling his heels ever since.

He tried to keep his mind on the business at hand, but it was difficult. He kept seeing the weed-covered mound he'd found behind the ruined houses in Croxton's Mill. He shuddered to think what would be found when the mound was dug up. He'd have his proof that something terrible had happened at the town, but nothing to tie Adam or James or any of the other soldiers to the dreadful deed, and that wasn't enough.

He wasn't suited for the role of avenging angel, but how could he stop pursuing this? There was a madman on the loose, a man who seemed to like killing and hadn't stopped. For that reason alone Morgan couldn't give up his pursuit. But there was a more important reason as well. Sarah.

The thought of her in danger chilled him to his marrow. Even now, not knowing what she was up to made him tense. The Prughs seemed innocent enough, but who knew how far the madman's tentacles reached? He'd managed to entangle Morgan in one of his murders, and Morgan knew he wouldn't stop there.

He only hoped Sarah would really learn something useful. He could see the toll each disappointment took, though he had to admit he was impressed with the way she was handling the entire horrible business. Adam had been the center of her life for so long that learning of his actions must be a real blow.

What would she think when she learned *his* secrets?

He stood up, needing to work off some of his tension by pacing. Just then, the front door opened.

"Thank you for your hospitality, Aggie," Sarah said

and smiled at the older woman. "And you take care of that rhumatiz. Try that mixture I told you about."

"I will and thank you. Have a safe trip," she called out before she closed the door.

Morgan waited as Sarah made her way to his side.

"Well?" he asked impatiently as they began to walk toward the rig.

"I knew it. I just knew it."

Her eyes were shining, and she tossed her head, barely able to contain her excitement.

"Are you going to tell me this big secret?"

"I've gotten the information we need."

"What information is that?"

"I know where Hedda Winslow is."

Morgan stared at her, unable to believe his ears. If were true—"But—" he started to say, only Sarah in her exuberance, interrupted him.

"I thought Aggie knew more than what Abner was telling. It was something in her eyes. I knew if I could get her alone, I might be able to get her to talk and have her tell me what she knew. And it worked."

Morgan gazed down at her. She looked so proud of herself. And she had done a wonderful job. She had all the instincts of a good journalist—that gut instinct that told you something was there even when everything pointed elsewhere.

"This is just what we've been looking for. I didn't even pick up on Aggie's unease. If you hadn't noticed we might have missed this altogether."

As he spoke he noticed her smile dimming slightly. "What is it?" he asked. "You did a wonderful job."

He put his arm around her shoulders and hugged her to him.

"I haven't told you *where* she is."

With her face turned up, he could see the sunlight reflecting in her clear green eyes. As always, she hid nothing. He saw her enthusiasm, her innocence, her frustration, and her disappointment.

"Where?" he prompted.

"In a sanitarium—a *sanitarium*, and I thought her being in New Orleans was bad. Aggie says she's crazy as a loon, but she goes through periods when she's lucid. Abner's ashamed that a relative of his is in a place like that. That's why he didn't want her saying anything. Aggie figured we wouldn't pity or embarrass Abner so she didn't mind telling. I reassured her that we wouldn't."

Morgan felt the usual tug of conflicting emotions every development in this case had engendered. Somehow, with very two steps forward, they slipped one back. Now they had found Hedda, only to learn she was crazy. Where would they be if they couldn't get any useful information from her?

With Ossy's passing, Morgan was afraid they'd reached a dead end—except for one thing. There was at least one more person who knew all about it—the person who was killing off all the men in the company.

"Where's the sanitarium located?" he asked as they headed back to the wagon.

"We're lucky with that. It's near Geneviève's summer home. We'll have a place to stay."

"She might not be too happy to have a fugitive hanging around her front door."

Sarah laughed. "You don't know Geneviève as well as I do. Once she makes up her mind about something, she doesn't let anyone tell her what to think. I'd bet all the money I have she's been defending you to everyone who even breathes your name."

"Is that so?"

She looked up at him with a smile. "You know it is. Though now that I think about it, I'm not sure I like the idea of her defending you quite so energetically."

"Are you jealous?" he asked as he helped her into the wagon.

She didn't reply as he walked around the wagon and pulled himself up into the driver's seat. When he realized she wasn't going to answer, he couldn't stop from probing. "You don't know that she'd defend me."

Twisting in her seat, Sarah turned to look at him. "She would, you know. She's liked you from the start."

"Unlike you, who found me too rough and uncivilized for polite society."

"That's not true. I never felt that way. As a matter of fact . . ." Abruptly she stopped speaking.

She'd answered instinctively, without stopping to think through her answer. What else had she been about to say? The possibilities tantalized Morgan as he drove off.

"I guess it isn't everyone who gets visitors wanted for kidnapping as well as murder." Geneviève said as she opened the front door of her summer house. She didn't seem at all surprised to see them though it was well past the dinner hour.

"Kidnapping! Who was kidnapped?" Sarah exclaimed as she hugged her friend and kissed her on both cheeks.

"You, *ma chère*," she replied, clearly waiting for Sarah's reaction. It wasn't long in coming.

"What?" Morgan and Sarah exclaimed in unison.

"Here I'll let you read about it in black and white. And in your own paper, Morgan," she said, opening the first door on her left and reaching inside.

"The *Picayune?* They wouldn't," Morgan denied, but he didn't say it with much conviction. Unfortunately, he knew how a newspaper operated.

"They did," Geneviève said, hearing his denial, and handed him a newspaper dated over a week before.

Morgan unfolded the paper, and Sarah read over his arm.

"They've taken up nearly the whole front page with this story. How could they say such things?" she asked finishing the first few paragraphs, then looking to Morgan for an answer.

"Because it sells newspapers, and that's the name of the game." When Geneviève had said the story was in the paper he'd known what to expect.

"But these are your friends, your fellow journalists," Sarah argued.

"Who'd sell their mother for a story that would generate an extra fifty dollars," he said as he continued to scan the page. "But I'm surprised at Nat."

Both Sarah and Geneviève looked at him questioningly.

"Nat's my editor—and my friend—or so I thought." He continued to read the article. "Though the story could have been a lot worse," he said as he finished.

"How?" Sarah asked angrily.

"Any number of ways, now that I think about it. Maybe Nat did the best he could."

"What do you mean? This is outrageous," Sarah fumed. "How could they do this to you? We can't let it continue. I'll have to go back to the city and tell them how preposterous this all is."

Morgan could understand Sarah's frustration, her sense of hurt at having her life exposed to all and sundry, and her need to make everything right, but he knew that wasn't possible.

"I'm afraid you can't," Morgan said, his voice quiet as he looked up from the paper. He wished he didn't have to tell her this next part. He looked over at Geneviève. She nodded her head, knowing what was coming next and that he couldn't keep it secret.

"Why not?"

"You didn't finish reading the article. They've implicated you as an accomplice rather than a victim."

"An accomplice to murder?" she asked in a dazed voice.

Her face paled and she swayed on her feet. Rage filled him, the kind of rage he hadn't felt in a long, long time. He threw the paper at the hall clothes tree. It scattered on the hardwood floor. "Those sons-a-bitches," he muttered, then put his arms around her and pulled her close, gently rubbing her back.

"We'll clear this up, darling, I promise," he said quietly. *If it's the last thing I ever do,* he added to himself.

"Come, let's go to the parlor," Geneviève suggested. "We'll have some tea and talk about our plan of attack."

Morgan half-smiled in Geneviève's direction. He appreciated her attempt at normalcy. "You're right. There's nothing we can do without a plan."

"Morgan, why don't you take Sarah in while I make the tea. It's the second door on the right."

Morgan didn't wait for Sarah's approval, but gently guided her into the room and seated her on the couch.

He sat next to her, and her head dropped onto his shoulder. He kept his arm firmly around her. He might be able to protect her physically, but the kind of hurt she was experiencing now was out of his control. And he didn't like things out of his control.

"Everything will be all right. We'll work it out," he tried to reassure her.

Her head came up off his shoulder.

"We can't work it out, don't you understand that? Nothing will ever be the same again. First, Adam dies before I have a chance to see him one last time, then we find out there was a conspiracy of silence and that Adam and his company were part of a massacre, and now this—you're wanted for murder and somehow I've been implicated. And, to top it all off, there's still some murdering madman on the loose. It can't be. It just can't be." Her voice broke and suddenly tears were rolling down her face.

When she would have pulled away, his grip tightened, not allowing her to hide her pain. He held her close, wanting to shield her from everything that could harm her. She'd been strong for so long—strong for her brother, strong for him. Now she just didn't have the strength left to be strong for herself. It was up to him to make sure she made it through, just as she had been there for him. And he would.

This time he would be more careful. He would not lose again.

Chapter Thirteen

Morgan had not been happy when she'd insisted she wanted to go with him to see Hedda the next day. Even Geneviève had been worried, but she at least had understood Sarah's need to see the investigation through to the end. She, too, had been shattered by the news about Adam and had retired early, needing some time alone.

Shortly after, Morgan and Sarah had also gone upstairs to their separate bedrooms. She'd lain in her bed for half an hour unable to sleep. Now she sat on a wicker settee just outside her room, on the gallery circling the second story of the house. A slight breeze had picked up, bringing in the cool sea air. She wore only her nightdress and had smoothed it over her up-drawn knees and tucked it around her toes.

Tomorrow they would resume their search for Hedda, and Morgan would be traveling to see his sister, Annie, to break the news about James. Then they would have to deal with the heart of the matter: the man who had started this chain of events, the man that reached out from the past to corrupt the present—and even the future.

She shivered.

"Cold?"

Morgan's voice came from just a few feet behind her. She hadn't heard him come out though his room also opened onto the gallery.

"Not really," she replied, the feeling of restlessness inside her growing more defined.

"Couldn't sleep?"

"No. How about you?"

"Me, either."

Their words bore no relation to the real conversation going on between them, the tentative reaching out to see what each wanted and needed.

"Come and sit a while," she offered, patting the empty cushion beside her.

When he neared, she saw that he wore only his britches. Even his feet were bare, as if he'd been lying naked in his bed and had just thrown on the pants before coming out. He moved like a dark shadow, his broad shoulders blocking the sky as he passed in front of her, his unique scent, musky and male, enveloping her. When he sat beside her, her skin prickled with awareness and she felt every fine hair on her arms stand.

The breeze blew more strongly and again she shivered, this time from the chill. He placed his arm around her shoulder and angled her back until she reclined against his chest, his heat warming her. His breath fanned against her skin as he placed a chaste kiss in the hollow where her shoulder and neck met. She leaned back against him relishing the peace of this moment stolen from the middle of the night.

His arms closed around her waist and he shifted and lifted her onto his lap. They sat in silence. Sarah felt sheltered by his undemanding embrace, and gradually a feeling of confidence came over her. With Morgan at her side they really might succeed after all. Not that things would be easy, but he shared her passionate commitment to their goal. He would not let her down.

She leaned her head back against his shoulder, and he rested his cheek on her hair. The restlessness inside her died away. Eventually he moved, replacing his cheek with his lips. She turned her face, catching his light kisses with her mouth. Suddenly the restlessness was back, a deep, dark force that ate at her from the inside, demanding satisfaction.

She opened for him, meeting his need with her own. His hands slid up from her waist and cupped her breasts. The soft fabric of her gown served as the thinnest of barriers. Her nipples puckered and a shudder ran through her when he rubbed his palms over them. She lifted her head and pulled away, then turned to kneel facing him. His eyes smoldered in the light of the moon, the dark orbs intent upon her.

His hand swept her clothing above her thighs and settled her astride his legs. He buried his other hand in her hair, undoing the long braid, and brought her mouth back to his. His lips were open, and she felt his hunger as he stroked his tongue in and out of her mouth, tangling and engaging hers in a heated duel.

Her own hands swept over the firm contours of his chest and over his powerful shoulders. She enjoyed the feel of the silky curling hairs gliding through her fingers and of the muscles beneath, taut and quivering at her touch. As her arms reached around him, her breasts fell forward until just their tips brushed against him. Even with the fabric of her nightdress between them, she felt a thrill of sensual awareness. She wanted to lie against him, skin to skin.

His back felt strong and supple as she ran her hands up and down along his spine. Just touching him like this melted her insides, filling them with liquid heat. With her knees anchored on either side of him and nothing under her gown, she felt vulnerable, exposed, but he pressed the small of her back until she was flush against him, and she found he was as aroused as she. The hard ridge of his erection lay just beneath her, the roughness of his pants exciting her as the material chafed against her most sensitive spot. Her hips flexed in involuntary response.

As if he understood her need, his hands slipped beneath her nightdress and slid it up her back and over her head. Suddenly she was naked, her breasts gleaming like veined alabaster in the moonlight.

Morgan caught his breath. She looked like a silver statue, perfectly proportioned in every detail, he thought as he stared at the beauty he'd unveiled. Her hair fell in dark waves, billowing in the breeze like seductive, beckoning fingers. A shorter lock blew into his face and he captured it with his hand, holding it in place while he breathed in the essence of her, then wrapped it around one finger while he dipped his head to taste her again. She was sweetness and fire, and like a night-blooming cereus, she blossomed just for him.

He touched her breast and felt it swell in response, the tight nub at its center reaching out for the center of his palm. When he ran the edge of his thumb over her nipple, she moaned into his mouth, the sound ringing sweetly in his ears. He crushed her to him, unable to get enough of her. She pressed herself eagerly against his body, her feminine core brushing against his manhood, tantalizing him with the promise of more.

He reached between them and gently stroked the swollen softness of her secret, most feminine place. She arched into his hand with another moan. She was more than ready, hot and liquid and urging him on. She leaned back and reached for the front of his britches, caressing his length with her palm. Exquisite pleasure shot through him, leaving him breathless and on the very edge of losing control. With the delicacy of a cat, she undid the buttons keeping him from her. When at last he sprang free, she pushed the waist of his pants down. He lifted himself, helping her to ease the garment from beneath him, then kicked it off.

This time, when he pulled her close, his manhood nestled against her feminine center, flesh to flesh, and he gloried in the heat that swept through him, surrounding him with the scent of their desire. Her hips rocked forward and then back as she rubbed herself against him. Spirals of need spun through him. He wanted to bury himself inside her as deep as he could. Just thinking about it was enough to make him close his eyes and gasp for air. Another second and he would lose all control, her effect on his senses was so potent.

Gently pushing her from him, he eased her hips higher until he was poised at the very brink of entering her. Her eyes opened wide as she felt him and understood what he wanted. With a smile she slowly eased downward, taking him inside, enfolding him in her special warmth, caressing him on every side as she accepted him, then lifted and settled again, enclosing him fully.

He loved the way she felt, and told her so, whispering

how wonderful she was, how good he felt inside her, how hot and tight she was,—made just for him.

She moved in tempo with him, lifting until they were barely connected, then sinking again until their bellies touched, her breasts swaying in front of his face. He lifted one hand to cup a soft mound, shaping it for his mouth, then lowered his head to lick and suckle the sensitive tip.

Sarah felt the tension build, the pleasure in her breast magnifying and echoing the pleasure down below. Her back arched as she offered herself to him. Her hands grabbed onto his shoulders as she rode him, her breath coming in gasps as the pleasure intensified. Morgan filled her again and again, each thrust taking her higher until she cried out his name and the explosion came. Tremor after tremor shook her as his desire met hers, and he thrust one last time.

Sarah collapsed onto him, her head nestling in the hollow of his shoulder. She matched him breath for breath as they floated back to reality, arms entwined, legs shaking with the force of their intimate embrace.

Their joining drove away the ugly images that had haunted her all day, replacing them with hope and life and a deep certainty that with this man, anything was possible. She lifted her head and gently kissed him, tiny butterfly kisses that covered his cheeks, his eyes, his jaw. He stroked her hair back and let her have her way with him until, suddenly impatient, he wrapped her hair around his fist and held her in place for a long, deep kiss.

She could feel him hardening inside her and marveled at his potency. She felt full and satisfied, yet hungry for more, eager to follow his lead back to that marvelous pinnacle of feeling, where emotion filled every empty place in her soul and brought her a peaceful healing.

He rolled over, maneuvering them both until she lay beneath him. This time he took control, setting the pace, driving her until she thought she couldn't climb any higher, then pushing her farther still. When their climax came, they greeted it together, each crying the other's name as they arched into that magic place.

The last thing Sarah remembered was thinking how wonderful she felt with his weight pressing her down, his warmth seeping deep inside her to his own special place in her heart.

The sanitarium stood on a slight rise surrounded by a tall wrought-iron fence. The building had clearly been a plantation house at some point in its existence though the grounds around it were greatly reduced. Beyond the gate, a double row of oak trees lined the drive leading to the house. Graceful pillars held up the second-floor gallery and framed the double doors of the entryway.

Sarah's scalp itched as she walked to those doors, Morgan at her side. Geneviève had helped her dye her hair this morning, turning the auburn tresses to a dull brown. Her friend had promised that the hideous color would come off after a couple of washes. She wore it in a simple knot at the back of her neck and had dressed in clothes typical of a country matron.

Morgan had also refined his disguise, trimming his beard and borrowing a set of britches and a shirt from Geneviève's gardener. The clothes didn't fit him, having been designed for a man of wider girth and shorter height. A braided leather belt held the pants in place and kept the extra fabric of the shirt from billowing out around him. To Sarah's eyes, he looked handsome no matter what he wore, but she knew no one else would recognize him in the unassuming, somewhat shy role he was playing.

They knocked on the front door of the main house and were greeted by an old man.

"How may I help you?" he asked in a neutral tone.

"We're here to see Miss Hedda Winslow," Sarah said.

The old man frowned. "Don't get many visitors for her. I'll have to check if you're on the list."

"The list?"

"Her visitors list, ma'am. Says who can and can't see her. Last I looked there was naught but one name on it."

"Who makes up this list?" she demanded.

"Either Dr. Corbin or his missus. They run the place. I just work here. Can't let you in if you're not on the list. Rules, you know. It's as good as my job if I slip up. Now you folks just have a seat in here, and I'll go check you out. What did you say your name was?"

"We didn't," Morgan said.

"It's Prugh," Sarah said quickly. "At least, mine used to be." She gave the man a shy smile and looked down at her left hand where a gold ring gleamed on her third finger. Geneviève had lent her the ring, and she'd turned it upside down, hiding the small pearl in her palm, so that the band resembled a wedding ring.

"Prugh?" the old man asked.

"Yes. Hedda's cousin. You may have heard of my family?"

The old man shook his head.

"From Barner's Creek. Hedda was raised near there," she added helpfully when the man still shook his head.

"Sorry," he said. "Didn't know she had any family."

"We lost touch, what with the war and all. I only learned recently that she was here. We were close when we were young." She looked at him with pleading eyes, as if this reunion with her supposedly long-lost cousin was a matter of deep concern. Which it was, in fact, but not for the reasons the caretaker thought.

"Well, let me just check the records," he said. "You and your husband just hang on a minute. I'll be right back."

He left, and Sarah shot Morgan a worried look.

"Don't worry," he said and took her hand, rubbing it between both of his. "If this doesn't work we'll try something else. At least now we know she's here."

"But, Morgan, it's terribly important that we see her soon. I couldn't bear having to wait now that we've finally found her."

"Don't give up yet. Every man's got his price, and my guess is the caretaker won't be that hard to convince. Now try to ease up a little. You'll make yourself sick if you let every little setback put you into a state."

He was right, she knew, but she couldn't help herself. She felt so close to solving the elusive and deadly mystery, and the thought of another delay was unconscionable.

The old man came in and Sarah stood eagerly. "Can we see her?"

"Sorry, ma'am. Ain't no one by the name of Prugh listed. You'll have to come back on Monday when Dr. Corbin will be here. He's the only one can let you in."

"But Monday is two days away! My husband and I

can't stay away from home that long." Tears filled her eyes and she blinked rapidly.

The old man looked sympathetic as he shifted from one foot to the other uncomfortably.

"Listen, honey," Morgan murmured just loud enough for the man to overhear. "Why don't you step outside for a minute and let us men talk?"

She looked at him with hope in her face and nodded. In a few minutes, Morgan called her back inside.

"What happened?" she whispered, hardly daring to believe what her eyes were telling her.

"Everything's set, but the old man is worried about his job. He'll only give us a few minutes."

Her knees felt weak with relief, and she stumbled. Morgan quickly grabbed her by the arm and steadied her, then held her to his side.

"This way," the old man called from the end of the hall at the rear of the house. "Miz Winslow's got her own cabin out back."

He led the way to a small, well-kept cabin several yards from the rear door, one of several that stood in a row.

"Used to keep the house slaves out here," he said conversationally. "Now a few of the special patients get these as private quarters."

The quarters might be private but they resembled a prison more than a palace. The windows were barred, and the door locked from the outside.

"Is she dangerous?" Sarah asked, not really sure about the exact nature of Hedda's affliction.

"Nah. Just don't want her wandering about when she gets into one of her states, especially on one of her bad days."

"Is today a bad day?"

He shrugged. "Don't know yet, not till we go in and find out."

The caretaker unlocked the door and opened it. He motioned them to follow him as he went inside. Sarah looked up at Morgan, and he gave her a reassuring smile. This was the moment she'd been waiting for, the moment when she would learn what really happened at Croxton's Mill.

She walked into the cabin and found herself in a small square room. In the corner by the window, a woman sat in a rocking chair, bobbing and weaving. A funny noise came from her, too faint to make out clearly.

"Miz Winslow, you got company, dear," the old man said rather loudly.

His words did not seem to penetrate Hedda's haze. She continued to rock back and forth, the chair's rockers making a squeaking sound against the floorboards.

"She gets like this, sometimes," he said with an apologetic shrug.

"Do you know what she's saying?" Morgan asked.

"Never paid her no never mind. She's always going on about something. Sounds like a song, a nursery rhyme, maybe, from her childhood. Been saying the same damn fool thing since '67 when they first brought her here."

"Mind if I try?" Morgan stepped in front of Hedda and squatted so they were at eye level to each other. He listened intently, then looked up at Sarah. "It's definitely words of some sort. Something about 'deep and cold' and the 'secret holds.' I can't make out the other parts. Come give it a try."

Sarah leaned over, placing her head next to his and

concentrated on the woman's mumbled remarks. She was repeating the same couplet over and over. Slowly Sarah began understanding some of the words. And then suddenly it all made sense.

"In a grave, so deep and cold, the town, my friends, the secret holds," Sarah recited in time with Hedda.

"Yes, I think that's it," Morgan said. "Unfortunately, that doesn't help us."

"Help you?" the old man asked. "With what?" His curious brown eyes darted from one to another.

Sarah searched for an explanation that might satisfy him without raising his suspicions, either about who they really were or why they had come here.

Morgan smiled blandly. "My wife is trying to find the rest of her family. You know how it was during the war. Families got separated and never found each other again. Sarah's looking for her brother. Thought Hedda might know something about him."

The old man shook his head sadly. "Don't reckon you'll ever know nothing from her, not the way she is now. Even on her good days she gets so excitable you can't do much with her."

"Well, we thank you. We had such high hopes. Come, dear." Morgan put his arm around Sarah's shoulders as if to lead her away. Then he turned back to the caretaker. "Oh, I just thought of something. You say Miss Winslow gets a visitor now and then? Who is it, if I might ask? Maybe they'll know something about the family."

The old man looked suddenly guilty. "Can't say as I know," he said briskly and rushed them to the door, stopping only to lock it from the outside before herding them toward the big house. "Maybe you can find your own way out," he suggested. "I can't answer none of your questions. I'll be fired for sure."

"I guess I'll have to come back on Monday, then, and see if Dr. Corbin can help."

"Dr. Corbin? I thought you said you couldn't stick around until Monday," the man whined.

"Didn't think I could, but I hate to disappoint the wife. And as you said, Miss Winslow might have a good day. We'll check with Dr. Corbin, tell him we don't want to see her if she's like today."

"But then he'll know you saw her!"

Morgan scratched his head. "I guess you're right," he said slowly. "But how else am I going to get the information I need?"

He was the consummate convincer, playing the caretaker like a fish on the line, leaving him no alternative but to come into his net, like it or not.

"All right, all right. Let's make a deal. You want something, and I want something. We can both come out ahead."

He looked at Morgan's pocket, and Sarah realized that Morgan had paid him for their visit to Hedda. That information both pleased and dismayed her. Apparently Morgan was right: every man did have his price, and she hoped the caretaker's wasn't too high. At the same time she couldn't help but wonder at world where honor was bought and sold so freely.

"I'm willing, if you really know what you're talking about. How will I know you're telling me the truth?"

The older man drew himself up to his full height. "I ain't lied to you yet, have I?" He gave Morgan an indignant look.

Sarah couldn't believe her eyes. The man was willing

to sell any secret for a price and then got prickly about his honor? She couldn't believe it, but she saw Morgan was taking it all very seriously.

"That's true," he said. "But I have to protect my wife, you know. We need an arrangement that's fair to both of us."

"What do you mean?"

"Well, let me ask you this. Are you willing to tell me your information and then I'll decide what to pay you?"

"Hell, no." He looked at Sarah and reddened. "I mean—"

"I know what you mean. I feel exactly the same way about paying you first. So here's what we'll do: I'll give you half the money now and the other half after you've told me what I want to know. How's that?"

An avaricious gleam shone in the old man's eyes. "Sounds fair enough."

"Good," Morgan said with a grim smile. He took a few greenbacks from his pocket and carefully tore them down the middle.

The old man looked at him as if he was crazy. "What you doing that for?"

"Here's your half, just as we agreed. You'll get the rest after you talk."

"What good is this half?"

"None, without my half. That's the point."

The man swore under his breath. "All right," he finally muttered, seeing the implacable look on Morgan's face.

Here was *Le Sabre* in action, the sword mercilessly cutting through all obstacles to get what he wanted. Sarah watched him in fascination, a chill running down her spine. He was a familiar stranger at such moments—

someone she thought she knew so well and yet with a side to him she neither knew nor fully understood. But there was no denying he was effective at getting his way.

"The man's name was Darber," the old man said reluctantly.

"What man?" Morgan asked.

"The man who comes to visit Miz Winslow. Who'd you think?"

"Darber, eh?" Morgan looked questioningly at Sarah and she shook her head. The name meant nothing to her either. "Where's he from? When does he come to see her?"

"How should I know?" the man retorted.

"Fine. Come along, dear, let's go," Morgan said to Sarah. "I'm afraid we'll have to come back on Monday after all." He took her arm and turned toward the front of the house where their carriage waited.

"Wait. I can tell you what he looks like," the caretaker called after them.

"That might help." Morgan faced the man.

"I ain't seen him but a couple of times, you know."

Morgan nodded impatiently. "Go on."

"Well, he's not quite as large as you. Kind of narrower in the shoulders, too, but a gentleman, you know? He's got manners and he dresses fit to kill. He's always very secretive, though, like he doesn't want anyone to know who he is or that he's come to visit. Usually comes at night when no one else is here."

"How do you know?"

"Told you. I seen him. He weren't too pleased neither. Got all angry that Dr. Corbin wasn't here instead. I told him the doctor had an emergency, not that he's any kind of doctor, if you ask me, but then no one's too curious since the war. Those Yankees just come down here and do what they please."

"Dr. Corbin is from the North?"

Sarah glanced at Morgan, noting his interest, though why it mattered where Corbin came from, she couldn't begin to fathom.

"Who else would have the money to fix the place up like this?" the caretaker replied with irrefutable logic. "Anyway, Mr. Darber said I wasn't to tell anyone I'd seen him if I knew what was good for me."

The man shuddered. "And he meant it, too. You should have seen the look in his eye."

"What did he do here?" Sarah asked.

"Just stopped in to check on Hedda and make sure she was getting her medicine all regular like."

"Medicine?" Morgan's voice had an edge to it.

"Yeah, she takes the stuff every day. Keeps her calm-like."

"Keeps her quiet, more likely."

"Huh?"

"Never mind," Morgan said. "Tell me more about what the man looks like. Was his hair light or dark? What about his eyes?"

"Funny you should mention that. His hair was real funny. Dark, you know, over most of his head. Darker even than yours. But on this one side"—the old man touched his right temple—"well, it's all light colored, not white, mind you, more like blond or something."

Sarah gasped. "Philip," she murmured.

She felt light-headed at the thought. Surely it was impossible—but how many people could have a swatch of light hair just there?

"The man's name," Morgan cut in, his eyes bright, "could it have been D'Arbereaux?"

"Ain't that what I said? Darber, that's his name all right."

Sarah had only the dimmest recollection of Morgan giving the man the other half of the torn money and promising not to tell anyone of their visit. The old man told them he wouldn't tell anyone either, which seemed to suit Morgan.

On the drive back to Geneviève's, Sarah simply sat in the corner, trying to take it all in. What could it mean that Philip regularly visited Hedda? And why did he check on her medication? Were they relatives or . . . ? Her mind shied away from completing the thought.

When they arrived at the summer house, Morgan helped her down from the carriage and inside the front door.

"Are you all right?" he asked when she just stood there feeling disoriented and strangely lethargic.

She looked at him blankly. How could she possibly be all right after what they'd learned?

As if he read her thoughts, Morgan added, "What I really meant was, is there anything I can do to help?"

"Help with what?" Geneviève asked as she walked into the room. "Oh, my goodness, Sarah. What happened?"

"She's had a shock. Do you have some brandy?"

Sarah didn't want brandy. She wanted answers and she wanted the truth, the *whole* truth, for she suddenly realized what had been bothering her most since they'd realized that Philip was the man visiting Hedda: Morgan's lack of surprise.

"What does Philip have to do with this?" Sarah demanded of Morgan.

"Philippe?" Geneviève asked. "You've seen him?"

Morgan shook his head and quickly told her of their discoveries at the sanitarium.

"But what does it mean?" Geneviève asked. "Sarah, you've been close to him. Has he never mentioned this woman?"

Sarah shook her head. "It seems Philip has kept a lot of secrets. And he appears not to be the only one."

Sarah stared at Morgan, challenging him to deny her suspicions.

"I'm sorry, Sarah," he said softly. "I never meant for you find out this way."

"Never meant for me to find out this way! What way *did* you want me to find out?"

"I didn't know for sure that he was involved. I only suspected it."

"Why didn't you even hint at it?" she asked, wanting to find a way out.

"Would you have believed me?"

Sarah looked away from him. He wasn't going to apologize for not telling her, sorry though he might be that she'd found out. And in a way she understood; she wouldn't have believed him if he'd implicated Philip without any evidence.

"No," she admitted in a small voice. "And neither will anyone else, will they?"

"Believe what?" Geneviève asked impatiently.

"Philip was in the army, you know," Sarah said. "A captain."

"So? I know all that. What does that have to so with his visiting Hedda Winslow?" She paled suddenly. "My God, you think he's the one, don't you?"

Sarah nodded miserably. "It seems so." The words slipped out, putting the thought she'd denied into sharp focus.

"But who will believe such a thing?" Geneviève said, making no attempt to hide her surprise and outrage. "It can't be true. I mean, I never liked the man, but this . . . it is outrageous. *Fou.* Crazy. *Philippe?* No, you must be mistaken."

"Perhaps," Morgan said noncommittally. "But a lot of it fits. He was in Lee's army as an officer; his company was involved in the battle Ossy told us of, and in the rout that followed. Who's to say he didn't get separated from them for a while? And Mrs. Prugh said Hedda left with an officer after the massacre."

"But why would she leave with him?" Geneviève demanded.

"Maybe he gave her no choice, not if she wanted her life spared. I don't know, but right now that's the most likely explanation."

"I still don't believe it," Geneviève asserted. "And what about you, *chérie?*"

Sarah didn't know what to say. "I don't want to believe it. After all, Philip was so helpful to me in trying to find Adam."

"Yes, and now Adam is dead," Morgan said harshly.

Sarah turned shocked eyes to him. In two steps he was at her side, his arms around her. "I didn't mean it like that. You had no way of knowing. No one did. Even now Geneviève can't believe it—and maybe she's right. Our evidence is not complete."

The word *yet* hung in the air, though it hadn't been said.

"What do you plan to do?" Geneviève asked.

"Find a way to get him to admit what happened. Or find someone who was there and is willing to talk just as I was doing before."

"I'll help," Sarah said. "If you're wrong, I want to clear Philip's name once and for all."

He clenched his jaw. "And if I'm right?"

Sarah had no answer, for then it meant she'd led Philip right to her brother. Had Philip simply been using her? And what about Morgan? Did he see her merely as a means for reaching Philip?

The betrayals ran so deep she couldn't begin to sort them out. She pulled out of Morgan's embrace, knowing she couldn't think straight when he held her. He stepped back, regarding her warily. Was he afraid of losing her as a link to Philip or was he worried about her? How could she tell?

Nothing was the same since she'd started looking for Adam. Adam. He was at the heart of her troubles. Had it not been for him, Philip would have shown no interest in her and she would never have dared seek out a man like Morgan.

"If you're right," she repeated in a hoarse whisper, "then damn you all, and Adam most of all!"

With one hand she reached for the locket that had hung around her neck virtually every day since Adam had given it to her. Wrenching it off with a hard jerk, she flung it at the stone wall behind the fireplace. It bounced off and landed on the slate floor.

"Oh, Sarah, don't," Geneviève said, her voice full of sorrow. She scurried over to the hearth and picked up the locket. "Adam wouldn't have wanted you to feel like this. He was trying to save you from this pain." Tears ran down her face as she bent over to pick up the gold pendant. "Oh, look, his picture has slipped. And there's something behind it."

"What?" Sarah asked in surprise.

Geneviève handed her the gaping locket. "Look," she said lifting the edge of Adam's picture where it had separated from the gold rim holding it in place.

Sarah peered under the photograph and saw a thin piece of neatly folded paper tucked beneath it.

"How did this get here?" she asked, thoroughly confused.

"It's not yours?"

Sarah shook her head and gently pried the paper loose, afraid it might tear. The paper was old and slightly brittle. She unfolded the page and held it by an edge.

"It's Adam's handwriting," she exclaimed.

"What's it from?"

"I don't know. It looks like a journal entry, but the writing is so small I can barely make it out."

"Come over near the window," Geneviève urged. "There's more light."

The three of them gathered round the end table by the window, and Sarah set the page down where they all could see it.

"Eighteen sixty-four," Geneviève read. "It's from the war. Can you make it out?" She looked expectantly at Morgan.

"Do you mind?" he asked Sarah. He gave her a quizzical look, and she realized he'd sensed her turmoil—and her anger at him, muted though it was.

"No, please, go ahead."

She stepped back so he could get in closer. He frowned at her and looked as if he were about to say something, but instead he leaned over the document and peered at it intently.

" 'Fought another battle today. The Yanks beat us good,' " he read haltingly. " 'They called the retreat, and we ran every which way. Men lay dying, screaming for help, and those damn Yanks kept shooting. The man running with me was hit. I couldn't even stop to help him. Several of us met at a small town. We were so angry and scared. These were the folks that helped the Yanks, someone yelled. The order came to kill them. 'Tweren't my captain, but still I obeyed. When we were done firing, no one moved. We'd killed them all, and not an armed man among them. Oh, God, we were scared now. We promised to not tell a soul what had happened. Swore on a Bible someone had found in one of the houses. Then we buried them all and burned the place down.' "

"Is that it?" Geneviève asked in a husky voice as she blinked back tears.

"No, there's a bit more." He looked back at the paper. " 'I can't bring myself to tell though I know I should. But I have to write it here. It can't be forgotten. Forgive me, God, for I have lost my soul today.' "

Chapter Fourteen

Breakfast was a quiet affair. The events of the past few days had so drained everyone that each sat lost in thought. Sarah looked particularly defeated, Morgan thought, eyeing her over the rim of his cup as he took a sip of the bracing coffee Geneviève's maid had prepared. He remembered Sarah from the first day they'd met, feisty and impetuous, so sure of herself and her quest.

He'd warned her then, that her impulsiveness would one day get her in trouble. Apparently that day had come. The thought gave him no satisfaction. He lowered his cup and looked at her openly. She didn't return his gaze, and a pain sliced through him. Was the messenger to be punished, then? After all, he *was* the one who'd destroyed all her illusions—first defaming her brother, then her close friend Philip. Whom could she trust?

As his thoughts swirled, the realization hit him, knocking his breath from his body. She didn't trust him! He dropped his gaze lest she or Geneviève see the turmoil inside him. How could she not trust him? He'd let her farther into his life than he had anyone. Feelings of indignation quickly veered toward anger. Of all the people in her life, he was the one who'd always been honest with her.

Have you really, an inner voice asked. He took a deep breath, quelling his anger while he thought things through more carefully. He hadn't confided in her beyond the most superficial aspects of this investigation. He'd thought to protect her. All he'd accomplished was to lose her trust and faith, that honest naïveté he'd always found so charming.

And as he watched her something occurred to him. She wasn't as much upset with him as she was with herself. She'd found her judgment had been faulty where it had most counted, and she didn't know where to turn.

He noticed now the purple smudges beneath her eyes and wondered if she'd slept at all. He cursed silently, damning himself for not going in to check on her. He'd let his own insecurities and petty angers overrule his good sense. He would not let that happen again.

"I have to go see my sister," he announced, ending the tension of the prolonged silence. "I'd like to leave today. I thought you might like to come," he added to Sarah.

When she didn't respond, Geneviève asked, "Where does she live?"

"Upriver a short way. In Madson. It's a fairly small town. You may not have heard of it."

"Will you be back tonight?"

"I'm not sure. Probably not. Annie can put us up for the night if necessary. She may need the company when she hears what we have to say."

"When do you want to leave?" Sarah asked.

"In about an hour, if that's all right."

For the first time, Sarah looked at him. "I'll be ready," she said, then pushed her chair from the table. Leaving her breakfast untouched she left the room.

Morgan stood to follow her, but Geneviève's hand came out and stopped him. "Don't. Give her some time." He sat down again heavily.

"I didn't mean for things to turn out this way, you know."

"What way is that?" Geneviève asked. "That you would find the answers to your questions or that you would find Sarah?"

Morgan ran his hand over the back of his neck. "Both. Neither. I don't know. She has me so confused . . ."

Geneviève smiled. "I think you have her confused, too. This business is ugly and painful for us all, I'm afraid. Did Sarah ever tell you about Adam and me?"

He shook his head.

"I would have married him if he had come back for me."

"Is that why you've remained single?"

Geneviève stared into the distance. "Perhaps. As long as there was the slightest chance . . ." She shook her head and blinked rapidly. "I'm sorry. I guess I always kept hoping. It seems like so much foolishness now, the dreams of girlhood. I thought I had put them behind me, but maybe I simply buried them where they wouldn't hurt so much."

"What will you do now?"

She shrugged. "What I have always done. Go about my life as best I can."

"You're too good a woman to spend your life alone. You should marry, have children."

She laughed. "How like a man! Do you think the only way to happiness is to be married? What about for yourself?"

"I'm a man." He looked away, uncomfortable with the direction the conversation had taken.

"Yes, and a good one. Don't let your masculine notions of what's right and wrong keep you from what's important. You men think that women are soft and fragile and in need of being sheltered to the point where you cut us off. We're stronger than you think, and more forgiving. If Adam had come back to me, who knows what might have happened? But running from the truth didn't help either one of us, now did it?"

Morgan knew she didn't want an answer to her question. She was simply making a point, a point he needed to think about before he could make any decisions.

"I have to get ready to go," he said.

"Yes." She stood and began collecting the breakfast dishes. "Just think about what I said. I don't know what you're running from, but it can't be as bad as you think. You're a good man, Morgan. And Sarah is a strong woman. She may be confused and hurt by the events of the past few days, but she'll survive this. I know that. And she'll survive whatever you have to tell her, too."

"You seem pretty sure of yourself," he replied, rising from his chair.

"I'm very observant. It's both one of my virtues and one of my faults. Now," she said, her tone brisk, "why don't you tell me what you'll need for this voyage in the way of food, and I'll pack you a hamper."

* * *

Sarah washed the last dish and rinsed it in the bucket of clear water. Drying her hands, she looked around the neat little kitchen to see if anything else was out of order. It all looked tidy.

"You didn't have to clean up," a soft voice said from the door. "I was going to get to it in a few minutes."

Annie Campbell was some years older than her brother. Her hair was a medium brown, and her eyes somewhere between green and hazel. She carried herself with a dignified sadness.

"It was no trouble," Sarah replied. "This has been a hard day for you, I know."

"Yes. Morgan told me about your brother, so you know what I've been going through. James was never the same after the war. Now I know why." She came in and sat on a chair by the small table. She looked up at Sarah. "I don't know if knowing what really happened is better or worse than just suspecting."

Her eyes filled, and she bit on her lower lip. "Don't mind me," she whispered, shaking her hand in front of her face.

Sarah handed her a dry dish towel, and she quickly wiped her cheeks.

"James was a good man, you know. It's hard to believe he was part of that madness."

Sarah sat on the chair across from her. "So was Adam. I think there was just something overwhelming about that time and place. And the other people there. They were good men who went berserk. That's not an excuse, I know, but look how eaten up they were with their guilt."

"Except for that Philip Darber—he seems to be handling it, making sure Hedda didn't have enough of her faculties to say anything to anyone," Annie said with anger. "He started the whole thing, and the other men suffered for it."

"His name is D'Arbereaux," Sarah said softly. "And ... I don't want to be cruel but ..."

"What?" Annie demanded when Sarah hesitated.

"They didn't *have* to listen, did they?"

"What else could they do?"

"They could have refused. Adam could have said no. I don't see Morgan capable of shooting up a town of helpless women and children no matter what someone ordered him to do, do you? The men might have been basically good, but they were also flawed."

Annie looked at her intently. "You love my brother, don't you?"

Sarah wanted to deny it, but couldn't bring herself to utter the lie.

"Morgan isn't perfect, you know," Annie went on. "You're right about him, though. He wants to do what's right, and it hurts him when he can't. You need to understand that if you want to make a life with him."

"He hasn't asked and even if he did—"

"He may never ask because of what happened," Annie interrupted. "You may have to persuade him."

"But—"

"Has he ever told you about our childhood?"

Sarah shook her head. "He's never said much about the past at all."

"That doesn't surprise me. Our mother was a very religious woman. She believed in the ten commandments above all and drummed them into us when we were young. Then the war came. Do you know what it's like to be a man and live by the commandments during the war? Our mother wouldn't let Morgan join in the conflict, not if it meant taking a life."

"But Morgan was in the war. At least, from what he's said now and then, it sounded like he's been in many battles."

"Oh, he was in the battles, all right. He just didn't fight. He administered aid to the soldiers that were wounded. Even helped the Yanks, now and again if they were badly injured. Nearly got court-martialed for his trouble."

"That sounds just like him, helping a wounded man without worrying about what side he fought on."

And staying around for the punishment it might entail—unlike James and Adam, Sarah thought, though she didn't voice the words for fear of hurting Annie. The other woman hadn't had the time to adjust to the news and must be feeling the loss of James—and his reputation—keenly.

"Morgan was always the one to help others. What I want to tell you has to do with just that kind of unselfishness. This happened after the war ended, and I thought it might destroy him. At the time I had my hands full with James and couldn't talk with Morgan the way I would have liked. But knowing how our mother could react, I know it had to hurt him deeply."

"I don't think Morgan would want you telling me all this," Sarah said, feeling torn. Despite her uncertainties about him, she hungered for even the tiniest scrap of information, anything that would help her judge if her impressions of him were right or wrong. But she also felt a certain loyalty to him.

"Probably not. But I think you need to know. More

importantly, I think *he* needs for you to know. You're the first person in whom he's shown any interest in years."

"Because of this investigation," Sarah explained.

Annie laughed quietly. "I hope you're just saying that because I'm his older sister and not because you really believe it. I've seen the way he looks at you."

Sarah chewed on her lip, wishing she could believe all Annie was implying but afraid to trust her own instincts after the way they'd betrayed her.

"I'm not sure I believe you, but we'll let it go for now."

"Fair enough," Annie said. "This is what happened. After the war there were a lot of soldiers with no homes to go back to. They frequented the bars, drinking and fighting and carrying on the way men sometimes will. One night Morgan caught a soldier in a back alley beating and having his way with a young woman. She was fighting him off something fierce but didn't have the strength to make an escape.

"When Morgan intervened, the man drew a gun and fired, wounding Morgan. Then he turned the gun on the girl, threatening to blow her head off. Morgan had no choice but to go after the man who kept firing his gun until he himself was killed."

"Morgan killed him?"

"After a fashion. It was unquestionably self-defense, and there never was any problem from the courts. It's Morgan's own sense of duty that haunted him over the death."

"But why? The man would have killed him or the girl if he hadn't been stopped."

"True enough from what the witnesses said."

"Witnesses? Then why didn't they help?"

305

"Down by the waterfront they only watch. Dangerous place to stay around."

Her words were an uncanny echo of Morgan's. Sarah remembered how adamant he'd been that she avoid the dangerous area, and now she knew why. For him, the danger wasn't hypothetical; it was a grim reality rooted in his past.

"But that wasn't the worst of it," Annie continued. "When Morgan finished with the soldier and knew it was safe, he turned to the girl, wanting to help her. She took one look at him and screamed, then took off. She ran along the levee for a while, and Morgan chased after her, afraid of what might happen to her in her hysterical condition. But he couldn't keep up. The loss of blood from his wound slowed him.

"The girl stopped at a place where the water was deepest, right along the levee wall, took one look over her shoulder, and threw herself in."

Sarah gasped. "But why?"

Annie shrugged. "Who knows? Maybe she saw Morgan as just another man out to get her, maybe she was so demoralized by what had happened she didn't want to go on living."

"Did she die, then?"

Annie nodded. "It was the worst thing that could have happened to Morgan, you know. The police treated him like a hero, but he didn't feel like one. He felt as if he'd abandoned the very principles at the center of his life to save a girl who refused to be saved. He always wondered if he could have stopped the man another way, short of killing him, and blames himself that two lives were lost that day."

"How awful." Sarah could see where Morgan would

have been deeply shaken by the events. In all their travels, he had carried a knife but she had never seen him use it. If he could talk himself out of a situation, he would. Even when he'd been tied up and locked in the cellar the night Bettine was killed, he'd merely knocked out the guard who'd stabbed him.

"It was awful. And it left a lasting mark. Morgan retreated into a hard shell after that incident. They called him *Le Sabre* because he was as hard and cold as that cutting blade. If I hadn't been desperate, I don't know if I would have gone to him over James's death, but I had no choice. And then I found that the Morgan I'd always known was still there, buried beneath the surface but still reachable.

"I can't tell you how wonderful he was, staying here when I couldn't stand being alone and going after your Mr. D'Arbereaux or whoever it was that killed James. But to the outside world, he was still *Le Sabre*. You're the only other person I know who has broken through to him. I hope you will give him the chance to come completely out of his shell. I'd like the old Morgan back."

The knock on the door was as abrupt as it was unexpected. Morgan shot a glance over at Annie. She looked as bewildered as anyone.

"Were you expecting callers this evening?" he asked.

"No. Not really."

"Let me answer then." He went to her door. "Who's there?"

He pushed aside the cotton curtain and peered through the small window in the door. A man stood there.

"Perry Armbruster," he called out. "Come to see Miz Campbell."

"Oh, Sergeant. Do come in," Annie said as she flung open the door. "I wasn't expecting you back before tomorrow."

"I thought it would take longer myself. If this is a bad time, I can return in the morning."

"No, no. Come in and have a seat. This is my brother, Morgan Cain. The sergeant knew James in the war."

As if she suddenly realized what all that meant, Annie paled and swayed on her feet.

The sergeant clasped her by the arm and said, "Here, now. Come sit yourself. Have you been unwell?"

The sergeant was a tall man with a shock of red hair and a matching mustache. His manner with Annie was carefully solicitous, and Morgan stepped back.

"I'm fine," Annie said in a small voice when she was finally seated. "I just had some very disturbing news today."

Sarah walked in then. "Is everything all right?" she asked, looking worriedly at Annie and at the stranger.

"A brandy might be nice for the lady," Armbruster suggested. "She's looking a bit peaked."

"I'll get it," Morgan said and went to the sideboard to get a glass. "How about you, Sarah? Sergeant?"

"Yes, sir, I'd be most grateful for a sip," Armbruster replied.

"None for me. Thanks," Sarah said.

"Permit me to introduce myself. I'm Perry Armbruster. I knew James Campbell in the war. Perhaps Miz Campbell mentioned my visit?"

"I'm afraid not. We've brought some troubling news,

and Annie hasn't had a chance to tell us what's been happening here."

"Ah, I see," said the sergeant. "Here, let me help with the drinks," he added and crossed the room. "She knows then, does she, about the incident?" he whispered as he neared Morgan.

Morgan nodded. "You were in James's company, were you not?"

"Yes. But I wasn't there that day. I got separated from the others during the retreat. By the time we all caught up again, the deed was done and over. But I heard the tale. 'Tis hard to keep a secret like that tied in a tight knot."

"Is that why you're here?"

Armbruster looked surprised. "Why on earth would you think so?"

"No reason. I just wondered what brought you. Annie's alone now. I feel protective."

"And well you should. It's a harsh world. Too harsh. My friends are dying, one by one. I came to see if James knew why, only to find he was dead, too. I told Miz. Campbell I wanted to check on another of my friends. And that's where I've just come from. He was killed two days ago. Fell in front of a speeding wagon."

"Or was pushed."

"Aye. That's what I've been thinking. It's the way of it that has me flummoxed."

"He was at the massacre?"

Armbruster's eyes opened wide, so wide that Morgan could make out the thin brown band circling the green irises.

"Ye-es," he answered slowly. "And so were the others, were they not?"

309

"Most, as far as I can tell."

"You've been looking into this?"

"Annie asked me to."

"Of course. I see." Armbruster stroked his mustache, looking lost in thought.

"Excuse me a moment. Let me take this to Annie."

The sergeant nodded absently, and Morgan returned to Annie with her brandy. "Are you all right?"

"Yes. Seeing the sergeant just reminded me all over again of what happened."

"Would you like to go up to your room? I can see to the sergeant's needs. I'd like to talk to him a bit more anyway."

"Was he there?" she asked with a shudder.

"No. But he's heard of it. It's possible he might know something we don't."

Annie nodded. "I'll go up then."

The two women left, Sarah helping Annie up the stairs as they talked in low voices.

Morgan glanced at Armbruster. He was still standing by the sideboard, a frown on his face, oblivious to the women's departure. Morgan decided he could be safely left for a couple of moments, and went to his room behind the stairs. Reaching into his bag, he pulled out a sheaf of notes. When he returned, the sergeant had poured himself a drink and was sitting in an armchair, waiting.

"Took the liberty," he said, holding up his glass. "Hope you don't mind."

"Not at all. I apologize for not thinking of it."

"No problem. Seems you've got a lot on your mind. Puzzling business, eh? Now who would want them all dead and gone?" he asked, returning to their earlier topic. "Could be someone plumb crazy or . . ."

Sarah came in then and looked questioningly from one man to the other.

"We're discussing the murders," Morgan told her. "Sergeant Armbruster was in James' and Adam's company, though he got lost during the rout."

"Does anyone know that or is he in danger?" Sarah asked.

"In danger?" Armbruster stood at Sarah's approach, waiting until she perched on the settee before resuming his seat.

"Someone seems to be killing everyone who was at the massacre," she said.

"And you think he'll come after me?"

"It's possible," Morgan answered, seeing no reason to hide the gruesome facts from the man. "I'd be careful if I were you."

"I'll do more than that. I'll look for the murderer myself. No one's going to intimidate Perry Armbruster."

"We think we know who it might be," Sarah said hesitantly. She glanced at Morgan, her eyes dark with worry, but at least she looked at him. Earlier in the day he'd felt cut adrift, as if some invisible but all too real barrier lay between them.

"Who?" Armbruster demanded.

"A man named D'Arbereaux," Morgan said, sitting in the second armchair. "He was a captain in the war."

"He's a powerful man. I've heard of him."

"Do you know if he was at Croxton's Mill?"

Armbruster shook his head. " 'Fraid not. I only know a few of the names, and then, just my buddies. What are you going to do about D'Arbereaux?"

Morgan shrugged and looked at Sarah. "We're trying to get proof one way or the other that he's the right man."

"You'll need plenty of that, that's for sure. You can't just go accusing a man of his stature on some soldier's say-so."

"But if it's true, he's committed these other murders, too," Sarah said. "Surely there must be a witness somewhere."

Armbruster sighed. "I don't know. The witness would have to be pretty reliable to convince a judge. Money talks, too, you know."

"Let me show you my notes," Morgan said. "Maybe you can help me with some of these names. I'm still hoping to find some of the soldiers."

They pored over Morgan's lists, talked about people he'd met or tried to find, poked and pushed and prodded the facts this way and that, but nothing definitive came of it.

"We need to catch him in the act," Morgan said with frustration. "There's no other way."

"But how can we? He moves like a shadow. No one knows where he'll strike next," Sarah said.

The sergeant leaned back in his seat. "Then we'll just have to make sure we know where he'll strike, won't we?"

"A trap?" Morgan said.

"Yes," replied Armbruster quietly. "A trap."

"But how can you possibly trap him?" Sarah asked. "You'd need some sort of . . . bait, wouldn't you?"

"You're looking at it," the sergeant replied. "What do you think?" he asked Morgan.

"I think it could work, but we'll have to plan it very

carefully. Couldn't have anything go wrong. It'll be risky, you know."

"It's a risk I'm willing to take. After all, there's no saying he won't come after me even without the trap, is there?"

"True enough."

The two men leaned over the coffee table reviewing Morgan's notes and making their plans. Sarah insisted on being included.

"How else will you get to Philip?" she challenged them.

"I won't let you put yourself in such a risky situation," Morgan said, his heart racing. She was still too impetuous by far. Hadn't the events of the past few days made an impression on her? Why couldn't she be more like Annie, willing to let the men solve the problem while she stayed safely out of the way?

"It's not for you to decide," she said sending him an angry look.

"Sarah, I'm not objecting for frivolous reasons. If I'm right about Philip, he's a formidable adversary. Our plan could go wrong at any point and Philip would have no hesitation in doing anything to save himself. Do you think that just because he was friendly to you once he'll spare you given what you know?"

"No more than he'll spare you or the sergeant. Why is it all right for you to take the risk and not me? If I ask you not to go after Philip will you stop?"

She had him there, Morgan had to concede, clenching his jaw until he thought his teeth would crack. Damn it, didn't she understand that he just wanted her safe?

"Do you think I don't want you safe, too?" she asked gently as if she read his thoughts.

"It's not that simple." he protested.

"It's exactly that simple," she countered. "Together we might have a chance against him, a better chance than either of us will have alone. I'll be very careful, I promise, and you better be, to."

Morgan looked to Armbruster for support. The man merely shrugged. "She's got a point. If we want this D'Arbereaux person to come after me, we have to point out the way so we can control where and when. Sounds like Miss Gentry is more likely than either of us to plant that seed in his mind. As long as she stays away from the scene when the attack comes, she should be safe enough, I'd warrant."

"I don't like it but I seem to be outvoted. Now, let's figure out exactly what we're going to do."

They stayed up half the night making their plans. By the time they quit, satisfied with their efforts, Sarah felt too tense to sleep. She sat in the bed, pillows propped behind her, and let her thoughts wander. She needed something stable to hold on to, but there was nothing. How naïve she'd been a mere two days ago, sitting in Morgan's arms and thinking that everything would work out. Naïve and blind. Everything was changeable; no one could be trusted.

No one? She thought of Morgan. She must trust him on some level or she wouldn't have insisted on participating in their dangerous mission. Her life was in his hands. But could she trust him with her heart?

Did she have a choice? He was everything she'd ever dreamed of in a man, strong, protective, handsome, concerned for others. But he was more, too, dark and brooding, filled with secrets he would not share, and if Annie was right, deeply hurt. So hurt that he no longer reached out to others, preferring to live on the fringes, a loner who went about the harsh business of living without a thought to himself. Could she break through his barriers?

Did she want to?

There had been something natural about pretending to be married at the sanitarium, even if they had used a fictitious name and disguised their true selves. Deep down she'd felt a flutter every time Morgan had called her his wife. And when he'd held her and kissed her at Geneviève's summer house, she'd known only bliss. But that was before she'd learned about Philip.

A confusion of thoughts and feelings weighted her down. Adam. Geneviève. Philip. Annie. Morgan. Always Morgan.

She needed his arms around her now, then she would have no doubts. His touch seemed to answer all her questions. His eyes told her all his secrets if only she was astute enough to read them. Her heart yearned for him, the hollow place inside her ached to be filled. Only her mind had reservations, reservations nothing could assuage, especially with Morgan at the other end of the house.

He'd been confused by her withdrawal, she'd seen that several times today, but there had been nothing she could do about it. She'd needed the time, the isolation, to come to grips with the profound upheaval in her life. Now she accepted that Morgan had been right: she would never have believed Philip was at the heart of this nightmare without some proof, and Morgan had been wise enough, and perhaps kind enough in his way, to want to spare her the doubts while he was unsure himself.

She wished she could talk to him of her doubts, of the changes in herself as she found the strength to cope. She knew he of all people would understand her struggle to reconcile her beliefs and hopes with the realities of a harsh world. But right now they had to concentrate on their plan. Everything had to work perfectly for them to all come out safe.

Her heart raced as she thought of the danger. She understood Morgan's reticence to let her participate more than she'd let on. She felt the same way about him. But just as he felt compelled to see this through, so did she.

Chapter Fifteen

Sarah paced the front parlor of Geneviève's home in New Orleans. Her palms were wet, and her heart beat so loudly she was afraid that anyone standing near her might hear it, including the one person she needed to convince of her sincerity—Philip. He was due any minute and then their elaborate game would begin.

She chewed on her lip. What if she didn't have what it took to pull this off? She closed off the thought. Others depended on her, their very lives were in her hands. Nervous or not, she would do this. She tried to remember the confidence she'd felt at Geneviève's summer house. Geneviève had been both supportive and terrified, understanding Sarah's need to see this through and warning her to be careful. Philip was not stupid. One misstep would be all it took.

A knock sounded at the front door, the knocking matching the pounding of her heart.

He was here.

Her stomach rolled over. How could she face him knowing what she knew? How could she look him in the eye and not show the horror that filled her heart? Closing her eyes, she willed herself to calm down. She stood for a moment, gathering her resolve. She could do this—if not for herself then for Adam and all the other Adams Philip had destroyed. And for Morgan. It might not set things right, but it would go some way to evening up the score.

Taking a deep breath, she stepped into the hall. With considered and deliberate movements she pulled open the door and flung herself into Philip's arms.

"Oh, Philip," she wailed. "I was wrong to have ever doubted you. You were right about Morgan Cain. I just got back to the city today and found out everything. *Everything.*" She sobbed against his jacket. "I'm just devastated. Can you ever forgive me?"

She tilted her head back and gazed up at him. Tears spilled onto her cheeks and her whole body trembled, conveying just the right amount of abject remorse. In truth, both the tears and trembling were induced as much by her fear and the terror of what he might do if he discovered her duplicity as any other emotion real or imagined.

"Now, Sarah, what's all this nonsense? Calm yourself, please." He glanced worriedly up and down the street. "Let's go inside so you won't make a spectacle of yourself."

He helped her back into the house, his hand on her elbow. She continued to sob and lean on him for support. Peering at him from beneath the shelter of her lashes, she looked for any signs of nervousness or suspicion on his face. She caught sight of the blond patch gleaming brightly against his dark hair and thought how it had given him away, but other than his discomfort with her tears, she saw no other emotion.

She breathed a small sigh of relief. The first confrontation had been successfully negotiated though she knew the hardest might be yet to come.

She allowed him to lead her into the parlor and fuss over her. "Come and sit down and tell me what you're babbling about."

"Babbling!" She pretended to be incensed. "How can you say such a thing? To come back from LucyAnne's and find that my good name has been bandied about in public as if it were of no account. Why, I just couldn't . . ." Her voice broke and once again tears rained down her face.

"Hush, now. Everything will be all right," he said, his voice oh so comforting. No wonder she'd been fooled. He sounded as sincere and concerned as a saint.

He pulled out his handkerchief and carefully dabbed at her cheeks. So far everything was working just as she'd planned. If she could keep the tears falling, Philip would fall right into line as he always did at the sight of a woman crying.

When her face was dry, he tucked the handkerchief into her hand and said, "There, now, that's better, isn't it? I'm sure you're blowing the entire affair out of proportion."

"How can you possibly think so with my good name splashed across the front page of the *Picayune?* Didn't you see it?"

"Well, yes. I do read the paper every day, but—"

"Couldn't you have done something?" she asked, softening her tone so her voice came out in a pleading whisper. "Oh, I was just so humiliated. You have so many contacts. Couldn't someone, your friend Mr. Palmer, maybe, have kept the story out of the paper?"

"Unfortunately, my dear, my contacts don't own papers."

He patted her on the back. It took all her control not to flinch away.

"How did they even come up with the notion that I was kidnapped? Geneviève did tell you I'd gone to LucyAnne's didn't she? Couldn't you have written a letter of protest when you read it?"

She watched for his reaction. She had to know if he believed Geneviève's story about her going to visit a friend. If he did, everything would be easier.

"Yes, Geneviève told me, but I was certainly upset that you would run off and not even have the courtesy to tell me yourself."

"Surely you can understand," she said with a catch in her voice. "I was so upset and confused by all that had happened that evening."

He looked uncomfortable at being reminded of his behavior the night before she'd disappeared with Morgan. Though it didn't suit her purposes to have him pull away from her, that piece in the newspaper nagged at her. She had to know if he'd had anything to do with it.

"What matters now is what to do about the *Picayune*. How did they even come up with such a preposterous supposition?" she pressed. "I just don't understand how the papers dare to print such ridiculous things, do you?"

She sniffed into the hankie he'd given her and looked expectantly up at him. He'd always enjoyed playing the role of knowledgeable man of the world, especially when he'd helped her search for Adam. She couldn't count the number of times he'd boasted of his contacts in high places or his influence with the publishing industry. She hoped now that he would be unable to resist.

His hand came up, and he ran his finger under the edge of his collar.

"One never knows how they come up with these things," he replied evasively. "Those reporters will print anything they hear. They never check their facts. If I could have stopped it, you know I would have."

As soon as his hand touched his collar she knew he was lying; he had been responsible in some way for the article. She'd noticed that nervous habit before: whenever something bothered him or he was telling an outright lie. His eyes certainly looked guileless enough and his manner seemed as concerned as she might wish. She marveled at his skill, sitting right there with his arm around her and lying to her face.

"But, Philip, they called me an accomplice. To murder. That's serious."

"Now, my dear, you're overreacting. Nothing all that terrible happened."

"How can I ever show my face again if this isn't cleared up? Murder isn't something to laugh away."

She watched him carefully as she spoke, noting that the mention of murder didn't perturb him. Was it because he was innocent or because the idea of murder held no mystery or fear for him?

She had spent the trip back to the city trying to deny Philip's role in the events they were investigating. In some small part of her, she'd hoped Morgan might have made a mistake, that the page from the journal they'd found in her locket didn't really indicate Philip at all but someone else.

They'd been friends for more years than she could count. He'd courted her and asked her to marry him. But now she realized he could have planted the lies about the kidnapping. And the only reason he would have for discrediting Morgan was that he realized Morgan's investigation was closing in on him.

She choked on the thought.

"Now, dear," Philip said. "Don't get so worked up over this. I'll look into the whole business tomorrow. As you said, John Palmer can probably help get them to print a retraction and maybe even fire the reporter who wrote the story."

"Oh, Philip, how wonderful of you. You know they really shouldn't be able to write those kinds of things about innocent people."

"I know and I'll take care of it."

"Oh, thank you. I knew I could count on you just as I always have."

He smiled. "Of course, you can."

"You've always been there for me, and I know you always will." She forced herself to smile back and look suitably grateful and helpless, in need of his masculine protection. Inside she felt ill at his touch. A very primitive urge to exact revenge tore through her. All she had to do now was to feed him Perry Armbruster's name and there would be no turning back.

The game would start in earnest.

She took a deep breath, like a diver waiting to go off the edge of a cliff. And then she jumped.

"There's one other thing I wanted to check with you," she said, looking up at him as though he alone could provide the answers to her questions. "Good news, actually."

"What's that, my dear?" he asked indulgently. The smugly satisfied gleam in his eyes told her that he thought he had her just where he wanted her—back by his side and telling him all she knew.

She pulled away from his embrace and sat back in the corner of the couch. "I think I have a clue regarding Adam's murder. You did say you'd help me find the person who murdered him, didn't you?"

"If he can be found. What's this new clue?"

He was pathetically eager. Sarah's stomach clenched, but she kept the smile on her face.

"I'm so excited about this. If it hadn't been for this terrible thing in the paper, we might have already found the murderer. Do you think my friends will believe what they wrote in the paper? I so hope not. How will I ever show my face again in polite society?"

"I'm sure your true friends won't believe a word. Now about this clue. What exactly is it?"

"Oh, yes, I was talking about that wasn't I. Lately, things have been so difficult. You will forgive me, won't you?"

"You know I will. Now, you were saying?"

"Right." She paused and pretended she'd forgotten what she was going to say. If Philip thought she was a totally scattered female, he would feel safer and less suspicious. "Now, what was it? Oh yes, I remember. I've come across a name. I was hoping it might lead to someone who knew Adam during the war. Don't you think that might be a good place to start?"

"I really couldn't say. Why don't you tell me the name, and I'll ask some of my contacts if they know of him or where he might be found. Though I don't want you to get your hopes up. You do realize there's no telling where this person might be. He might have even died during the war."

"I know I mustn't let myself get too excited, but it's so important to me to clear Adam's name."

She studied him covertly and noticed that her words had startled him though he quickly recovered.

"What do you mean *clear his name?*" he asked.

"Why of the suicide, of course." His shoulders relaxed almost imperceptibly. If she hadn't been purposely looking, she would have missed the tiny, telltale sign. "I could never let the world think Adam would take his own life. You don't believe that, do you? Tell me you don't."

"Of course not. Adam was a fine man just down on his luck. If you could have found him I'm sure he would have come home with you, and everything would have been back to normal."

"I'm sure you're right." She smiled again though it was one of the hardest things she'd ever done. She knew he was lying; his hand was back at his collar. Now that she knew what to look for, the signs were becoming more and more obvious. He knew Adam would never have fit back into a normal life; that was one of the reasons he'd had to be killed—before his conscience finally goaded him to speaking out, oath or no oath. Had Philip done the dirty deed himself or had he hired someone to do it for him?

It didn't really matter. All that mattered now was stopping him.

"Now tell me about this man you've found," he prompted, and Sarah had the satisfaction of knowing he'd taken the first part of the bait. Now she had to feed him some line and make sure he was truly hooked.

"I don't know, maybe you're right," she said. "The more I think about it, the more I realize what you said is true. This is probably just another dead end."

Philip sat forward on the couch and grasped her hands in his. She quelled the feeling of panic that threatened to engulf her. She had to keep acting the grateful, helpless female until everything was set.

"Give me his name anyway," Philip coaxed, "and I'll check him out just to be on the safe side. He might be somewhere near, and then we both can go and talk with him."

"Oh, Philip, that would be so wonderful. Do you really think we could?"

"As soon as I find something out. Now, all I need is the name."

"Of course, how silly of me. Just give me a minute." She paused, tilting her head to the side as if she were deep in thought. "I knew this would happen. His name is so unusual."

"What do you mean?"

"I can't remember it exactly."

"You can't expect me to investigate someone if I don't have their name," Philip said impatiently.

"You're right, of course," she said, enjoying his discomfiture. Let him think there was an unknown threat just out of his reach. He deserved to suffer a bit. She put a frown on her face. "I'm sure I wrote it down and put it with the things the police gave me of Adam's."

His eyes lit up. "Why don't you give me everything you have," he said smoothly. "There might be something helpful there, you never can tell. We want to get to the bottom of this as soon as possible."

"But I thought I'd like to read his journal before anyone else," Sarah said, wanting Philip to think she'd hadn't had a chance to look at it yet.

"I can understand that, but it will probably just upset you. Why don't you let me check it out for you? Then

I can prepare you for any difficult parts. The war was brutal, you know."

"Yes, it was, wasn't it," she murmured and shivered.

"Besides, it will speed up the investigation from my end. You do want to find out what happened to him as quickly as possible, don't you?"

"I guess you're right."

"Of course, I am. Why don't you run and get the name and journal?"

Sarah hurriedly left the room, but not for the reason Philip thought. She knew if she stayed around him another minute she would be sick. How on earth was she going to continue with this charade? The thought of being in the room with him, much less having him touch her, was almost more than she could bear.

She made her way up to her room to get the journal Adam had kept and which the police had returned to Geneviève after she and Morgan had left for the bayou. Of course she'd already read it, even finding the place where Adam must have torn out the page they'd found in her locket.

She'd hoped to read it with some detachment, but even with all that had happened, his words had reached her. She ached thinking about the pain he'd gone through in those years he'd been away from her. The journal had started during the war, the entries written sporadically, whenever he felt he had something to say, and continued up until a few months before his death.

He must have put the torn page in her locket on one of his last visits home. She remembered his asking about it, whether she wore it and what she did with it when she didn't have it on. She'd told him it never left her—at least almost never, but she must have mislaid it for him to have had a chance to hide his secret entry there. Had he intended her to find it? She thought so.

It had been his confession, a way of keeping his word to his fellow soldiers while ensuring that the episode would not be completely forgotten. Some day she would have found it, perhaps not as soon as she had, but one way or another, the truth would have emerged.

Philip would be disappointed when he combed through the faded pages. Adam had been careful to give no names even before the massacre. Most of his impressions had shown the gradual brutalization of a young soldier, the sinking from a high-minded idealism to a world-weary cynicism, then to despair that humanity held any good at all.

She got the journal out from beneath her pillow, then caught sight of herself in the cheval mirror standing in the corner. She looked as highly strung as she felt. Philip would sense something was wrong if she wasn't careful. Walking to the washstand, she poured some water into the basin and quickly washed her face.

While she patted her face dry, she planned exactly what she would say when she got back downstairs. She wanted to be as subtle as she could. She quickly straightened her hair, then scooped up the journal and headed back downstairs.

"I knew it was a good thing that I wrote his name down," she said, walking into the room. "I have it here. His name is Perry Armbruster. Have you met him?"

When she'd said the sergeant's name, she thought she detected some recognition in Philip, but she couldn't be sure.

"No, the name doesn't ring a bell. But then I knew a lot of men back then. It's hard to remember them all."

"I'm sure it is. But Mr. Huggins seemed to think he might be important."

"Huggins?"

"The private investigator I hired to help find Adam. He managed to come up with Perry Armbruster's name."

"Then I should speak to him. Where is he?"

"I'm not sure. I've just been so scattered since Adam's death. I'm having a terrible time sleeping, and every waking minute I see his face. I can't seem to remember anything these days. Poor LucyAnne was at her wit's end with me."

"I'm sure, but did this Huggins fellow come up with an address?"

"Not yet, but he said he thought he might have something in a few days—which should be any day now."

"Well, let me know the minute he contacts you. It will speed things up considerably."

She nodded. Philip was hooked. She took a deep breath.

"I don't want you going off on your own again," Philip told her. "You saw what a mess it made of things before. Before you go anywhere, be sure to tell me. Is that clear?"

"Yes. I'm sorry about what happened, believe me. Reading about yourself in the paper like that is enough to worry anyone."

"Yes, well, I'll see what I can do about that. Now, if that Huggins fellow calls on you, you be sure to let me know. I'll try to free up my schedule, though it may take a few days."

Sarah allowed disappointment to fill her voice. "I've waited this long, I guess I can wait a little longer, but see if you can get through with your business as quickly as possible."

"I'll do my best," he said, patting her hand. "Why don't I take the journal and be on my way. The sooner I get back to work, the sooner we'll be able to start our investigation."

"I don't know how I can ever thank you."

"Don't thank me until we have some answers, but you know I'll do the best I can."

And so will I, Sarah thought, so will I.

Morgan waited in an alleyway across the street from the *Picayune*. Soon Nat would be coming out for dinner, and he didn't want to miss him. So far things had gone his way. He'd delivered Sarah safely to Geneviève's house and stopped by Smoky Row to check with some of his contacts. None of them knew much, which could be a good sign. Maybe the police weren't looking so actively for him anymore.

The hardest part had been setting up a convincing front for Perry Armbruster. He needed a "home" somewhere in the city, in a place accessible to Philip yet easy to defend. Morgan had no intention of losing his quarry to carelessness at this point. Armbruster had left them at the city limits, not wanting anyone to see them together. He would be sneaking into the city and contacting Sarah in a couple of days to find out where to go.

Morgan had already found a vacant house in the Vieux Carré that suited their purposes. When he was sure no one would notice, he would send the address to Sarah so she could relay the message.

Morgan checked the alley and the street again. Nothing. Where was Nat? Morgan was getting impatient. He needed to convince his friend to help him determine who'd set him up for Bettine's murder. Not that he had any doubts where the blame would ultimately fall: D'Arbereaux. But the man hadn't done it on his own. He seemed to keep a certain distance from his dirty work where Morgan was concerned.

Every time he thought about Sarah with that swine it set his teeth on edge. He wanted nothing more than to rush to her side and make sure she was safe. He hadn't liked D'Arbereaux from the moment he'd heard of him and his affiliations with the damn carpetbaggers. The man had gone out of his way to ingratiate himself with the enemy, to cheat rather than help his fellow Southerners. When Morgan thought how Philip traded on his "illustrious" war record, he saw red.

The man was a consummate liar and had absolutely no moral scruples. And Sarah was alone with him. Morgan swore under his breath. He'd only given in to her argument because time was of the essence. With each delay, Philip had another opportunity to murder again and set himself up as invincible. He had to be stopped quickly, before he realized just how close they were to getting him. Desperate men took desperate chances. And Morgan could think of nothing more desperate than risking Sarah's safety.

He checked the street again and saw Nat heading down the banquette in the direction of the alley. Just as he was about to pass, Morgan called out softly.

His editor turned at the sound of his name, then seeing who was signaling him, stopped dead in the middle of the sidewalk.

"What the hell?"

"Shhh," Morgan hissed and motioned him into the alleyway.

Taking a quick look over his shoulder, Nat scurried to Morgan's side.

"Where the hell have you been?"

"It's a long story."

"They usually are." Nat stared at him. "It's good to see you."

"Thanks, but let's get out of here. I don't feel too secure standing out here in front of the paper. It wouldn't surprise me if they have this place under observation."

"Where do you suggest since you're wanted all over town?" Nat commented dryly.

"Ellie's?" Morgan suggested, giving the alley and street a careful scrutiny.

"Are you crazy?" Nat looked at him as if he'd lost his mind, and then he snapped his fingers. "You may be right. Ellie's been worried about you. Asks after you every time I go in. What is it with you and women?"

Morgan ignored his friend's last statement. "Did you tell her there wouldn't have been anything to worry about if the *Picayune* hadn't spread my name all over the front page?"

"Don't get on your high horse, Cain."

When he would have said more, Morgan stopped him. "Let's save this conversation until we get to Ellie's. Follow me."

Morgan took him through the alley and out the other side, then wound around the back until he ended up at Ellie's rear door. They knocked and peered in, catching Ellie at the stove.

"Mr. Cain, it sure is good to see you. We've been worried sick ever since you disappeared," she said as she

331

wiped her hands on a towel and came over to greet him. "How'd you get yourself in such a godawful mess?"

"I wish I knew, Ellie. It looks like someone has it in for me. Do you think we could get a meal served back here? I don't think it would be too wise for me to sit in the public dining room, and Mr. Bayard and I have some business to discuss."

"You sure do have your worries now, that's for sure. I'll have Boudin fix you up a table off the kitchen. No one will see you, and you'll be away from the bustle of my people."

Within minutes a table was ready, and they sat down to eat. Morgan buttered one of the rolls and took a bite. He hadn't eaten since leaving Geneviève's summer house early this morning with all the other activities he'd been involved in.

Before he could swallow, Ellie was setting bowls of soup in front of both of them. "I been thinking, Mr. Cain, where are you staying with the police after you?"

He hadn't thought that far ahead. He certainly couldn't go back to the boardinghouse. He would surely be found there. He couldn't imagine the police not having it watched.

"I haven't thought about it yet, Miss Ellie."

"If you like, you can use the room in the attic. It's a mite hot, but no one'll look for you there."

"Miss Ellie, I'm wanted by the police. Having me here could put you in danger. I don't think it's a good idea."

"Where else you got to go?"

"Nowhere, but—"

She interrupted him. "Mr. Cain, I never told you. Too embarrassed I guess, but that story you did on them girls being sold into prostitution helped me find my cousin's child. I owe you." There was a catch in her voice as she finished, then abruptly changed the subject. "Why don't I just fix you both up a special meal of my own choosing. How'd that be?"

"I appreciate everything," Morgan told her.

"You just finish that soup, and I'll be back with your meal."

"Does your offer include dessert?" Nat asked.

Ellie laughed. "With you, Mr. Bayard, I'm surprised you even want a meal before going for those sweets."

Nat took her kidding good-naturedly. Morgan smiled. Now that he had a roof over his head and a good meal, he could relax a bit. His stomach growled, reminding him that it had been sorely neglected all day, and he dug into the thick soup.

Nat was slower to start, and Morgan felt his friend's gaze on him. He raised his eyes from the soup he was devouring.

"About the article in the paper," Nat began. "I was overruled. They said it was just the story to sell a lot of papers. And they were right. It did. I'm sorry I couldn't do anything."

Morgan could see the regret in his editor's eyes. Sometimes there were things that were just beyond your control. He certainly knew about that. "Who broke it?"

"A fellow who used to write for the paper but left about six months ago. You might remember him. George Fuller."

George Fuller. That might explain it. Six months before Morgan had accidentally come across a scheme George was running. For a few extra bucks, George would slip the names of merchants into his articles.

When Morgan had found out about it, he'd gone to George and given him the opportunity to confess on his own or have Morgan go to Nat with the facts. George had opted to quit rather than own up. Morgan hadn't mentioned the episode to anyone, considering it over. Now it appeared George didn't forget quite as easily.

"What kind of proof did he bring with the story?"

"He had a witness who said he saw you running from the scene right before they discovered the body."

"Did you get the witness's name?"

"I told him there was no way we'd print the story without the name. And he gave it to me. One of the fellows checked it out, and everything was corroborated."

"That name is somewhere to start."

"What are you planning to do?"

"To clear my name and trap the person who's behind the story I've been working on."

Morgan told Nat of the massacre and his subsequent investigation, leaving out the more personal details such as Sarah's involvement. Nat was a newspaperman first and foremost, and Morgan didn't trust him not to exploit any information that might be converted into more sales. By the time he'd finished, they were almost done with their meal.

"So what are you planning to do next?" Nat asked.

"Get the man behind it all. But first I need to get my name cleared so I can move about without any problems. You think you have someone who can handle that?"

"I would imagine the source for the original story would change his line if he knew he might go to jail for perjury. We might want to start there and see where it leads us. Now, are you going to tell me whom you suspect?"

"This is my story, Nat. I need to know where I stand. Do I still have a job?"

"You know you do, but stay low until I get in touch with someone I know at the police station and see what they can do. Now that I know more of the background they might put more faith in what I have to say. Sometimes they can be damned stupid bastards."

Morgan nodded. It felt good knowing that Nat had gone to bat for him when all this had first started. Without even an explanation, he'd thought Morgan innocent.

"All right. I'll tell you, but I expect you to keep this under your hat. Our quarry is skittish and *very* well connected. Probably has someone in your own office feeding him information. I need your word that you won't tell a soul. I don't want him finding out until I'm ready for him."

Nat's eyes widened and he leaned forward. "You have my word. Who is it?"

Morgan trained his gaze on the older man not wanting to miss his reaction when he said Philip's name. "Philip D'Arbereaux."

"The guy that's thinking about running for congress?"

"The very same."

Nat whistled softly. "This could be some story."

"Or it could be a fiasco. D'Arbereaux takes no prisoners. He fights to win."

"You're playing a dangerous game, my friend. Do you need any help?"

"As I said before, I need my name cleared, and I can't do that alone. I'll let you know if anything else comes up."

"I'll get on it right away."

Morgan leaned back in the chair after Nat left. With

a full stomach and Nat heading to the police station, it appeared everything was finally falling into place. His only concern now was Sarah and how safe she was with Philip D'Arbereaux.

Philip walked down Conti Street. Everything was finally falling into place. He'd planned everything carefully, and he would take care of this latest wrinkle, too. All he had to do was find this Armbruster person before anyone else did. He hoped the man was not in New Orleans. Too many unexplained deaths, especially of former soldiers, might raise someone's suspicions. After all, that Cain fellow had started to raise some questions before he was conveniently scared out of town.

Thinking of Morgan Cain brought Sarah to his mind. He smiled to himself. Even she was falling into place again. He'd been furious when she'd thwarted him, angry enough to plant that stupid newspaper article just to get back at her for leaving him. Now he'd have to do some fancy footwork to get a retraction. And, he'd have to deal with George Fuller and that drifter he'd hired to frame Cain in that Smoky Row bitch's murder. A dead drifter wouldn't cause much of a stir at all. As for Fuller, he'd think of something. Hadn't he taken care of practically everyone who'd known the secret?

Before long he'd have Sarah for his wife and a seat in Congress. He'd guessed she wouldn't want to be connected with a wanted man, and the events of the morning proved him right. All women cared about was their reputation and a man who could give them status. He would be able to give her both—and then she'd be his. He laughed out loud, pleased with himself.

Only a few loose ends remained to be taken care of, starting with Armbruster. If the man had really known Adam then he was a risk, a risk Philip couldn't afford. He'd have to be taken care of quickly, whatever it took, and Philip had an assortment of methods to choose from, methods tried and true. He laughed again, his cleverness knowing no bounds.

And then he'd take care of that bastard Cain once and for all. The laughter left Philip's face. Just this morning he'd heard that Cain was seen on Smoky Row. How had he gotten back into town? The man was too curious by far, a dangerous adversary, but nothing Philip couldn't handle. He'd already turned Sarah away from him, and he'd do even more.

Of course he would have to be extra clever about it since Sarah had once been sweet on the man. It wouldn't do to have her think he had anything to do with Cain's downfall. No, he'd have to be more subtle than usual, destroying whatever was left of the man's reputation so even Sarah would be glad he was gone. If he did things right, the police would handle the problem for him; all he needed to do was plant some evidence here and there to set them looking for him double-time—and take the heat off of himself. Yes, that would work out fine.

He continued walking down the street, a slight smile on his face. Things really were going his way at last.

Chapter Sixteen

The next morning when Morgan went downstairs to Ellie's kitchen he learned Nat had sent word that he was coming over with good news. Morgan could use some. His night had been filled with images of Sarah and D'Arbereaux, images that had him waking up in a cold sweat. They had to get D'Arbereaux to show his hand and soon. Morgan couldn't take knowing that Sarah was in that bastard's company any longer than necessary.

Ellie's son agreed to take a message to Sarah, telling her that the house had been readied and as soon as Armbruster arrived he should get over there. Once Armbruster was settled, she could contact D'Arbereaux and then pull herself out of this dangerous game. The boy promised to talk to no one of his mission. To make sure no one suspected his true purpose, Ellie packed one of the meals she provided for the residents of the surrounding boardinghouses. Her son would pretend to be delivering it to Sarah as a cover.

"He'll be fine," Ellie said when the boy left. "He has a clever head on his shoulders."

"Thank you for all your help."

"I told you already. We're even. Now come and eat before you get back to all your worries. Everything looks better on a full stomach."

Morgan sat at the same table he'd used the night before and drank the coffee Ellie set before him. He wished he could have come up with another way to trap D'Arbereaux, but Sarah was the only contact they had that the man would trust, and even that wasn't a sure thing. Damn, but the worry was eating him alive.

As he finished the last piece of toast, Nat came through the kitchen door, smiling broadly. He didn't waste any time delivering his good news once he was seated.

"The police have dropped all charges."

"How did you manage that?" Morgan hadn't expected results this fast, but he wasn't about to complain.

"From an unexpected source. Seems there's been someone following you."

"Following me? What are you talking about? Who would be following me?"

"A private investigator."

"What? That's crazy. Why would a private investigator be trailing me?"

Nat shrugged. "Seems he saw everything that happened to you the night the prostitute was killed. How you were jumped and tied up. How you escaped out of the cellar and ended up stabbed. The police followed up on his story and the drifter who'd said he'd witnessed everything was found dead in a gutter. I managed to find George Fuller, and he told me the only source he'd had was the drifter."

Morgan couldn't believe it was coming together so

quickly. "Why didn't this private investigator come forward sooner?"

"Claims he was trying to find you out in the bayou, but didn't have any luck. He only got back to town a day or two before you."

Morgan shook his head. Something was funny here. "Was Fuller able to implicate D'Arbereaux?"

"He said he didn't know anything."

"Did you believe him?" Morgan certainly had no reason to believe the man, but since he'd never told Nat his part in George's departure from the paper, he couldn't voice his suspicions.

"He didn't look nervous. And I certainly would have with both the prostitute and the drifter turning up dead. He's smart enough to figure he'd be the next one on the list if he knew who was behind everything. It stands to reason he's telling the truth."

"Damn. I knew it wouldn't be that easy. What did the police say? Are they going to pick up D'Arbereaux for questioning?"

"They said they didn't have enough to go on."

"Not even to question him?"

"You know as well as I do that in any investigation that has to do with someone as well-connected politically as D'Arbereaux, they'll just pussyfoot around until even a goose could see their guilt. They want their jobs tomorrow, and you know how these carpetbaggers operate."

If the situation hadn't been so frustrating Morgan would have laughed at the way Nat managed to bring those dreaded Northerners into every conversation. As it was, he didn't see any hope of getting Sarah out of harm's way until they had D'Arbereaux dead to rights.

Morgan brought his thoughts back to Nat when his friend pushed his arm to get his attention.

"So, what should we do next?"

"You're in this with me?"

Nat laughed with an embarrassed expression on his face. "I liked the excitement of being back out on the street, going after a story. If you'll have me, I'm ready to start."

"We can use all the help we can get." Morgan appreciated Nat's offer. Hopefully, the more people who worked on this the faster they could wrap things up and he and Sarah could be together.

The idea startled him. Until this moment he hadn't given the future any thought and certainly not a future with any one person. Now he couldn't conceive of life without Sarah. In just the one day since they'd been separated he'd done nothing but worry about her every minute. She'd become a part of him, a part he didn't want to be without.

For someone who had lived the last ten years without any attachments, not even a pet, he'd certainly changed in a very big way. The funny thing was he didn't know what she felt ... or what she wanted. Sarah had been as reticent as he.

"I say, Cain, are you all right?" Nat asked in a tone that indicated he'd tried to get Morgan's attention several times. "Have you come up with something?"

"Sorry, just thinking," he apologized unwilling to share such intimate thoughts. "What was that investigator's name? Did you get it?"

"His name was Huggins—Neubald Huggins. Do you know him?"

Morgan didn't answer.

* * *

Sarah had had him followed. Two hours later the words were still churning in his mind. He was standing outside John Palmer's club waiting for him to appear. The man was closely connected to D'Arbereaux, supporting his election plans and smoothing the way with finances. Finding out everything they could about him made sense. Palmer could be a source of information. Morgan had set himself the task of following the man and sent Nat off to look into the man's business interests.

As he waited in the shade of an oak, Morgan had nothing better to do than to think back on his conversation with Nat. He'd recognized the name of the investigator as soon as Nat had said it—Neubald Huggins wasn't a name you forgot. Sarah had spoken of the investigator the first time they'd met. But he'd assumed the man was off the case since Sarah hadn't mentioned him again.

Was Sarah having him followed? Did she trust him so little? He didn't want to believe it, but what else could he think? Even at this very moment he could be under someone's watchful eye though he'd been very careful. He was sure no one knew he had come back to New Orleans except for the people he wanted to know. But did that mean Sarah had contacted Huggins once she was back in the city and put him back on the case? Morgan might be able to understand her misgivings before they'd gotten to know each other, but not now, not after all they had shared.

He shifted to another position under the tree. Where was Palmer, anyway? He was tired of wrestling with his thoughts and suspicions and wished he'd never found out about Huggins. He realized what he was feeling was hurt; it wasn't an emotion he usually had to deal with. Before someone could hurt you, they had to be close, important in your life, and in the last few years he'd kept everyone at a distance. Even Annie had barely breached his defenses, at least before James's death.

Now Sarah had the capability of wounding him with the smallest actions. He wanted her trust, completely and unequivocally. As she did his, he realized, finally understanding her hurt when he'd hadn't told her his suspicions about Philip.

He shifted again, impatient with the lack of progress. Waiting was always the hardest part of any assignment, and this kind of waiting was the worst. He looked up just in time to see Palmer coming out of the Andover Club. The club was one of the newer ones in the city, located in the American section of town. It was frequented primarily by transplants from the north and their southern cronies.

As Morgan watched, Palmer walked toward his carriage, spoke a few words to his driver, and climbed inside. The driver turned at the first corner and headed toward Canal Street, in the direction of the Vieux Carré.

Morgan spied a hansom cab just down the road. He sprinted over, threw some coins into the driver's hand and told him to follow the other vehicle discreetly. Before long they were in an area Morgan knew only too well.

When Palmer's driver stopped outside a well-appointed house, Morgan had his cab pull up a side street. He paid the driver his fare and casually strolled around the corner, walking in Palmer's direction.

By the time he reached the house, the carriage had gone and Palmer had disappeared inside.

Morgan looked around. He couldn't just stand here on the street for long. He'd be too conspicuous. But where could he conceal himself? Just then a voice interrupted his contemplation.

"Whatcha looking for, Mister? I might be able to supply it."

The boy standing before him looked no more than twelve or fourteen. He held his head at a confident angle. This was his street, and he knew all its ins and outs.

"Is that right?" Morgan said.

"You tell me what you want, and I'll see what I can do," he offered with a cocky self-assurance.

"How about some information?"

"I don't know." The boy looked at him warily, ready to bolt down the street. Apparently he got few such requests—and most of them were probably from the police.

"You won't get into trouble. I'm not with the police," Morgan assured him. "Besides, I'll make it worth your while."

The boy eyed him speculatively. "We can't talk here," he said nervously, then glanced over his shoulder to see if anyone was around. "How much will you give me?"

"You'll benefit, I promise. How much do you make a day doing this?" Morgan gestured with his hand up and down the street.

"Four bits," the boy replied proudly.

Morgan laughed. "I'll give you four times that."

The boy's eye widened at Morgan's words. "We can't talk here, though."

"Where do you want to go?"

He knew he was taking a chance going off with the boy. The youngster could be leading him into a trap that could cost him his life, but he needed information, and he'd bet this boy knew everything that was happening on the street.

"There's a place around the corner, an abandoned house. I've been there once or twice. We could talk there."

Morgan nodded for him to lead the way.

The house had once been much like the one Palmer entered, but time and neglect had had their effect. Most of the windows were broken and the front door was completely missing. As soon as the boy entered the building through a side window, his swaggering veneer returned. He stopped in the middle of a large room littered with paper and bottles. Morgan figured the boy lived there and felt safe in his own environment but didn't say anything.

"How can I be sure you'll pay me?" the boy challenged him, hitching up his pants in a typically arrogant manner.

"How can I be sure you have anything of importance to say?" Morgan countered. It was the same story whether they were young or old—everyone trying to cut a deal.

The boy walked to the corner of the room all the while looking Morgan up and down.

"Whatcha want this for?" he finally asked.

Morgan decided to tell him half the truth. "I work for a newspaper, and I'm doing a story."

The boy's manner quickened. "A story. What kind of story?"

The prospect of having his name in the paper had excited the boy. This was a nice change.

"White slavery."

The boy's eyes widened. "I don't know nothing about that, no sir," he said, starting back to the window where they'd entered. His swagger disappeared and the pitch of his voice had gone up an octave.

The words scared him, Morgan thought as he watched the boy back away. He smiled to himself. A little fear went a long way in getting information. He just didn't want it to scare him completely off.

"Maybe you know some of the people who visit, though."

"Those men like to keep to themselves."

"I'm sure they do, but not all of them. Did you recognize the man who pulled up in the carriage before you saw me?"

"You mean at Miss Odette's house?"

Well, so she was back was she? He hadn't heard her name mentioned since he'd done his story. She'd gone north, rumor had it, but it didn't surprise him that the woman was back in New Orleans and in business again. "You work for Miss Odette?"

"No sirree. You bet I don't. Only a fool would play around with that there stuff. My boss, she keeps everything legal, you understand. We don't mess with that kind of thing. Too many people gets hurt, you know what I mean?"

Morgan understood too well. "The man that went in, do you know him?"

"I keeps my nose out of such. It ain't healthy if you catch my drift."

"Oh, I understand, but I bet a smart boy like you

knows something." Morgan flipped him one coin and then another.

The boy jingled them in his hand. "I might." The feel of the money was getting to him

Morgan threw another coin. Again the boy caught it.

"Well?" Morgan demanded in a harder-edged tone. He was tired of playing cat and mouse, disillusioned by the greed, defeated by the thought that no matter what anyone did, the exploiters always seemed to win.

"What he does inside I don't know, but he comes maybe three—four times a week."

"How long does he stay?"

"Not long. An hour, maybe less."

"You know any of the girls?"

"I only see them from a distance. Odette don't allow them out by themselves."

"Do you know the cook or the maid?"

"They come from Bayou Nègre. We don't have nothing to do with them."

Morgan thought for a moment. He had to get inside that house. John Palmer's activities inside could be of great interest. And the only way he could gain entry himself would be as a potential customer. He had enough money. Nat had seen to that.

He looked down at his clothes. He could pass as a gentleman. After Nat had left last night, he'd snuck into his old boardinghouse and gathered up all his clothes. At least his landlady had left him those. Everything else of value had already been removed—at least anything Mrs. Ogden could find. He'd quickly checked under the floor and found his money untouched. For the moment he was content to leave it there, figuring that it was as safe a place as any.

His only problem would be if Odette recognized him—if it was even the same Odette. He reached up and smoothed his beard. It was full grown and covered half his face and the trimming had shaped it up nicely. His hair was longer now, too, almost down to his collar, the front falling over his forehead. Chances were his own mother would not recognize him. He'd have to hope so.

"Here's your other four bits," he said to the boy. "I'll be on my way now."

"Don't you want to know nothing more?"

"No, thanks. I think I'll have to be getting my own information."

The boy shrugged. "It's your funeral. Just don't mention me."

"Don't worry. I won't."

The boy followed him to the window. "If you like, I'll keep an eye out for you."

"That's kind of you. I'll give you another four bits when I come back out."

The boy grinned. "It's a deal."

They left the dilapidated house together, the boy falling behind as they neared Miss Odette's. He wandered across the street in a seemingly aimless pattern, but Morgan saw him position himself where he could see down the alley that ran along the side of the house as well as watch the front door. The boy had clearly been on the streets a long time. He knew all the tricks.

Morgan felt a pang of sadness at the boy's fate, but now wasn't the time to solve his problems. Maybe when this was all over . . .

The boy gave him a slight wave, then pretended to be absorbed in some game he made up, while Morgan marched up the front walk to the house. He rapped briskly on the front door. A young woman answered and ushered him into a large vestibule.

"I've come for some enjoyment," he said using an English accent. It was one of many he'd perfected over the years to disguise his true identity in his various investigations.

"Yes, sir, have a seat. Miss Odette will be with you shortly," she said with a curtsey and pointed to one of the chairs sitting in a row by the wall.

Morgan sat down on the tufted red velvet. They obviously didn't do much business in the early afternoon. He looked around with interest. Miss Lamonte had come up in the world. This place was much different than her last. Instead of a small office and living quarters in the back, this establishment housed the women with plenty of room left over for entertaining.

Even with the quiet of the front hall, he could hear no one else in the house. He wondered if Palmer had left while he'd been talking with the boy. He hoped not.

A slight rustling noise came from the end of the hall and a woman entered through a beaded curtain on his left.

"What can I do for you, honey?" she asked as she neared.

He stood, his hat in his hand. It was Odette, all right, a little older, a little more overweight, but the same woman.

"I'd be most interested in some afternoon recreation," he said stiffly.

"Well, I think we can handle that."

"I'd like a certain type."

"That's no problem. We have all shapes and sizes."

"Can I look at some photographs?"

"Oh," she said and looked at him more closely. "How'd you come by here?"

"A man at the Andover Club sent me." Morgan gave out John Palmer's club's name hoping it would be the entrance signal he'd need. And at the mention of the name, Odette's face opened into a smile.

"Why, of course, honey, we've got everything you'd ever want. Come with me. I have a little room where you can do your picking."

Reluctantly Morgan followed her deeper into the house. He didn't have the stomach for this, but until he found exactly who Palmer's contacts were and how they related back to D'Arbereaux, he had to appear interested.

"How much do you wish to spend?" she asked.

"It depends on what you have to offer."

"I told you, we have it all. Here look through these. I'm sure your *type* is here." Just like the last time, she handed him a large book filled with pictures. "I have someone in the back I have to see. As soon as I'm finished I'll come and see who you've picked. They're all fresh and sweet and . . . untouched."

She gave him another, more lascivious smile before turning to go through a small door in the back.

From this room he could hear a murmur of voices, then Odette's began to rise in anger. It became clearer and more easily understood as her temper rose.

"I don't want him involved anymore. I told you."

The other voice answered much more quietly.

"You haven't been here," Odette said with some impatience. "You don't realize that he's going to get us all into trouble."

Again the other person replied, apparently at some length, for it was a while before Odette spoke again.

"I don't care if he's going to be president! I'm the one that's going to end up in jail if D'Arbereaux keeps on getting so damn rough with the new girls. He's ruining the merchandise. We need them for the paying customers."

So D'Arbereaux was involved in this reprehensible place. And he had a reputation for being rough. Damn, things couldn't get any worse! What if he got rough with Sarah?

This was a side of Philip with which Sarah was completely unfamiliar, Morgan was sure. She wouldn't know how to protect herself. Hell, she still wasn't convinced Philip was even the right man. Oh, she'd tried to hide her doubts, but Morgan knew her too well to be deceived. When he'd dropped her off, she still harbored some vague notion of proving Philip innocent.

He wanted nothing more than to go to her, to pull her into his arms and make sure nothing hurt her ever again, especially a lowlife like D'Arbereaux. But he couldn't go near her house. Chances were good that Philip was having it watched, just to make sure Sarah was his again.

Morgan couldn't believe he'd let himself be talked into this plan. Then he remembered Sarah's determination. She'd been through a lot and handled every adversity with surprising aplomb. What was it Geneviève had said? Women were stronger than he thought. She was right, at least about the women close to him. Annie had handled the news about James better than he'd feared, and he could only admire Sarah's spirit in the face of the setbacks they'd encountered.

He would have to trust in her.

He was through at Miss Odette's for the moment. As quietly as he could he let himself out the front door and waited for John Palmer.

If things did not work out the way he'd planned, he now had an alternative direction to strike at D'Arbereaux. One way or another, he would get the man.

Sarah sat in the kitchen, Morgan's note in her hand. Just holding it brought him closer to her. She missed him. After sleeping next to him for nearly two weeks, she'd wakened several times last night reaching for him, only to find he wasn't there, the bed beside her empty. They'd barely been apart three days, playing out this deadly charade, and she could hardly bear to be another minute without him.

She would never have believed the presence of another person could have such an impact on her life. Without realizing it, she'd turn to ask Morgan's opinion only to remember he wasn't there. He'd become an essential part of her life, and she knew she didn't want to be without him. She loved him with all that was within her.

And if anything happened to him ... her breath caught in her chest and her heart pounded at the thought. She got up to pace off some of her tension. Things were moving so slowly, as if they were all trapped in molasses on a cold winter's day. She wanted this adventure to be over. She wanted Morgan safe and by her side. She wanted so much—she wanted love.

To love him *and be loved* by him. She knew her own feelings; she wasn't sure of his. There were so many things they had to straighten out, secrets to unravel, promises to make. They needed time together, not this enforced separation, this plunge into dangerous waters with no clear way out.

It was too late to do anything about it now. She'd given Perry the address of the house when he'd come by this morning, and he'd promised to head there right away. Now all she had to do was give the information to Philip and wait for him to make his move.

She shuddered. This would be one of the hardest parts, for she would be setting up Morgan and Philip for a direct confrontation, one in which there would be only a single victor. And the advantage would be Philip's for he enjoyed the battle and the kill. Morgan had surprise—and Perry Armbruster—on his side. She hoped it was more than enough to even the odds.

She sat back in the chair, fingering Morgan's note. It was her only link with him and better than nothing. But she wanted so much more, to feel his touch, to hear him whisper in her ear, to smell his unique scent and know he was close, so close she could reach out and—

"Are you sitting in here moping?" Geneviève asked as she walked into the kitchen. She'd arrived back in New Orleans late the night before, saying she wasn't about to miss the most excitement the city had seen in many a day.

Sarah was so startled by her friend's sudden words she nearly fell off her chair. She pretended to read the paper in her hand so she could regain her control.

"I'm not moping. I'm waiting."

"Waiting and drooling over Morgan's letter. Though I have to admit he certainly is something to drool over. Do you think he has a brother?"

Sarah laughed as she was supposed to, shaking her head in answer, but Geneviève's question made her think. Even with everything Annie had told her, she still didn't know much about Morgan, though she had begun to understand him a little better.

"No, only a sister."

"I knew I couldn't be as lucky as you. Now tell me, what are you waiting for?"

"For Philip. I've sent word I have Perry's address."

"There's an interesting man."

"I presume you mean Perry, not Philip. And I did notice your rapt attention to everything he had to say this morning. Do I see a smidgen of interest in those blue eyes of yours?"

"Merely showing interest in a guest in my house," she answered with a sniff.

"I know you well enough to know you wouldn't pay that much attention to the governor should he come to call. Now tell me, are you interested in the man?"

"There's a possibility. Did you notice if he ... did he seem ... ?"

How unlike Geneviève to feel so insecure in her charms. Usually it was the man who had to worry if Geneviève would give him the time of day, not the other way around. This was a very promising change, not that Sarah would say so.

"Has there ever been a man who didn't find you most appealing?" Sarah said with a laugh.

"Don't be ridiculous. I know I am not unattractive, but ..."

"But this one might interest *you?*"

"I already admitted that," she said with a nonchalance that was very revealing. "And what about you and Morgan?"

Sarah heard the determination in Geneviève's voice. Not only was she turning the conversation away from Perry Armbruster, but she was turning it in a direction that interested her immensely. In the past, they'd spoken often about the gentlemen who had come to call, exchanging opinions and girlish confidences. But this time they were grown women, and Sarah had a woman's deep emotions, not the frivolous feelings of a girl.

She looked at Geneviève not knowing how to begin to describe the complex range of emotions coursing through her.

"I love him ... and sometimes I hate him ... and then I love him again," she said at last, knowing how inadequate a description it was. Still, it felt good to admit her feelings out loud.

"I'm glad you're so decisive. What do you love-hate-love about him?"

"Everything. He's caring and protective, yet he allows me to do things that I feel I have do—not always without an argument, but he listens to what I have to say. Then I'll discover he's kept things from me that I should have been told. And finally when he touches me, I ..."

She couldn't go on. Much as she loved Geneviève, what she had with Morgan was special, intimate—not to be shared.

"I understand," Geneviève said, her eyes dimming for a moment. "When you're with that special someone everything seems right—nothing you can do is wrong."

That was exactly the way she felt; she just wasn't sure he felt the same. "But what if he hasn't told you that he loves you? Or that he expects anything beyond today?"

Geneviève squeezed Sarah's shoulder. "Sometimes you can't be sure—you just have to let yourself go. It's like the first time you ever jumped into the river. You knew it was over your head, but you did it anyway, knowing that you would more than likely come up and start swimming. I think love is like that. You can't always play it the safest way. You have to take the chance and hope you come up. Otherwise, you may miss the most important experience of your life."

Was Geneviève right? Should she have confessed her love not knowing what he would say, how he would react? She was so confused. And the answers to her questions lay with Morgan, no one else. She needed him.

When the knock sounded on the door, Sarah realized she'd spent the morning thinking about Morgan instead of worrying about Philip.

Geneviève looked questioningly at her.

"Philip, most likely," Sarah said suddenly nervous again.

"Do you want me to stay?"

Sarah wanted to say yes, she could use the support, but she didn't want Philip to sense her uneasiness or to balk at the sudden presence of a third person.

"It's probably better that I see him alone. I don't want him suspicious."

"You're probably right. You know I could never keep my distaste for *Philippe* to myself. I'm afraid I might spoil everything by punching him in the middle of the conversation. I'll be upstairs, though, if you need me for anything."

Sarah smiled gratefully. Knowing Geneviève was in the house gave her some small measure of comfort. If Philip got out of hand for any reason, her friend would come to her rescue. She waited until Geneviève had disappeared up the stairs, then hurried down the hall to the door.

Philip stood before her on the stoop, dressed as immaculately as ever, but the only thing she could see was the patch of white in his dark hair.

"So the private detective came through, did he?" he asked first thing, before he'd even hung his hat on the rack in the hall. If she'd truly cared for him, she would have found his emphasis on business to the exclusion of all else hurtful. As it was, she was glad they would not need to make small talk. She wanted to be free of him as soon as possible.

"Yes, Mr. Huggins got back to me last evening," she said and gestured to the front room. He preceded her there and took the same seat he had the other day.

"Did you write everything down?" he asked. He must be remembering how flighty she'd been the other day.

"Yes, here it is," she said, reaching into her pocket and pulling out a slip of paper. Their fingers touched, and she shivered in revulsion, but he didn't notice. He was too intent on the contents of the page where she'd copied the address Morgan had sent.

"Good, I'll go see him as soon as I can, though some of the rumors I'm hearing might make the trip unnecessary."

"What do you mean?" Sarah asked, her heart in her throat.

They'd planned this so carefully, sure that Philip would jump at the chance to plug another possible leak. If this didn't work, she wasn't sure what they'd do.

"I've heard they have a suspect. A friend of yours. Or should I say a *former* friend."

She was tired of his dallying. "Who are you talking about, Philip?"

"Morgan Cain."

What was Philip up to now, Sarah wondered She knew he wasn't telling her the truth, but what reason could he have for telling her such a lie? "I'm sure I read somewhere that he'd been cleared of the murder he was charged with before I left town."

"So he was. This is another. I'm sorry I have to be the one to break it to you, but I've been told Morgan Cain is under investigation for Adam's murder."

"But how? I don't understand."

And then it came to her. Just as he'd planted the evidence in the first murder, he was planning to frame Morgan for Adam's murder, too. And he could do it, she knew. After all, he'd gotten those lies about her and Morgan in the paper once already. He must have bought off a number of people. They could be bought again—she'd seen such things with her own eyes, she thought, remembering how Morgan had convinced the caretaker at the sanitarium to let them see Hedda.

"I know this must be painful for you," he was saying. "After all, didn't you point him in Adam's direction?"

Nausea and fear rose in a solar tide, nearly engulfing her. She had never known such evil. She had thought the devil would show his horns, that the signs of his misdeeds would be written clearly across his face. But Philip looked as calm and convincing as he ever had. It was all Sarah could do to keep from flinging herself at him and scratching his eyes out. To sit there and accuse Morgan of the very thing he had done was the most vicious, depraved thing she'd ever heard.

"What a terrible thing to say, Philip," she said, her

voice shaking as she struggled for control. "How could you even bring something like that up? Don't you have any regard for my feelings?"

"My dear, I'm so sorry. It's just that I did hear there was some evidence against him. You'll have to put my wayward tongue down to the jealousy that fills me when I think of the two of you together."

"We were never together," she lied, not wanting to give Philip yet another reason to go after Morgan. "I thought I needed him to further my search for Adam. Nothing more. You know the only thing I've ever wanted was to find Adam and, now that he's dead, his murderer."

"You're right, and I humbly apologize. I've spoken out of turn. Will you forgive me?"

Sarah nodded, afraid that if she spoke she'd tell him exactly what she thought.

"Shall we change the subject then? Has Geneviève returned with you?"

"She arrived last night. I sent word from LucyAnne's I'd be coming back to town."

"I'm not sure she's such a good influence on you. She's rather too straightforward for my taste," he said, shifting in his seat.

"You have to understand that I've known Geneviève for a very long time. She's my best friend and I've learned that you have to allow a few flaws to those who are closest to you."

As she said the words she knew they were true. Whatever Morgan had or hadn't done, she would allow him his flaws as she hoped he would allow her hers.

"Of course you're right. Where would I be if you

didn't allow me my foibles?" He chuckled, as though his foibles were few and far between.

"Exactly," she said and forced a smile. "Now tell me when you're going to visit Perry Armbruster."

"Well, since you're so eager to hear what he has to say, I thought I might go over this evening."

"Maybe I should just go myself. I can clear some time tomorrow, then you won't have to be bothered," she said, hoping it would solidify his plans. If he thought she might go on her own, he was sure to want to get there before her.

"You wouldn't want to do anything like that," he said quickly, clearly alarmed by her suggestions. He looked at the slip of paper again. "Besides, this isn't in the best area. No, I'll go this evening and call on you tomorrow. That will be just as quick, don't you think?"

"I guess, but knowing you've already spoken to him will keep me tossing and turning all night. Do you think you might come over directly after you've spoken with him? I know I couldn't wait until tomorrow to find out what he said."

She watched him debate the cost of the favor and then decide to grant it. "How late may I call?"

"It doesn't matter. I'll wait up for you." She had to be sure he went tonight. With any luck the police would have him in custody before he could think about coming back.

As soon as he left, she sent her order to Miss Ellie's—dinner for two. It was the message they'd agreed upon: now Morgan would know tonight was the night.

Chapter Seventeen

Morgan stood in the small dark back room and waited. He reached down and placed his hand on the gun he'd slipped in his belt. After he'd sent Nat off to contact the police, he'd pulled the gun from the back of the bag he'd taken from his room at the boardinghouse.

"Morgan, everything's set," Perry said in a low tone as he came into room.

"Good," Morgan replied looking up as the former sergeant entered the room. He'd arrived at the house in the Vieux Carré a few minutes earlier. "Now all we have to do is wait for D'Arbereaux to show up."

"I hope everything goes according to plan."

"You can never be too sure, so stay alert. He'll be pumping you for information as well as you him."

Armbruster nodded, though Morgan could barely make him out in the darkness.

"I thought you said we'd have the police here when D'Arbereaux came," the sergeant said.

"I'd hoped Nat would be able to convince them to come, but ..." Morgan shrugged. He'd known better than to try and get the police to come on his own—

they'd have laughed in his face. He'd hoped Nat's reputation would have some bearing on their decision, but it didn't appear as if it had.

He walked to the doorway and looked down the hall to the front. "We'll just have to handle this on our own, I guess. If you'd rather not see this through I understand."

"Hell no. I'm in this to the end. The captain was good to me. I'm doing this for Miz Campbell and all the other widows who are crying their hearts out because of this bastard."

Morgan appreciated the man's dedication. They wouldn't have had a chance of getting D'Arbereaux without him.

A banging on the front door brought both men's attention to the business at hand.

"This is it," Morgan said and stepped back into the dark depths of the small room.

Armbruster started down the hall to the front door. Just before he reached it, he turned and gave Morgan a thumbs-up sign, then turned again and opened the door.

"Perry Armbruster? Sergeant Perry Armbruster?"

"Maybe. Who wants to know?"

"My name's Philip Darber and I have some information for you, Sergeant."

"I don't go by sergeant any longer. The war's been over a long time." Perry moved in front of the door, blocking Philip's entrance.

"Not for some. For some it gets replayed every day."

"What does that mean?"

"It means you should listen to what I have to say. It could save your life."

"What the hell are you talking about? Are you drunk?"

Morgan smiled in the dark. Armbruster was a damn fine actor.

"I'm telling you your life is hanging in the balance. Let me in, and I'll tell you everything I know."

Morgan could just make them out as he peered around the corner of the door. Perry had backed away from the front entrance, and D'Arbereaux now stood in the hall.

"If you have something to say, we might as well be comfortable, especially if I'm about to hear my death warrant. Why don't we go in here?" Perry offered and pointed to the front parlor.

"I think I could use a drink if you've got one," Morgan heard Philip say as he slipped from the small back room and out into the hall. Quietly, he edged his way toward the front of the house along the wall that separated him from the room the two men were in.

"Good whiskey," Philip said after a while.

"Mmm," Perry returned noncommittally. "Now, you were saying you had some information that I might be interested in?"

"It's a good thing I got to you when I did. I think you're next on the list."

"What list? You're talking in circles."

"I've only come to warn you." Philip paused and Morgan imagined he must be taking another sip of the whiskey. "It's the least I can do for a fellow veteran." He cleared his throat, then continued, "There's a man out there who has a grudge against your company. I don't have all the details, but he's murdering you one by one."

"Murdering? That's crazy. You say this is happening to the whole company? Do you know who he's gotten so far?" Perry's voice came from different locations each time he spoke as if he were walking around the room. D'Arbereaux's voice always came from the same place—against the wall Morgan was leaning on. He could hear him as clearly as if he were standing alongside him.

"About eight of the men, or so I've been told. From all around the state."

"Do you know his name and where he is?" Perry asked.

"This is the scary part. He's here in New Orleans, and that's why I think you're in danger."

"What did you say his name was?"

"I didn't, yet. But it's Cain. Morgan Cain."

Morgan caught his breath. He couldn't believe his ears. What the hell was the bastard up to? He put his ear against the wall, straining to hear every word.

"Is this the same Morgan Cain who writes for the papers?"

"Oh, you've heard of him, have you?"

"I follow his pieces when I'm in town. I can't imagine—"

D'Arbereaux interrupted him. "Those are always the ones. They appear normal, but . . ."

When D'Arbereaux didn't continue, Perry asked the question Morgan wanted to blurt out. "Why would he do something like this?"

"Seems he was a bit of a coward in the war. Now he's trying to make up for it by taking the lives of good honest men who fought for their country."

"My God, this is amazing!"

"I know. I've talked with one of the victim's sister, Sarah Gentry—did you know her brother, Adam?"

Perry thought for a moment. "Not that I recall. There were a lot of men coming and going. Some I knew, some I didn't."

"Anyway I've told her everything I know, and she'll be going to the police with what I've given her. She now knows all about Cain's war record—about what a coward he was, how he wouldn't even take up a sword and defend his country. They nearly court-martialed him, you know."

A deep, dark anger slowly grew inside Morgan, consuming his thoughts. Had D'Arbereaux really told Sarah all that? And if he had, what was Sarah thinking now? The court-martial story was true, as far as it went. Had D'Arbereaux been able to use it to convince her of his guilt? Morgan's hand automatically went down to his belt and the gun he'd put there before leaving Ellie's. He curled his fingers around the grip, then jerked them away as if he'd been burned. He looked at his hand as if it were an alien entity with a will of its own. What had he been thinking of? How could he allow a man like D'Arbereaux to push him so close to the edge?

When Morgan heard D'Arbereaux's voice again, he realized he'd missed part of the conversation.

"I'm going back over to her house. Want to come along and talk with her yourself?"

"You know something doesn't seem right."

"How's that?"

"There's only one thing our whole company had in common, one thing that all of us vowed never to talk about."

"Yeah? And what was that?"

Morgan could hear the wariness in D'Arbereaux's voice. He hoped Armbruster knew what he was doing. They couldn't afford to get this close and have everything blow up in their faces. If the police had gotten one of their men here, they would have had an impartial witness to corroborate their accusations. As it was, they would need some kind of overt act on D'Arbereaux's part to get him. Was that what Perry was angling for with his provocation?

"An incident near the end of the war," Perry replied. "It happened in a small town not far from here."

"Is that so?"

"Yes, Croxton's Mill. Ever hear of it?"

Morgan held his breath. There was silence for several seconds. He couldn't tell what D'Arbereaux was doing, but finally he spoke.

"So what happened there?"

"A travesty. But, then, you probably know better than anyone, don't you think?"

"Smart, aren't you?" Philip's voice was no longer by the wall. He'd moved to the center of the room "How long have you known?"

"That you were behind the massacre or the murders?"

Philip laughed nastily. "It doesn't matter anymore, does it? Now you'll have to join the rest of them. And no one will ever know what happened back in Croxton's Mill. You'll just be another soldier who couldn't live with the aftereffects of the war. I think you'll have a really bad case of nostalgia. You'll even put it in the note. That sounds reasonable, doesn't it?"

"I've told the police the whole story, D'Arbereaux. You might as well put that pistol away."

Armbruster's voice was as strong now as it had been before, but Morgan was worried. D'Arbereaux sounded at the end of his tether. It wouldn't be long before he snapped and used the gun, especially if Armbruster wasn't doing things according to his plans.

Morgan listened for sounds outside the house, sounds that would indicate the police had arrived, but heard nothing.

"I didn't want to do it this way, but you leave me no choice." D'Arbereaux's voice had changed, it was more menacing. "Let's step out into the hall."

At that moment, Morgan knew he could no longer wait. Saving Perry's life was all that mattered.

"Oh, my God," Sarah whispered as she stopped in front of the address she had given to Perry Armbruster. She could see shadows behind the curtains at the window, the shadows of two people. And one of the shadows was holding a gun.

Whatever doubts she'd harbored about Philip's involvement had long since evaporated. In all honesty, she'd known the truth for some time but couldn't admit her own bad judgment. Now there was absolutely no question.

Frantically she looked around for someone to help, but the narrow street was deserted. She had thought the police would have been here by now. The plan had been for one of them to be in the house before Philip arrived to hear what he had to say. The rest were to wait outside, ready to act when the situation called for it. But there were no police around, and the time to act seemed to be at hand.

She had to get help, quickly. One of the houses down

the block had a light shining in a window, and she turned to run to it just as a gunshot sounded from inside Armbruster's house. Whirling she turned in time to see one of the shadows fall to the floor. A scream filled her throat.

Suddenly the door flew open, and a man came running out.

By the time Sarah realized the danger she was in, it was already too late to escape. Philip had caught her by the arm and pulled her in front of him, then shifted his hold and grabbed her around the neck, squeezing her so tightly she almost couldn't breathe.

"Don't make a sound. I'd hate to be forced to kill you here in the street. Now start walking toward that alley," he ordered, motioning with his head to the left.

He quickly shoved her ahead of him, not stopping until they were around the corner, out of sight of the house. Breathing heavily, he thrust her against the wall of a darkened house and leaned against her, holding her in place while he craned his head around the corner to check the street.

"Philip, have you gone crazy? What's the matter with you?" Sarah gasped as he eased off her. She frantically looked around for help but saw nothing but darkness. None of the nearby houses had lights showing.

"That act isn't going to work this time, my dear," he said through gritted teeth. "You were very persuasive when you flung yourself into my arms, crying and carrying on. But I'm not stupid enough to be fooled by your little game twice. Cain wasn't in that house by accident. I know when I've been set up. You were the only one who could have told him I'd be there tonight." He jerked her up until the side of her face was pressed against his. "Do you think I'd be so easily duped?"

"No, I don't think that at all. You're smart, very smart," Sarah said, her voice no more than a whisper. The way her heart was beating, she was surprised she got that much out. Her impulsiveness had gotten her into trouble again, only this time the trouble was much more serious than any she'd ever faced. Her very life was at stake.

"Don't lie to me, bitch. I know everything. How do you think I've gotten this far?"

He grabbed her again, and she nearly whimpered as he choked off her air but swallowed the sound when he eased the pressure. She'd seen the feral gleam in his eyes a minute before. He was like a wild animal, any sign of weakness might send him into a killing frenzy.

"What do you know, Philip?" she asked with as much calm as she could muster, hoping to gain some time.

"I know you and Morgan have been in this together from the beginning. That first night at the ball, I could see something between you. It just goes to prove I was right to set him up for the murder of that whore. I should have realized, though, just how hot you were for him, so hot you'd do anything, even leave with him when you knew he was a murderer."

"He wasn't a murderer," she interjected.

"You didn't know that then—you went with him anyway, didn't you?"

She was afraid to lie to him, afraid to tell him the truth.

When she didn't answer, he shook her and asked again, "Didn't you?"

She could hear the edge of madness in his voice. The

suave, sophisticated man she'd thought she'd known had disappeared without a trace. She was in the devil's hold now.

"Yes, I did."

If she were going to die, she'd die telling the truth.

"Did you go to bed with him, too, when you were out on your run from the law?"

Again he shook her when she didn't answer. "Well?"

"I love him."

"Bitch," he spat out. Then in a low growl right beside her ear, he whispered. "You're gonna find it's real hard to love a dead man."

"No," she cried, and his hand closed over her mouth, muffling her screams. She tried to twist away from him, to free herself so she could run back to the house, but he wouldn't let her go.

She couldn't believe what was happening. All her hopes for the future, all her plans to tell Morgan what was in her heart, were for naught. Now she didn't want him to save her, didn't want him anywhere near the deadly monster holding her for fear he would be killed.

"Shut up and keep moving," Philip commanded. "Or you'll be lying beside him."

Sarah tried to think rationally, to stifle her panic and find a way to free herself before Morgan arrived. She stumbled and Philip jerked her up with an oath.

"Move your feet, damn it. I don't want to drag you, but I will if I have to. Or better still I could put the bullet in you right here just like I did to your friend." He raised the gun to her temple. She could smell the acrid odor of gunpowder. This was the gun that had been fired. Suddenly his words took on a different meaning.

Had he already shot Morgan? Was that why he'd called him a dead man?

The horror of it clouded her eyes and made her knees weak. It couldn't end like this, it just couldn't. She hadn't even told Morgan she loved him. And she did love him, with all her heart and soul.

Tears rolled down her face, out of her control. How was she going to go on if he wasn't there beside her? How could she face the nights knowing he wouldn't be there to hold her?

At that instant, she knew she didn't care if she lived or died. The pain of losing Morgan overrode everything else. All she wanted to do was lash out at the person who had harmed him—to punish Philip as he had punished her.

Morgan was kneeling over Perry's body when Nat and a burly man came rushing in through the back door.

"The son-of-a-bitch shot Perry and got away," Morgan said as he motioned for Nat to drop down by his side. He'd raised Armbruster's head and shoulders and was cradling his head in the crook of his arm. Perry's eyelids fluttered open as he spoke.

"Go after him, Morgan, I'll be all right," Perry managed to say through gritted teeth. "I took enough lead during the war to know this one ain't too bad."

The wound might not be bad, but Morgan could tell the pain was intense. And he blamed himself. In the end he hadn't been able to use the gun. He'd left it on the hall table where it still lay.

Nat had opened Perry's jacket and was pressing his handkerchief to the man's shoulder. "The wound doesn't look too bad. We'll see about getting a doctor and finding the police. You get going."

Morgan gently laid Perry's head on the cushion the burly stranger had brought in from the front room.

"Hurry now," Nat said. "Before you lose track of him."

"I have a pretty good idea where he's gone," Morgan replied. As he started for door, he thought of Sarah safe at Geneviève's house, far from all danger. Thank goodness she was nowhere near.

"You're such a coward, Philip," Sarah taunted. "Are you going to shoot me like you did all those women and children in Croxton's Mill? Is that what it takes to make you feel like a man? Shooting helpless women?"

"What do you know about it?"

"Everything. You led a group of battle-weary soldiers down a road straight to hell. And you didn't even look back, did you?"

He laughed in her face. "You don't know anything. I wasn't the only one. It was all the men, men your brother fought with, all his friends. You just can't face the fact that that's the kind of man your brother really was. Your precious Adam was as much a murderer as I was," he said as he pushed her farther into the dark alleyway. "But I had a reason. That whole damn town deserved everything it got. They ruined my early life with their holier-than-thou ways. Hedda and I were never good enough for them. Being born on the wrong side of the blanket gave them all the excuse they needed to look down on us. But now they'll never do it again. I made sure of that. And your brother was my revenge. His gun blazed with the best of them."

"He was a murderer, but you were something far worse," she managed to say as he tightened his grip around her neck. "Adam left me a page of his journal telling me about all that happened. He paid for his sin, Philip, he paid for it with his life, a life of incessant wandering, of tortured nights and endless days. And you'll pay, too. I guarantee it. You'll pay if it's the last thing I do."

"Yeah, I'll pay. I'll pay by going to Washington and becoming a very important man." He laughed again, an evil, vile sound.

"Don't fool yourself. You can't keep this a secret much longer. You don't think we were working alone, do you?" she mocked him. "There are at least ten other people who know exactly what we were planning tonight. Are you going to shoot all of them?" Her derisive words were finally touching him, angering him; she could feel it in the way he moved, the way his breathing changed. But before he could react to her goading, a voice came out of the darkness behind them.

"Even John Palmer doesn't want anything to do with you now, D'Arbereaux. Not since he heard what you did during those hours in Croxton's Mill."

It was a voice Sarah knew like her own.

"Morgan," she screamed and fought Philip's hold with new strength. He was alive! Philip hadn't shot him. The relief that surged through her left her exhilarated and a new sense of conviction pulsed through her.

Philip twisted around, dragging her with him, then brought the gun up toward her head. She turned her head at the last moment and caught his wrist with her teeth. With all the power she had in her, she bit down as hard as she could. She heard his scream and the sound of his gun hitting the cobbled roadway behind them.

The salty taste of blood touched her tongue and then she was free. And she ran—ran with everything that was in her straight toward Morgan. He caught her in his arms and just as quickly pushed her over to the wall and started after Philip.

She could hear the echo of Philip's footsteps as his feet pounded against the packed dirt of the alley. Morgan took off after him and, with a running leap, managed to grab Philip around the knees. They both hit the ground with a loud thud.

Sarah left the relative safety of the wall to follow the two men. She wouldn't leave Morgan now, not even to run for help. She would have to help him herself rather than risk Philip doing something while she was gone.

She watched as Morgan scrambled to his feet, but Philip was just as fast. They were evenly matched as they stood crouched, staring at each other. She searched frantically in the darkness, looking for the gun Philip had lost when she bit him, but the alley was too dark.

"Give it up, D'Arbereaux. This is the end," Morgan said as he circled his opponent.

"Not very likely," Philip said, his breathing labored. "Everything I've ever wanted is finally at my fingertips, and no one's going to take it away from me—no one."

"You're wrong. Everything's over."

"Not yet it isn't," Philip shouted and drew his fist back. His swing went wild and Morgan hit back, striking Philip square in the jaw. The man staggered backward, but didn't fall.

Shaking his head, Philip regained his balance. He charged toward Morgan who neatly sidestepped and brought up his fist to connect with Philip's stomach. Philip doubled over with pain and fell back against the building.

"I'm going to stop you here and now, D'Arbereaux," Morgan said walking toward him. "You won't get the chance to hurt others like you hurt Sarah and my sister."

"Your sister?" D'Arbereaux said between grunts of pain.

"Annie Campbell you bastard. James Campbell's wife."

Philip began to laugh. He leaned his head against the wall and held his stomach, "That's funny, so funny," he managed to say, between grunts of laughter and pain. "You stayed on this because of James Campbell?" His voice was incredulous, and he started to laugh again.

"What are you laughing at?" Morgan said, jerking him away from the wall by the lapels of his jacket. Morgan's anger showed in his stance, in his eyes, and in his voice.

"You, me, everything."

D'Arbereaux stopped speaking and Morgan gave him a shake. "Tell me. What's so funny?"

"James Campbell wasn't even there that day."

"You're lying." Morgan shook him again and D'Arbereaux's head flopped from side to side.

"He'd been pulled to advise another company in the area. So he missed that entire battle."

"Then why did you kill him? Why?"

"Because somehow he found out about it. And he started questioning his old friends. I couldn't let him get any answers. I didn't have any choice. He had to die like the rest of them."

"Just like that," Morgan murmured.

375

Sarah watched as a strange stillness came over Morgan. She could see a thousand emotions pass over his face. And then with slow, deliberate movements his hands came up around D'Arbereaux's throat. Slowly, very slowly, he began to squeeze.

Philip's hands clawed at Morgan's as his air was cut off, but he didn't have the strength to free himself. For a moment Sarah watched, not in the least unhappy to see Philip suffer from his own tactics. Her own throat still ached from his harsh grip. Then she saw that Morgan wasn't stopping.

"Morgan, what are you doing?" she shouted, running up to him, hoping she could reach him in whatever place he had gone. "You have to stop. Please. Morgan! Listen to me. This won't prove anything. Killing Philip won't bring James or Adam back, or any of the others."

She watched Philip's eyes widen with the realization that Morgan wasn't going to let him go. He tried to speak but only a gurgling sound came out.

"You bastard. You'll never ruin the life of another person I love. I won't let you."

Tightening his hands, he let the life drain out of D'Arbereaux. Sarah felt her own life draining out, too.

"Morgan, this won't change anything," she cried, pulling at his hands. "Please stop, for my sake. I can't live without you. Don't you understand? I can't go on if you aren't here. I love you. I love you." She sobbed as she tried to reach him any way she could even if it meant baring her soul for all the world to hear.

When she thought there was nothing more she could do, that he would never listen, never hear her, he suddenly stepped back, letting go of his opponent. He looked down at his hands and over at Philip as the other man slid down the wall gasping for breath.

"Miss Gentry, are you all right?" a voice called out from the road. She recognized it as Neubald Huggins's.

"Please, we need your help," she called back, putting her arms around Morgan as he stood beside her. She could feel him trembling.

The older man came running toward them and quickly assessed the situation.

"It's over now, D'Arbereaux," he said as he pulled Philip to his feet and twisted his arm behind him in case he had any thoughts of fleeing. "I'll take care of him for you if you like."

While Huggins took over, Morgan pulled from her embrace and walked back up the alley. Worriedly she watched him while listening to what the investigator had to say.

"Thought you might like to know that Armbruster's doing fine. The doc just got there and says it was a clean shot and easily managed. I'll just walk our friend here out to the street and wait for the police. They should be here any moment."

While she appreciated the information the man was giving her, all she really wanted to do was get back to Morgan. She thanked him for his help and watched as he half pulled, half dragged Philip to the end of the alley.

"It's over, Morgan. You did it," she said to him. "You stopped Philip just like you wanted."

But Morgan didn't seem to hear her. He was leaning against the wall with his head bent, a gun in his hand. He should have looked triumphant. Instead, he looked defeated.

Chapter Eighteen

Morgan didn't move. He just stared at the gun.

"Are you all right?" Sarah asked, coming over to stand by him though she was careful not to touch him. Something told her he needed to be separate for a while.

He didn't speak, only nodded his head. At least he'd heard her.

"I'd like to stay here a while longer and let the house clear out, if that's all right with you," she said. "I don't think I could face all those people right now." Without stopping to think she reached out for the gun. "Here let me take that. The police might want it."

She held out her hand, but Morgan didn't offer her the gun.

"Do you know the damage something like this can cause?" he asked, turning the gun over in his hand.

Sarah nodded, afraid to interrupt him for fear he would close up again. His voice sounded strained, not at all like him, and she knew he was still half lost in another world, a world of painful remembrances. She put her hand back down.

"It's just so easy. Too easy." He sighted down the barrel. "One pull of the trigger and lives are changed forever. One shot and the whole world is different." He lowered the weapon and stared at it. "Looking at it you'd never suspect that, would you? It looks almost harmless. The metal's so smooth and shiny, cool to the touch." His fingers moved over the barrel and then down to the stock. "The wood of the handle feels warm in your hand, the grain polished to bring out its beauty. But it isn't harmless, is it? It's deadly . . . but it isn't just guns that take lives." For the first time he gazed at her, but his eyes belonged to a Morgan of another time, a fragile, caring Morgan who'd been betrayed by an unjust world. "Oh God, Sarah, hands take lives, too."

"Sometimes they do, my love," she said, putting her arms around him and pulling him into her embrace. His hands fell limply to his sides. "But not today."

She felt a tremor pass through him. The gun fell from his hand and hit the ground with a clatter. Then his arms closed around her, crushing her to him.

"Hold me, Sarah. Hold me and never met let go."

"I won't, my love. I'll hold you for as long as you want."

For the longest time they stood there in the alley, neither of them speaking.

"I killed a man once," he said finally in a lost voice. "It was just like this—in an alley, at night. He'd grabbed a girl, forced himself on her. She was screaming and struggling, and I couldn't just walk by, could I?"

For the first time Sarah saw Annie's wisdom in telling her this story. Now she understood Morgan's struggle, knew what to say.

"No, you couldn't," she confirmed.

"He had a gun. As soon as he saw me he fired. I was so angry, the rage just exploded inside me. I went after him not caring that he was still firing, at me, at the wall, at anything that moved.

"The other men laughed, cheering him on, and I got angrier, and he kept firing."

"He could have killed you," Sarah said, leaning back so she could look up into his face.

"But he didn't. I killed him instead."

"I don't think he gave you much choice, did he?"

"I don't know. I was so filled with . . . rage and panic and . . ." He stopped speaking, not knowing what to say.

"Anyone would have felt the same. You'd been shot, after all, and the man was in the wrong. You know that, don't you? He certainly didn't worry about what he did to you or the girl."

He stayed silent for a while. Would he tell her about the girl? Was he ready to put this whole, terrible episode behind him?

"No," Morgan conceded. "He was like Philip. Filled with his own lust for power, thinking he was invincible. But maybe there was another way to reach him."

"If Philip hadn't dropped his gun, he wouldn't have hesitated to kill you. He told me so before you came. There was no way you could have reached past Philip's crazed intentions in time to save yourself. My guess is it was the same that other time, too."

He gave no answer. In the dark, she could barely make out his expression so she relied on her other senses, listening to his troubled breaths, feeling the tension in his body, the stiff way he held himself. As he thought over her words, she felt him relax his vigilant stance.

"Maybe you're right," he said on a sigh. "I don't know. Whatever the case, I couldn't save the girl, either."

Her heart broke for him. He'd sold his soul in a bargain with the devil, and the devil hadn't held up his end of the deal, stealing a second soul in his greed.

"I know," she said softly, resting her head against his chest. "It wasn't fair. You did the right thing, but sometimes even that isn't enough. What happened with her had nothing to do with what you did."

"How do you know?"

She shrugged, knowing he would feel the movement against his arms. "Maybe because I'm a woman, maybe because you saved me tonight and I know what I feel. It's Philip I hate, not you, Philip who hurt me, who made me rage—I was just like you that night, filled with anger and fear, ready to do anything to stop him from hurting you, *anything.*"

"That's how I felt, too. I was ready to kill him to save you, but . . ."

"There's no but. To save someone else, sometimes you have no choice but to act. Philip knew what he was risking."

"I know, but the rage I felt was so strong, so all-consuming."

"But you did stop, you know."

"Only because of you," he whispered. "I heard you calling me, and the rage began to lose its grip. God, Sarah, what would I have done if I'd lost you?"

He held her more tightly so that she could barely breathe, but that was fine with her. She felt the same desperate need to be close to him, to assure herself that he was really fine. She splayed her hands across his back and hugged him to her.

They stayed together until they heard someone clearing his throat at the end of the alley.

"Excuse me, but the police are ready to leave now." It was Neubald Huggins. "Would you care to make a brief statement before they disappear?"

Morgan was the first to pull back, but he didn't let her go. "We'll be right there," he said, sounding stronger, more like his usual self.

"Fine. I'll let them know," Huggins called back and disappeared from view.

"We'd best go back to the house," Morgan said.

"All right."

She smiled softly at him as he put one arm around her shoulders. They walked out of the alley and down the street to the house he'd let for Perry Armbruster.

A couple of policemen were still in the front hall. They had most of the story from Nat and Perry and just needed a few details from Morgan and Sarah. Philip was already on his way to jail, much to Sarah's relief. She didn't think she could handle seeing him again, even if he was in police custody.

As they closed the front door behind the policemen, a voice called from the kitchen. "Morgan, is that you?"

"It's Nat Bayard," Morgan whispered. "My editor. I'll see that he doesn't stay long."

The older man peered down the all from the kitchen door. "Is everything all right?"

"Yes, we're fine." Morgan glanced over at Sarah as he spoke and gave her an encouraging smile. "How's Perry?"

"He'll be fine. He said to tell you he'll see you as soon

as they release him from the hospital. Probably be tomorrow or the next day."

"Good."

"I hate to bring up business, but there's no time to waste. Once word gets out that Philip is in jail, the papers are going to have a field day. We need our first story in tomorrow's paper. We can do a whole series on various aspects of the case in the next several issues, but I want to be sure we break the story before anyone else. So . . ." He took a deep breath, as though he realized the enormity of what he was about to ask after all that had occurred this evening, not that it would stop him. "Will you need my help to write it up or would you rather do it alone?"

Sarah wanted to protest the man's insensitivity. Didn't he know what Morgan had just been through? But before she could say a word, Morgan said, "I can do it myself, thanks. When do you want it?"

"I'll send a runner around ten. Can you have it ready by then?"

"I'll have something to start with."

"Good. Then I'll leave so you can get to work. Can I drop you off somewhere, Miss Gentry?"

"Sarah's staying with me," Morgan answered for her. "If you wouldn't mind, I'd appreciate it if you could let her friend, Miss Michaud, know that everything's worked out. I wouldn't want her to worry."

"No problem," Nat replied.

"And one other thing. I need to write my sister a note and let her know that Philip said James wasn't involved in the massacre. Can you have someone take the letter to her?

"Do you want me to wait now?"

Morgan shot Sarah a questioning look.

She nodded. "Annie should be told as quickly as possible. It would be cruel to keep her in ignorance a minute longer than necessary."

"Give me a second, Nat. This won't take long."

Within minutes, the editor had the note in his hand and was on his way.

When the front door closed, Sarah and Morgan were finally alone. They stood staring at each other. Sarah could see longing and desire in Morgan's eyes, but also the pull of obligation.

"Why don't you go on up and get started," she said, putting a reassuring smile on her face. "I'll just straighten out down here and then come along."

"Are you sure? You don't have to straighten anything, it's—"

"I won't do too much, don't worry. Now get going. Last I heard, you had work to do."

He gave her a careful look, as if trying to gauge whether she really meant her words.

"Go on," she said with an exasperated laugh. "The sooner you start, the sooner you'll be done."

He smiled back. "True enough. Don't take too long down here."

"I won't," she promised.

After a last lingering look, he headed up the stairs. Her gaze followed him. She felt a oneness with him, a blending. Tonight they had run a gauntlet of danger and fear, of pain and, she hoped, redemption. Once Morgan finished writing his story they could move on with their lives, lives unencumbered by the pressures of the past—not that she would ever forget Adam or what had happened at Croxton's Mill. Nor would Morgan ever forget that he'd killed a man.

But those events would be in the past where they belonged.

She went into the kitchen and set water to warm so she could wash the few dishes left on the table. Morgan had apparently rented the place fully furnished. Having her hands in the warm water relaxed her, and Sarah's thoughts returned to Morgan. She'd never been so terrified as when she saw him facing down Philip. And afterward, when he looked so defeated.

It was the first time she'd been the one who had to be strong, to cushion the blows. Before Morgan had always taken on that role. But it had felt good that he'd allowed her to ease him through his pain instead of shutting her out. They were now on an equal footing, each giving and taking as needed, each knowing the other would be there no matter what. She liked that, liked feeling she was needed, that she could make a difference rather than always being the burden. And Lord knew she had been a burden to Morgan more than once.

She smiled as she remembered their trip to the bayou, their visit with Etienne and Octavie, the birth of Adam's namesake. They worked well together, she and Morgan, even when things didn't go well. She thought back to Ossy's death, the smile leaving her face. Whether he knew it or not, he'd been a big help. Without him, she wasn't sure they would have ever broken through the secrecy. They would have to find out where he was buried and take him some flowers.

When the kitchen was set to rights and the front room tidied, she looked around. She liked this little house. With a few touches it could be very homey. Smiling to herself, she headed up the stairs to Morgan.

The bedroom took up nearly the whole second floor. Morgan was working at the desk so she tiptoed in and sat on the bed, watching him. He was intent on his work, his pen moving across the piece of paper as if he couldn't write fast enough to keep up with his thoughts. His hair curled around the top of his shirt collar. She knew now just how silky it felt. Her fingers tingled with the memory.

She yawned and blinked rapidly. Maybe she would just lie down for a second, she thought. She could watch Morgan just as well if she rested her head on her arm. From this position, the lamp behind him set a glowing aureole all around him, highlighting his broad shoulders and the masculine lines of his face. He was so beautiful, she thought, she could watch ... for ... hours ...

Morgan put the pen down. The story was one of the strongest he'd ever done—and one of the most painful, touching his family and reaching into his own past. But he would never have met Sarah if it were not for Philip, so some good had come of it all. He looked over his shoulder. He'd been aware when she'd entered the room, trying to be so quiet. Her presence had filled him with warmth, comforting him without her saying a word.

Now she lay sprawled over the bedcovers, sound asleep at the foot of the bed, her hair escaping the confines of a braided knot at her nape. The light caught on the auburn tresses, turning them to flame. Her eyelashes, a shade darker, rested just above her lightly flushed cheeks.

He crossed the room and gently stroked one finger across her cheek. Her skin was soft, womanly, calling to him. He wanted to touch her, not just on her face but all over, along her sleek back and ripe hips, down her legs to her slim ankles. He wanted to cup her breasts until her nipples puckered for him ... and then he wanted to taste her, to dive into her feminine shelter and find his soul.

Instead, he pulled back the light coverlet, then gently lifted Sarah into his arms and set her more comfortably in the bed. He removed her shoes as she slept and loosened the ties on her dress. The dress was dark in color and simply cut, designed for working in the house or garden rather than visiting. He guessed she'd chosen it so she wouldn't be easily seen. He was relieved that she wore no corset; surely he would have wakened her if he had to loosen any stays.

He sat on the edge of the bed and removed his own boots. Then stood to take off his trousers and shirt, crossing the room to lay them over the chair. It was still dark out, though close to dawn, and he dimmed the lamp, leaving only enough light to make his way back to the bed. He slipped under the covers next to Sarah.

As if she knew he was there from some sixth sense, she turned toward him and snuggled against his shoulder, laying one arm across his chest. He liked feeling her slender weight on him, her warmth easing the chill of the evening from his bones where it had settled so deeply he'd thought he would never be free.

Free. That was how he felt, he suddenly realized. Free of the past and the guilt, free of the self-imposed loneliness, the isolation from warmth and human contact. Free to make of his life what he wanted. And he knew just what that would be. For with the freedom came another emotion: the need to be tied, tied to this woman he held in his arms, bonded in ways that would never break, never leave him prey to the devastating aloneness that had held him prisoner for so long.

She was his freedom, his soul, his love. He remembered now that she had told him she loved him. But had he answered back?

No. It was her love that had stopped him when he would have killed Philip, her love that had reached past his hatred and rage and found the core of goodness inside him. He'd felt his own love reaching for her, but first he'd had to fight through his past mistakes so he could be free to love her.

And now he had. He turned his face to press a chaste kiss in her hair and saw that she was awake, watching him.

"I love you," he said, and the words seemed right, the rightest words he'd ever said.

"I love you," she replied.

He leaned toward her and she tilted her head back so their lips could meet. Her sweet taste made him hungry for more. He slid farther down in the bed so their faces were level and he could deepen the kiss. His tongue met hers, velvety and soft, and gently dueled while his hands made quick work of her disheveled hair, removing every last pin and clasp until it flowed through his fingers like warm silk, its flowery fragrance filling his nostrils with every gasping breath he took.

He held her head in place so he could plunder her mouth even more deeply, and her hands slid over his shoulders and around to the back of his neck. Her skin felt smooth against his, warm and vital. As she pressed herself against his chest, he could feel the soft mounds of her unbound breasts flatten beneath the fabric of her dress. He turned her onto her back, his hand desperately searching for a way to remove every barrier between them. As soon as she realized his intent she broke off the kiss to help him.

When they were both naked, he held out his arms and she rolled into his embrace. For a moment it was all he could do not to come apart at the myriad sensations assaulting him—her feminine scent, her luscious curves fitting so perfectly to his body, the sweet moans that escaped from deep in her throat when he stroked her.

Her mouth felt hot and wickedly seductive as she nibbled and licked her way from his mouth down to his chest, pausing to flick her tongue at each male nipple as she moved down his body. Her hair dragged along his skin leaving each nerve ending achingly aware as it passed over his chest and down his abdomen.

Never had he yielded control to a woman in such a way. Never before had Sarah taken the lead in their lovemaking, yet he reveled in the pleasure she was giving him, much to his surprise. As the intensity grew, he clutched at the feather bed with his fists. When she kissed him intimately, his back arched and his heels dug into the bed. Her caress was hot and loving, turning his insides into a fireball of need, ready to explode.

He pulled her up, unable to take another second of wanting her, of waiting for fulfillment. He began his sensuous assault on her body, kissing her as she had kissed him, covering every square inch of her skin with kisses, molding her body to his every need until she felt fluid in his arms. He took her to the brink, then eased back, each time building the pitch of feeling until he sensed that she, too, had reached the limit.

Slowly he entered her, teasing them both with an agony of anticipation, a surging wave of unbridled desire.

"Please," she begged him and he slid a little deeper.

"Does this please you?" he murmured.

"Yes, oh, yes." The words were broken with need.

She moaned and grabbed his hips with both hands, pulling him closer. He yielded to her demand, sliding in to the hilt. She lifted her knees, taking him even deeper.

He groaned, ready to explode inside her, yet wanting to prolong the moment. He'd never felt this before, as if he never wanted to be separate again. If he could he would stay like this forever. With her arms and legs wrapped around him and the heart of him buried deep inside her, he would be forever happy. But the moment refused to wait, carrying him with it like a wave cresting near the shore.

She moved beneath him, a quick, demanding thrust of her hips, and he was lost. He began to move with her, riding the wave as it swept both of them to a different place, racing toward the end of their journey. The wave exploded with a final surge and so did he.

But the moment didn't end, the pleasure didn't die. Even when the wave slowly ebbed, leaving him breathless and spent, he still felt a part of her, as if they'd exchanged a portion of their souls and now would be joined together forever.

"Marry me," he whispered in her ear. "Spend the rest of your life with me. I need you and want you and love you. Will you have me?"

"Oh, Morgan, I love you so much."

"Is that a yes?" he had to ask though he knew it was. He just wanted to hear the words.

She laughed and tears ran down her cheeks all at the same time.

"Yes. Yes, yes, yes."

"Good," he said, a deep well of satisfaction swelling inside of him.

He wanted her again with a hunger that would never be fully assuaged, not as long as she looked at him that way, her eyes shining green, filled with passion and love and desire. They made love again, oblivious to the world outside until they heard the pounding at the door.

"Who could that be?" Sarah asked worriedly, sitting up in the bed and pulling the sheet over her. "Sounds like an emergency of some sort."

"At the paper, they undoubtedly think of it that way—I have their lead story, don't forget."

"Oh, right, the runner." She dropped back onto the mattress. "I forgot."

Morgan leaned over her and dropped a kiss on her forehead. "Don't move. I'll be right back."

He slipped out of the bed and into his pants, grabbed the pages off his desk, and took the stairs took at a time.

"Enough already," he shouted. "I'm coming."

He flung the door open.

"Nat! What are you doing here?"

"Come for my story. Didn't want to trust it to anyone else. Well?"

"Well what?"

"Do you have the story?"

"Here." He thrust the pages into his editor's hands.

Instead of taking off at a run the way Morgan expected, Nat looked him up and down. "It's like that, is it?" he asked. His eyes narrowed. "You marrying her?"

"As soon as I can."

Nat grinned. "Sounds like you'll need a raise, then. Being a family man, and all."

"To say nothing about breaking the best story you've had in years."

"I said nothing about it, did I?" Nat laughed as he moved out of reach of Morgan's mock punch. "All right, all right," he called over his shoulder. "I'll add an extra consideration for that, too, as long as you invite me to the wedding. Oh, and I nearly forgot, Miss Michaud asked me to tell you that she expects you both for dinner tonight. No excuses."

Dinner was a cozy affair. Geneviève had invited Perry Armbruster to recuperate in her house since he was right-handed and his right shoulder was injured, incapacitating him. Sarah accepted the explanation with a straight face, knowing Geneviève had not reached the point where she could be teased about her budding feelings for the redheaded sergeant.

Afterward, Sarah and Morgan went outside to sit on the gallery and drink their coffee while Geneviève insisted that Perry retire for the evening and get some rest. She was still inside helping him.

Nettie brought the coffee out on a tray laden with pastries and a rum cake. She put the heavy tray on the low table and started to set out the cups and plates for dessert.

When she finished, she stood and clasped her hands in front of her.

"I'm afraid I owe you an apology, Mr. Cain," she said. "Miss Geneviève told me what happened back then with that story you wrote."

"That's all right. Misunderstandings often occur."

"Well, I'm afraid I had a bushel of misunderstandings that day, Mr. Cain. Tante Zabelle was shocked when I went to see her and told her how afraid I was that Sarah had gone with you. I thought you were the one in the prophecy, but she told me it was someone Sarah had known a long time. I hope you can find it in your heart to forgive me."

"I'm glad you cared enough to be upset for Sarah's safety. I'm glad she has such loyal friends."

"Tante also said her Lafcadio heard stories of one of the men who came at night asking questions. Remember she was going to find out for us, Miss Sarah?"

She nodded.

"Well the name he came up with was Huggins. Have you heard of him?"

Sarah laughed. "I'm afraid so. I hired him to help me find out what happened to my brother, but I guess I never told him to stop."

"I am happy that it was nothing important, then. I was worried when I couldn't give you the message."

"Thank you for trying. I really appreciate your concern."

Nettie smiled. "Oh, and one other thing. Tante Zabelle says not to throw out the cradle after the first two. There will be a third surprise later."

"What does that mean?" Sarah demanded.

"I already told you, miss, it is not done to ask. Tante Zabelle tells you just what you need to know, no more, no less. Now, if you will excuse me, I must help in the kitchen."

After she left, Morgan pulled Sarah into his arms. "Sounds like three children, if you ask me. What do you think?"

"About children? I just hope they don't come too quickly. We don't even have a place to live, and if you think I'm going back to that boardinghouse of yours, you can think again."

Morgan laughed. "I don't think either of us wants to deal with Mrs. Ogden again. I'll go back only long enough to retrieve my cache from under her floor. How's that?"

She nestled against him, reveling in her happiness. "Where will we live?"

"How about that house I rented for Armbruster? I understand it's for sale, and it's not far from Geneviève so we can visit often."

"It sounds wonderful."

She lifted her lips to his for a kiss, and he obliged, taking her quickly to their special, magic place. Her arms crept around his neck and she felt the warmth of his hands at her waist. She remembered the last time they'd been on this gallery and desire raced through her. After this morning, she'd thought it would be a while before she felt this all-consuming need, but just one touch of his mouth and she was ready to go up in flames, to burn for him.

She pulled away with some reluctance. "We'd better be careful or Geneviève will be shocked."

"To say nothing of your Mr. Huggins. Have you told him he can stop following us around yet?"

"Oh, my goodness! Surely he knows now—I mean,

he was there when we caught Philip last night. You don't think—"

He started to laugh. "No. I don't think he's still following us, though to tell you the truth there were a couple of times when I wasn't sure what the man was up to."

Sarah sighed. "I guess I never told him that I no longer needed his services once I'd met you. Then, once you were shot, it never occurred to me that he was still around. Everything happened so quickly."

"Well, it wasn't all bad. He had an uncanny knack for turning up when he was needed."

"Yes. But only after it was safe." She laughed. "I'm afraid to see my bill. It didn't sound like he had a good time chasing through the bayou looking for us."

"Not as a good a time as we had, that's for sure."

He held her close and she leaned her head against his shoulder, remembering the first time they'd made love. Life was suddenly good, the future full of promise. She smiled to herself, filled with plans and ambitions. Three children—that sounded like a nice number, not too many, not too few. She'd have plenty of time for other things . . .

"What are you thinking about?" Morgan whispered.

"You and me."

"Mmm. Sounds good so far." He nibbled at her ear. "How late does Geneviève expect us to stay?"

"I don't think she has any set time."

"Good. Then let's leave now."

Sarah giggled. "We can't. She'll guess why we're going."

"So? We'll be married before you know it. Do you think she doesn't know how we feel?"

He traced a path of kisses along her jaw and trailed to a stop just short of her mouth. Her lips ached for his touch, but when she tried to kiss him back he whispered, "Are you sure we can't go?"

With his mouth so tantalizingly close to hers, she was sure of only one thing—how much she wanted him.

"I think you're right. We'd better leave right away."

They left word with Nettie that they were going and ran outside. In the shadowed lee of the house, Morgan grabbed her for a quick kiss that quickly threatened to get out of control. Laughing like children, they raced through the streets to the house they would make their own.

"I wonder how soon we'll start our first child," Sarah mused as Morgan tumbled her into the bed. "Maybe I should check with Tante Zabelle."

"Never mind Tante Zabelle. You want your first child, check with me. It'll work a lot better that way."

"All right," she agreed. "When should we start our first child?"

"How about right now?"

Epilogue

Nine months later, James Adam Cain was born. Followed by his sister, Abigail, a year and a half later. Sarah had nearly forgotten Tante Zabelle's promise when no children came over the next few years. She was busy raising her children and working with Morgan's sister, Annie, to help other soldiers who could not recover from the war.

Morgan stayed with the newspaper, gathering enough evidence to once again close down Odette Lamonte and her ilk as well as make sure John Palmer never again stepped out of line.

Their lives were rich and full, their love even stronger and more passionate than before. And then one day, when James was nearly eight and Abigail six, Jenny was born, sunny and golden, with a smile no one could resist and her mother's bright green eyes.

Tante Zabelle smiled when she saw her. "This one will drive the men crazy. You don't need the gift to see that. I wonder, though, how she will like it when you move to Washington."

"Now what did that mean?" Sarah demanded when she and Morgan sat down to dinner that night.

Morgan smiled sheepishly. "I was approached by some men to run for Congress a few days ago. I told them I had to talk it over with you and decide if I even have a chance at winning."

"Of course you have a chance. You have the only chance. Tante Zabelle said so. What do you think we should take along?"

She looked around the room at the various furnishings, trying to decide what was worth taking and what could be left.

"Just so you take our bed, I don't care."

She caught the gleam in his eye. "I don't know. You think it's in good enough shape to bother with?"

"Of course it is."

"I'm not so sure. Maybe we should test it."

"Now?" The gleam brightened.

She laughed. "No time like the present."

She got up from her chair and raced up the stairs, Morgan right behind her.

"I wonder what Tante Zabelle would say about this," Sarah said with a satisfied sigh a long time later.

"I don't care about Tante Zabelle. All I need is your opinion."

"You're everything I ever wanted, Morgan."

"That's all that matters," he said and sealed the promise with a kiss.

Authors' Note

The legends concerning Spanish moss are taken from *Louisiana: A Guide to the State* compiled by Workers of the Writers' Program of the Work Projects Administration in the State of Louisiana, Hastings House, New York, 1935.

Descriptions of locations in and around New Orleans and historical information on various sites were obtained in part from the *New Orleans Guide,* James S. Zacharie, F. F. Hansell and Brothers Publishers, 1893, and *The Picayune's Guide to New Orleans, Fifth Edition,* 1903, and *Storyvill, New Orleans: Being an Authentic Account of the Notorious Red-Light District,* Al Rose, The University of Alabama Press, 1974.

Biography for Phyllis Herrmann

Phyllis Herrmann is the pseudonym of the New Jersey writing team of Nira Herrmann and Phyllis DiFrancesco. When they aren't writing, Phyllis teaches piano and is President of the local Historical Society, while Nira teaches at the university level. Between them, they have two husbands, three daughters, four cats, two mice, assorted fish, and a variety of computers, all of which have been taught to communicate peaceably (more or less). They also write as Anne Harmon.

You can write to them at P.O. Box 4694, Highland Park, NJ 08904.